Louis Spohr

A critical biography

Louis Spohr: portrait by Roux, 1838
Signature from a letter of 6 March 1835

Louis Spohr

A critical biography

CLIVE BROWN

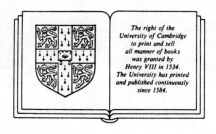

The right of the
University of Cambridge
to print and sell
all manner of books
was granted by
Henry VIII in 1534.
The University has printed
and published continuously
since 1584.

CAMBRIDGE UNIVERSITY PRESS

Cambridge
New York   New Rochelle   Melbourne   Sydney

Published by the Press Syndicate of the University of Cambridge
The Pitt Building, Trumpington Street, Cambridge CB2 1RP
32 East 57th Street, New York, NY 10022, USA
10 Stamford Road, Oakleigh, Melbourne 3166, Australia

First published 1984
Reprinted 1987

Printed in Great Britain by
Antony Rowe Limited,
Chippenham, Wiltshire

Library of Congress catalogue card number: 83-26206

British Library Cataloguing in Publication Data

Brown, Clive
Louis Spohr.
1. Spohr, Louis
2. Composers – Germany – Biography
I. Title
780'.92'4   ML410.S/

ISBN 0 521 23990 7

ME

To my parents

Contents

Illustrations

Acknowledgements

In preparing this book I have received invaluable help and encouragement from many colleagues and friends, and have benefited from the courteous assistance of a number of libraries and institutions. I should like particularly to thank Herfried Homburg (Kassel) and Hartmut Becker (Würzburg) for their generosity in supplying material from Germany. For advice on and help in preparing the typescript for publication I am indebted to Lynn Binstock, David Harris, Hugh Macdonald, Jan Smaczny (who read the whole of the first draft and made many pertinent suggestions), Stephen Wilson and various members of my family, who applied their critical faculties to the work in progress. Georgina Clarke, David Constantine, Ruth Evans and Jane Walling offered helpful guidance on German translation, and Siân Jones exercised admirable forbearance while typing out my barely legible roughs. Finally, I am grateful to Rosemary Dooley and Eric Van Tassel of C.U.P., who have smoothed the path to publication with unfailing tolerance.

I

Early life
1784–1803

In 1843 Olivia Dussek Buckley, daughter of the composer Jan Ladislav Dussek, published a book in London entitled *Musical Truths*. Considering the great composers of the past, she enthused:

Beethoven, the kingly master of composition, prince of genius (like Dante in poetry), super-excellent in all deep and somber conceptions of musical idea, in which no one could compete with him, admirable in all the softer effusions of composition; his fancy seemed to flit from earth to heaven, as though to feed his soul with heavenly melody; the depth of his thoughts was profound, his judgement stupendous, his passionate imagination superb: he was soul in soul, yet this great and gloomy genius was not so universally appreciated as Mozart, probably because his works were too scientific to be understood by all; but he was the adoration of many, and re-exists now in the sublime Spohr.[1]

Mrs Buckley's concluding statement is likely to be met with amusement if not incredulity by present-day readers, but her high estimation of Spohr would not have been considered at all eccentric by her contemporaries; for a period of more than thirty years – from the death of Beethoven in 1827 to his own death in 1859 – he would have been regarded by many musicians and music-lovers as the greatest living composer, while very few would have denied him a prominent place in the first rank of great composers. Yet within little more than a quarter of a century after his death the bulk of his music had disappeared from the repertoire, and not only were his achievements disparaged but also the magnitude of his reputation and the extent of his influence on musical developments during his lifetime were largely forgotten.

The history of music provides no parallel case of a composer upon whom posterity has so decisively reversed the judgement of his contemporaries. Whether or not Spohr's aesthetic achievements are currently undervalued, his historical importance certainly is. The sway which his music exercised over the hearts and minds of many of his contemporaries is abundantly attested by numerous expressions of admiration from musicians and critics. Such major composers as Chopin, Mendelssohn, Schumann, Brahms and Wagner, along with a host of minor composers in Germany and England, including Burgmüller, Gade, Raff, Sterndale Bennett, S. S. Wesley, Bishop,

Henry Smart and Sullivan, gave utterance to the sincerest form of flattery in their own music;[2] but today Spohr's contribution to their styles goes unrecognised because so little of his music is familiar even to the majority of nineteenth-century scholars. There is no doubt that during the 1830s and 1840s Spohr was widely seen as a dominant force in German music. As J. W. Davison wrote in 1854, at a time when a new generation of young musicians and critics had found fresh idols,

Not many years ago the bias was quite the other way. The musical mind of Germany, and of all the followers of the German school, was thoroughly imbued with Spohr. Their light was but a reflection of his light, their ideas were the natural offspring of his, their forms but imitations of his own. He had pointed out a high road to excellence in which the rest endeavoured to walk; he had invented a new style with whose attractions the others were intoxicated. From one well alone was drawn the German inspiration; and that well was Spohr's. Even the critics were as mad on one side, as now they are mad on the opposite. Mozart and Beethoven were on the point of being deposed, and Spohr was to reign in their stead. No composer was more idolised, emulated, and pillaged; the young musicians regarded him as a prophet; his method of harmony was lauded to the skies, and his knowledge of orchestral combinations pronounced unparallelled.[3]

And many others, including Eduard Hanslick and Emil Naumann, echoed Davison's opinion. Spohr undoubtedly made a distinctively individual contribution to nineteenth-century music; a knowledge of that contribution is essential to any adequate understanding of the development of music during this period.

At the time of Louis Spohr's birth his ancestors had been living in the vicinity of the Harz mountains for at least five generations, having probably migrated to central Germany from the Spanish Netherlands during the religious persecutions of the mid sixteenth century. The earliest member of the family about whom anything definite is known is Christoph Spohr (1605–79), who established himself in Alfeld as surgeon and director of medicinal bathing. Christoph's descendants over the next century were burghers and landowners, and as doctors and pastors were concerned with ministering to the corporal and spiritual needs of the inhabitants of the region.

Louis' grandfather Georg Ludwig Heinrich Spohr (1729–1805) was a Lutheran pastor at Woltershausen, while his father, Carl Heinrich (1756–1843), reverted to the family's earlier interest in medicine. Before settling down to practise, however, Carl Heinrich had spent an adventurous youth. At the age of fifteen he ran away from home to avoid punishment at school and maintained himself in Hamburg for some time by translating and teaching languages, for which he had a remarkable gift. Subsequently he worked his way through several universities, initially without support from his parents, returning to Brunswick in 1782 as a qualified doctor. Reconciliation with his family had by this time taken place, and on 26

November 1782 Carl Heinrich Spohr married his cousin Juliane Ernestine Luise Henke (1763–1840). The young couple, he aged twenty-six and she nineteen, spent the first years of their marriage in Brunswick, in the spacious house attached to the church of St Aegidius of which her father was minister. Their first child was born on 5 April 1784 and seven days later was christened in his maternal grandfather's church, where the baptismal register recorded his name as Ludewig. His parents, however, adopting the French fashion prevalent among the educated classes in Germany at that time, called the boy Louis – the name by which he always chose to sign himself in later life and under which his compositions were generally published. In 1787 the family moved to nearby Seesen, where Carl Heinrich had been appointed district physician, and there the household was gradually increased by the births of four more sons and one daughter.

Louis Spohr's genetic inheritance gave him both a sound constitution and a herculean frame (he was about six feet six inches tall, with a correspondingly powerful build), together with high intelligence, a determined nature and remarkable artistic gifts. During his childhood and early years he was strongly influenced by his father. Carl Heinrich Spohr was in many ways a child of the Enlightenment, adding to the sturdy independence of his burgher ancestors a spirit of cosmopolitan enquiry; his activities as a translator brought him into contact with foreign ideas – by 1792 he had translated some thirty-six texts from English, Italian, French and Spanish – and his receptiveness to new ideas is illustrated by his friendship with, and interest in the theories of, Samuel Hahnmann, the founder of homeopathy. He showed his awareness of the ideals of such spokesmen of the Enlightenment as Diderot, Rousseau and Voltaire in the rearing of his children, in whom he instilled a consciousness of humanitarian principles, the equal rights of all men, and a code of morality which required the individual to be responsible to his own conscience for his actions. Adherence to the Lutheran faith was tacitly accepted but does not seem to have played a dominant part in their lives; moral convictions appear to have been based as much on rational precepts as on divine injunction, and there was certainly no hint of sectarian intolerance.

Both Carl Heinrich and his wife were keen amateur musicians; the former played the flute, the latter was a talented pianist and singer, at one time a pupil of the Brunswick Hofkapellmeister J. G. Schwanberger. Music was an important recreational activity for the Spohr family, as it increasingly became for many other members of the German middle classes during the second half of the eighteenth century. At the age of three or four Louis, who had a clear treble voice, was able to take part in duets with his mother at the family's regular soirées. Louis' obvious musical ability soon persuaded Carl Heinrich to accede to his son's repeated requests for a violin, and at the annual fair of 1789 he purchased for him the instrument which is still preserved in the Brunswick Staatsarchiv. Encouraged by his mother's accompaniment on the piano, Louis soon taught himself to play on the violin the melodies he had previously sung with her, and having proved his aptitude for the violin he was sent for lessons to the local assistant schoolmaster, J. A. Riemenschneider, under whose tuition he rapidly made sufficient progress to take part with his parents in trios for flute, violin and piano by Kalkbrenner and others at their musical evenings. At one of these gatherings, in 1790 or 1791, Louis was so moved by the expressiveness of the violin playing of Lieutenant Dufour, a refugee from the French Revolution, that he burst into tears and afterwards begged his father to be allowed to take lessons from him. In view of Spohr's later concern with expressiveness rather than virtuosity for its own sake it is not surprising that this quality in the Frenchman's playing should have attracted him so strongly.

Dufour played an important part in putting his new pupil on the way to becoming a professional musician. When the idea that Louis should follow a musical career was first suggested, his grandfather, pastor Georg Ludwig Heinrich Spohr, strenuously opposed the proposal. To him the social implications of such a course seemed disastrous, and voicing the conventional prejudice of his class, he averred that a musician was nothing better than 'a tavern fiddler who played to dancers'.[4] Carl Heinrich, however, much to his father's displeasure, adopted a more enlightened attitude and, despite his hopes that his son would become a doctor, continued to support Louis' musical studies. The conflict of opinion undoubtedly left its mark; throughout his life Spohr remained sensitive to any suggestion of a slight on the social position or artistic integrity of the professional musician. Indeed, his unswerving refusal in later years to compromise his position in this respect played a significant part in improving the status of musicians in Germany. During these years, though, the boy's love of music was untroubled by such considerations. With Dufour's encouragement he made rapid progress in his violin playing and began to try his hand at composition, writing duets for two violins which he played with his teacher at the Spohrs' musical evenings. Spurred on by their success he devoted most of his spare time to composition, and even attempted an opera based on Weisse's *Kinderfreund*. This proved too grand an undertaking, though, and was given up after a meticulously decorated title page and an overture, chorus and aria. His father expressed strong disapproval of his abandoning a work once begun, and his injunction always to finish what he started made a deep impression. Spohr's adherence to the paternal precept is attested by Moritz Hauptmann, who wrote in 1845: 'Once he has planned a new scheme he is sure to execute it unfailingly.'[5] Carl Heinrich also objected to his son's scratching out mistakes, and, referring to the holes he made in the music paper, would grumble half seriously: 'now the stupid boy is making windows again'.[6] Spohr believed that it was his sensitivity to this gentle chiding that had led him to acquire the habit of putting his ideas down on paper only after they were fully worked out in his head; and indeed his extant scores are remarkably free from erasures, while sketches are conspicuously rare, until the last years of his life. It is clear that Carl Heinrich was at least partly responsible for inculcating the perseverance and systematic habit of work which Spohr was to display in so great a measure. He took a keen interest in his son's work, allowing him to compose in his own study, apparently oblivious to the humming and whistling of the young composer.

In 1796, when Dufour left Seesen to take up the post of Kapellmeister at the monastery school in Holzminden, he suggested that Louis should be sent to Brunswick to receive more advanced tuition. But first, in accordance with the law of the Duchy, Louis had to be confirmed, and so between October 1796 and April 1797 he went to stay with his paternal grandfather in Woltershausen. During this period he walked twice a week to nearby Alfeld for violin lessons, though he considered his temporary teacher less accomplished than himself, and later admitted in his memoirs that he derived considerable pleasure from getting the better of him. Despite this element of childish conceit, Louis seems to have been a readily likable youth with an open and ingenuous nature. Few normal boys would have resisted the temptation to exhibit their skills, especially when rewarded with coffee, cakes and fruit, as was the case at the house of a miller who lived between Woltershausen and Alfeld. Once, taking shelter there from a heavy shower, he made such a good impression on the miller's wife that she made him stop for refreshments every time he passed. Louis generally repaid her by playing something on the violin, and on one occasion so enthralled her with Wranitzky's variations on the old German song 'Du bist lieblich' that she kept him with her all day.

Shortly after his thirteenth birthday, having been confirmed by his grandfather, he was sent to Brunswick where he lodged with the family of a wealthy baker, J. M. Michaelis, whose wife Carl Heinrich had successfully treated for dropsy several years earlier. In Brunswick he received a good general education at the Collegium Carolinum, took lessons on the harp, and began to study the violin with Gottfried Kunisch, a member of the ducal orchestra, while harmony lessons were given by Carl August Hartung, the organist of the Reformed Church. The choice of Kunisch was extremely fortunate, for he took an almost paternal interest in his pupil. That of Hartung was less so: when Louis showed the old organist one of his compositions, soon after his harmony lessons began, Hartung was crushingly dismissive, and even when some months later he encouraged his pupil to make attempts at composition his criticisms were unpalatably severe. Spohr remarked in his memoirs, 'he corrected me so mercilessly and scratched out so many ideas which to me appeared sublime that I lost all desire to show him anything further'.[7] These lessons, which were the only formal instruction he ever

5

received in theory, were discontinued within a year because of the old man's ill health, but through Kunisch's good offices Spohr was able to borrow scores from the library of the Brunswick Hoftheater, and by studying these and books on theory he rapidly acquired a command of standard harmonic resources and compositional techniques.

The earliest compositions which Spohr included in the catalogue of his works date from the year 1803, but a few pieces survive from before that date to give an impression of his early development. Three duets for two violins, dating from around 1796, show Spohr's lack of instruction in their peculiar phrase lengths, awkward part-writing and primitive tonic/dominant harmony. The themes themselves are conventional and reminiscent of the German *Singspiele* of Hiller, Dittersdorf, Weigl, Mozart and others, though cast in a suitably instrumental mould. The first duet in F, for instance, opens with a theme that recalls Papageno (ex. 1); however the theme, though it is

Ex. 1

typical of *Singspiel* in general, is found in much earlier sources than Mozart. The first movement of a second duet in C shows more confidence, but Spohr's inexperience is evident in an abrupt dominant modulation at the eighth bar (ex. 2). A fourth duet in E flat, probably dating from 1797, shows

Ex. 2

greater fluency and a burgeoning awareness of convention; its Rondo begins with the sort of 6/8 theme which is almost archetypal in that key (ex. 3). His continuing progress can be seen in a violin concerto dating from about 1799, which is technically more assured than the duets and musically more coherent (see illustration on p. 8).

Ex. 3

Whereas the theoretical side of Spohr's musical education was left largely to chance and his own perseverance, Kunisch took greater care with his violin playing. Within the first year of his tuition he recognised that he could no longer provide the level of teaching that his pupil's rapid progress required. He therefore pressed Spohr's father to find the extra money for his son to have lessons with Charles Louis Maucourt, Konzertmeister of the Brunswick court orchestra, who was considered to be the best violinist in Brunswick at that time. In 1803 Cantor Dr W. L. Müller of Bremen wrote of Maucourt that he was 'the most cultured musician I have seen; he has taste and much knowledge'.[8] Under Maucourt's instruction Spohr will have been introduced to a wide range of works. He was able to gain further valuable experience by playing in public concerts, first at the Collegium Carolinum, then at the well-established subscription concerts in the Deutsches Haus and also in the theatre orchestra.

After Spohr had been studying with Maucourt for about a year, the increasing expenses of a growing family led Carl Heinrich Spohr to decide that it was time for his eldest son, now aged fifteen, to make his own way in the world. He therefore suggested, prompted perhaps by the memory of his own youthful adventures, that Louis should undertake a concert tour to Hamburg, where Carl Heinrich still had a number of friends to whom he could address letters of introduction. Furnished with these, a little money, his violin and a good deal of advice about the snares of city life, Louis was put on the coach to Hamburg in the early summer of 1799, full of the blithe self-confidence which his youthful successes in Brunswick had encouraged. However, his mother's misgivings proved only too well founded; the season was wrong for such an undertaking since most of the rich people were in the country at that time of year, and in any case Louis had neither the money to arrange a concert nor the reputation to secure an audience. All this was explained to him when he delivered his first letter of introduction. With his illusions shattered and his self-confidence dissipated his only thought was to

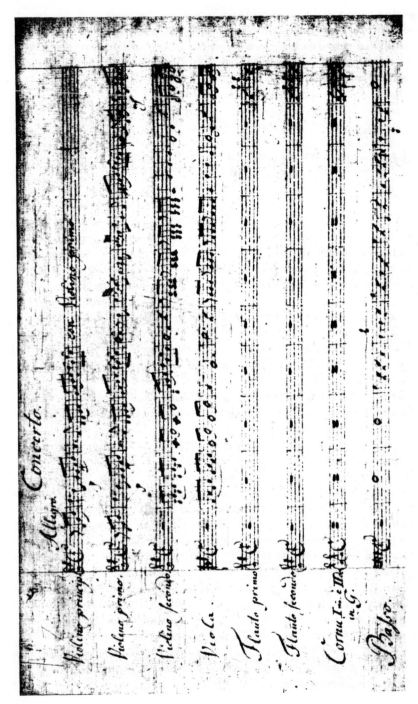

First page of the autograph score of Spohr's first surviving violin concerto (c. 1799)

get back to Brunswick, but having spent his meagre allowance he was unable to afford the return fare, so began to walk the hundred-mile journey. On the way the prospect of such a humiliating return home stimulated his initiative, and he hit upon the notion of petitioning the Duke of Brunswick for patronage.

Spohr was fortunate to have been born in the Duchy of Brunswick, for Duke Carl Wilhelm Ferdinand was one of the most enlightened and cultured princes of Europe. A nephew of Frederick the Great, the Duke inherited many of his uncle's qualities both as a soldier and a musician, though he did not pursue either of these occupations with quite the same egomaniac persistence. Von Sybel described the Duke's qualities at the time of his accession in 1780, remarking:

Those who saw him at this period at his little court were astonished to find in the champion of Krefeldt and Minden a careful manager of the state, a zealous partaker and patron of every kind of intellectual progress, and an active and unpretending administrator.[9]

Personally, the Duke was polite almost to the point of affectation. His almost legendary generosity in assisting those who appealed to him for help was commented on even by his enemies; Beugnot, sent by Napoleon to take over the Duchy in 1806, remarked that 'his acts of charity were not to be reckoned up, for it would have been an endless repetition'.[10]

Spohr was doubtless aware of the Duke's affability and generosity, and knew also that he had played the violin in his youth (having taken lessons from the Brunswick Hofkapellmeister, C. A. Pesch). The Duke remained passionately fond of music and, though not a particularly accomplished player, had frequently been known to sit up late into the night performing music.

In his memoirs Spohr gave an amusing account of the result of his petition to the Duke, which nicely illustrates his youthful pride and lack of servility. Knowing that the Duke regularly took a morning walk in the palace grounds, he sought him out there with his hastily concocted petition. Spohr recalled:

After having glanced over it and asked me some questions about my parents and former instructors, which I fearlessly answered, he enquired who had worded the petition. 'Well, who but myself? I need no one's help for that,' was my reply, half offended at the doubt as to my ability. The Duke smiled and said: 'Well, come to the palace tomorrow at eleven; we will then speak further about your request.' Who so happy as I! Punctually at eleven I presented myself before the groom of the chambers and requested to be announced to the Duke. 'And who may "he" be?' snarled the groom to me in an unfriendly tone. [The use of the third person, 'Er', in eighteenth-century German was a contemptuous form of address used to menials and children.] 'I am no "he". I am here by the Duke's command, and "*he*" has to announce me!' was my indignant reply. The groom went to announce me, and before my excitement had subsided I was introduced. My first words to the Duke were therefore, 'Your Serene

Highness! your servant calls me "he"; I must earnestly remonstrate against that.' The Duke laughed aloud, and said: 'Come, calm yourself; he will not do it again.' Then, after having put several questions to me to which I gave the most unembarrassed answers, he said 'I have enquired about your abilities from your last teacher Maucourt and would now like to hear you play one of your own compositions; this can take place at the next concert in the apartments of the Duchess. I will have it intimated to the director Schwanberger.'

Overjoyed, I left the palace, hastened to my lodging and prepared myself for the concert in the most careful manner.[11]

Spohr's performance greatly impressed the Duke, who offered him a post as Kammermusicus and promised that if he continued to make progress he would send him to a first-rate violinist for instruction in a few years' time. Thus, at the age of fifteen, Spohr became one of the second violins in the Brunswick court orchestra at a salary of 100 thalers per annum, the decree of his appointment, which was drawn up later, being dated 2 August 1799. This newly acquired financial independence even enabled Spohr to assist his family by taking in and teaching his seven-year-old brother Ferdinand, who had also shown a talent for music.

During the next three years Spohr participated enthusiastically in the varied musical activities of Brunswick, acquiring and deepening his knowledge of a wide range of music. According to his own recollections his activities in the theatre provided a particularly powerful stimulus. He remarked in his memoirs that a French company had been employed in Brunswick shortly before his appointment as Kammermusicus, and that 'I therefore became earlier acquainted with French dramatic music than with German; and this was not without influence upon the tendency of my taste and upon my compositions of that time.'[12] According to Moritz Hauptmann, the composer whose music made the most profound impression on Spohr at that period was Cherubini. Hauptmann observed many years later: '[Spohr] told me himself that he remembered the day when he valued Cherubini more than Mozart'; and on another occasion he postulated that 'Spohr probably got his tendency towards what he calls "interesting harmonic progressions" from Cherubini.'[13] Spohr claimed that it was not until later that he had the opportunity to hear any of Mozart's operas. He recalled:

At last, when at the time of the two fairs a German operatic company from Magdeburg was also engaged, the grandeur of Mozart's operatic music burst upon me, and Mozart now became for my whole lifetime my ideal and model. Even now I well remember the transport and dreamy enchantment with which I heard for the first time *Die Zauberflöte* and *Don Juan*; and that I had no rest until I had got the scores lent to me, and had brooded over them half the night long.[14]

The facts, however, cannot be entirely reconciled with his account of events. A French company, under the direction of Mme Aurore Bursay and conducted by A. le Gay, gave their first performance in Brunswick on 17 March 1800, which was after Spohr's appointment. Before that a German company had been resident, and if, as Spohr claimed, he had played in the theatre orchestra before his ill-fated trip to Hamburg, he could hardly have failed to become acquainted with some of Mozart's operas as well as ones by such composers as Dittersdorf, Müller, Winter, Salieri and Hiller. The following performances of Mozart's operas were given in the Brunswick Theatre between 1797 and 1800:

15 Feb.	1797	*Die Hochzeit des Figaro*
23 Aug.	1797	*Die Zauberflöte*
3 May	1798	*Die Zauberflöte*
14 Feb.	1799	*Die Zauberflöte*
6 Aug.	1799	*Don Juan oder der Steinerne Gast*
12 Aug.	1799	*Die Entführung aus dem Serail*
25 Sept.	1799	*Titus der Grossmüthige*
6 Feb.	1800	*Die Zauberflöte*

It will be noted that the last four of these performances took place after his appointment as Kammermusicus, and since it was part of his duty to play in the theatre orchestra it seems unlikely that Spohr could have failed to hear some of these operas. If he did hear them they seem not to have made much of an impression on him at that time, either because they were badly performed or because he was not musically ripe for them. In 1802, when the Magdeburg company were engaged in Brunswick for a short while and staged *Die Entführung*, *Die Zauberflöte* and *Don Giovanni*, it may be that the musical experience he had gained over the previous two years had put him in a better position to appreciate them.

Bursay's company, which was resident in Brunswick during the rest of Spohr's time there, performed very few German operas. Among the most frequently represented composers in their repertoire were Grétry, Dalayrac, Méhul and Boieldieu. The only opera by Cherubini to be given by them was *Les deux journées*, first produced in Brunswick on 30 July 1801; but it was repeated more frequently than any other opera except Dalayrac's *La maison isolée* and *Montenero*. Each of these three operas received nineteen performances between 1800 and 1805.

In the Brunswick quartet circles which Spohr frequented, his imagination was fired by the chamber music of Haydn and Mozart and, shortly after their publication in 1801, by Beethoven's op. 18 string quartets. Contact with music of this order helped to sharpen his sense of style and spurred him on to practise with renewed zeal. At these private gatherings his playing was also stimulated by encounters with visiting violinists such as Carl August Seidler and the young Friedrich Wilhelm Pixis.

Spohr's need to perform and compose was an inner compulsion, and fortunately, after the ill-fated Hamburg venture, he was able to take these experiences at his own pace and to absorb them into his playing and his com-

positions, none of which, however, survive between 1799 and 1803. The lack
of a composition teacher, which might have hampered someone with a less
highly developed analytical and critical instinct, was not a problem for
Spohr. He applied his formidable powers of concentration in a single-
minded quest for self-expression and quickly acquired a mastery of the
musical vocabulary of the day which was to be apparent in the published
works of 1803. He was rapidly developing an individuality different from,
but no less marked than, Beethoven's.

Some of Spohr's most valuable experience was gained through his association with the court orchestra, as he was allowed to try out new compositions
with them and thus had an ideal opportunity to judge their effect. The Duke
encouraged this, giving his young Kammermusicus permission to inform
him whenever he intended to produce a new work at one of the weekly court
concerts, to which he sometimes came to listen. In the Duke's presence the
concerts were rehearsed beforehand and listened to in silence; when, as was
usually the case, he did not attend, the situation was quite different. Then,
in order that the Duchess's card party should not be disturbed, the orchestra
was forbidden to play *forte*, timpani and trumpets were omitted, a thick carpet was spread under the musicians to deaden the sound, and the bidding of
the card players was often louder than the music. Spohr was deeply affronted
by such a slight on the dignity of his art. Already as a youth he had the
courage to rebel against this sort of humiliating treatment, which his fellow
musicians accepted so tamely, and throughout his life continued to fight it
strenuously. He gave the following account of his first act of defiance over
this issue, which occurred in 1801 or 1802:

One day when the Duke was not there, and for that reason nobody was listening to
the music; the prohibition regarding the *forte* being renewed, and the dreadful carpet
again spread, I tried a new concerto of my own. Engrossed with my work, which I
heard for the first time with the orchestra, I quite forgot the prohibition, and played
with all the vigour and fire of inspiration; so that I even carried the orchestra with me.
Suddenly, in the middle of a solo, my arm was seized by a lackey, who whispered to
me, 'her Highness sends me to tell you that you are not to scrape away so furiously'.
Enraged at this interruption I played, if possible, still more loudly; but was afterwards obliged to put up with a rebuke from the marshal of the court.[15]

He did not let the matter rest there, however, for the next day he complained
to the Duke, who once more calmed his excitable protégé and laughed good-
humouredly at the incident.

The Duke had not forgotten his promise to send Spohr to an eminent
violinist, and moves were made to find a master to take him. Neither Viotti,
who was first applied to, nor Friedrich Johann Eck, who was later
approached, were willing to take on a pupil. Eck, though, recommended his
younger brother and former pupil Franz Eck, who agreed to take Spohr.
Franz Eck was therefore invited to Brunswick, where he gave a successful
concert in the Hoftheater on 24 April 1802, and when he had thus satisfied

the Duke as to his suitability it was arranged that Spohr should accompany him on his projected concert tour to Russia.

Franz Eck was one of the last representatives of the Mannheim school. His father, Georg Eck, had been a horn player in the Mannheim orchestra, and his brother Friedrich Johann was Konzertmeister with the orchestra for some years after its removal to Munich in 1788. The only detailed source of information about Franz Eck's character and abilities which has survived is the meticulous diary kept by Spohr during the fourteen months of his travels with Eck. From this emerges a picture of a man of lax morals (according to the standards inculcated by Spohr's upbringing) whose health was badly impaired, probably by syphilis; he was incapacitated for weeks at a time on several occasions during the trip by recurring attacks of his illness. Yet Eck clearly had an attractive personality and treated Spohr more as a friend than a pupil, though it soon became apparent to Spohr that his musicianship left much to be desired. Eck was unwilling to tackle anything he had not already learned, while for want of ability as a composer he passed off his brother's compositions as his own. Nevertheless, Eck was a polished violinist, and Spohr quickly appreciated that there was much he could learn from him. Their first lesson, which took place in Hamburg on 30 April 1802, convinced him of this, for Spohr remarked in his diary:

alas! how I was humiliated! I, who imagined myself one of the first virtuosos of Germany, could not play a note to his satisfaction, but was obliged to repeat it ten times at least before I could begin to satisfy him. My bowing particularly displeased him, and I see now that it is very necessary to alter it. It will be difficult for me at first, of course, but I am convinced of the great advantages of the change and hope eventually to achieve it. [16]

At Eck's insistence Spohr purchased a Tourte bow in Hamburg and, aided by his remarkable stamina and powers of concentration, set himself a strict routine of practice, working each day until 3 o'clock at whatever Eck had set for him. In this he was urged on not only by youthful ambition, but also by a determination not to betray his patron's generosity – a determination which was strengthened by information from Brunswick that there were those who believed he would prove as worthless as most of the Duke's protégés.

The detailed and charmingly naive diaries which Spohr kept during his absence from Brunswick give a vivid and lively picture of places, people and events, providing a primary source of evidence on the state of music in the places he visited. They travelled through Hamburg, Ludwigslust, Strelitz, Danzig, Königsberg, Mittau, and Riga, arriving finally in St Petersburg in December 1802. In each of these places Spohr turned an observant eye and ear on his surroundings. He carefully noted his opinions of operas and concerts, demonstrating a sharply critical attitude to both performers and music. His remarks about violinists were particularly severe and indicate (apart from the arrogance of youth) his acutely analytical approach to violin playing, which allowed him to derive the maximum benefit from Eck's tuition, and ultimately made Spohr his own best teacher. He was also fortunate to meet a number of distinguished musicians during this journey. In Hamburg he encountered Dussek for the first time and laid the foundations of further acquaintance. His opinions of Dussek's music, however, were not entirely complimentary; of the piano quintet which Dussek played at one of the soirées they attended he remarked: 'it did not entirely please me; for despite the numerous modulations it became tedious towards the end [a significant remark in view of Spohr's delight in modulation], and what is worse was that it had neither form nor rhythm, and the end could quite as well have been the beginning'.[17] But a cantata by Dussek (composed for the English community in Hamburg in celebration of King George III's birthday, and now lost), which he heard a few days later, impressed him much more. In Königsberg they encountered the Pixis family returning, disgruntled at their lack of profit, from a concert tour to Russia. It was not until they arrived in St Petersburg that they met any other notable musicians. There Spohr was soon on good terms with Muzio Clementi, whose lively temperament and avaricious nature fascinated him. The piano playing of Clementi's pupil John Field made a profound impression. Spohr recorded in his diary his admiration for Field's 'perfect technique and ardently melancholy expression'[18] – a significant indicator of Spohr's own musical temperament.

Spohr's observations on the state of musical life in the places he visited provide evidence of the early formation of views which were to become characteristic in later years. His name was to become almost synonymous with high artistic ideals and the assertion of the independence and dignity of the musician. Already in this diary there are numerous instances of these attitudes. When a lady in Danzig ventured to suggest that he might have been better to have followed his father's profession of medicine, as had originally been intended, he replied indignantly: 'As high as the soul is above the body, so high is he who devotes himself to the ennobling of the mind above him who only attends to the mortal frame.'[19] In Ludwigslust, when he heard that the court orchestra was required to play for dancing he asked ingenuously: 'how is it possible that the Duke can require such a thing from the members of his orchestra, and that they have so little feeling of honour and artistic pride as not to refuse it?'[20] For Spohr, music was something far more important than mere entertainment; throughout his life he steadfastly refused to compromise this ideal. This was apparent not only in his concern for social recognition but also in composition and violin playing, where he was unwilling to seek popularity at the expense of artistic integrity.

Already in 1803 he made a public, though anonymous, statement of his position in an article on the state of music in St Petersburg, in which he made clear his high-minded expectations and his disgust at the prevailing lack of musical appreciation. The article began:

The present state of music here does not allow one to be very encouraging. I do not think there is any other city where people have a less genuine love of music. It is true that almost every rich Russian has his children instructed in music for several months, but only in order to say: my children learn music, or: they have been taught by this or that celebrated virtuoso. But there are also several houses where art is treasured and studied diligently; where one can hear music several times a week, and where one does not, as is usually the case at the Pharoe-Bank, drown the music with chatter, but sits in the circle of performers and attends to each beauty of the composition or the performance and rewards it with applause.

I am very well aware that in Germany people have a very different notion of the state of music here, believing it to be universally loved and on the highest cultural level. It may be because of this that almost all the celebrated and not-so-celebrated virtuosos come here in the hope of making their fortune; but most of them find themselves disappointed in their expectations and leave St Petersburg dissatisfied. For it is not sufficient here to possess a reputation and an outstanding talent to be sure of being able to give a public concert in a large auditorium; one must have made oneself socially acceptable beforehand, must have visited those to whom one is recommended several times a week and played music in their houses as often as they want, and at last, before the concert, one must know how to force the tickets on them with an amiable impudence; only then is one sure that expenditure will not exceed receipts.[21]

He continued with a description of the various musical enterprises that took place in the city, commenting constantly that people came only out of habit, not for the enjoyment of the music. He was particularly scathing about the German Opera, which he observed was 'only frequented when such operas as *Die Zauberzither*, *Das Donauweibchen* and other similar trifling things* were given'; adding that 'because of the terrible orchestra operas such as *Don Juan* or *Die Entführung aus dem Serail* cannot be given at all'.

The seriousness found in Spohr's views on music is also evident in his personal relationships. During his time in St Petersburg he formed a close friendship with a young Frenchman of about his own age called Remy, who played the violin in the Imperial Orchestra. The two young men met and ate together almost every day, and on evenings when they had no other engagements they spent hours playing duets. The great affection which Spohr inspired in his friend is shown in Spohr's entry in his diary on his nineteenth birthday, 5 April 1803:

Remy again invited me to play duets with him, and today I was able to bring him a newly completed one of my own. After we had played this through for the second time he embraced me and said: 'You must change violins with me so that we may each possess a souvenir of the other.' I was overcome with surprise and joy; for I had long preferred his violin to my own. But as it was a genuine Guarneri and worth at least twice as much as my own I felt I had to refuse the offer. However, he would not accept my refusal and said: 'Your violin pleases me because I have heard you play on it so frequently, and even though mine is really a better one you must accept it from me as a birthday present.' Now I could not refuse any longer and, overjoyed, carried my new treasure home with me.[22]

* *Die Zauberzither*, by Wenzel Müller (1767-1835); *Das Donauweibchen*, by Carl Friedrich Hensler (1759-1825).

On the eve of his departure from St Petersburg Spohr wrote: 'The parting from my dear friend Remy was very painful and cost us both many tears. He promised that he would seek me out in Germany when he made an intended visit to his own country in a few years' time, and I am sure that he will keep his word.'[23] But he appears not to have done, and nothing more is known about his life.

Further insights into Spohr's character are gleaned from his relationships with young women. His diary described, with charming thoroughness, a number of chaste flirtations which generally ended in disillusionment. In Hamburg he had undertaken to paint the portrait of Henrietta Lütgens, the thirteen-year-old daughter of a local music teacher, and was quickly attracted by her. (Spohr was a gifted artist, as his surviving self-portraits indicate.) The effusive sentimentality of his account is leavened by a fair measure of wry humour, as in his description of a rival for the girl's attentions, who is depicted as having 'an orang-utan face, always distorted into a sweet smile'.[24] And on another occasion he wrote: 'Her father, whose hobby is harmony and counterpoint, entertained me continually with the resolution and combination of chords, finding in me the most patient listener to his sermon, while I would much rather have preferred to speak with his amiable daughter about the combination of hearts and lips.'[25] Eck, who doubtless watched his pupil's infatuation with amusement, warned Spohr that Henrietta Lütgens was a coquette. The justice of the observation was soon brought home to him, for the diary recorded:

Henrietta begged me to paint her portrait in the dress which she was wearing, assuring me that she had chosen it specially, for her other dresses were not cut low enough and covered her bosom too much. I was astonished at her vanity, and the sight of this truly charming bosom which would otherwise have enchanted me now saddened me, being convinced that she was already infected by the vanity and shamelessness of the Hamburg ladies.[26]

(It is interesting to note that in the *Selbstbiographie*, published by Spohr's family after his death, the word *Busen* (bosom) in this extract was changed to *Hals* (neck).) The conversation which then ensued between the girl and her cousin about the dresses they were to wear for the next evening's ball so irritated him that he determined not to attend it himself, and several days later commented in his journal: 'It is really a thousand pities that this girl with so much talent and good sense lives in such a vulgar society and is thus being drawn into the follies of Hamburg.'[27] At the height of his disillusionment he had complained: 'My sociable heart, which could so willingly attach itself to anyone, finds nobody here. In this girl I thought I had found something on which to set my affections, but I see that I am once again deceived.'[28] But he nevertheless lamented that because her parents were present when he took his leave, he did not receive any 'kisses from her rosy lips'[29] as payment for his labours.

16

In Strelitz Spohr was involved in an abortive love affair, the course of which was again meticulously recorded in his diary. Many pages of the journal were filled with conversations in dialogue with his inamorata, and there were even outbursts of jealousy against Eck, whose flirtatious behaviour had attracted the lady away from him. (Fortunately these complaints were confined to the diary and did not result in an open breach between master and pupil.) As before, the affair ended in disillusionment, for Spohr's sense of propriety had already been shaken by reports that she was the recipient of presents and attention from a local nobleman. His low opinion of her character was confirmed by her response to Eck's advances.

In Königsberg, where Spohr's romantic susceptibilities were inflamed by a young girl called Rebecca Oppenheim, the customary disillusionment was prevented by his early departure for Mittau, on the eve of which he confided to his diary: 'It is fortunate that we leave tomorrow, for Rebecca is a dangerous girl! He who loves his freedom and his peace must fly from her, and the sooner the better.'[30]

Spohr's object in all these relationships was social rather than consciously sexual; his convictions in matters of sexual morality were firmly held. But he was no bigot. He was well aware of human frailty and had a deep fund of tolerance and kindliness in his nature which generally allowed him to accept people for their better qualities even when their behaviour fell short of his own standards. This is well illustrated by his reaction to an affair in which Eck had become involved with the daughter of one of the members of the Imperial Orchestra. Knowing Eck's propensity for philandering, and his infectious condition, Spohr became concerned about his teacher's increasingly dubious relationship with the young lady. He felt it his duty to approach her parents and warn them that Eck was only trifling with their daughter and had no intention of marrying her, a warning which they received with coldness and disbelief. It is clear that Spohr's intervention was motivated by genuine concern about what he considered to be the immorality of Eck's behaviour and the welfare of the parties involved; certainly his disapproval of Eck's actions in this and other cases involving young women did not destroy the affection and gratitude which he felt towards him as a person and a teacher. On leaving St Petersburg he wrote in his diary: 'The parting from my teacher to whom I owe so much was also a very sad one, the more so because for some time past he has been very ill and I am afraid I shall not see him again.'[31] His fears were correct, for Eck died in an asylum in Strasbourg the following year, almost certainly the victim of syphilis.

Spohr returned to Brunswick in the summer of 1803 with greatly enriched experience, a command of violin playing that enabled him to play any of the concertos in the repertoire, and a number of compositions. In Strelitz he had completed the first of his works which were to appear in print - the Violin Concerto in A major, published as op. 1, and one of the duets of op. 3. The concerto had been tried out a couple of times in St Petersburg with an orchestra of serfs directed by one of Spohr's friends, Christian Leveque. When Spohr had been satisfied that the orchestration was effective he made arrangements to send the manuscript to Breitkopf & Härtel for printing. The conditions under which they agreed to publish the work seemed so humiliating to the young composer that his initial reaction was to reject them. Far from accepting his proposal that he would give up all claim to payment for the work and only required some free copies, the publishers stipulated that he would actually have to buy 100 copies at half price. However, he had already asked the Duke of Brunswick's permission to dedicate the concerto to him, and his desire to be able to present the Duke with a printed copy on his return induced him to accept the terms.

Spohr's op. 1 is a solid workmanlike achievement for a youth of eighteen. It does not indicate the sort of precocious genius shown by Mozart or Mendelssohn, but it displays a well-developed lyrical gift, a feeling for formal balance and a thorough grasp of technical resources. The orchestration, which is conventional but adroit, is for a small orchestra of two flutes, two bassoons, two horns and strings. Melodically the concerto shows a mixture of influences. Mozart is close to the surface, but so too are Viotti, Kreutzer and Rode, whose concertos Spohr had certainly studied in depth. Viotti's Violin Concerto no. 13 in A major, mentioned by Spohr in his diary, suggests itself as a particular model, especially in the outer movements. Both Spohr's and Viotti's first movements begin with a similar dotted rhythm, and both last movements are polonaises. (Viotti's Thirteenth Concerto may well have been the work which started the fashion for polonaise Finales in violin concertos.) Spohr's liking for chromatic inflexions in the melody, later to become a prominent feature of his style, is apparent throughout the concerto. Having rejected three attempts at a slow movement as unsuitable for the context, he settled on an attractive Siciliano in which the theme is twice varied with elegant embellishments that provide a good example of his partiality for chromatic ornamentation (ex. 4). Also evident in this concerto is Spohr's lik-

Ex. 4

[Siciliano]
[violin solo]

ing for modulation to mediant and submediant keys. In the Siciliano (in F major) the cadence into A minor at the eighth bar is a characteristic nuance, frequently to be found in Spohr's later works. This sort of cadence into the mediant minor has parallels in the violin literature of the period; for example, the second subject of the opening movement of Kreutzer's Nineteenth Concerto in D minor. In the Polonaise with which Spohr's concerto concludes there is an abrupt switch from A minor to F major, which can be seen as a rather naive precursor of a device he was subsequently to handle much more effectively (ex. 5). The use of remote keys and enharmonic modulation

Ex. 5

which was to become such a distinctive characteristic of Spohr's music is also found already in this Polonaise (ex. 6).

Ex. 6

The difference in style between the op. 1 concerto and the op. 3 duets, which he completed in St Petersburg, is remarkable, and illustrates the sharp distinction that Spohr drew between various categories of music. The concerto is first and foremost a vehicle for displaying his qualities as a violinist, and though form and purely musical interest are given greater weight than in the majority of virtuoso compositions of the period the peculiarities of the performer are prominent in the work. To some extent it suffers from the fact that its most obvious antecedents are the concertos of men with a greater talent for violin playing than for composition, whose rather mechanical alternation of lyrical sections and unrelated virtuoso passagework was initially accepted by Spohr as a formal principle. The duets, however, are firmly in the classical chamber-music tradition where virtuosity is firmly subordinated to considerations of design. Other violinist–composers had made a distinction between concertos, which were for their own performance, and duets, intended primarily for amateurs. Thus the level of difficulty in Viotti's and Rode's duets is much lower than in their concertos; double-stopping is generally straightforward, and the higher positions are used sparingly. Spohr's duets, on the other hand, are much more difficult than this, but do not gratuitously exploit virtuosity for its own sake. As in Beethoven's op. 18 string quartets, the difficulties arise from the pursuit of purely musical aims. Spohr's three duets op. 3 are clearly differentiated from the op. 1 concerto by the nature of his basic material and the tautness with which he uses it. There is very little affinity here with the music of the violinist–composers whose influence permeates the concerto. Many of the themes in the duets have a terse motivic quality reminiscent of Beethoven's early quartets and violin sonatas (which Spohr certainly knew); for example, the opening of the Allegro vivace of op. 3 no. 1 (ex. 7). The final bars of this theme show both the

Ex. 7

economical use of this motive and the exploitation of the violin's highest register (ex. 8).

Ex. 8

Another Beethovenian phrase is found at the beginning of the first movement of op. 3 no. 2, and he again seems uppermost in Spohr's mind in the
second subjects of these duets, particularly op. 3 nos. 1 and 2 (ex. 9). In the

Ex. 9

third duet the opening theme of the Allegro vivace shows Spohr's liking for
chromatic scales (ex. 10) – a device conspicuously rare in the works of other

Ex. 10

violinist–composers of the period but not uncommon in the chamber music
of Mozart and Beethoven. Here too he makes the most of his initial idea, by
inverting the chromatic scale to provide an answering phrase (ex. 11).

Ex. 11

None of the op. 3 duets has a fully fledged slow movement, though all have
slow introductions to the first movement, and those in nos. 1 and 2 are substantial. In no. 2 the first movement is followed by a set of free variations,

beginning andante and progressively speeding up; while in no. 3 the second of the two movements consists of alternating Andante and Allegretto sections, an idea possibly inspired by the last movement of Beethoven's op. 18 no. 6, or Haydn's op. 76 no. 5.

Overall these duets are a remarkable achievement; the only feature which betrays Spohr's inexperience is his almost invariable use of eight-bar themes. But in their range of sonorities, vitality of material, harmonic subtlety and skilful construction, the duets are arguably the equal of anything that had been composed in the genre up to that time (with the exception of Mozart's two duets for violin and viola K. 423/4), and they give a sure indication that Spohr was capable of being more than a violinist who merely composed for his own performance.

II

First concert tours
1803–1805

In company with Leveque, Spohr returned to Germany by sea in June 1803. During the journey they ran into a storm which resulted in universal sea-sickness among the passengers. Spohr's account of this manifestation of nature's power, as recorded in his diary, illustrated his strong reaction to the dramatic in nature and his physical courage which sometimes bordered on foolhardiness. He wrote:

I crept, ill as I was, on deck, to see this terribly grand spectacle. I got thoroughly drenched, it is true, for the waves broke continuously over the deck, and I could not endure the piercing wind and cold above deck for long. But it was worth the effort to see how the waves like mountains came rolling on, threatening to submerge us; how they suddenly seized us, lifting us high in the air, then just as quickly let us plunge into a deep abyss![1]

He arrived back in Brunswick on 5 July and was excited to learn that the great French violinist Pierre Rode, whose concertos he already knew and admired, was passing through on his way to Russia intending to give concerts at court and in the Hoftheater. The impression which Rode's playing made on him was tremendous, and after he had heard him play twice he was confirmed in his feeling that here, above all violinists he had previously heard, was a worthy model to follow. He recalled:

The more I heard him play the more I was captivated by his playing. Yes! I soon had no hesitation in placing Rode's style of playing, then still reflecting all the brilliance of that of his master Viotti, above that of my teacher Eck, and in applying myself sedulously to acquire it as much as possible by carefully practising those of Rode's compositions which I had heard him play at court and in private concerts. In this I succeeded by no means badly, and up to the time when I had by degrees formed a style of playing of my own, I was the most faithful imitator of Rode among all the young violinists of the day. I succeeded particularly well in performing the Eighth Concerto, the first three quartets and the world-famous Variations in G major wholly in his style; in these, both in Brunswick and afterwards on my first concert tour, I achieved great success.[2]

Spohr's absorption of all the best features of Rode's style marked his final phase as a student of the violin. By the time of his concert tour of North Germany in 1804 he was already a master who could stand comparison with the finest players; from then on his development came from within, and proceeded hand in hand with his development as a composer.

Rode's influence was important not only for Spohr's violin playing, but also for its contribution to his style as a composer. It was particularly strong in his writing for violin, of course, but because violin figurations colour Spohr's melodic thought in general, there is a tendency for it to seep into other areas of his work. The reference above to Rode's Eighth Concerto is noteworthy, since this concerto contains an especially large amount of passagework which is strikingly similar to Spohr's. (exx. 12 and 13). Much of this

Ex. 12: Rode, Violin Concerto no. 8, 1st movement

Ex. 13: Spohr, Violin Concerto no. 7, 1st movement

was the stock-in-trade of violinists, but it was largely through Rode's agency that Spohr acquired it. Another rhythmic and melodic idea which constantly appears in Spohr has unmistakable antecedents in Rode and other French composers of the period (ex. 14). It has several variants, and usually

Ex. 14: Rode, Violin Concerto no. 7

occurs in the last movement of an instrumental piece in which the violin is prominent (ex. 15). It is less likely that Rode had any important influence on Spohr's harmony. Rode's own feeling for harmony was not nearly as highly developed as Spohr's, but passages are occasionally encountered in Rode's music which can be paralleled in Spohr's earlier works.

Ex. 15: Spohr, String Quartet op. 4 no. 2

There was one other important respect in which Spohr seems to have been influenced, in part at least, by Rode: his taste for what was described in so many contemporary reports as 'noble melancholy'. He commented in his *Violin School*, when discussing concerto playing, that the first movement of Rode's Violin Concerto op. 9 should be played in such a way as to emphasise that it has a 'serious, elevated, and in the . . . subject and its repetition a somewhat melancholy character';[3] and he described the Rondo as 'fanciful and melancholy in its theme'[4] (see ex. 14 above). The similarity of such themes in the works of these two composers can clearly be seen from two extracts: in both cases this sort of opening theme may be regarded as typical (exx. 16 and 17). This 'noble seriousness', which pervades much of his music in all genres, was carried to a higher artistic level in Spohr than in Rode, and was one of the features of his music most admired by contemporaries.

Ex. 16: Rode, Violin Concerto no. 8

Ex. 17: Spohr, *Quatuor brillant* op. 61

After Rode's departure from Brunswick, Spohr made arrangements to give a concert of his own in the Hoftheater, in order to perform his op. 1 Violin Concerto and to provide the Duke with evidence that his faith in him had not been misplaced. It was with a degree of trepidation that Spohr made an appearance so soon after the celebrated French violinist, but in the event his nervousness evaporated almost as soon as the concert began, and both

his performance and the composition were very well received. The success of
the concert and the Duke's warm congratulations in particular caused Spohr
to remember the evening as one of the happiest of his life. As a mark of his
satisfaction the Duke made Spohr a substantial present for the dedication of
the concerto and appointed him to a position as first violin in the court
orchestra with a threefold increase of salary.

Spohr spent the next twelve months consolidating what he had learned
from Eck and from Rode's example. At the same time he applied himself to
composition with characteristic energy, producing a concertante for violin,
cello and orchestra, three violin concertos, and a potpourri for violin with
string trio accompaniment. Spohr did not publish the concertante and in
later years had lost his copy of it, so that it was omitted from his thematic
catalogue (although a copy of the score has survived and is now in the Kassel
Landesbibliothek). The work is in two sections, Adagio maestoso (C minor)
and Allegro (C major), with a repetition of the Adagio in A minor in the
middle of the Allegro. The Adagio is remarkably prophetic of the mood of
'noble seriousness' which, building on Rode's example, Spohr was to make
peculiarly his own. The opening tutti and the first solo entry (exx. 18 and 19)

Ex. 18

Ex. 19

show the genuinely Romantic quality that he was able to achieve even in this early work. The concertante was written for performance with J. P. Benecke, a Brunswick cellist, with whom he began a concert tour to Paris in January 1804, but because of the theft of Spohr's Guarnerius violin from the back of the coach in which they were travelling the tour was abandoned after a single concert in Göttingen.

The Duke of Brunswick's generosity allowed Spohr to acquire the best violin available in Brunswick at that time (probably a Guadagnini) as a replacement for the Guarnerius (which was never recovered), and by diligent practice he familiarised himself with the new instrument. Throughout the spring and summer of 1804 he continued to compose assiduously with a view to making another concert tour in the autumn. His enthusiasm for Rode had made him dissatisfied with his previous concertos; even the most recent one in E minor (unpublished), which he had composed immediately after his return from Russia, no longer seemed satisfactory, and after a few performances in November and December 1804, when it was given in a remodelled version with a newly composed Adagio, it appears to have been discarded.

The works which Spohr wrote specifically for his forthcoming concert tour were the concertos in D minor (op. 2) and A major (unpublished), and the potpourri on an air from Pierre Gaveaux's opera *Le petit matelot* (1796) (op. 5). The potpourri (a favourite form at the time) was scored for violin with string trio accompaniment and was clearly designed for use at the music parties which were an essential element of any concert tour. The situation may not have been as bad in Germany as it seemed to be in St Petersburg, but it was nevertheless necessary for an artist to make himself known among the principal musical households in any town where he hoped to give a concert, and the impression which he made at these gathering was of vital importance to the success of his public concert. An accompaniment for string trio in potpourris and other such salon pieces for violin was normal at this period. The use of the piano as the accompanying instrument did not become common for some years; it was not until 1811 that Spohr began to include an optional piano accompaniment in this sort of piece. The two concertos are of sharply contrasting characters. The A major remained in manuscript until its publication by Bärenreiter in 1954, though whether this was because of Spohr's own dissatisfaction with the work or because at the time he could not interest a publisher in it is uncertain. It is, in fact, interesting and attractive. The first movement begins, unusually, with a slow introduction and continues, even more unusually for a violin concerto at this period, with an Allegro in 3/4; the conclusion that Spohr must have had Mozart's Symphony no. 39 at the back of his mind is hard to avoid, especially in view of the strikingly Mozartian quality of much of the material. Rode, however, is apparent in the elevated style of the melody with which the first solo begins and in many of the figurations with which the solo part is embellished. These same influences are present in the other two movements, and the overall form of the work owes much to Spohr's obvious familiarity with Mozart's piano concertos. Nevertheless there is a strong sense of the composer's own individuality. The opening Adagio in particular seems already characteristic of its composer, with something of the same Romantic quality that is to be found in the concertante for violin and cello, while the slow movement's sustained lyricism looks forward to the mastery in this style which Spohr was to achieve in his later concertos. Despite its eclecticism the work as a whole shows how rapidly he was forging a unified and distinct style of his own.

Many of the same features are to be found in the D minor Concerto, though in this work the debt to Rode is more pronounced. However, in most respects Spohr's concerto is superior to Rode's compositions; it has greater cohesion and a surer control of harmonic and tonal resources. The first movement begins with a march-like theme which gradually builds up to a fine climax before the solo violin enters with a declamatory theme loosely based on the opening motive (ex. 20), which once again reflects the noble

Ex. 20

melancholy of Rode. From this point the movement pursues its course with unflagging vigour. The Adagio which follows is, like that of the A major Concerto, a lyrical movement of considerable charm and expressiveness which must have been specifically designed to display these qualities in Spohr's playing while at the same time giving him an opportunity to show his skill in double-stopping. The Finale is, as in the op. 1 concerto, a polonaise, but this time handled with much greater assurance. An abrupt shift to the submediant is here managed far more effectively than in the earlier work (ex. 21).

With this concerto Spohr had produced his first masterpiece – a work which was to lay the foundations of his fame as both violinist and composer during the concert tour of Central and North Germany which he began in October 1804. His itinerary took him to Halberstadt, Magdeburg, Halle, Leipzig, Dresden and Berlin. In the first three cities he achieved consider-

Ex. 21

able artistic success, especially with the D minor Concerto. His playing seems to have made a strong impression on many of those who heard it; Adolf Müller, a student at the university in Halle and a competent violinist himself, wrote to a friend after Spohr's concerts of 21 and 23 November:

Several weeks ago there was a very remarkable violinist here, Spohr, who as a virtuoso achieved much, much more than Pixis or Fränzl. He played in the Kreutzer manner, and had a very powerful tone that was probably so strong because he kept the bow close to the bridge. I learned much from him, not least to distinguish clearly between an artist and a mere technician.[5]

In Leipzig, however, Spohr achieved his most important triumphs of the tour. There the *Allgemeine musikalische Zeitung* (*AMZ*) was already well established, under the editorship of Friedrich Rochlitz, as perhaps the most influential musical journal in Germany, with a wide circulation outside Leipzig. Spohr was well aware that a good report of his playing from such a source would be of inestimable value in gaining recognition for his talent. But his stay in Leipzig did not begin auspiciously. He arrived in the city on 27 November and was somewhat chagrined to discover, on delivering his letters of introduction, that his artistic reputation had not preceded him. In a city such as Leipzig, which was visited by the most notable musicians, little interest was taken in an unknown twenty-one-year-old violinist. At the one important soirée to which he was invited he almost ruined his chances by an injudicious choice of music. When asked to play a quartet he produced his favourite of the Beethoven op. 18 set, but quickly perceived that the music was unknown to the other players, who seemed baffled by its unfamiliar idiom; what was worse, the audience rapidly lost interest and people began to talk among themselves. Totally unrehearsed music was commonplace even in the best soirées, and presumably the audience had a high degree of tolerance for inaccuracy, but it is hardly surprising that a performance of such complex and demanding music as these quartets of Beethoven, in which three of the players were sight-reading, should fail to hold the attention of the listeners. Someone less forceful than Spohr, or who lacked his passionate commitment to the dignity of his art, might have struggled to the end of the piece and retired into obscurity for the rest of the evening, having lost his chance to impress the musical amateurs of Leipzig. Not so Spohr: in the middle of the first movement he broke off abruptly and, without saying a word, packed up his violin. When his host approached he remarked, loudly enough to be heard by the rest of the company, that he had previously been accustomed to being listened to in silence and that he interpreted their inattention as signifying that they would prefer him to desist. Having apologised to the other musicians, he was about to leave the gathering when the embarrassed host returned to him and suggested that if he would play something more adapted to the taste and capacity of the audience he would be listened to attentively. Spohr recognised that he had misjudged the occasion in bringing forward the Beethoven, and readily complied. He played Rode's E flat Quartet, which was so greatly relished that he was easily induced to follow it with the same composer's G major Variations and, as he later recalled, he became the object of the most flattering attention for the remainder of the evening.

As a consequence of this incident the Leipzigers undoubtedly showed more interest in Spohr's concert than would otherwise have been the case. The rehearsal was numerously attended, and the favourable report which was spread by those who were there, especially of his D minor Concerto, helped to ensure a good audience for the performance. At the concert on 10 December his playing was so successful that he was persuaded by 'the requests of many friends of the musical art'[6] (according to the *AMZ*) to give a second concert a week later. The concert of 17 December was, by his own account, the most numerously attended of any that had ever been given in Leipzig by a visiting artist. Whether or not this was an exaggeration, Rochlitz's review of the two concerts in the *AMZ* is unequivocal about the profound admiration evoked by Spohr's playing and compositions. Rochlitz considered that 'he gave us a treat such as, so far as we can remember, no violinist but Rode ever gave us'; and he added that 'Herr Spohr may without doubt take a place among the most eminent violinists of the present day; and, especially when his youth is considered, his powers would arouse astonishment if it were possible to go from rapture to cold astonishment.' He felt that the concertos (the D minor and the E minor) ranked with the finest, and that he knew of none which could surpass the D minor (which had to be repeated at the second concert by request) 'either with regard to inventiveness, soul and charm, or seriousness and profundity'.[7] He added that Spohr's preference seemed to be for the 'grand and for a soft dreamy melancholy' (*sanfter Wehmuth Schwärmenden*). It is noteworthy that this sort of description was repeatedly applied to Spohr's music throughout the next eighty years or so during which his works remained a part of the standard repertoire.

The tendency which produced this quality in Spohr's compositions also led him in his playing to stress expression over execution. Thus Rochlitz noted:

As regards, first, accuracy of playing in the broadest sense, it is here, as it were, as a sure foundation; a perfect purity, certainty and precision, the most remarkable fluency, every manner of bowing, every variety of tone, the most unembarrassed ease in the handling of all these things even amid the greatest difficulties – these make him one of the most skilful virtuosos. But the soul with which his playing is inspired – the flights of fancy, the fire, the tenderness, the intensity of feeling, the fine taste; and then his insight into the spirit of the most different compositions, and his art of giving each its own spirit; this makes him a real artist.[8]

After the success of his first concert Spohr had become a notable figure in Leipzig musical circles and was eagerly sought to play at soirées, where the impact he made was perhaps even greater than that produced by his concerto playing. He was even able now to secure a hearing for his favourite Beethoven quartets. After hearing his chamber-music playing, Rochlitz was further impressed by Spohr's ability to express the individuality of each composer whose music he performed. He observed in his review:

He is altogether a different person when he plays, for example, Beethoven (his darling, whom he handles exquisitely) or Mozart (his ideal) or Rode (whose grandiosity he knows so well how to assume, without any scratching and scraping in producing the necessary volume of tone), or when he plays Viotti and *galant* composers: he is a different person because they are different persons. No wonder therefore that he pleases everywhere and leaves scarcely any other wish behind than that one might keep him and listen to him always.[9]

In Leipzig Spohr had once more succumbed to the lure of female beauty. The object of his attentions this time was a young Italian singer, Rosa Alberghi, whom he had heard at a Gewandhaus concert and had engaged to sing in his own concerts. Spohr began to spend an increasing amount of time at the house where she and her mother had taken lodgings, and assisted Rosa in her practice, accompanying her on the piano so far as his limited keyboard ability allowed, and writing embellishments for her arias. His diary, which recorded the initial stages of this relationship, was not continued beyond 9 December, but it is clear that their affection for one another soon developed into more than a casual flirtation. By the end of the tour, though, Spohr's infatuation with Rosa Alberghi had begun to cool, partly on account of her Roman Catholicism, which led her to attempt 'the conversion of the Lutheran heretic',[10] as Spohr put it, and partly because with characteristic clear-sightedness he had seen that she would not make a suitable marriage partner. Unfortunately Rosa's infatuation with Spohr persisted as strongly as before and, as he was unable to bring himself to dash her hopes, the relationship dragged on inconclusively until his engagement to Dorette Scheidler in 1806, when he was finally forced to write to Rosa to tell her that he could never marry her.

After his triumph in Leipzig Spohr travelled on to Dresden where, with the assistance of Rosa's father, who was a member of the Dresden Chapel Royal, he arranged two successful concerts. But he declined to play at court when he learned that the concerts, without exception, took place during dinner; as he remarked, 'my youthful artist's pride was kindled with indignation at the idea that my playing would be accompanied by the clattering of plates!'[11]

Still accompanied by Rosa, Spohr travelled on to Berlin, where his old teacher Kunisch, then a member of the Berlin Hofkapelle, proudly introduced his former pupil to many of the distinguished musicians in the city and facilitated arrangements for his concert. This took place on 3 March 1805, and thanks to Spohr's shrewdness in inviting the thirteen-year-old Jacob Beer (the future composer Meyerbeer) to appear in it, the audience was greatly swelled by members of the city's Jewish community, making it one of the most numerously attended of a busy season. In the *Berlinische musikalische Zeitung*, however, Johann Friedrich Reichardt, the Royal Konzertmeister, did not give Spohr so flattering a notice as he had received in Leipzig. Reichardt considered Spohr's playing to be 'too cold and monotonous', and expressed the wish that in his compositions he 'might keep less scrupulously to a number of forms in the Rode fashion and use them less frequently'.[12] He also objected to Spohr's portamento as an exaggerated copy of Rode's, and his freedom with respect to tempo. Though Spohr initially felt pained by these criticisms he concluded on reflection that the last remark, at least, was justified and set himself to develop a more disciplined control of tempo without diminishing the expressiveness of his performance; the portamento remained a prominent feature of his style, as a review in 1808 indicates (see below, p. 47). On the whole it seems unlikely that many of those who heard Spohr play would have shared Reichardt's reservations, which are not echoed in other reports at this period. Rochlitz's enthusiasm probably reflected much more closely the reactions of the majority of Spohr's auditors; certainly his review in the *AMZ* had aroused sufficient interest in the young man to bring him invitations to many important music parties in

Berlin. He renewed his acquaintance with Dussek at a soirée given by Prince Louis Ferdinand (of whose household Dussek was then a member) and elsewhere met some of the most distinguished musicians of the day, though he discovered when he played one of the Beethoven quartets that even in such company as this Rode was preferred to Beethoven; the celebrated cellist and composer Bernhard Romberg complimented him on his playing of the Beethoven, then remarked disparagingly: 'But my dear Spohr, how can you bear to play such baroque rubbish?'[13]

Returning to Brunswick, Spohr could be well satisfied with the outcome of his concert tour, which had been both an artistic and a financial success. The excellent reception that his D minor Concerto had met with must have helped to confirm his faith in his powers as a composer, and he immediately began working on a new concerto in B minor (later published as his no. 4, op. 10). Here a growing individuality of style can be seen, though there is still a feeling that some of the influences are not yet thoroughly digested. Haydn, Mozart, Beethoven, and Rode rub shoulders with other, less easily identifiable elements. It would not be fanciful to assume that the contact with Dussek (whose use of chromaticism and modulation has parallels with Spohr's) and Prince Louis Ferdinand (whose music contains some remarkable anticipations of Romantic expression) had added another dimension to Spohr's musical experience, which was the process of assimilation in the B minor Violin Concerto.

At about this time Spohr also received his first pupil from outside Brunswick, so beginning his lifelong activity as a teacher which was to result in his instruction of a large number of pupils and the exertion of an enormous influence on the development of violin playing in Germany.

In June 1805 Rochlitz's review of his concerts in Leipzig the previous winter bore fruit in an invitation from Gotha to compete for the vacant post of Konzertmeister. The review had made no mention of his age, and when Spohr arrived in Gotha the Intendant, Baron von Reibnitz, was somewhat taken aback to see so young a man. However, the brilliance of his performance and his self-assured bearing in rehearsing the orchestra so impressed the Baron that he advised him to give his age as twenty-four when introduced to the court, since at twenty-one he might be considered too young for the post. In the event, though, his playing before the court made such an impression that the appointment was not in doubt. Thus with a fivefold increase in salary Spohr became, by a decree dated 5 August 1805, the youngest Konzertmeister in Germany.

After having given a concert at Wilhelmsthal near Eisenach, the family residence of the Grand Duke of Weimar, and a final concert in Gotha, he set off on his return to Brunswick, stopping on the way to receive the congratulations of his parents in Seesen. Unfortunately a fall from his horse between Seesen and Brunswick resulted in such severe lacerations to his face that he was unfit to resume his orchestral duties in Brunswick for three or four weeks. But in the meantime he had received a letter from Dussek inviting him to join Prince Louis Ferdinand's household in Magdeburg for the duration of the military manoeuvres which were taking place there, so that he could participate in the regular evening music parties. He obtained leave of absence from Brunswick from his indulgent patron and travelled to Magdeburg. There he found himself involved in experiences quite unlike anything he had previously encountered. For a brief period he hovered on the periphery of the cataclysmic events which were then reshaping the map of Europe. But Napoleon's great campaigns on German territory had not yet taken place; and though the bloody battles of Austerlitz and Jena lay in the near future, the brilliant uniforms and military pageantry had more immediacy than shattered limbs and corpses. Spohr thoroughly enjoyed the thrill of riding to manoeuvres as a member of the Prince's suite until one day, having been hemmed in by a battery for more than an hour, he began to fear for his hearing and thereafter took to spending the time, when not required for the Prince's music-making, with acquaintances in Magdeburg. The realities of war must, however, have been brought home to him when early in the following year Prince Louis Ferdinand was killed in action near Saalfeld, and when later in the same year Duke Carl Wilhelm Ferdinand of Brunswick was mortally wounded at the battle of Jena. Spohr was not insensible of the great debt he owed to his generous patron, nor was his gratitude untouched by genuine affection. Recording the Duke's death in his memoirs, he wrote: 'I mourned for him as for a father.'[14]

III

Konzertmeister in Gotha: marriage
1805–1808

In 1805 Gotha was one of the most cultured and politically liberal states in Central Germany. Duke Ernst II of Saxe-Gotha-Altenburg, who had died in the previous year, had been a Freemason and an ardent supporter of the ideals of the Enlightenment. Under his rule the Illuminati, a branch of Freemasonry whose progressive political aims caused them to be proscribed in most of the German states, had taken root firmly in Gotha. However, the revolutionary agitation which followed in the wake of the French Revolution led to the suppression of Masonic lodges throughout Germany, and in 1793 the Gotha Lodge too was disbanded. But under Ernst's successor Emil Leopold August, whose enthusiasm for cultural and intellectual pursuits and abhorrence of military affairs and hunting ensured the court's continuing liberal and artistic tendencies, it was refounded in 1806 with the name *Ernst zum Kompass*, and on 12 October 1807 Spohr was admitted as a member. In such an environment Spohr's independent character found a fertile soil for its development; his beliefs in essential human dignity and in the supremacy of merit over privilege, of which the foundations had been laid in his parents' house, were confirmed and strengthened during his time in Gotha. Spohr will have come into contact with the ideas of the Illuminati, who were certainly active again in Gotha between 1807 and 1812 (as is clear from August Reichard's *Selbstbiographie*), and among his acquaintances in the Gotha Lodge was Rudolf Zacharias Becker,* known as the *Gothaer Jakobiner*, some of whose radical political views were later to be reflected in Spohr's own opinions.

Musically, Gotha had a distinguished history. Pachelbel, Telemann, Stölzel and Georg Benda had all worked there, and the Duchess Caroline Amalie, who was far more stable and practical than her eccentric husband, together with the Duke's music-loving younger brother, Prince Friedrich, continued the court's special interest in music. Gotha possessed no opera company, but weekly concerts of vocal, instrumental and orchestral music were given at court throughout the year, and music was not, as in Brunswick, Dresden and many other courts, merely an accompaniment to cards

---

* R. Z. Becker (1752–1822), editor of the *Deutsche Zeitung für die Jugend*, the *Allgemeine Anzeiger der Deutschen* and the *Nationalzeitung der Deutschen*.

or dinner, but was performed for its own sake. The *Kammermusici* who formed the bulk of the orchestra had no official duties apart from the weekly court concerts; only the court oboists, who augmented the orchestra, were expected to play at balls and banquets. In such a congenial situation Spohr set to work with enthusiasm to mould the players at his disposal into a fine ensemble. He scheduled three or four rehearsals each week, and by the firmness of his control he soon began to achieve excellent results.

At this period the concept of a conductor whose sole task was to direct the orchestra was barely envisaged. The normal practice was for the initial tempo and minimal direction to be given either from the keyboard or from the first violin. At Gotha, when Spohr first arrived, both systems were in use, direction from the first violin being given in orchestral music, and from the piano in vocal music with orchestra. In many places the use of, and direction from, the piano in orchestral music continued well into the century (at the Philharmonic Society in London, for instance, the pianist, who after 1820 was designated conductor, played in symphonies and overtures until the early 1830s). It is unlikely that this practice existed in Gotha in 1805, for Spohr observed in his memoirs that the court pianist Reinhard played viola in the orchestra. In orchestral music therefore Spohr's direction from the violin would have been unchallenged. When vocal pieces with orchestra were to be performed, however, Reinhard (who, out of respect for his seniority and long standing as the Duke's music master, had been designated Konzertmeister at the same time as Spohr) took part as pianist, and at first, in Spohr's words, 'he made some weak attempts to assume the direction of the vocal performances'. This division of authority was not acceptable to the forceful young Konzertmeister and, as he recalled, 'I knew so well how to overawe him by my decisive bearing as first violin that he soon succumbed as willingly to my lead at the piano as on the viola'.[1] After a certain amount of resentment from one or two of the older members of the orchestra had been overcome, Spohr's direction was decisively established. Whether at this stage he took to directing rehearsals with his violin bow rather than playing continuously with the first violins is undocumented, but it seems likely that he did; it is improbable, though, that he used a baton at this time, for at the Frankenhausen Music Festival of 1810 he is reported to have directed with a roll of paper. The peak of excellence to which Spohr brought the Gotha orchestra before he relinquished his post there in 1813 is attested by no less a critic than Carl Maria von Weber, who wrote, after attending a performance of Mozart's Symphony no. 41 in C major just before Spohr's departure for Vienna in the autumn of 1812,

it is a rare experience to hear this difficult work so well played. Tempos were spirited and well chosen, and light and shade assured by careful observation of *piano* and *forte* markings. Wind and strings vied with each other to produce complete unity of feeling.

The present writer's pleasure was only modified by his awareness of the fact that perfection such as this is not likely to come his way again for some time, since Spohr is leaving on 5 October.[2]

The major event in Spohr's personal life during his first year in Gotha was his marriage to Dorothea (Dorette), the eighteen-year-old daughter of one of the court singers, Susanna Scheidler. Dorette had been given a good general education by her recently deceased father and was also a brilliant harpist, accomplished pianist and competent violinist. Spohr described how, at their first meeting, he asked her to play something for him on the harp and recalled that after she had played with the greatest confidence and the finest shades of expression, 'I was so deeply moved that I could scarcely restrain my tears. Bowing in silence, I took my leave – but my heart remained behind.'[3] He then forwarded his suit by composing the vocal scena *Oskar* for Susanna Scheidler, and a sonata in C minor for harp and violin, which would provide a good reason for him and Dorette to spend time together. Then, during the court's stay in Altenburg for a session of the Diet, towards the end of 1805, he proposed to Dorette and was accepted. On 2 February 1806 their wedding took place in the presence of the Duchess in the court chapel at Gotha. The match was an ideal one; throughout the twenty-eight years of their marriage they remained devoted to one another and there is no evidence that Spohr's affections ever strayed during that time. Their correspondence with each other even after so many years of marriage was filled with expressions of affection which radiate a genuine warmth. The strength of their marriage lay partly in their shared musical lives. As a harpist Dorette became a distinguished virtuoso in her own right who, even in an age when fine harp players were not uncommon, stood out as an exceptional artist. At the same time her well-developed critical instinct allowed her to take an informed interest in – and exert a beneficial influence on – her husband's creative work.

It is appropriate that so important an event in Spohr's personal life should have coincided with the emergence of a more strongly personal element in his musical style. The Violin Concerto in C major op. 7, which he completed in Altenburg around the time of his proposal to Dorette, is perhaps the first work in which his own distinctive mode of expression seems clearly to predominate over the diverse influences to which his style had hitherto been indebted. Spohr's confident assertiveness, which pervades the whole of the first movement, is seen in the declamatory theme, based on a figure from the opening tutti, with which the soloist enters (ex. 22), while the Siciliano second movement has a truly Romantic character. Only in the third movement, a Rondo alla polacca, is Rode's influence still apparent to a marked degree; but even here there are important differences, most notably in the greater emphasis on chromaticism and the use of cadential pedal points. Elsewhere numerous examples of violin figurations which reflect the development of a personal style of playing can easily be found.

Louis Spohr: self-portrait, (c. 1806)

Ex. 22

The other works which he composed during his first twelve months in Gotha – two sets of variations for violin and string trio in D major and A minor (opp. 6 and 8), three sonatas for violin and harp, and the scena and aria *Oskar* – show a continually growing self-confidence and indicate how early he acquired the essential elements of his mature style. In *Oskar*, for instance, there is much which immediately proclaims his authorship, such as a woodwind passage from the opening section of recitative (ex. 23). An

Ex. 23

enharmonic modulation in the concluding Allegro, too, is indicative of the direction in which he was moving (ex. 24). The sonatas for violin and harp in C minor (1805), B flat major op. 16 (1806) and E flat major op. 113* (1806) show a progressive expertise in handling the medium and especially in the fluency of his writing for the harp. In the E flat sonata he lighted upon the idea, which he adopted in his subsequent compositions for violin and harp, of writing the harp part a semitone higher than the violin part and tuning the strings of the harp down a semitone; this had two advantages, for it allowed each instrument to play in the sort of key which suited if best (i.e. the violin in sharp keys, the harp in flat keys) and also minimised the possibility of the harp's strings breaking in performance. Spohr showed a much sounder grasp of sonata structure in the first movement of op. 113, which is far more assured than those of the two earlier sonatas; the themes lend themselves

---

* The high opus number resulted from the fact that it was only in 1840–41 that Spohr published the sonatas which he and Dorette had kept in their repertoire.

Ex. 24

better to motivic development, and the material as a whole has greater individuality and cohesiveness. In all these works the final movements are the least satisfactory, relying too heavily on Rode-like dotted rhythms and, as in many of the works from this period of his life, light-heartedness too often descends into triviality and commonplace.

The three sonatas for violin and harp, especially the one in E flat, provided Louis and Dorette Spohr with a repertoire in which their joint virtuosity could be brilliantly displayed. With these and the newly composed violin works they hoped to make their first concert tour in the Autumn of 1806 but were overtaken by events both political and domestic. Napoleon's campaign against Prussia made travelling hazardous if not impossible, and in addition Dorette found herself pregnant. Forced by these circumstances to forgo the projected tour Spohr threw himself with redoubled energy into his musical activities in Gotha. His continuing admiration for Beethoven is attested by the repeated performances he gave with the court orchestra of the first four symphonies, which up to that time were hardly known outside Vienna, and with Dorette as pianist he also performed Beethoven's Second and Third Piano Concertos. In the field of composition his mind turned towards a more ambitious project than he had so far attempted: a one-act opera entitled *Die Prüfung*. Up to this stage, with the single exception of *Oskar* his works had all centred on his own instrument; his desire now to write an opera indicated that his ambition to be taken seriously as a composer was strengthening, and that he recognised the desirability of success in that genre as a means of establishing his credentials before the world. The timing of such an undertaking might seem unpropitious, for during these months Gotha was occupied first by billeted Prussian troops and after the terrible battle of Jena was troubled by a constant stream of French troops and Prussian prisoners. Fortunately, though, the townspeople were unmolested, little damage was done to property, and the battle zone rapidly shifted away from Gotha. During all these events Spohr, calling on his deep reserves of self-discipline, was able to sit quietly in the study at the back of his house where he could not hear the constant noise in the streets and, blocking out all thoughts of reality, immerse himself in his own world of imagination. It was entirely consistent with his character that, seeing he could do nothing to ameliorate the situation, he should turn to art as the expression of mankind's higher qualities. Under these conditions the opera rapidly took shape.

The libretto of *Die Prüfung* (The Test) was by his uncle Eduard Henke (1783–1869), though the subject matter and layout were jointly worked out during Henke's visit to Gotha during the Autumn of 1806. However, during his stay Henke completed only the texts of the musical numbers, promising to send the linking dialogue later. The autograph* does not contain the dialogue which, if it was ever sent, is now lost. For this reason the plot can only be roughly reconstructed from the libretto of the two arias (with accompagnato recitative), three duets, terzetto, Romance and Finale which, with the overture, constitute the musical numbers. The action is centred on four characters: Count W., his daughter Natalie, her lover Edmund, and Charis, who incites Natalie to put her lover to the test. This is done by Natalie disguising herself and, under the name of Ida, attempting to seduce Edmund. After Edmund has shown his constancy and proved Natalie to be similarly faithful the opera comes to a happy ending. The kinship of this plot with *Così fan tutte* and many other operas of the period is obvious, and on the surface it seems rather unpromising, but in one respect at least it reflected the changing intellectual climate, for Count W. and his daughter represent the conflict of old and new ideas. The Count is an old-fashioned rationalist who has little sympathy with art, while Natalie is an enthusiastic Romantic and a lover of poetry. Their different stances are brought out in a duet (no. 3) where Natalie sings: 'Do you know a maiden called Romanticism? She adorns our earthly life. She is sent from Heaven to men, to lift our hearts on high. She teaches me to revel in heavenly pain and disposes the joyful heart to melancholy. I have given myself to her service.' Her father answers: 'Do you know a goddess called Reason? . . .' etc. The ending of the opera shows that Spohr's and Henke's sympathies lay with Natalie.

Musically the work has a number of interesting features. The overture is a

* In the Louis-Spohr-Gedenk- und Forschungsstätte in Kassel.

substantial piece – Spohr's first purely orchestral composition – and it shows his indebtedness to both Mozart and Cherubini. The rich harmony and wind writing of the opening Andante recall the former, while the thematic material and its handling, especially an abrupt modulation to the flat submediant (ex. 25), are reminders of Spohr's early devotion to the latter. Much

Ex. 25

of the thematic material in the vocal numbers of the opera is rather bland and conventional, indicating a degree of tentativeness in writing for voices, but there is also much that reveals Spohr's individuality, particularly in chromatic nuances. The concluding bars of Charis and Edmund's Andantino duet (no. 1) are an example of the 'soft' endings for which Spohr showed so marked a predilection throughout his life (ex. 26). Tonally there are some

Ex. 26

surprises, such as Natalie and Edmund's Andantino duet (no. 7) which, after a dramatic recitative, begins with a slow section in E flat major 2/4, followed by an Allegro in F major 4/4, which in turn gives way to a final section in A flat major 12/8. In the Finale there is a repetition of part of no. 7, the lovers' duet, giving emphasis to the solution of the conflict, and a neat formal touch is the return of the main theme of no. 1 right at the end, giving a sense of roundness to the whole piece. This type of repetition of a complete extract is similar to the technique employed by Georg Benda, though Spohr probably derived it from the operas of Cherubini, Dalayrac and others of the French school. In the instrumentation Spohr strove for variety. The E flat section of no. 7, for instance, is accompanied only by two clarinets, bassoon and pizzicato basses. Charis' Romanze (no. 5) begins with two solo horns and includes a cello obbligato, while Natalie's aria (no. 6) has a virtuoso violin solo which vies with the voice throughout. This violin solo, judging by its difficulty, was almost certainly intended for Spohr himself to play and thus indicates incidentally that he probably directed the opera from the violin.

At first, in rehearsal, Spohr was well pleased with his new work, but as time went by he began to discover more and more things in it with which he felt dissatisfied, so that by the time he came to give the opera a concert performance at one of the court concerts he had already decided to suppress it. Despite its good reception by performers and audience he laid the work aside, with the exception of the tenor aria (no. 4), which he probably presented as a concert aria in a few subsequent concerts, and the overture, which was later published as op. 15.* Having, on his own admission, taken Mozart as the standard by which to measure the success of his opera, Spohr could hardly have failed to be disappointed with *Die Prüfung*; but it had been a valuable exercise and was a sure pointer to his wider musical ambitions. Spohr possessed the capacity to put both his failures and his successes behind him within a very short time, and was soon immersed once more in composition. 1807 was a prolific year for him, seeing the production of a fifth violin concerto in E flat (op. 17), two concertantes for harp, violin and orchestra, a trio for harp, violin and cello, a fantasia (op. 35) and variations (op. 36) for harp, a potpourri on themes of Mozart for violin and string trio (op. 22), two string quartets (op. 4), a *quatuor brillant* (op. 11) and an overture in C minor (op. 12). By far the majority of these works were intended for his own and his wife's performance, but the two string quartets and the overture are evidence of his continuing desire to explore new territory. The distinction between the op. 4 string quartets and the op. 11 *quatuor brillant* is an important one: the former are in four movements with a classical layout and a conscious attempt at equality between the parts, while the latter, in three movements, is essentially a violin concerto with string trio accompaniment, and is in the tradition of Rode's three quartets op. 11, the first of which, in E flat, Spohr had often played to the delight of audiences that did not relish Beethoven. He maintained a similar clear distinction between his seven subsequent 'solo' quartets (opp. 27 and 30, though not specifically called '*quatuor*

---

* The opus number 15 was subsequently applied to the string quartets of 1808, and Spohr altered the overture to 14 in his own catalogue. It appears in Schletterer as op. 15a.

brillant', are clearly in that category), which were published singly, and the rest of his string quartets which, except for the last four, were published in sets. The op. 4 quartets, however, failed to satisfy the exacting criteria of fine quartet writing which his knowledge of Haydn's, Mozart's, and Beethoven's masterpieces had set for him. It is probable that he would have consigned the manuscript to oblivion along with *Die Prüfung* had it not been for the publisher, Kühnel of Leipzig, who had already issued his Violin Concerto op. 2 and Duets op. 3, and who, having heard Spohr play at a music party at his house in Leipzig in the autumn of 1807, succeeded in persuading him to allow the quartets to be published.

The op. 4 quartets, which had probably been composed over the previous two or three years, reveal a mixture of influences: turns of phrase, especially in the first movements, indicate the impact of Beethoven's op. 18, but the influence of Haydn and Mozart is closer to the surface, while Spohr the violinist can be seen in many of the melodic ideas, particularly at cadences (ex. 27), which he was to use almost unchanged in works of twenty or more

Ex. 27

years later. On the whole the handling of material in the first movement is somewhat stiff, and the Minuets are lacking in individuality, though that of no. 2 has a degree of humorous vitality. The Finale of no. 2 is again in the French dotted fashion; that of no. 1 is in a more successful Mozartian style. The most interesting movements are the slow movements. The Poco adagio of the second quartet has an attractive and well-sustained lyricism, though there is a very obvious origin for one of its principal ideas (ex. 28). The Adagio of the first contains a prophetic passage of harmony (ex. 29). In general the quartets do not, as Spohr himself recognised, achieve a successful

Ex. 28

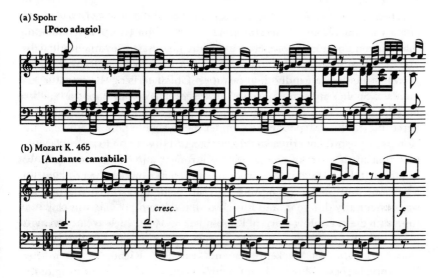

(a) Spohr
[Poco adagio]

(b) Mozart K. 465
[Andante cantabile]

cresc.

Ex. 29

[Adagio]

balance between the instruments; the lion's share of the interest is in the first violin and there is little sense of the conversational quality that distinguishes the classical works in the genre. The op. 11 *quatuor brillant* has no pretensions to be other than a chamber concerto, and as such is an attractive work.

In his handling of the orchestra in the concerto, the concertantes and the overture, Spohr showed the benefits of his experience as Konzertmeister in increased dexterity and imagination. The balance is almost unfailingly well judged and there are some unusual effects, as in the final movement of the E minor concertante where a cadenza for the harp and violin, in which the theme of the previous movement is recalled, is accompanied by solo timpani. The E minor concertante is a work of considerable musical worth and, unlike the first concertante in G major, it avoids falling into banality in the final movement. The most notable features of the violin concerto are a fine impassioned section in the middle of the Adagio ma non troppo, and a brilliant and effective cadenza in the Rondo. (Spohr always wrote out his cadenzas in full, though in many of his concertos he dispensed with the formal cadenza entirely.)

When the Overture in C minor was published in 1808 the *AMZ* reviewed it along with the Violin Concerto op. 10 and the Quartet op. 11, concluding that this composition for orchestra alone did not attain the same standard of excellence as Spohr's violin music, though it was conceded to have a good overall structure and individual beauties. Characterising the essential elements of Spohr's style, the reviewer observed: 'His compositions as a whole have, more or less, a character of spirited yet temperate seriousness and an agreeable mixture of gloomy and tender melancholy. If one should call this Romantic the present critic would not object.'[4] He went on to say of the overture that in this sort of composition a stronger and bolder approach was required. Taking Haydn, Mozart or Beethoven as a model, the criticism was a just one; but Spohr was aiming to create something which was in many ways essentially different, and it is clear that the end product was closely in tune with the prevailing spirit of Romanticism. Music such as this was capable of inducing the same sorts of reaction in Spohr's impressionable younger contemporaries that Wackenroder and Jean Paul Richter depict in their Romantic heroes.* Moritz Hauptmann's reaction to his first hearing of this overture gives a vivid illustration of this:

Once long ago, I bought an Overture of his (in C minor), and Franz . . . happened to see it at my house. Energetic as ever, he contrived that the people at the Baths should hear it at once. That was in 1809, eighteen years ago therefore, and I was at an age when one of La Fontaine's novels could make me infinitely happy or miserable. After hearing that Overture I cried, cried again the whole way home, cried at home by the pailful, and cried for several days afterwards. I see myself even now, sitting alone in my room, steeped in that music, kneeling on the ground with my head on a chair, weeping like mad in a delirium of joy and despair. Nothing in later life can compare with this . . . In those days Spohr was my idol.[5]

In May 1807 Dorette gave birth to a daughter, christened Emilie in honour of Duke Emil Leopold August, who stood godfather to the child. When Dorette had fully recovered her strength, Spohr was able to make plans for their long-deferred concert tour and, leaving Emilie in her grandmother's care, they set off from Gotha in October 1807. Their journey took them to Weimar, Leipzig, Dresden, Prague, Munich, Stuttgart, Karlsruhe, Mannheim, Heidelberg, Darmstadt and Frankfurt. In the various places they visited they gave public concerts and court concerts and played in private salons, winning enthusiastic acclaim for their performances and sowing the seeds of a considerable reputation. In Leipzig, where their concert on 27 October included the overture *Die Prüfung*, the Fifth Violin Concerto (op. 17), one of the concertantes for violin and harp, one of the potpourris and the

---

* For example, Joseph Berglinger in Wackenroder's *Herzensergiessungen eines kunstliebenden Klosterbruders*, and Victor (to some extent a self-portrait) in Jean Paul's *Hesperus*.

Fantasia for harp op. 35, a critic wrote that the concert was 'on account of the worth of the compositions as well as the performance one of the most outstanding of all that we have heard here for many years by visiting virtuosos'.[6] In Prague a lengthy review went into considerable detail on the manner of Spohr's performance and the character of his compositions from a more critical viewpoint. It is particularly interesting since it indicates that Spohr played an important part in disseminating the practice of expressive portamento which dominated violin playing up to the time of Kreisler. The critic observed:

It is known that Herr Spohr ranks with the most outstanding violinists of our age, and in particular his strength and purity are wholly incontestable in adagio, where he ravished us with irresistible magic to follow his feelings; yes, one could call him unsurpassed in this genre if he did not often disturb us in this enjoyment, and sometimes very unpleasantly, by a mannerism much too frequently employed, that is by sliding up and down with one and the same finger at all possible intervals, by an artistic miaow as one might call it if that did not sound teasing.

The critic also complained of mannerism in his allegro playing and noted in addition that he lost some of the allegro character by executing all the passagework with 'long-drawn-out uninterrupted bowstrokes'. This latter feature he identified as characteristic also of the celebrated violinists of the current Parisian school. Of the compositions, while admitting their excellence, he made a number of criticisms which were frequently to be echoed in the future. He commented:

The compositions of this able artist (almost all in minor keys) possess almost universally a character of enthusiastic melancholy [*schwärmerische Melancholie*]; they are rich in beautiful harmonies and surprising modulations; they are clearly organised and very conscientious in structure. We have only one wish which we express out of love for the art and for the artist, that Herr Spohr should not so often employ enharmonic modulation by means of diminished seventh chords; for it is in the nature of things that anything which is intended as it were to seize the soul suddenly with force should not occur too often if it is not to fail in its aim.[7]

On this tour Spohr made contact with many distinguished men, including Goethe and Wieland in Weimar, the composer Peter von Winter who was Kapellmeister in Munich, and in Stuttgart Franz Danzi and Carl Maria von Weber. Of Weber Spohr did not form a very high opinion. Applying the same high critical standards that had caused him to reject his own operatic effort, he considered some extracts from *Der Beherrscher der Geister* (The Ruler of the Spirits) which Weber played to him 'insignificant and amateurish'.[8] Spohr's relationship with Weber, which lasted until the latter's death in 1826, seems to have been a decidedly one-sided affair; for while Weber clearly recognised Spohr's deep musicality, Spohr was never quite able to dissociate Weber's flair for writing popular music from charlatanry. In an article on German opera published in 1823 he remarked of *Der Freischütz* that it was just as well that its popular elements were accompanied by 'beauties of a higher sort',[9] but it is clear from other sources that Spohr never had a very high opinion of Weber's work.

In Stuttgart, capital of the small kingdom of Württemburg, Spohr gave another characteristic example of his artistic pride by insisting that he would not play at court unless the customary card games were suspended during his performance; and contrary to his expectations the condition was agreed to. During the rest of the concert, however, cards were played as usual and, to Spohr's utter disgust, as soon as the king had finished his game the music was instantly terminated in the middle of a cadence. The petty tyranny and squalid corruption which Spohr observed in Württemburg can only have helped to strengthen his dissatisfaction with the political state of Germany and to fuel his misgivings about unchecked monarchical government.

Spohr returned to Gotha in April 1808 after an absence of more than five months, with profits at least four times his annual salary, and resumed his various activities. His spreading fame as a violinist has already attracted pupils to Gotha (between 1807 and 1811 the list includes nineteen names), and as at this time there was little difference in age between master and pupils Spohr spent much of his leisure time with them, 'played at ball and other games with them and taught them to swim'.[10] He encouraged them also to join him on hiking excursions, and in the summer of 1808 a temporary absence of the Duchess from Gotha, which resulted in the suspension of some of the court concerts, enabled them to make a longer excursion to the Harz mountains. Spohr vividly recounted the idyllic trek, on which the enjoyment of nature, sightseeing, violin lessons in the open air, singing male-voice part-songs, an ascent of the Brocken and a visit to his parents in Seesen were ideally combined. He recalled too the pleasure of returning home: 'I still think with emotion of the intense joy with which my dear little wife welcomed me back, and never did I feel more acutely the happiness of being loved.'[11] The warmth of Spohr's character, his humour and his delight in simple pleasures is clearly brought out in his account of these events. At this time the long struggle to maintain artistic integrity against the exigencies of uncongenial masters and the personal troubles he was later to experience had not created the hard outer shell which misled some of his younger contemporaries into thinking him self-centred and insensitive. In Gotha the impression he made was very different; the writer Friedrich Ludwig Wilhelm Mayer, visiting Gotha in 1810, described him as 'the handsome and charming Konzertmeister Spohr'.[12]

Spohr's friendly relations with his pupils was shown by some of the works written in 1808. The masterly concertante for two violins and orchestra (op. 48) was inspired by the ability of a pupil, Friedrich Wilhelm Hildebrand, with whom he was fond of playing, while the duos for two violins op. 9 were dedicated to five of his pupils (Wizemann, Hildebrand, Franz, Lampert and Krall). Comparison of these duos and the contemporaneous duo for violin and viola (op. 13) with op. 3 shows clearly how far Spohr had developed as a composer and violinist during his time in Gotha. Some real advances in the handling of materials and form are apparent in these works. The first movement of the concertante, which begins with a slow introduction where the typical Spohr sentiment of *schwärmerische Melancholie* is established, has a fine sense of pace, and the appearance of a beguiling new theme in the development section is nicely judged. Throughout the work the writing for soloists and orchestra is well conceived and there are some particularly imaginative moments, such as the section in the Andante where the bass instruments have pizzicato semiquavers while the two soloists sustain a series of expressive suspensions in double-stopping. The Finale is a *tour de force* of humour and brilliance which Spohr himself described as 'saucily playful'.[13] Compared to the concertante, the two Duets op. 9 are lightweight works, and in common with most duets of the period neither has a slow movement (though no. 1 has an eleven-bar Poco adagio introduction to the second movement); but from the point of view of workmanship they are perfect gems of their kind. The adaptation of sonata form to the medium is neatly accomplished, so that both instruments are able to share the melodic interest equally. The op. 13 duet, composed later in the year, is a work of far greater weight. It seems probable that Spohr was inspired by the wider range of the viola, and the consequently increased textural possibilities, to adopt a more serious tone in this work and to include a substantial slow movement. The contrast between the vigorous opening bars and the rhapsodic continuation of the theme sets the tone for the whole of the duet (ex. 30). It is noteworthy that in

Ex. 30

(Ex. 30 cont.)

the first movement Spohr uses the opening idea as a unifying factor, its constant reappearance serving to bind the structure of the movement together. The evidence of the op. 9 and op. 13 duets, and of other works composed at about this time, shows that Spohr had become seriously preoccupied with ways of achieving greater cohesion within movements. In a few cases he indulged his interest in the thorough working out of a single motif to such an extent that the concentration on detail tends to obscure the listener's view of the movement as a whole.

A potpourri for violin and orchestra on themes of Mozart (op. 23) written early in the year illustrates another aspect of Spohr's concern with detail, in its ingenious combination of variation and free fantasia, and also shows his unwillingness to let the virtuoso element predominate over musical considerations. Both these concerns are apparent, too, in the Clarinet Concerto in C minor (op. 26), written for Johann Simon Hermstedt in the Autumn of 1808. This was composed in response to a commission from Hermstedt's employer, Prince Sonderhausen, who was willing to pay handsomely for a piece which would display his Konzertdirektor's abilities to the full. The resulting concerto was all that could be desired; as a critic wrote after Hermstedt had performed it in Leipzig in November 1809: 'Since no composition whatever existed in which this excellent artist could display all the superiority of his playing, Herr Konzertmeister Spohr of Gotha has written one for him; and setting aside this special purpose, it belongs to the most spirited and beautiful music which this justly famous master has ever written.'[14] Not only did the concerto further Spohr's and Hermstedt's reputations, it also led directly to technical improvements in the clarinet, for Spohr confessed in the preface to the printed edition, which appeared in 1810:

Since at that time my knowledge of the clarinet was pretty nearly limited to its range and I therefore paid little attention to the weaknesses of the instrument, I have thus written much that will appear to the clarinettist at first sight as unpracticable. Herr Hermstedt, however, far from asking me to alter these passages, sought rather to perfect his instrument and soon by continuous industry arrived at the point where his clarinet had no faulty, dull, uncertain tones.

He then appended a list of Hermstedt's technical specifications for adapting the instrument.* The solo part, though brilliant, is skilfully integrated with a sensitively scored orchestral accompaniment, and when not engaged in virtuoso display the soloist often joins democratically in dialogue with the wind instruments of the orchestra. A notable feature of the first movement is again the pervasiveness of a single melodic cell which is announced at the beginning of the Adagio introduction and dominates the ensuing Allegro, serving as the basis for both first and second subject (ex. 31).

Ex. 31

Hermstedt gave the new concerto its first performance at a concert in Sondershausen, where Spohr also premièred his Sixth Violin Concerto (op. 28), which he had finished only a few days previously, as well as a new potpourri for violin and orchestra on themes of Mozart (op. 24). The Sixth Violin Concerto is of a very different character from the Clarinet Concerto. Whereas the first movement of op. 26, despite its considerable virtuosity, is essentially reticent, that of op. 28 is extrovert in mood, as the bravura opening to the solo part implies (ex. 32). But since Spohr never entirely forsakes his lyrical

Ex. 32

* For these see F. Göthel, *Thematisch–bibliographisches Verzeichnis der Werke von Louis Spohr*.

nature, there are numerous examples of affective chromaticism. The second movements of the two concertos are even further apart; op. 26 has a calm, song-like Adagio accompanied only by strings, while op. 28 has a highly original second movement with the form Recitativo andante – allegro molto – adagio – Recitativo andante. This use of dramatic instrumental recitative, which was to be further exploited in Spohr's later concertos, is an early example of a device frequently utilised by a host of later Romantic composers. In the last movement of op. 28 Spohr also anticipated a large number of later violin concertos by his use of folk song. In this case the source was Spain. He had noted down the melodies sung by a Spanish soldier who was quartered in his house in Gotha and wove them into a Rondo alla spagnola, imitating the guitar accompaniment in the orchestra.

The two String Quartets op. 15, were also completed in 1808 (he had probably begun work on them in 1806, soon after the composition of op. 4). They show some advance on the earlier set in the technique of quartet writing, but are still tentative in their handling of the medium. They do not display anything like the same sureness of touch which Spohr had shown in his duets or orchestral music. His biggest problem seems to have been in achieving variety of texture and in restraining the dominance of the first violin; nor did he yet seem capable of creating sufficiently idiomatic material to be successful in this exacting form. To some extent similar criticisms could be made of almost all his many subsequent string quartets. But he was far from alone among nineteenth-century composers in failing to come up to the high standards which the Classical masters had set; the emphasis on melody and harmonic colour together with the loss of rhythmic vitality, which were significant traits in much Romantic music, combined to produce a style ill adapted to the austere demands of quartet writing. Curiously enough, though less distinguished musically than the finest of Spohr's later string quartets, the op. 15 set are in some ways a more satisfactory example of the genre simply because they are closer to their Classical models.

On a visit to Gotha towards the end of 1808, J. F. Reichardt heard the quartets at Spohr's house and commented in his account of the visit: 'Herr Spohr let me hear three of his inspired [genialen] and well-written quartets and had the opportunity therein to display his great and masterly playing.'[15] Spohr's own recollection of Reichardt's attitude to the quartets was somewhat different; he recalled that Reichardt made many criticisms delivered with a 'smug look of infallibility', most of which, despite his chagrin, Spohr was forced to confess were justified. One remark seems to have had considerable effect, for Reichardt, observing in an Adagio Spohr's preoccupation with working on a single motif throughout a movement, had severely criticised him for it, concluding with the words 'you could not rest until you had worried your motif to death'.[16] A direct consequence of this seems to have been that Spohr rejected the offending movement (op. 15 no. 2 in D major has no slow movement), and because of his need for money at that time sent the quartets straight off to his publisher Kühnel without composing a replacement. In the longer term, Reichardt's criticism had the effect, if not of stifling this trend in Spohr's compositions, at least of making him think again about the extent to which he had been carried away by it.

At this stage in his life Spohr was too severe a self-critic to be satisfied for long with his new string quartets, and within a short time he regretted having published them. He was similarly dissatisfied with his second attempt at opera, *Alruna die Eulenkönigin* (Alruna the Owl-Queen), a 'grand Romantic opera in three acts', also composed during this prolific year. The disillusionment, however, was not immediate. He finished the work full of enthusiasm, and extracts from it performed at court concerts during the winter of 1808–9, which were received with considerable enthusiasm, encouraged him to make efforts to interest a theatre in staging the work. To this end he travelled to Weimar to see Goethe, who at that time was Intendant of the court theatre, and the prima donna Frau von Heigendorf (Caroline Jagemann), who was the Duke of Weimar's mistress. Provisional support for the project was obtained, and when, after a few months' delay, rehearsals were mounted, Spohr, in company with his librettist (whose identity it has been impossible to discover), went once more to Weimar to direct a public rehearsal of the work. Goethe, Wieland and the many amateurs who were present overwhelmed Spohr with praise for the music, but Goethe disliked many features of the libretto and insisted that all the spoken dialogue should be altered from iambic verse to prose. As a result of the delay occasioned by this requirement, misgivings about his music, which Spohr had already felt at the Weimar rehearsal, grew stronger; he became more and more convinced that he lacked a gift for operatic composition and was increasingly reluctant to allow *Alruna* to be staged. Consequently he withdrew the work before it could be put into production.

In later years Spohr himself recognised the considerable advances in operatic writing that he had made between *Die Prüfung* and *Alruna*. The latter opera is in many ways a milestone. For one thing it was his first excursion into the field of the supernatural which was to feature largely in five of his subsequent operas and which became a hallmark of German Romantic opera. The sort of story on which *Alruna* was based was already widely popular in the first decade of the nineteenth century; Weber had been working on a similar theme in his *Der Beherrscher der Geister*. The admitted model for the plot of *Alruna* was Carl Friedrich Hensler's popular opera *Das Donauweibchen*, though there are clearly strong influences from Mozart's *Don Giovanni* and *Die Zauberflöte*. In the absence of the spoken dialogue it is only possible to give the outline of the story, but this shows that it contains many of the stock characters and situations of the German magic-opera, as well as of the *Singspiel* in general.

53

In Act I the human characters in the drama are introduced and their relationships established. A knight, Herrmann, loves Berta, the daughter of Count Bruno. His love is reciprocated, but the Count will not let them marry unless Herrmann recovers the Count's property which has been stolen by robbers. The character types of these three are very similar to Edmund, Natalie and Count W. in *Die Prüfung*. Another element is introduced here, though, with a pair of less serious, socially inferior lovers, Herrmann's squire Franz and Berta's maid Clara. Franz possesses the typical buffo attribute of cowardice; Clara is portrayed as coquettish. In Act II the supernatural characters make their appearance. The act opens with Herrmann and Franz wandering in the forest in a storm. They stray into the realm of Alruna, whose habit is to seduce and then bewitch errant knights. She attempts to exercise her wiles on Herrmann, but with little success, so she arranges a magic play in which Berta is portrayed as unfaithful. The effect of this is not as anticipated, for Herrmann remains impervious to her advances and slips away to return home to discover the truth or otherwise of Berta's infidelity. The superficial resemblance of Alruna to Mozart's Queen of Night is strengthened by her musical treatment: Spohr gives her elaborate coloratura passages at the end of no. 5 (almost certainly written with Caroline Jagemann in mind). Alruna's chief companion, Tio, has more success in seducing Franz, and they sing a duet, the theme of which was later used for a set of variations for clarinet and orchestra (1809). Act III opens with Alruna and her female entourage engaged in a hunt for the fugitive Herrmann; horn calls and thematic reminiscence are used here to bind the first four numbers of the act into an extended scene-complex in which female chorus, melodrama, recitative and arioso are woven into a continuously developing unit. Alruna fails in her search for Herrmann, who has meanwhile been reunited with Franz beside a gravestone, which proves to be the tomb of Herrmann's ancestor Udo, whom Alruna had previously ensnared. Udo's ghost suddenly speaks from the grave (recalling the statue scene in *Don Giovanni*) and, having cursed the treacherous Alruna, offers Herrmann a magic shield with which to break her power. The final scene takes place in Bruno's castle where, after an extended aria by Berta and a scene with her father, the Finale begins. Alruna and Tio, who have plotted to abduct the Count and his daughter, arrive to carry out their plan, but Herrmann appears at the crucial moment and overcomes Alruna's power with his magic schield. Udo's ghost then joins them and seals the lovers' bond.

Though the libretto has little or no literary merit, it provided the composer with plenty of situations and ample opportunity for effects. The musical dimensions of the opera show the seriousness with which Spohr approached his task. Many of the numbers are surprisingly extensive; the introductions and finales, and especially the continuous first scene of Act III, indicate Spohr's concern to create a genuine musical drama rather than just a string of musical numbers linked by dialogue. This approach may possibly have been encouraged by his contact with the ideas of Weber, Poissl and others during his visit to Stuttgart, which at that time was an important centre of German opera, but the overriding influence on the musical substance of the opera was still clearly Mozart. Spohr's allegiance is announced by the fugal opening of the Allegro of the overture, whose kinship with the overture to *Die Zauberflöte* is obvious (ex. 33). The resemblance was not lost on contemporaries and was admitted by Spohr, who confessed unrepentantly:

Ex. 33

it is an exact imitation of the overture to *Die Zauberflöte*; for that was the object I had in view. In my admiration for Mozart, and the feeling of wonder with which I regarded that overture, an imitation of it seemed to me something very natural and praiseworthy, and at the time when I sought to develop my talent for composition I had made many similar imitations of Mozart's masterpieces, among others the aria full of love complaints in *Alruna* [no. 13] from the wonderful aria of Pamina 'Ach ich fühl's, es ist verschwunden'.[17]

Like the overture to *Don Giovanni*, that of *Alruna* links into the first scene. Other reminiscences of Mozart abound; the opening of the Finale to Act II, for instance, recalls the aria 'Dies Bildnis ist bezaubernd schön' (no. 3) from *Die Zauberflöte*, which is also in E flat major (ex. 34). As Spohr himself went

Ex. 34

Noch kannt' ich nicht die__ Lie · be der Freund-schaft lebt__ ich__ nur

on to say, however, the overture is no slavish imitation; the chromaticism in the fugue subject is not Mozartian, while Spohr's distinctive *romantische Seele* is revealed at the very start in the surprising keys through which the overture's nine-bar adagio introduction passes (E flat minor, C major, F minor, B flat minor, F sharp major, G major). Elsewhere in the opera, too, he uses chromaticism and enharmonic modulation with characteristic freedom.

In *Alruna*, Spohr also went a stage further in his use of reminiscence motifs. In the Finale of the first act he recalled part of the music of the lovers' duet (no. 1) as a way of emphasising their devotion to one another; then towards the end of the act he made Bruno sing his farewell words to Herr-

mann with a phrase from the same duet changed to the minor key, thus sub-
tly underlining the lovers' sorrow at parting. In Alruna's scena in the third
act, where she expresses her feelings, Spohr recalls a number of themes and
phrases from earlier in the opera to give musical support to her recollections.
This use of reminiscence is clearly related to Cherubini's use of it in *Les deux
journées*, an opera which Spohr certainly knew and admired. But despite the
surer grasp of dramatic technique and the attractiveness of much of the
music in *Alruna*, Spohr could see that he had not yet found his own voice in
operatic writing. He may also have perceived that he had failed to draw the
characters convincingly or consistently in the music. Tio's polacca Cavatina
(no. 6), for example, seems quite out of character, as does Alruna's tender
Cavatina at the beginning of the second Finale.

The suppression of the opera after the Weimar rehearsal was not total.
Spohr published the overture, for which he retained considerable affection in
later life, as op.21, and he included Berta's aria (no. 13) in concerts over the
next few years. The adagio opening of this aria was later used as the basis of
the Adagio of his Notturno op. 34 (1815), while parts of nos. 8 and 9 were res-
cued for use in his next opera, *Der Zweikampf mit der Geliebten* (1811). Though
Alruna as a whole was abortive, its composition had been a necessary step on
the path to writing a successful opera. Despite its many deficiencies it gives
sure indications of the direction in which Spohr's development was leading
him. His employment of thematic reminiscence, the building up of scene-
complexes and the expressive use of chromaticism were all elements that
were to figure importantly in Spohr's considerable contribution to the future
development of German opera.

Though operatic success was as yet beyond his grasp, he was able to deal
more convincingly with smaller vocal forms. The six Lieder op. 25, which he
wrote during the second half of 1809 and dedicated to Caroline Jagemann,
are attractive in their own right and show how in this field, too, he was in the
vanguard of musical developments. Writing to the publisher Peters in 1816,
Spohr himself claimed that: 'in form and in other essential things they are
very different from those of all other earlier composers'.[18] His claim is clearly
an exaggeration; they are not, in fact, as revolutionary as he liked to think,
but they are in many respects progressive. Three of the songs (nos. 1, 2 and 4)
are strophic, though no. 2 has a short piano prelude and postlude which are
not repeated between verses. No. 5, a setting of Goethe's 'Zigeunerlied', is
more unusual; the harmonic framework stays the same for all four verses,
but Spohr substantially changed the vocal line and the piano accompaniment in each verse. The final song of the set is through-composed with a
return of the opening material towards the end. The third song, another
Goethe setting, 'Gretchen am Spinnrade', is the most striking; here the music
for the repetition of the refrain, 'Meine Ruh' ist hin', remains the same, but
each verse is set differently, giving the form *AB AC AD*. There are also

significant changes of speed and expression: the direction at the beginning is 'Langsam und schwermütig', for the second verse it changes to 'Geschwind und sehnsuchtsvoll' (bar 38), at bar 47 the marking is 'Langsamer', at bar 66 'Erster Bewegung', at bar 74 'mit steigender Leidenschaft', at bar 78 'kräftig', and at bar 81 'wehmütig'. In the other songs of the set the initial performance directions are similarly expressive. No. 1 is 'Sanft', no. 2 'Mit innigem, tief bewegtem Gefühl', no. 4 'Feurig', no. 5 'Flüchtig und mit ängstlicher, gedämpfter Stimme', and no. 6 'Schwärmerisch fröhlich'. These directions indicate the essence of Spohr's approach – his concern to illustrate, where appropriate, the emotional nuances of the text by musical means rather than leaving it to the expressive delivery of the singer. In this context his use of chromatic harmony is of special significance. Here lay his original contribution to the Lied – not, indeed, in the creation of unprecedented harmonies or progressions, but in their concentrated use. No earlier composer had employed chromaticism in his Lieder to anything like the same extent as Spohr did in several of this set. Though some of the chromaticism is essentially colouristic, much of the time he employs it to genuinely expressive effect, as in the whole of 'Gretchen'. The final bars of this setting are a good example of the sort of thing which he was to develop a few years later in his next sets of Lieder (ex. 35).

Ex. 35

(Ex. 35 cont.)

wollt   an   sein - en   Küs-sen   ver - ge - hen sollt.

IV

Virtuoso and composer: spreading reputation
1808–1813

In November 1808, after the birth of a second daughter, Johanna Sophia Louise (known to the family as Ida), Dorette fell victim to what was described as a 'nervous fever' – an affliction to which she was periodically subject for the rest of her life and which was eventually to prove fatal. On the occasion of this first attack her life seemed in danger for some time and Spohr stayed by her bedside day and night. He recalled:

What I suffered by her sick bed is indescribable! Alarmed by her fits of delirium, by the serious face of the doctor who evaded my questions, and tortured by self-reproach for not having taken better care of her, I did not have a moment's rest during Dorette's illness. At last the doctor's more cheerful expression intimated that the danger was past and I, who had for the first time become fully aware of what I possessed in my wife and of the intense love I had for her, now felt inexpressibly happy.[1]

Even after she was out of danger her recovery was slow. In the spring of 1809, so that she could have the benefit of the country air, Spohr rented a house in the countryside near Gotha. There her strength gradually returned and she began once more to practise the harp which had been neglected for almost six months.

By the autumn of 1809 they were ready to contemplate another concert tour, for which their repertoire was enriched by the new Violin Concerto in G minor (op. 28), the Potpourri op. 24, and a fourth sonata for violin and harp (op. 115). They set out from Gotha in October, travelling first to Weimar, where Spohr hoped to obtain letters of recommendation from the Grand Duchess, sister to Czar Alexander II, for he planned to visit Russia once again. A traveller from St Petersburg had told him that his and Dorette's reputations were now well known there, and he surmised that a visit at that time would be highly profitable. There were two serious obstacles to this scheme, however; for one thing, it was unlikely that the court at Gotha would agree to his taking as extended a leave of absence as would be necessary (he had already been granted three months); and for another, Dorette was extremely reluctant to be parted from her children for such a long time. With Spohr, devoted to his family though he was, the lure of travel and acclaim outweighed all other considerations at this time and he was unwilling to allow any such obstacles to deter him. Dorette was finally persuaded to agree to the scheme; and, as to the court's objections, Spohr hoped simply to overcome them by a *fait accompli*, trusting that the Duchess of Gotha's partiality would keep him secure in his post.

Having given a successful concert in Weimar and obtained the required letters from the Grand Duchess, Spohr and his wife continued their tour through Leipzig, Dresden and Bautzen, augmenting their reputation and their purse in each city. Towards the middle of November they reached Breslau, a city noted for its love of music, where at that time of year the theatre was open daily and concerts took place almost every evening. With the friendly assistance of the Cathedral Kapellmeister, Schnabel, Spohr was able to arrange three extremely successful concerts. Shortly after his arrival in Breslau, however, he had received a letter from the Duchess of Gotha, who having heard from Weimar of his plans to visit Russia, wrote to indicate her displeasure at losing their services for so long and offered Dorette the post of court soloist and music teacher to the Princess if they would relinquish the proposed journey. This offer and Dorette's obvious eagerness to return to her children induced Spohr to give up his plans and, after negotiating a definite salary for his wife's appointment, he agreed to return to Gotha as soon as possible. They left Breslau in December 1809 and, having given two concerts in Golgau on the way, arrived in Berlin just before New Year. A concert there on 4 January was well received and they gave another a week later, the day after the royal family returned to Berlin for the first time since Napoleon's occupation of the city in 1806. This second concert attracted an exceptionally large audience after it became generally known that the Queen of Prussia had sent for tickets.

From Berlin Spohr successfully applied to his long-suffering patroness in Gotha for a few weeks' extension of leave so that he and Dorette could give concerts in Hamburg. Clearly his talents were so highly valued in Gotha that he could enjoy a remarkable degree of freedom. As it turned out, the visit to Hamburg was especially fortuitous. Spohr formed lasting friendships with Andreas Romberg and Christian Friedrich Gottlieb Schwenke, spending many pleasant hours at their houses enthusiastically playing and talking about music, while the three concerts which he and Dorette gave there produced receipts equal to a year's salary at Gotha. More important, Friedrich Ludwig Schröder offered Spohr the libretto of *Der Zweikampf mit der Geliebten* by Johann Friedrich Schink, which was to be one of four new operas given in the opening season of his new theatre company in 1811. Spohr was so pleased at the opportunity to try his hand again at operatic composition that he accepted the proffered libretto without making very thorough enquiries about either the text or the terms for setting it to music. The terms proved to be fair enough, but on careful reading of the libretto Spohr was to discover much that dissatisfied him.

It was not until March 1810, after almost five months' absence, that Spohr returned to Gotha, somewhat anxious about the nature of his reception by the Duchess. But, having performed some of her favourite music at the earliest opportunity, he was quickly re-established in her good graces, and after settling back into his accustomed routine he set to work energetically on the new opera. Its success meant a great deal to him. His reputation as a violinist–composer had been firmly established in the various German cities he had visited on the concert tours of 1808 and 1809, while the almost invariably enthusiastic reviews which regularly appeared in the *AMZ* had spread his fame throughout the German-speaking world. But he had ambitions to be known as more than a composer for the violin. So far, he had failed to gain acclaim in other fields – his scena *Oskar* had been found 'too long and somewhat monotonous' when given at one of his concerts in Leipzig in 1806,[2] he himself had soon recognised the shortcomings of his two earlier operas, and neither the op. 4 nor op. 15 string quartets had satisfied him for long. Playing the op. 15 quartets before a gathering of distinguished musicians in Hamburg, he had apologised in advance for their deficiencies but was nevertheless slightly nettled when, after hearing them, Romberg concurred with Spohr's own assessment, saying: 'Your quartets will not do yet; they are far behind your orchestral compositions.'[3] He therefore reposed great faith in a success with *Der Zweikampf mit der Geliebten* as a means of establishing his reputation as a composer.

Before beginning work on the opera he felt the necessity of making substantial changes in the libretto and, having obtained Schröder's permission to make the alterations, he enlisted the assistance of an unidentifiable Gotha poet (possibly the same one who had written the libretto of *Alruna*). Since neither the original libretto nor the spoken dialogue is extant, it is impossible to know the sort of changes Spohr thought would make the text more suitable for operatic purposes; nor, without the dialogue, is it possible fully to unravel the intricacies of the plot. The action takes place at the court of Flanders during the sixteenth century. Donna Isabella has arrived in Brussels disguised as a young knight in order to test the supposed unfaithfulness of her beloved Don Enrigue. The two of them meet at a hunting party presided over by the Princess Matilde, who has taken a liking to the disguised Isabella. A quarrel ensues between Enrigue and Isabella (whom he has not recognised) over who should have the honour of retrieving the Princess's dropped handkerchief, and a duel is demanded. After much intrigue and misunderstanding in which another of the Princess's admirers, Gaston, is involved, everything is clarified and the lovers are happily reconciled. In addition to the main characters there is a sub-plot involving two servants, Decio and Laurette, who fill the traditional buffo roles; like Franz and Clara in *Alruna*, they have the conventional characteristics of cowardice and coquettishness.

It is doubtful whether, given a free choice, Spohr would have chosen to set such material, which was so closely in the tradition of Italianate *opera semi-seria*. It offered little in the way of situations for dramatic musical portrayal, the high points of the opera being a fight in the second Finale between Enrigue, Isabella and two members of the court, and the abortive duel at the end of the third act. On the other hand, with the external action providing so little opportunity for startling musical effects, Spohr was forced to concentrate more on the portrayal of character. This was a useful lesson for him and he met the challenge remarkably successfully. The character of Princess Matilde is particularly well drawn in the music, for she is shown in her private moments (as in the fine scena 'Ich bin allein' in Act I) as tender and human, while in her public appearances she always keeps up a haughty nobility befitting her rank. Elsewhere the musical portrayal of conflicting and shifting emotions is skilfully accomplished by the composer, especially in the second Finale.

Taken as a whole *Der Zweikampf mit der Geliebten*, though still strongly indebted to Mozart, as Spohr admitted, is a most attractive work. Almost all the individual numbers are musically excellent; in the first act alone, apart from 'Ich bin allein', the terzetto (no. 2) and the bantering duet between Decio and Laurette (no. 3) are outstanding, and this level is generally maintained throughout the opera. That *Der Zweikampf* failed to hold the stage was not due to any lack of musical merit, but rather to the fact that the genre in which it was written was already becoming old-fashioned. In response to the conventional constituents of the libretto Spohr had reverted to a more stereotyped musical format than in *Alruna*. *Der Zweikampf* consists of the standard succession of set pieces; there is no attempt to create scene-complexes, nor any use of thematic reminiscence as in Spohr's previous opera. As a result *Der Zweikampf*, while vital experience in many ways for Spohr as a writer of operatic music, added nothing to the development of German opera.

In the middle of writing *Der Zweikampf mit der Geliebten* Spohr was interrupted by an invitation from Georg Friedrich Bischoff, cantor at Frankenhausen, to direct a music festival there in June 1810. The vocal and instrumental forces for this venture, one of the earliest instances of the sort of middle-class festivals which were to become so distinctive a feature of German musical life during the nineteenth century, were drawn from towns and cities in the Thuringian region, and numbered 101 singers and 106 instrumentalists. That Spohr at the age of twenty-six, by far the youngest musical director in the region, should have been offered the direction of this festival shows clearly how considerable his reputation had already become. As well as being asked to direct, Spohr was requested by Hermstedt to write him another clarinet concerto for performance at the festival. Suspending his work on the opera, therefore, he composed his Second Clarinet Concerto in E flat major (op. 57) in a few weeks, but it shows no signs of hasty workmanship.

This concerto is in many respects his finest up to that time; throughout the work Spohr showed a remarkable fertility of invention and achieved a depth of musical substance far greater than Weber did in his almost exactly contemporary clarinet concertos, without in any way yielding to them in brilliance. As with so much of Spohr's music the beauties, ingenuities and harmonic subtleties follow one another with such frequency that it is impossible to do justice to them in anything less than a full analysis. A few may, however, be singled out. The first entry of the solo clarinet in the fourth bar of the first movement is almost unperceived as it joins for four bars with the woodwind of the orchestra before retiring from the scene and allowing the full orchestral tutti exposition to proceed. During this exposition a characteristic moment occurs when towards the end of a dominant preparation for the key of the second subject (B flat) there is a sudden harmonic side-slip which introduces the new theme in D flat major (ex. 36). Via E flat minor, D

Ex. 36

minor and B flat the music then makes its way back to E flat major and the exposition continues on its way. In the richness of its thematic material this movement is in sharp contrast to the First Clarinet Concerto. Spohr's liberality here extends to the introduction by the soloist of a new theme, towards the end of the development, which has a typically Romantic dreamy quality, creating a point of repose and allowing the clarinet to show another side of its nature (ex. 37). The Adagio second movement in A flat begins with a con-

Ex. 37

templative section of great beauty in which the clarinet dwells on its rich chalumeau register. An enharmonic modulation initiated by the horns then takes the music rapidly through E major and G major to C minor, where the clarinet begins a new dramatic section which seems to look forward more than eighty years to Brahms' Clarinet Quintet (ex. 38). At the return of the A

Ex. 38

flat section Spohr shows his feeling for contrasts of tone colour with a dialogue between the solo clarinet in its chalumeau register and the flute almost two octaves higher. The Rondo alla polacca also displays Spohr's skilful and imaginative orchestration. The opening with solo timpani (which continue to play a prominent part in the movement) answered by solo horns is arresting, and the later repetition of the timpani rhythm by pizzicato upper strings while oboe and solo clarinet answer each other with a whimsical phrase has a piquant effect. The wit and high spirits which are thus established at the beginning of the movement are brilliantly sustained to the end.

At the orchestral concert on 22 June 1810 which comprised the second half of the two-day Frankenhausen festival, the new clarinet concerto was given its first performance and was described by Gerber in his review of the festival as 'indisputably one of the most perfect artistic works of the kind'.[4] Also performed in this concert were Spohr's concertante for two violins and orchestra (op. 48), which Gerber considered a 'masterly work', and his overture to *Alruna*, which the critic did not care for, as well as Beethoven's First Symphony and various shorter items. On the first day of the festival a fine performance of Haydn's *Creation* had taken place under Spohr's direction, which Gerber described as 'the most powerful, most expressive and in a word the most successful I have ever heard', and he attributed its excellence largely to Spohr's method of conducting 'with a roll of paper, without the least noise, and without the slightest contortion of countenance'. This was the first time Spohr had conducted so numerous a body of performers, but it presented him with no serious problems, and by the efficiency of his direction he laid the foundations of his future fame as a conductor.

The whole festival took place amid a general holiday atmosphere, and with his usual amiability Spohr made many new friends among the performers and listeners. One of these was Christian Friedrich Lueder, who along with Schwenke helped to rouse his interest in the works of Bach, and whose friendship Spohr enjoyed for almost fifty years during which they kept up a constant correspondence on historical matters. When the festival was over, Spohr, and a number of others who were unwilling to separate so soon, organised a hiking excursion to the Kyffhäuser where, doubtless with the politically fragmented and war-weary state of Germany in mind, they sang an appeal to Friedrich Barbarossa to fulfil the ancient prophecy that he would one day awake and come to the rescue of Germany. On the whole, though, the excursion, which was blessed with fine summer weather, was a light-hearted affair, and it was with reluctance that the company separated to return to their own homes.

Over the winter of 1810–11, having completed his opera, Spohr composed a new violin concerto (op. 62), a fifth sonata for violin and harp (op. 114), and a concert aria 'alla polacca' for tenor with violin obbligato. After that he set to work to produce new compositions for a second Frankenhausen festival to be given in June 1811. In response to Hermstedt's request for a new work he composed a set of variations on themes from Peter von Winter's *Das unterbrochene Opferfest* for clarinet and orchestra (op. 80). Bischoff made a more challenging suggestion; he asked Spohr to write a symphony for the festival. The idea of trying his hand at symphonic composition was something which must have been in Spohr's mind for some time. The C minor Overture of 1807 seems to indicate a tacit recognition that he was not then equal to tackling so exacting a task as a symphony, but with the experience he had gained in the meantime he was, by 1811, ready to make an attempt.

The Symphony in E flat (op. 20) clearly shows Spohr's continuing debt to Mozart, whose Symphony no. 39 in the same key may plausibly be seen as its spiritual ancestor; but the differences are as important as the similarities, and indicate how far Spohr had already moved beyond the position of a mere epigone. Mozart and Spohr both begin their E flat symphonies with an Adagio introduction in 4/4, of approximately the same length; Spohr's Adagio, like Mozart's, reaches a strong cadence on the dominant at the ninth bar, but the routes by which they arrive there are quite dissimilar. A comparison of the harmonic skeletons of the first eight bars of both works is revealing of the extent to which Spohr had committed himself to a degree of harmonic complexity far beyond what Mozart or any of Spohr's contemporaries employed except in rare instances (ex. 39). In Mozart's Adagio the music proceeds from the ninth bar over a dominant pedal with expressive suspensions; Spohr, however, continues his tonal adventures with a passage which E. T. A. Hoffmann considered of particularly good and novel effect, before finally arriving at a dominant pedal for the final seven bars, and concluding with a

Ex. 39

(a) Spohr

(b) Mozart

characteristic alternation of dominant and tonic minor over the pedal. The intricacy of the Adagio gives a foretaste of what is to come, for though the Allegro (3/4) begins, like Mozart's, with a calm and ingenuous theme, the chromatic elements increasingly make their presence felt and a striking concentration of detail in the scoring and use of thematic material is soon apparent. Mozart's influence may be detected in the four bars (17–21) of V ♭9/11, which recall bars 5–6 of the first movement of his E flat String Quartet K. 428 (V 9/11), but despite such features and the similarity of some of the melodic material, Spohr's own individuality is clearly predominant. The second subject is particularly characteristic (ex. 40). A number of typical

Ex. 40

harmonic devices occur in the exposition, such as the enharmonic modulation at bar 84, the shift into D flat at bar 100 after several bars of dominant preparation in B flat, and a surprising sequence of chords at bars 121–2 (ex. 41). Much of the development is based on a fugato treatment of a variant

Ex. 41

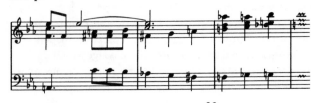

of the first bars of the Allegro's opening theme. When this has been finally relinquished, a version of bars 17–21 recurs at bar 174, leading to a dominant pedal in E flat which ushers in the recapitulation. Because of the extensive use of the first-subject material, which was only briefly ousted in the exposition by the second subject, Spohr considerably shortened the first part of his recapitulation, reaching the second subject after only twenty bars. But the key, C major, in which the theme appears *pianissimo*, is unexpected; it is immediately repeated in C minor before finally bursting out *forte* in the home key. From this point the movement proceeds as expected, concluding in a short, climactic coda.

The Larghetto con moto which follows, like the Andante of Mozart's Symphony no. 39, is in A flat 2/4, and a similar dotted figure plays an important part in the movement. The two movements are, however, quite different in character. The theme of Spohr's Larghetto, first stated by cellos and basses alone, has a simplicity which recalls Haydn rather than Mozart (ex. 42). This, together with a second idea (ex. 43), provides the material for the

Ex. 42

Ex. 43

whole movement. These two ideas are alternated and combined, with an abundance of expressive harmonic inflexions. Towards the end of the movement the main theme recurs in the violas and cellos with elaborate filigree decoration in semiquaver sextuplets from the first violins, who then take it over while the lower strings accompany it in a *piano* dynamic, with fragments of the theme in the wind instruments and threads of the accompanying figures tossed from one group of strings to another before fading into silence.

The Scherzo is far more elaborately written than those of the String Quartets opp. 4 and 15, Spohr's only previous essays in the genre. It stretches to 605 bars including the repeats, reflecting perhaps the influence of Beethoven's 'Eroica' Symphony, which he had performed in Gotha; though since Spohr's Scherzo must be taken at a considerably slower pace it lasts much longer in performance. The range and frequency of modulation is greater than in any of Beethoven's scherzos. A characteristic passage occurs at the beginning of the second section, where Spohr abruptly moves into G flat major and introduces a melodic countertheme in the wind (ex. 44).

Ex. 44

Rhythmically, too, there is considerable interest; twice the metre changes to 2/4 with piquant effect. The Trio, in C minor, drives forward harmonically and rhythmically, making much use of triplet figurations and descending chromatic bass lines. A codetta over a C pedal leads eventually to dominant preparation for the return of the Scherzo in E flat. Notwithstanding its admirable qualities, the Scherzo is marred by its excessive length. This was commented on by E. T. A. Hoffmann and recognised by Spohr, who wrote to his publisher, Peters, on 1 January 1812 that Hoffmann was 'absolutely right to say that the Scherzo is too long, and I have therefore already in Frankenhausen and recently in Hamburg made the first two parts go straight through, whereby this drawback is largely obviated. Would it not be possible for the repeat marks to be deleted from the as yet uncirculated copies?'[5]

The allegretto Finale begins innocently enough with a rather conventional theme, which provides the basic material for much of the movement (ex. 45). This movement shows Spohr's continued liking for thematic econ-

Ex. 45

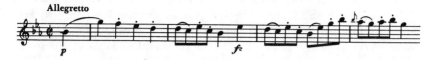

omy, which despite Reichardt's strictures sometimes led him to overestimate
the potential interest of his material. In this case he again relies heavily on
chromaticism and harmonic ingenuity to sustain impetus. The first theme is
adapted and colourfully harmonised to form the second subject (ex. 46).

Ex. 46

The substantial development modulates rapidly and widely: utilising enharmonic changes it passes through E major to G minor and then rapidly via
B major, C sharp minor and E flat minor to a dominant preparation for the
essentially regular recapitulation. The use of clarinets, bassoon, horns and
bass trombone only, joined in the fourth bar by pizzicato strings, for the
statement of the main theme at this point, is an example of Spohr's finely
judged orchestration, apparent throughout the symphony. His understanding of the orchestra, here displayed for the first time in a major work, shows
how well he had profited from his years of experience as Konzertmeister in

Gotha; his consummate mastery of orchestral technique was to be among the many qualities which awakened the admiration of his contemporaries.*

The second Frankenhausen festival was as successful as the first, and Spohr's symphony in particular made a striking impression. His own catalogue of compositions gives the information that the Frankenhausen performance was the symphony's première, but in fact it had already been performed from manuscript parts at Leipzig in April 1811, when the *AMZ* remarked of it:

We not only place it *far* higher than any of this master's orchestral music that we know, both in invention and in perfection of workmanship, but also confess that we have not heard a new work of this kind for many years which possesses so much novelty and originality without singularity or affectation, so much richness and skill without bombast or artifice.[6]

When the Symphony appeared in print later that year, E. T. A. Hoffmann contributed two leading articles to successive issues of the *AMZ*, which, though not uncritical, hailed it as a highly significant work that raised great hopes for the future.[7]

During the following few years Spohr's First Symphony received performances in most major musical centres from Vienna to Amsterdam. At the Gewandhaus in Leipzig it was given almost annually until 1830, after which his Third and Fourth Symphonies replaced it in the repertoire, but in London it remained a regular item in the Philharmonic concerts and elsewhere from the 1820s to the 1860s. As late as 1871 a manuscript score of the Symphony was compiled in Liverpool, on which the copyist explained the reason for his labour with the comment 'There being no printed copy of this work shame be it said'. (Spohr's First and Second Symphonies were issued in parts together with a 'Partie pour la direction' which was written on three staves, the middle one in full-size print containing only the first violin part while the outer ones in smaller print contained a reduction of the other parts.)

Shortly after the First Symphony had been launched on its successful career at Frankenhausen, Spohr received notification that *Der Zweikampf mit der Geliebten* was scheduled for production in November 1811 and, having obtained the necessary leave of absence from Gotha, he travelled to Hamburg to supervise rehearsals and conduct the first performances. After a number of hitches which for a while put the staging of the opera in doubt, it was eventually premièred on 15 November 1811 with a strong cast and an orchestra containing Hermstedt, as well as many of his Hamburg musical friends. Fears that the first night might be disrupted by hostile claques were unfounded, and it was highly successful. Schwenke wrote a glowing review

---

* S. S. Wesley, for example, in a conversation recorded in C. H. H. Parry's diary (6 January 1866), asserted that Spohr excelled Mendelssohn in the ability to produce a marvellous tone from his orchestra.

in which, as Spohr remarked, 'he adroitly combated the well-founded opinion of its opponents that it contained many reminiscences of the operas of Mozart, and while admitting that the form of the separate numbers as well as the whole design recalled Mozart he cited that as a positive feature and proof of its excellence'.[8] For Spohr, however, the triumph was a hollow one. As with his two previous operatic ventures he had already become dissatisfied with much of the work at rehearsal; but on this occasion, rather than feeling that he had no talent for opera, he was convinced that he could see the precise nature of the weaknesses and the means whereby he might have remedied them.

Despite its initial success in Hamburg *Der Zweikampf* did far less to further Spohr's reputation than the First Symphony, for after a relatively short run it was taken out of production. Subsequently it seems only to have been produced at Kassel in 1840, where Spohr himself revived it, though it may also have been produced in France. A vocal score was printed about 1813 by Böhme of Hamburg with a new edition about 1820, and a French edition was published by Marescot of Paris in 1828.

On his return to Gotha from Hamburg, Spohr found a letter from Bischoff awaiting him, informing him that the French governor at Erfurt, prompted no doubt by the success of the Frankenhausen festivals, had requested him to organise a similar event to celebrate Napoleon's birthday in August 1812. Bischoff asked Spohr to direct the festival once again and also to compose an oratorio for it. For this he suggested a text by August Arnold entitled *Das jüngste Gericht*. As oratorio was now the one major branch of composition, apart from keyboard music, at which Spohr had not tried his hand, he welcomed the commission with open arms. But before starting work on it he made an intensive study of Marpurg's *Kunst der Fuge*, realising that his earlier course of self-instruction in composition had not included strict fugal writing, and taking the conventional view that at least one fugue was obligatory in any self-respecting oratorio (not, however, a view shared by Beethoven in *Christus am Ölberg*). Having mastered the necessary technique, he completed the work between January and June 1812. The première at Erfurt on 14 August was, with the exception of an appalling performance by the bass soloist who sang the part of Satan, successful and well received. Spohr, however, was once again left with mixed feelings about his work; parts of the oratorio he considered equal to anything he had so far written – some of the choruses and the part of Satan in particular – but he soon recognised that most of the arias, which are written in an undigested amalgam of Haydn's oratorio and Mozart's opera styles, were inappropriate to their context and detracted from the overall unity of the work. After performances in Leipzig, Prague and Vienna in December 1812 and January 1813 Spohr suppressed the oratorio, which remained in manuscript and was never performed again.

The Autumn of 1812 saw the resurgence of Spohr's *Wanderlust* and, when the Duchess Caroline Amalie's reluctance to lose his services yet again had been overcome, he and Dorette set out on another concert tour in October. Their destination on this occasion was Vienna, partly because Spohr considered that it had been little disturbed by the depredations of the war, but also because he felt that success in Vienna was essential for the firm establishment of his reputation. As he observed in his memoirs:

Vienna was at that time indisputably the capital of the musical world. The two greatest composers and reformers of musical taste, Haydn and Mozart, had lived there and produced their masterpieces there. The generation which had seen them rise and had their tastes formed by them was still alive. The worthy successor to those artistic giants, Beethoven, still lived there and was now at the height of his fame and in the full strength of his creative power. In Vienna therefore the highest standards for art works existed, and to gain acclaim there was to prove oneself a master.[9]

On the way they stopped in Leipzig and Prague, gaining the customary acclaim for their duet playing, but some criticisms were raised about Spohr's compositions. A Leipzig reviewer, while praising the Adagio of his Violin Concerto op. 28 as 'the very finest that was ever produced by any virtuoso',[10] found the first movement too long for its material and considered it over-elaborate. In Prague, in an otherwise extremely laudatory review of a concert which included the overture to *Alruna*, a violin concerto, the first movement of his symphony and a sonata for violin and harp, a general criticism of his music was made. The writer observed: 'We cannot suppress the wish, which we share with several music-lovers, that Herr Spohr would employ more economy in modulation and surprises in his ensemble pieces, and that in general he might be more inclined to *find* than to *seek*.'[11] Such reservations about Spohr's more recent compositions were not isolated at this time. Gerber, who was in general a profound admirer of his music, had made very similar criticisms of the overture to *Alruna* when it was given at Frankenhausen in 1810. He had remarked that 'Almost with every bar one *Inganno* succeeds another so that it may be looked on as a series of studies in modulation'; he went on to say that 'music which continually disappoints the expectations of the ear never satisfies'.[12] Much the same objections were raised to the Second Clarinet Concerto when it was performed in Kassel in 1812, where a critic observed that 'despite its modulating into almost all twenty-four keys it was somewhat cold and monotonous . . . and ultimately the quantity of dissonances and enharmonic changes became too much'.[13] The rest of this review, however, makes it clear that the performance of the clarinet concerto was not a good one, confirming Spohr's own conviction that his music was less able to survive a poor performance than that of most other composers.

In Vienna Spohr's compositions were not to escape criticism, but at the same time it was generally recognised that they possessed a quality which raised them far above the usual productions of virtuosos and entitled him to serious consideration as a composer of exceptional talent. About his violin playing there was unqualified enthusiasm. After his first concert on 17 December, at which his old idol Rode, who had just arrived in Vienna, was present, his performance with Dorette elicited the observation that their 'masterly playing roused universal rapture'.[14] Rode's playing at a concert on 6 January 1813 disappointed Spohr greatly; he felt that during the nine years since he had last heard him there had been a sad decline in his powers as both violinist and composer – a view which was shared by the critics. After Spohr's second concert on 14 January there was little doubt that he had proved himself the superior artist. Of his performance on this occasion it was observed: 'in the pleasing and tender, Spohr is indisputably the nightingale of all living violinists known to us. It is hardly possible to execute an Adagio with more tenderness and yet so clearly, combined with the purest good taste; added to this he overcomes the most difficult passages in fast movements and effects the greatest possible stretches with wonderful ease.' The reviewer also noted that he 'received a general and unanimous applause and was repeatedly called forward'.[15]

At private music parties where he often played alongside Rode and the Viennese violinist Joseph Mayseder, Spohr also achieved notable success. His musicianship in the performance of quartets by Haydn, Mozart and Beethoven was particularly admired, but he seldom lost the opportunity to astonish his audience with his technical prowess in more showy music. Spohr's account of an incident which occurred at one of these gatherings is revealing of his character. He wrote:

With frequent opportunities of hearing Rode I became increasingly convinced that he was no longer the perfect violinist of earlier days. From the constant repetition of the same compositions mannerisms had gradually crept into his playing that now bordered on caricature. I was rude enough to point this out to him and asked whether he had forgotten the way in which he played his compositions ten years before. Yes! I carried my impertinence so far as to put the variations in G major in front of him and said I would play them exactly as I had heard him play them so frequently ten years earlier. After I had finished playing the company broke into rapturous applause and Rode, for decency's sake, was obliged to add a *bravo*; but one could plainly see that he felt offended by my indelicacy. And with good reason. I was soon ashamed of it and only mention the incident now to indicate what a high opinion I then had of myself as a violinist![16]

The combination of arrogant impetuosity, regret for the insensitivity of his actions and simple honesty in recounting a discreditable incident illuminate basic elements in Spohr's personality.

As a result of the acclaim he had earned in Viennese musical circles as both violinist and composer, Spohr received an offer from Count Palffy von Erdöd, lessee of the Theater an der Wien, of a three-year engagement as *Orchesterdirektor*. At first he firmly declined the offer, being unwilling to leave his congenial post in Gotha. When, however, he was told that the salary would be more than three times as much as he and Dorette together received in Gotha, that he would have a free hand in choosing the orchestra, that the Count intended to make the Theater an der Wien the finest in Germany, and that he would again have the opportunity to write for the stage with the certainty of an excellent production, he reconsidered the proposal. Though Dorette was reluctant to be parted from her mother and family in Gotha, she recognised the importance of the move for her husband's career, and when her consent had been given Spohr signed a contract. This committed him to play in all grand operas, to perform violin solos in operas and ballets and to conduct whenever the principal conductor, Ignaz von Seyfried, was not present; but he was not required to take part in minor operas, ballets, or the incidental music to plays.

Dorette remained in Vienna while Spohr travelled back to Gotha to arrange for the removal of their possessions and to collect the children, who had been left in the care of Dorette's mother. The journey was somewhat impeded by troop movements and marred by a nearly disastrous misadventure. At dinner in an inn, while Spohr was cutting a loaf of bread the knife slipped, slicing off a large piece of the ball of his left index finger together with part of the nail. To most people it would have been an unpleasant but trivial accident; for Spohr the threat to his livelihood was so appalling that he fainted for the only time in his life. For some time he suffered the greatest anxiety, but the injury proved not to be as serious as he feared. The wound healed remarkably well and with the aid of a leather finger stall he was able to assume his orchestral duties on his return to Vienna several weeks later, though not to play solos for some time.

His reception by the court in Gotha was frosty; the Duchess especially was incensed at losing his services. Nor were Dorette's family happy about the impending separation. Anxious to escape the unpleasant atmosphere of reproach he hurried ahead with the arrangements for departure, and accompanied by the children, their nursemaid and his brother Ferdinand, whom he had appointed to a place in the orchestra of the Theater an der Wien, he left Gotha early in May 1813. Favoured by excellent weather they enjoyed an idyllic voyage down the Danube in a hired boat, travelling continuously for four days and nights. Natural beauty always touched a deep chord in Spohr, and he vividly recalled the journey many years later, saying:

We were in the month of May, the moon was full and the deep blue sky spread out over the enchanting country around! Spring had just decked all nature in her first dress of tender green and the fruit trees were still laden with their beautiful blossom. The bushy banks of the majestic stream were the resort of numerous nightingales which, especially in the bright, calm nights, poured forth an unceasing melody. It was indeed a delightful voyage, and I have striven continually during the whole of my long life to make it again under similar favourable circumstances; but alas! in vain.'[17]

V

Vienna
1813–1816

The move to Vienna marked the beginning of a new phase in Spohr's life. Stimulated by constant contact with musicians of great ability and urged on by his ever-increasing determination to gain recognition as a composer, he produced a group of compositions in which all the threads of his previous experience were drawn together. In 1812 he had composed only the oratorio *Das jüngste Gericht* and a string quartet of the *brillant* type (op. 27). During the next two years he added fifteen new works to his catalogue of compositions: an opera, a cantata, a violin concerto, three string quartets, two string quintets, an octet, and a nonet, as well as a number of shorter pieces. Almost all of these reach new peaks of achievement.

The first task to which he applied himself after his return from Gotha was the opera *Faust*. Soon after he had accepted the appointment at the Theater an der Wien he had begun eagerly to look for a suitable libretto, and in February 1813 the young poet Theodor Körner, whom Spohr had frequently encountered at music parties and whose enthusiasm for music immediately attracted him, had agreed to write a libretto based on the Rübezahl legend. However, before he could begin, Körner, despite earnest attempts at dissuasion by Spohr and his other friends, enlisted as a volunteer in Lützow's regiment of light horse and was killed in action later that year. After Körner's departure from Vienna, the Viennese author Joseph Carl Bernard came to Spohr with the tempting offer of a libretto on the Faust legend. Spohr required a few changes, but these were made during his absence in Gotha, and he was able to begin work immediately on his return. In his memoirs he described how enthusiastically he set to work on the music for the opera, giving a revealing account of his method of composition. He wrote:

I now led a very active and very happy life enjoying the company of my family. The early dawn found me at the piano or at the writing table, and every other moment of the day which my orchestral duties or the tuition of my pupils allowed was devoted to composition. Yes, my brain was so continually absorbed at that time that on my way to my pupils and when taking a walk I was constantly composing and by that means acquired a facility in working out mentally not only long sections but whole pieces of music so completely that without any further effort they could immediately be written down. As soon as this was done they were as though effaced from my mind and I then had room for new things. Dorette frequently chided me in our walks for this perpetual thinking and was delighted when the prattle of the children diverted me from it. Once this had occurred I happily gave myself up to external impressions; but I was not to be allowed to relapse into my thoughtful mood again and Dorette was very skilful at preventing it.[1]

The white heat of his inspiration was so great that despite a multitude of other activities he completed the score of *Faust* in less than four months, between the end of May and the middle of September 1813. Because of his limited facility at the piano he would periodically take completed sections of the score to Meyerbeer, who was at that time resident in Vienna, and then, with Meyerbeer playing and himself undertaking the voice parts, the music was tried out for the first time. Hummel, Pixis and von Seyfried, to whom he also showed the score at this time, all encouraged him in his belief that he had produced something worthwhile.

For the material for his libretto Bernard drew upon elements from different versions of the Faust legend and moulded a number of bizarre but dramatic incidents into an effective story for musical treatment. The outline of the plot is as follows: Faust, disgusted with his life of sensual pleasure, determines to reform himself and use the powers which he derives from his compact with Mephistofeles for good purposes. The drama hinges upon his inability to transcend his own human weakness and the corruption which is necessarily attendant upon the use of diabolic powers. His first good intention is to marry Röschen, for whom he has genuine affection. His plans are disrupted by Röschen's rejected suitor, Franz, and a band of citizens who, suspecting Faust of having encompassed the death of Röschen's mother in order to possess the girl, force an entry into his house to apprehend him and free Röschen. Mephistofeles spirits Röschen away, and Faust and his friends escape by the use of his magic powers. The location then changes for the second half of the act, and Faust is shown making another attempt to do good by assisting Count Hugo to rescue his betrothed, Kunigunde, from the clutches of Sir Gulf, who is holding her captive in his castle. This is achieved with Mephistofeles' help, but the evil consequence which inevitably follows is that Faust conceives a passion for Kunigunde. Here the first act ends. The second begins with a witches' sabbath on the Blocksberg, where Faust obtains a magic potion with which he intends to gain Kunigunde's attentions. For his part in rescuing Kunigunde, Faust is invited as a guest to her wedding to Hugo, and at the celebration he begins his seduction of the bride. Mephistofeles draws Hugo's notice to what is going on, Kunigunde flees in confusion, and in an ensuing duel Faust kills Hugo. In the turmoil which follows, Faust and his friends escape. In a short scene Mephistofeles exults with the witches on the Blocksberg over the evil they have wrought. The action then shifts back to Faust: after he has spent the night with Kunigunde, Röschen, who had attended the wedding disguised as a youth and witnessed Faust's infidelity, commits suicide. An armed band arrives to take Faust prisoner and Kunigunde, freed from the spell and discovering that he has killed Hugo, attempts to stab him, but Mephistofeles prevents her, saying that Faust is his victim. When the origin of Faust's powers is revealed everyone flees, leaving him alone with Mephistofeles, who summons demons to drag him off to hell through a flaming abyss.

With no comic characters and its almost unremitting tension, *Faust* does not fit comfortably into any of the usual categories of opera in this period. An account of Spohr's treatment of the work is complicated by the additions and alterations which he made to it at a later date. The 1813 version was in two acts with spoken dialogue; for performance in Frankfurt in 1818 he added another aria for Faust; for performance at the Royal Italian Opera, Covent Garden in 1852, he revised the dialogue considerably and set it all to music, remodelled the opera into three acts, adding additional music including another scena and aria for Kunigunde, 'Ich bin allein', taken from *Der Zweikampf mit der Geliebten*. The division of the opera into three acts was conventional long before 1852, however; at Berlin in 1829 a notional third act was begun after the murder of Hugo, with Spohr's overture *Macbeth* (1825) used as an introduction and the aria from *Der Zweikampf* inserted. The same division into three acts was used for the Paris production of 1830.

The plot has four main points of dramatic tension: the confrontation between Faust and the citizens over Röschen's disappearance, the rescue of Kunigunde and the burning of Gulf's castle, Hugo and Kunigunde's marriage celebrations followed by the murder of Hugo, and the final dénouement. All these are treated by Spohr as substantial and connected musical pieces, as are the introductory scene of the first act and the Blocksberg scene with the witches at the beginning of the second act. Among the remaining numbers there is a wide variety of forms. As well as a number of recitatives and arias and duets, there is a *Trinklied mit Chor* no. 2(4),* a scena and aria with chorus no. 6(9), a Terzett no. 7(10) in which none of the characters sing together, a chorale from within the cathedral no. 10(13) – a device employed later by Halévy, Meyerbeer, Wagner and many other composers – which leads via a melodrama into a cavatina no. 11(13) for Röschen (the difference in social status between Röschen and Kunigunde is nicely emphasised by the contrast of this number with the latter's extended scena and aria no. 5(7), and an aria for Mephistofeles which leads into a scene with witches, no. 15(18) (this being later extended to form the introduction to Act III of the 1852 version).

In its 1813/18 version, *Faust* was a milestone in the development of German opera whose significance has too often been overshadowed by Weber's *Der Freischütz* (1821). The wider and more lasting popularity of Weber's opera has tended to obscure the radical nature of Spohr's achievement in *Faust* and its

---

* References to numbers are to the first version 1813/18, with those for the 1852 version given in brackets.

impact on contemporaries, including Weber himself. Spohr's intention in this opera was, first and foremost, to aim for dramatic truthfulness and to use the music as a means of welding the work into a coherent whole. This is immediately indicated by the overture, to which he appended the following note:

The composer has tried to present in the overture a musical impression of the circumstances of Faust's life. In the Allegro vivace it is Faust's sensual life and the riot of debauchery that is suggested. With satiety comes an awakening of his better self, and pricks of conscience, though these are overwhelmed by the return of sensual impulses. In the Largo grave he at last pulls himself together and seriously attempts to renounce the evil of his ways; and in the fugato there is a suggestion of good resolutions being formed. It is not long, however, before he is again the prey of new and stronger sensual temptations (tempo primo) and, blinded by the deceptive power of the Evil One, he abandons himself more completely than ever to the most uncontrolled desires.[2]

The opening scene, into which the overture leads without a break, is handled with imagination and skill. As the curtain rises, disclosing a square in Strasbourg by night, the overture gives way to a minuet coming from a lighted mansion at the back of the stage (played by a small band behind the scenes). Faust, dishevelled from a night of debauchery, comes out of the mansion and begins to soliloquise in recitative accompanied by the main orchestra while the minuet continues in the background; he is joined by Mephistofeles, and when the minuet has finished a further section of recitative leads into their duet 'Ja ich soll mir Wonne schaffen'. In this duet the musical characterisation is finely conceived; at only one point do they both share the same material, that is when Mephistofeles imitates Faust's phrases at a bar's interval, clearly suggesting mockery. Apart from this their music is quite different and emphasises their opposing characteristics; Faust, full of good intentions, tends to sing assertive diatonic phrases in major keys, while Mephistofeles introduces a more sinister dimension (ex. 47). The musical characterisation and illustration of shifting emotions are carried out with similar attention to detail throughout the opera. The exceptional nature of Spohr's treatment in this respect was recognised by contemporaries. After hearing *Faust* in Berlin in 1829, Zelter wrote to Goethe and having discussed the weaknesses of the libretto he continued:

Now as to the work of the composer who is clearly recognisable more as a tonal artist than as a musician or melodist, everything is carried out most artistically and, astonishingly enough, in the most minute detail, in order to overreach, to outbid the most alert ear. The finest Brabant laces are rough work in comparison. A copy of the libretto is almost indispensable to the performance, for the expression of the words in respect of high and low, light and dark, tense and lax, and so on, is worked out with hair's-breadth precision like the honeycomb in a beehive.[3]

There is no lack of powerful effects in the opera; only the Blocksberg scene at the beginning of Act II seems to fall short of its aims, and fails to conjure

Ex. 47

79

up an impression of real evil – it is certainly less convincing in this respect than the Wolf's Glen scene in *Der Freischütz* – but even here there are passages of considerable tension and power, as when Mephistofeles invokes the witch Sycorax (ex. 48). The witches' music in 2/8 which returns periodically during this scene and in no. 15(18) may clearly be seen as a precursor of the elfin lightness of Mendelssohn's supernatural music, and the whole scene undoubtedly influenced the Walpurgisnacht music of Lortzing, Loewe and Mendelssohn.

Perhaps the most remarkable feature of *Faust*, however, is its use of leitmotif, which is employed with a degree of subtlety that was not matched until Wagner. Its use was recognised by Weber in his 1816 preface for the Prague première, where he observed: 'A few melodies, felicitously and aptly devised, weave like delicate threads through the whole, and hold it together artistically.'[4] Spohr went far beyond the mere thematic reminiscences which he had used in his first two operas, though there are also instances of this in *Faust*, as for example in Faust's scena no. 13(15) where several previously heard themes are recalled as he takes stock of his situation. But genuine leitmotif, in the sense of a musical phrase occuring in a variety of guises, which stands as a symbol for a person or an idea, is clearly to be traced in *Faust*.

Ex. 48

(Ex. 48 cont.)

bring' in wohlge-waschner Scha - le   ein-en Trunk zum lust'-gen Mahle!   Sy-co-rax

The two phrases which are treated most consistently in this manner are the 'hell' motif and the 'love' motif. The 'hell' motif is based on a descending triad in which the notes are preceded by a rising semitone appoggiatura (ex. 49). The 'love' motif is built from an ascending third with a rising semitone

Ex. 49

appoggiatura to the first note and a falling tone or semitone appoggiatura at the end (the interval between the third and fourth notes is variable); it has a more distinct rhythmic character (ex. 50). A third phrase (ex. 51) which is less

Ex. 50

Ex. 51

pervasive but seems to have some of the characteristics of a leitmotif is associated with Faust and appears to stand for his inner turmoil.

In the overture all three of these are used. The opening phrase (ex. 52) is a

Ex. 52

veiled version of the 'hell' motif; this is followed immediately by the 'Faust' motif which dominates the overture. The 'love' motif, associated with Faust's thoughts about Röschen, occurs as a second subject, but is darkened by sinister chromatic passages in the woodwind and is finally swamped by the resurgence of the 'Faust' motif (ex. 53). The C minor tonality of the recapitulation emphasises the sense of impending doom, especially through the semitone appoggiatura which then comes at the end of the 'love' motif. The 'love' and 'hell' motifs next appear in Faust's aria 'Liebe ist die zarte Blüthe'

Ex. 53

(Ex. 53 cont.)

no. 1a(3). Just before Faust refers to 'the power of hellish night' the 'hell' motif is heard in the orchestra; later, before he sings the phrase 'but even hell's dreadful sneers can be counteracted by the bonds of love', the 'love' motif makes its appearance in the accompaniment. There is a particularly subtle use of the 'hell' motif in Kunigunde's scena no. 5(7): she sings the words 'love gives the heart courage and strength'; then as she goes on to sing 'through it the works which cunning and evil create fail', the 'hell' motif, in an apparently innocuous major key, appears to mock her confidence (ex. 54). In the

Ex. 54

first Finale the 'love' motif is heard in consecutive thirds at the moment when Hugo and Kunigunde are reunited. At the very end of the act, when the castle has been destroyed by demons invisible to the onlookers, the orchestra makes clear the agency of destruction by boldly sounding the 'hell' motif descending through two octaves. Act II begins unambiguously with the same motif, emphasising the hellish allegiance of the witches. Faust's recitative and aria no. 13(15) makes considerable use of his 'turmoil' motif along with various other thematic reminiscences, though the other two motifs are not present. The 'hell' motif again insinuates itself by degrees into the wedding celebrations of Hugo and Kunigunde, becoming clearly recognisable at the point where Hugo is made aware of Faust's seduction of his bride. Another effective reminiscence earlier in this scene is the appearance of a rising bass arpeggio which is heard as the magic potion takes effect on Kunigunde (ex. 55) (she sings 'he holds me near him as if in a magic circle');

Ex. 55

Wie   in ein-em Zau-ber-kreis hält es   mich in sei - ner Nä - he

this phrase had previously occurred during the Blocksberg scene when Sycorax produced the potion for Faust (ex. 48). The 'love' and 'hell' motifs appear again in the Finale. Human love has succumbed to the powers of the devil and its motif appears in an anguished form as Röschen rushes off to kill herself (ex. 56); it is heard again, later, in this form as Kunigunde vows to follow her. When Faust sings 'but my will is my protection', openly admitting

Ex. 56

Weh!   Es   ist   um mich__ ge - sche - hen

the diabolic origin of his power, his music is the 'hell' motif (here sung by him for the first time), showing that contrary to his belief he is now irredeemably ensnared (ex. 57).

On completion of *Faust* Spohr immediately offered it for performance at the Theater an der Wien, and Count Palffy accepted it without hesitation. But before it could be put into production, relations between the two men

Ex. 57

were to deteriorate to such an extent that the Count, on the grounds that some of the principal parts were too difficult for his singers, withdrew his offer (see p. 103 below). Only the overture was performed during Spohr's time in Vienna, at a concert in the small Redoutensaal on 11 December 1814, when it elicited from a critic the comment that it 'gave rise to the wish that we could see this opera, which was finished more than a year ago, very soon'.[5] Spohr was not to hear a performance of *Faust* for five years, and in the meantime it was premièred in Prague on 1 September 1816. Subsequently *Faust* was produced on many stages both inside and outside Germany; it was published in German, Italian, French, English, and Czech versions, and held its place in the repertoire for more than half a century.

After he had finished *Faust*, Spohr cleared his mind of it and turned immediately to other projects. Far from having exhausted his creative energy, his intensive labour on the opera seems to have stimulated his productivity, for in the remaining three months of the year he composed two substantial masterpieces and a rondo in D for violin and harp, written to augment his and Dorette's joint repertoire. The two major works resulted from a curious commission: shortly after Spohr's acceptance of his post at the Theater an der Wien had become generally known, in the spring of 1813, he had been approached by the cloth merchant Johann Tost, an eccentric music-lover and patron, who years earlier had been the dedicatee of Haydn's opp. 54, 55, and 64 string quartets. Tost proposed that in return for an agreed scale of charges (thirty ducats for a quartet, thirty-five for a quintet, and so on in proportion to the number of instruments involved), Spohr should assign to him for a period of three years all the chamber music which he wrote in Vienna. In return he would have sole possession of the works for the three-year period, after which he would return the manuscripts so that Spohr could dispose of them as he wished. At first, perplexed over Tost's motive for so strange a proposal, Spohr hesitated to agree, but accepted the arrangement after Tost had explained that his reasons were, first, that he wished to be invited to the music parties at which the works were to be played, and secondly, that he hoped to use them when he was away on business trips as a means of making useful commercial contacts among music-lovers. Before leaving for Gotha Spohr was able to deliver two string quartets to Tost: the one in G minor which he later dedicated to Beethoven's patron Count Razoumovsky and published as op. 27, and another in F minor which he was subsequently to publish as the third of his op. 29 set. With these, Tost had to be content for some time, but on finishing *Faust* Spohr enquired of him what sort of chamber work he would most like him to compose next. Tost's suggestion was a nonet for wind and strings (obviously money was no object), and he particularly requested that Spohr should write it in such a way as to emphasise the individual character of each of the nine instruments. The challenge of tackling an unfamiliar medium almost always brought out the best in Spohr, and in this case he succeded brilliantly; the Nonet (op. 31) quickly became a favourite with performers and audiences and has rightly maintained a place in the repertoire up to the present day.

Apart from the finely judged and imaginative scoring, which unequivocally fulfilled Tost's request, a noteworthy feature of the Nonet is the use of a single motif in three of the four movements. This is the four-note figure with which the work opens (ex. 58): it pervades the first movement, appearing in a number of guises including a fugato in the development section (exx. 59 and 60). In the deeply felt Adagio third movement it lies at the root of the

Ex. 58

Ex. 59

Ex. 60

main theme (ex. 61): the relationship is emphasised in the codetta to the exposition (ex. 62) and this is expanded upon in the coda. Finally, the high-spirited last movement makes joking reference to it in the second subject introduced by the oboe (ex. 63). The second movement of the Nonet is a

Ex. 61

Ex. 62

Ex. 63

Scherzo in D minor with two Trios, one for strings and the other for wind with double bass; it is a beautifully crafted movement.

The other composition which Spohr presented to Tost before the end of the year was his First String Quintet in G major (published, as a result of the publisher's error, as op. 33 no. 2). It does not deserve its current obscurity; fresh, vigorous and skilfully scored, it fully merits a place in the repertoire. The addition of a second viola to the usual string quartet prompted Spohr to allow the lower parts more freedom than in his quartets. The first viola is often given an important melodic role, though the other instruments come forward prominently only in the variation movement. Like almost all Spohr's chamber music, the Quintet was written with his own participation in mind, and the temptation to give free rein to his virtuosity was seldom resisted, but only in the Trio section of the Scherzo does he permit the first violin to hold the stage entirely. As in the best of his chamber music the brilliant violin writing is not detrimental, and is certainly not at the expense of melodic, harmonic or textural interest in the composition as a whole. The first movement provides another good example of Spohr's ability to make a whole movement seem as if it grows almost entirely from a single idea. Virtually every bar of the movement contains an element of the principal theme or one of its derivatives, but interest is maintained throughout by the composer's fertility in devising new ways of presentation. Exx. 64–66 show the

Ex. 64

Ex. 65

Ex. 66

simple first statement in the opening bars, the transformation of the idea into a second subject (bars 44–8) and its reappearance in a more plaintive mood (bars 52–6). Elsewhere it pervades the music in a more or less subordinate role. During the transition to the second subject it is contrasted with triplet quaver arpeggios in the first violin and cello; in the passage which follows on from the second subject it is used as a counterpoint to the bravura semiquavers of the first violin (ex. 67), after which it again assumes dominance in the codetta. In the development the second-subject version undergoes

Ex. 67

another transformation to produce a poignant passage which Spohr marked 'con molto espressione' (ex. 68). The second movement, a Scherzo in G minor, exploits bold leaps derived from its vigorous opening phrase (ex. 69), while the theme of the graceful Trio in the tonic major grows out of

Ex. 68

Ex. 69

a legato quaver figure prominent in the second part of the Scherzo. The charming and resourceful set of variations which follows is in B flat major. When the Quintet was reviewed in the *AMZ*, a critic observed that this movement should 'be held as a model for all time, so long at least as the taste for true art does not perish; Haydn Mozart and Beethoven themselves have created nothing more magnificent of this kind'.[6] The Finale is a substantial sonata-form movement in G minor where, as if to offer a complete antithesis to the first movement, a host of contrasting ideas jostle for pre-eminence. An extraordinary passage occurs in the development section, where an angular motif clearly related to the Scherzo (ex. 70) is tossed from one instrument to another, while a diminished harmony is sustained for seven bars, before finally breaking loose in D major (ex. 71). Taken as a whole this quintet

Ex. 70

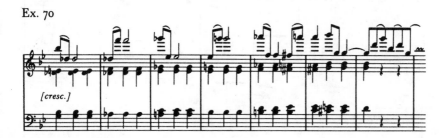

Ex. 71

(Ex. 71 cont.)

represents Spohr's first completely successful piece of string chamber music; in it he achieved a satisfactory balance between brilliance and a true chamber-music idiom, and as with most of the Vienna works it gives clear evidence that he had now consolidated his own entirely individual style and was able to employ it with increasing flexibility and confidence in almost every medium to which he turned his attention.

Amid all this creative activity occurred a domestic sorrow, for the son, Friedrich, to whom Dorette gave birth on 1 July 1814 died less than three months later. But the pace of their lives in Vienna did not allow either of the parents to grieve for long. Dorette sought distraction in practising the harp, and Spohr continued to fill almost every spare moment of his day with composition. The defeat of Napoleon at the battle of Leipzig in the previous October had resulted in a flurry of patriotic fervour throughout Germany. Writers and composers hastened to produce works in celebration of the victory, and Tost, cárried along by the general euphoria, proposed that Spohr should compose a cantata to celebrate the Emperor of Austria's return to Vienna. The composition of *Das befreite Deutschland* – a substantial work of eleven numbers, lasting about two hours in performance – took two and a half months, but for want of a suitable hall it could not be performed until after Spohr had left the city. (As a result he was to hear it for the first and only time at the Frankenhausen festival of October 1815, by which time it was celebrating the victory of Waterloo.) However, as in the case of his disappointment over the shelving of *Faust*, the similar fate of his cantata did not deter Spohr from further labours; he followed it up immediately with another *quatuor brillant* (op. 30) in which he could continue to astonish the salons of Vienna as much by his superlative lyrical and expressive gifts as by his brilliance. There is a great deal of very attractive music in this quartet, but it is unequivocally a piece for violin with the support of a string trio, and in this respect stands in sharp contrast to the other quartet of 1814. Here, rather than virtuosity and the rhapsodic statement of themes by a single instrument, a conversational working-out of motifs is the chief aim. The main theme of the first movement resulted from an incident at a musical evening where one of Fesca's chamber works, which began with a theme derived from the composer's own name,* had been played. Spohr recalled that he, Hummel and Pixis had been teased on account of their unmusical names and that this had spurred him to see whether he could make something musical out of it; using the abbreviation '*po*' for piano and a crotchet rest which resembled an 'r', he produced the two-note motif (ex. 72) with which

Ex. 72

he began his String Quartet in E flat op. 29 no. 1. The quartet is one of Spohr's finest. There is freshness of invention in the melodies, novelty in the harmony and masterly organisation of material. The development section of the first movement contains a passage of extraordinary harmonic effect (ex. 73). The second movement, an Andante con variazioni in C minor is constructed with his usual grace and skill. The Scherzo is a fugato in E flat with a charming Trio in B major (this calls to mind the same relationship in the Scherzo of Dussek's String Quartet in E flat op. 60 no. 3 of 1806/7). The Finale is a worthy conclusion to the quartet; the opening sixteen bars provide a good example of the way Spohr's harmonic method stamps a conventionally cheerful theme with his own peculiar individuality (ex. 74).

The String Quartet in C major, which he composed several months later at the beginning of 1815 and published as op. 29 no. 2, is also a fine work. The

---

* Fesca was able to represent the 's' in his name by exploiting the German convention whereby 'es' stands for E flat and can be used to spell 's' in personal names. Spohr too could take advantage of this convention and also of the German use of 'h' for B natural (b = B flat).

Ex. 73

Ex. 74

critic Fröhlich, who heard Spohr perform all three works in Würzburg in December 1815, wrote in a review of op. 29 that he thought the C major 'one of the most significant works which this branch of music possesses'.[7] It is less intricate in many respects than op. 29 no. 1, with an amiable, almost Mozartian quality established by the opening theme of the first Allegro; a deeper note is struck, however, with the second subject, which is marked 'con molto espressione' and takes an unexpected tonal direction (ex. 75). The third

Ex. 75

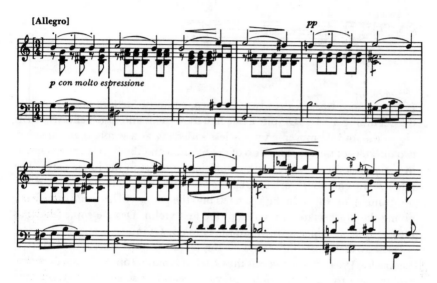

movement is a fine martial Menuetto in C minor with a Trio in the tonic major, and the Finale an ebullient helter-skelter. But the most typical movement is the second, a tender Adagio in F major in a style which is wholly Spohr's own (ex. 76); it contains a notable passage in which the first violin

Ex. 76

executes a series of expressive figurations that have an operatic quality (ex. 77).

Ex. 77

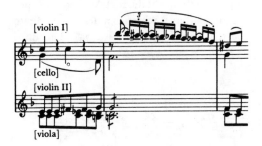

Op. 29 no. 3 was, as already mentioned, composed before nos. 1 and 2, at the beginning of 1813. Despite a fine first movement and much effective writing in the middle movements it is less satisfying as a whole than the other two quartets of the set. The Trio of the Scherzo and the Finale are too much in the *quatuor brillant* style, with insufficient interest in the lower parts. The other string chamber work of 1814 was a second string quintet (published as op. 33 no. 1), in which Spohr again fell into the pattern of his *quatuors brillants*, giving the lion's share of interest to the first violin. Despite some felicitous ideas it is far less interesting than the G major Quintet.

Perhaps the most impressive of the chamber works composed during Spohr's final year in Vienna was the Octet in E major (op. 32), a worthy companion piece to the Nonet of the previous year. It is scored for clarinet, two horns, violin, two violas, cello and bass. The scoring was inspired by the playing of the clarinettist Friedlowsky and the horn player Herbst from the Theater an der Wien orchestra (Spohr could not recall the name of the other horn player when he came to write his memoirs). The choice of two violas rather than two violins seems deliberately to have been intended to match the mellow tone of the horns and clarinet (whose lower register Spohr used in a way which had hardly any parallel at that time). This instrumentation also had the advantage of emphasising the brilliance of the violin. The structure of the first movement differs considerably from that of the Nonet. An Adagio introduction presents a number of thematic germs: the first bar announces the two elements out of which the first theme of the Allegro is built, but in reverse order (ex. 78). The closing bars of the introduction allude to the second subject. A formal peculiarity of this movement is that, following the exposition, there are only ten bars of development material before the music of the Adagio reappears, written in allegro tempo in long note-values, after which the first-subject group is omitted and a transposed version of the

Ex. 78

bridge passage from the exposition leads straight into the second subject. The Menuetto second movement has a scherzo character and is notable for its syncopated rhythms which, combined with Spohr's chromatic harmony, give it an affinity with the scherzos of Mendelssohn and Schumann. The theme of the Andante con variazioni is Handel's 'Harmonious Blacksmith', which Spohr used at Tost's request; Tost intended making a business trip to England and thought that this would make the work more interesting to the English. The variations again show the fecundity of Spohr's invention at this time, allowing the members of the ensemble to display themselves in a range of different lights. The surprising and beautiful coda brings Schubert strongly to mind (as does so much of the chamber music which Spohr wrote in Vienna) by its leaning towards the Neapolitan key (ex. 79). The relaxed and light-hearted Finale in rondo form is given an almost rustic quality by its principal theme, though there is nothing rustic about its perfection of detail and immaculate construction.

There can be no doubt about the importance to Spohr of his time in Vienna. Through his participation in the busy musical life of the city he came in contact with a large number of distinguished musicians. The violinists Schuppanzigh and Mayseder, the pianists Hummel and Moscheles, the imperial conductors Weigl and Salieri were among the resident musicians with whom he established friendly relationships; while Weber, Fesca, Pixis and Meyerbeer were for varying periods a part of the musical circles in which he moved. Beethoven, too, became a frequent guest in Spohr's apartments, where the happy family atmosphere seems to have provided him with a welcome relief from his own domestic disorder. The two musicians often met also in restaurants or at the Theater an der Wien, where Beethoven had a free seat, and the cordiality of their relationship can be

Ex. 79

gauged by the unusual care with which Beethoven inscribed Spohr's album with a canon and the message: 'May you, dear Spohr, wherever you find real art, and real artists, think with pleasure of me your friend Beethoven.' It is clear that Beethoven and Spohr were in complete agreement about the exalted worth of their art and the dignity of the artist.

With some of his orchestra from the Theater an der Wien Spohr took part in the performance of Beethoven's Seventh and Eighth Symphonies on 27 February 1814. The Allegretto from the former made a particularly powerful impression on him; his attitude towards Beethoven's compositions, however, was not uncritical. There could hardly have been a greater admirer of Beethoven's early works than Spohr, as his vigorous championship of the op. 18 quartets and his performances of the symphonies and piano concertos in Gotha indicate, but while finding much to admire in Beethoven's later works he became increasingly out of sympathy with what he saw as a striving for effect and the sacrifice of musical beauty for the sake of melodramatic gesture. Already in Gotha he had developed reservations about Beethoven's more recent music,* and in Vienna he became seized with the conviction that Beethoven was 'wanting in aesthetic feeling and a sense of the beautiful', and along with many of his contemporaries he was to feel that works such as the late quartets and the Ninth Symphony were 'eccentric, unconnected and

* See Spohr's letter to Peters of 24 November 1810 (*AMZ*, new series ii (1867), 299).

incomprehensible'. There is a certain honest courage in Spohr's admission, more than thirty years later, of his attitude to Beethoven's late works: 'It is true there are people who imagine they can understand them and, in their pleasure at that, rank them far above his earlier masterpieces, but I am not of the number and freely admit that I have never been able to relish the last works of Beethoven.'[8] The reason for this lack of sympathy is not far to seek. Stylistically Spohr's and Beethoven's development as composers took them in diametrically opposite directions. The op. 18 quartets are the point at which they were closest, but from there their paths diverged. Beethoven moved away from the chromaticism of late Mozart towards a broader harmonic style; it is significant that his only preserved comment about Spohr's music should have been 'He is too rich in dissonances; pleasure in his music is marred by his chromatic melody.'[9] Spohr's increasing preoccupation with harmonic detail and chromaticism as the principal vehicle for expressiveness, though ultimately a source of weakness in his own music, was perhaps in the long run to prove as fertile a source of inspiration for his younger contemporaries as Beethoven's more massive achievements. In this context it must be borne in mind that for several decades of the nineteenth century there were many who would have maintained that Spohr was Beethoven's equal and few who would have denied that he must be numbered among the great composers.

In 1814 this eminence lay some distance in the future, but the series of works which Spohr had produced in Vienna played a significant part in gaining it for him. Not the least of these was the only important composition of this period which remains to be considered – the Seventh Violin Concerto in E minor op. 38, which he completed in July 1814. In this concerto Spohr reached a peak which none of his later violin concertos was to surpass. Its freshness and originality bear witness to the powerful creative impact which Vienna had made upon him. He was aware that he was writing for an audience which would contain many connoisseurs who paid attention to the composition just as much as to the virtuoso. His strong desire that it should be listened to in this way is indicated by his diary entry for 20 October 1815, where, after performing the concerto at Frankenhausen, he wrote regretfully: 'today I again became convinced that the masses are far more taken with the skilful and brilliant execution of the virtuoso than by the merits of the composition. All were delighted with my playing, but few commented favourably on the work.'[10]

The first movement of the E minor Concerto draws together all the threads of Spohr's past experience. It is rich in melody, but through the masterly integration of its thematic elements and their subtle use as accompanying figures to the soloist's passages of display, the movement gives an impression of both expansiveness and conciseness. The three principal themes bear Spohr's unmistakable fingerprints, covering a range of charac-

teristic Romantic moods from 'noble melancholy' through emotional agitation to tender yearning (ex. 80).* The entry of the solo violin, initially
accompanied only by flutes and clarinets, is beautifully conceived (ex. 81).

Ex. 80

Formally the movement is irregular: during development the soloist introduces a new assertive theme in C major, after which passages of display
lead straight back into the second subject and finally to a coda where, following an echo of the first solo entry, the music drives inexorably to a violent
conclusion. The impact of the powerful emotional tone of this movement on
contemporaries is summed up in an *AMZ* reviewer's description of it as
giving 'an overall impression of glowing in dark red fire'; its genuinely
Romantic quality certainly sets it apart from anything else which was being
written at this time. The same reviewer went on to say of the second move-

---

* It is interesting that the harmonic and melodic outline of the opening of the movement
(ex. 80a) is quoted at the beginning of the song 'Der erste Kuss' op. 41 no. 5 (composed the following year), where the performance direction is 'Leidenschaftlich'.

Ex. 81

ment that it was 'a wonderfully beautiful, wholly original, very artful but not artificial Adagio', and stressed the new field of Romantic expression that Spohr had opened up in it. The violin seemed to the critic to give the impression of 'floating as if in a dream'. This Adagio is certainly one of Spohr's most beautiful. It is an equivalent on the violin of many of Chopin's nocturnes; the whole movement shows all the essential techniques of that style in a state of full maturity (ex. 82). The sensibility of the harmonic language again has

Ex. 82

(Ex. 82 cont.)

analogies with Schubert. After two such fine and original movements the Rondo finale seems less significant; it is retrospective rather than prophetic, still recalling the influence of Rode and Viotti in the character of several of its themes. This was recognised by the *AMZ* reviewer who, however, pointed out that it is 'constructed with far greater qualities of spirit and art'.[11] This is by far the most difficult movement technically and contains some breathtaking examples of Spohr's up-bow staccato.

The outstanding quality of the E minor Concerto was recognised immediately. After its first performance on 19 February 1815 it was described as 'a splendid, perfect composition'.[12] Its performance at Frankenhausen in October of the same year elicited an even more decisive accolade; there it was hailed as 'the greatest of all' violin concertos.[13] And two years later, on its appearance in print, a reviewer opined that 'in originality of invention and management of instruments it is truly in its own unique and enduring category'.[14]

The concert of 19 February 1815 at which the Seventh Violin Concerto was first performed was Spohr's farewell to the Viennese public. His position at the Theater an der Wien proved to be less congenial than he had expected. Count Palffy, having become lessee of the two court theatres, had begun to restrict the repertoire of the Theater an der Wien to the performance of spectacles and popular *Singspiele* in which the terms of Spohr's contract did not require him to play, and personal relations between Spohr and the Count had become strained over breaches of contract (on the management's part) which, with his well-developed sense of personal rights, Spohr bitterly resented. It soon became clear that it would be in the interests of both parties to terminate the agreement, so an arrangement was reached whereby the three-year contract would be cancelled at the end of the second year and in compensation Spohr would receive half of the third year's salary. In addition to this change of circumstances, Tost was on the point of bankruptcy and, being unable to pay for Spohr's latest batch of compositions, had returned all his manuscripts to him so that he could sell them. He insisted on giving Spohr a promissory note for 100 ducats which could be cashed when his financial affairs improved; this Spohr accepted reluctantly, and only when he saw that Tost's pride would be hurt by a refusal. Spohr's attitude in this instance is an example of one of the character traits which caused him to be so widely admired for his personal qualities, and prompted the reviewer of his farewell concert to end his article with the comment: 'May he, who by his talent and his open, manly character has left an honourable memorial of his worth in our hearts, meet always and everywhere with success!'[15]

It was not altogether disagreeable to Spohr that his departure from Vienna should have been precipitated by events, for, stimulating and enjoyable though his time there had been, the old urge to travel was stirring again.

Napoleon's exile to Elba and the ensuing European peace seemed to indicate that the time was propitious for an extended concert tour, and in March 1815 Spohr left Vienna with his wife and daughters. They travelled through Brünn to Breslau, where they gave two concerts on 4 and 12 April, but these were not well attended, for the news of Napoleon's escape from Elba had plunged the continent back into turmoil and turned people's attention away from concert-going. There was no lack of private music-making, though, and Spohr was able to delight the musical amateurs of Breslau with his recently written chamber works. He also found time to compose for his friend Schnabel (the cathedral Cantor) an Offertorium for soprano and chorus with obbligato violin and orchestra, in the performance of which he took part on 16 April in Breslau Cathedral.

Since even in less troubled times the summer was unprofitable for concert-giving, Spohr had happily accepted an offer to spend the summer months with the Prince of Carolath-Schönaich on his Silesian estates. The pleasant prospect of a complete break after the constantly busy life he had been leading for the past two and a half years was sufficient to induce him to give up his intention of going to Prague for Weber's production of *Faust*. The circumstances of his stay at Carolath are interesting. The invitation had come to him through a mutual friend, Baron von Reibnitz, the former intendant of the orchestra at Gotha. Dorette was to teach music to the young princesses but in every other respect she and her husband were guests of the family, dining with them and sharing in all their social activities and excursions. Spohr would certainly not have consented to come if there had been any suggestion that they would be discriminated against socially, but it is an indication of the changing status of musicians that they should have been treated on terms of such equality.

In this relaxed atmosphere Spohr devoted himself to giving his own children their first instruction in music and composed a number of pieces which could be performed at musical evenings in the castle. To texts selected by the Prince's sister-in-law he wrote the majority of the twelve songs that were later published as opp. 37 and 41.

The claim which Spohr made in his letter to Peters of June 1816, that his Lieder were different in form and other essentials from those of other composers, is much more justifiably applicable to these sets than to op. 25. Only five of the twelve songs opp. 37 and 41 are strophic (two of these with prelude and postlude); in the others Spohr responded to the nature of the text with a variety of formal procedures and musical treatments. Op. 37 no. 1 is a setting of Goethe's 'Kennst du das Land' (doubtless chosen because he was on the verge of realising his long-cherished wish to visit Italy), in which changes of time and different modulations are ingeniously made to illustrate the shifts of mood in each of the poem's three verses, without destroying the strophic feeling. The refrain 'Dahin! dahin!' is a constant, for which the music each time returns to the home key of F major, and each verse begins similarly; but thereafter there are significant changes: verse 1 goes to G major, verse 2 to F minor and verse 3 to D minor. Goethe complained to Tomaschek in 1822 that Spohr had misunderstood the poem by through-composing it, but he made the same criticism of Beethoven's setting which is in fact strophic with only a slight thickening of the accompaniment for a few bars in the last verse; his observation, with regard to these two settings, that Mignon could sing a song but not an aria is indicative of his musical conservatism and increasing alienation from Romantic trends. The finest of Spohr's op. 37 set is 'Die Stimme der Nacht' (poem by 'Cäcilie von W.'), a passionate song about the pains of love, in the setting of which Spohr achieves an intensity not normally associated with anyone but Schubert at this time. The sound of distant bells in the valley, referred to in the first stanza of the poem, is conjured up in the piano part at the beginning, then the key and the pattern of the accompaniment change dramatically as the poet turns to inner feelings of anguish. Here, as in others of these Lieder, Spohr shows his ability to portray the changing and developing mood of a poem with great subtlety and skill through melody and accompaniment, but above all through harmonic nuance. 'Die Stimme der Nacht' is such a coherent whole that no brief extract can adequately illustrate its qualities, but ex. 83 gives an indication of the style, and ex. 84 shows a particularly telling use of Neapolitan harmony. The fifth song of the set 'Liebesschwärmerei' (Cäcilie von W.) is an unusual strophic setting where each of the three verses begins 'Schwärmerisch fröhlich' (enthusiastically happy) but at the words 'Doch ach!', which occur in each verse, the key changes from G major to minor and Spohr gives the direction 'In Wehmuth versinkend und nach und nach immer langsamer' (sinking into sadness and getting gradually slower all the time). The first song of op. 41, 'Das Mädchens Sehnsucht' (Kind), is notable for a passage (ex. 85) which is strikingly similar to the question 'wo bist du?' at bars 54f of Schubert's 'Der Wanderer' (Oct. 1816). Op. 41 no. 3, 'An Mignon' (Goethe), is perhaps too full of subtle modulation, but the following song, 'Klagelied von den drei Rosen' (Buri), is touchingly direct and effective. The final song of the set, 'Vanitas! Vanitatum Vanitas' (Goethe), has the simplicity of a folk song, as does the final song of the op. 37 set, 'Lied beim Rundetanz' (von Salis), with its drone and imitations of yodelling in the piano accompaniment.

The other works written at Carolath were the Grande Polonaise for violin and orchestra (or piano) op. 40, with which Spohr frequently delighted the Prince and his occasional visitors, and the Notturno op. 34. The Polonaise is certainly a piece in which the technique of the soloist is displayed to advantage, but as usual the virtuosity is not achieved at the expense of purely musical considerations. The Notturno in C op. 34 – scored for flute (doubling E flat flute and first piccolo), second piccolo, two oboes, two clari-

Ex. 83

[Feierlich]

still in Nacht die Flur ver_sin-ken; Ach! Und mir gedrängt im

Her - zen to - ben wild der Lie - be Schmerzen! Un - gehort erschallt mein

Kla - gen durch die Nacht vom Wind ge - tra gen; ahn-det sie, die hoch ich

eh - re, wel - che Glut mein Herz ver - zeh - re? Nein

Ex. 84

Ex. 85

nets, two bassoons, two horns, two trumpets, post horn, bass horn (or double-bassoon), bass trombone, and 'Turkish' percussion – was written for the wind band of Prince Günther Friedrich Carl of Schwarzburg-Sondershausen, of which Hermstedt was director. It is in six movements: a Turkish March, Menuetto, Andante con variazioni, Polacca, Adagio and Finale. Mozart's wind-music style was clearly one of the influences on the work, but combined with this is the characteristic concertante writing which is found in Spohr's chamber works. The variations give each of the principal instruments an opportunity to show its capabilities, while in the beautiful Adagio in A flat Spohr creates a richly homogeneous sound. The post-horn solo in the Trio of the Polacca has a graphic effect, and the yodelling themes of the Finale conclude the work in high spirits. The Notturno did not appear in print until 1826 but thereafter achieved wide popularity, and numerous arrangements for various instruments were subsequently made.

At last, with the approach of autumn, the Spohr family bade farewell to their kind hosts at Carolath and journeyed to Gotha, where Dorette was overjoyed to be reunited with her family. There they remained until the end of October, during which time they made a number of short excursions. The first was to visit Spohr's parents in their new home at Gandersheim, where Carl Heinrich Spohr had been made district physician; another was to Frankenhausen for the festival, at which his cantata *Das befreite Deutschland* was performed. With Napoleon's defeat at Waterloo in June 1815 the cantata could celebrate, as Spohr put it, 'the now-complete emancipation of Germany'.[16] But he was by no means complacent about the internal state of Germany. In the following twelve months, during which they travelled through Germany and Switzerland, his diaries contain a number of remarks which show his dissatisfaction with the inefficient and often tyrannical governments of the German states. Meeting Conradin Kreutzer in Freiburg, he was disgusted by the account he was given of the insufferable despotism which still prevailed in Stuttgart.

With Dorette and the children Spohr had left Gotha at the end of October on the first stage of their journey to Italy. Travelling in their own specially designed coach, they made a leisurely progress giving concerts in Meiningen, Würzburg, Nuremburg, Munich, Frankfurt, Darmstadt, Heidelberg, Karlsruhe, Strasbourg, Münster, Bern and Zurich. Towards the end of April they took up residence in the beautiful village of Thierachern in the Bernese Oberland, where they were to remain throughout the summer months of 1816. Dorette, whose health had suffered from almost five months of continual travelling, was greatly in need of a period of recuperation, and Spohr was not loth to spend some time in what he described as 'one of the most beautiful spots that we had yet seen'.[17] By mid May they had settled into a routine of which Spohr gave the following account in his diary:

In the morning, while I compose, Dorette gives the children instruction in arithmetic, writing, geography etc.; in the afternoon I teach them the piano and singing. Then away we sally out into the fresh air. If the weather permits an extended excursion we take our frugal evening meal in some Küher's (so the shepherds are called here) and do not return till late in the evening. Should the weather be uncertain we go provided with umbrellas at least as far as Thun to enquire after letters from home, procure some amusement for rainy days from the lending library and purchase our little necessities. The daily exercise in the beautiful pure balmy air strengthens our bodies, enlivens our spirits and makes us joyous and happy. In such a disposition of mind one works easily and quickly, and several completed compositions already lie before me, namely a Violin Concerto in the form of a vocal scena and a Duet for two violins.[18]

The violin concerto which he had composed so quickly was the eighth, in A minor (op. 47), subtitled 'In modo si Scena Cantante' (which Spohr always referred to as his *Gesangsszena*). Its unusual form was suggested by the forthcoming Italian tour. Knowing how difficult it was for an instrumentalist to make an impression in the land where opera reigned supreme, he had determined upon meeting the prima donnas on their own ground. He was well aware, too of the reputation for unparalleled awfulness which Italian orchestras possessed and was careful to ensure that the accompaniment should be straightforward enough to minimise the chance of the performance being ruined from that quarter.

The concerto closely adheres to the three main sections of a scena and aria, and the movements follow each other without a break. The first movement is a dramatic recitative where, after twenty-seven bars of typically operatic introduction, the violin enters with recitative in the manner of a singer; the movement then proceeds with alternating sections of strict and free tempo, the solo part blending vocal ornament with idiomatic violin figurations whose brilliance is far beyond the capacity of any soprano. The Adagio which follows has a lively middle section, and on the repetition of the first part the soloist produces new ornamentation. A recitative-like Andante then links into the concluding Allegro moderato, towards the end of which Spohr includes a written-out cadenza. Along with Weber's Conzertstück in F minor for piano and orchestra of 1821, Spohr's *Gesangsszena* was an important influence on the development of new formal approaches in the later Romantic concerto.

The duet which Spohr mentioned in his diary along with the concerto was one of the set of three published as op. 39. In these works he raised the medium to a new level of artistry. The range of sonorities and sheer musical substance of these technically demanding duets is remarkable. The other compositions completed at this time were all repertoire pieces for the Italian tour; it had been decided that because of transport difficulties Dorette should not take her harp to Italy, so Spohr composed an Introduction and Rondeau for violin and piano (op. 46) which they could perform together, as well as arranging some earlier pot-pourris (opp. 23 and 24) for the same combination (subsequently publishing the second of them as op. 42). With these additions to their repertoire they set off on 2 September 1816 on the first stage of their journey to Milan.

VI

Italy
1816–1817

The Italy in which they found themselves was very different from the ideal land of Spohr's imagination. The art treasures, the fine buildings and the relics of antiquity contrasted grotesquely with the filth and poverty in which the majority lived. In Rome Spohr observed:

In no city in the world, I think, is the contrast so striking between the most luxurious splendour and the most abject misery as here. On the marble steps of the palaces, among the statues for which thousands have been paid, near the altars of the churches which are laden with golden ornaments and utensils – everywhere, in fact, one sees half-starved beggars lying who moan for bread and gnaw the stumps of cabbages or the peel of lemons which they have picked out of the gutter. At first I thought this merely a trick to excite the compassion of strangers, but I became convinced afterwards that many of the poor must subsist for days on such horrid food or perish with hunger.[1]

The ceremonial of the Papacy was another thing which disgusted him and roused his egalitarian instincts. After attending a service in the Sistine Chapel he wrote:

I saw that the priests who read the mass and the preacher before he ascended the pulpit threw themselves upon their knees before the Pope and kissed his red slipper, and how every time prior to this two assistants fell upon one knee, spread out his capacious mantel and lifted his sacerdotal frock to enable him to raise his foot for them to kiss. Nor did any of his attendants hand him anything, not even his pocket handkerchief, without previously kneeling before him. What is this but a degradation of humanity?[2]

Like most tourists, however, much of their time was taken up with visiting museums and notable buildings, of which Spohr left discriminating descriptions in his diary. In Venice the paintings by Veronese and others celebrating the history of the city, which adorned the Doge's Palace, inspired more than artistic appreciation. He commented:

In my opinion there is no kind of decoration so befitting and worthy of a princely palace as this, in which both the deeds of the nation and the names of the most skilful national artists are immortalised at the same time. At the present day how little feeling exists for this kind of patriotism! Where yet is to be seen any painting, produced by the order of a sovereign, to illustrate the modern deeds of heroism of the Germans? But how greatly the artists of the present day are in need of such encouragement and support! And I am here speaking only of painters and sculptors; poets and musicians too ought to have been invited to immortalise the deeds of the German people.[3]

While, on the whole, Spohr was deeply impressed by the artistic past of the Italians, their musical present made a very different impact. In the instrumental sphere he was in no doubt as to their great inferiority to the Germans, and even in the field of vocal music was far from convinced by their claims to superiority. He was constantly irritated by their complacent arrogance. After an experience with an orchestra in Venice, whose performance of Beethoven's Second Symphony was so dreadful that his ears 'rang the whole night with the infernal noise', he remarked that though the Italians might admit the German pre-eminence in instrumental music, 'they do not thoroughly believe it, and only acknowledge it in order to be able to boast with more freedom of their superiority in song and vocal compositions (!!)'; and he went on exasperatedly: 'The self-satisfaction of the Italians, despite their poverty of inspiration, is in fact unbearable; whenever I performed any of my things to them they thought they could pay me no higher compliment than to assure me that they were quite Italian in taste and style.'[4]

At La Scala in Milan, though, he found a better orchestra than usual under the efficient direction of Alessandro Rolla, with whose help he arranged a concert there on 27 September 1816. He was pleased to find that he had correctly calculated the Italian taste with his *Gesangsszena* Concerto, though he was annoyed by the audience's habit of applauding the solo passages and thus drowning the tuttis. There was no doubt, however, of his success. A Milanese critic observed: 'Rolla and several others have spoken to me of this artist with genuine admiration';[5] and after his concert it was remarked by the local critic of the *AMZ*: 'Here they cannot admire Herr Spohr enough; they rank him without hesitation at least equal to the here so celebrated and all-bewitching violinist Paganini. I say 'at least', for in *beauty* of playing Spohr certainly surpasses him.'[6] Much the same thing was said of Spohr's performance in Venice, though since these *AMZ* reviewers were probably Germans it may well be supposed that there was an element of partiality in the assessment. But there were undoubtedly many Italians who held the same opinion; indeed, Spohr was somewhat embarrassed by a letter which was published in a Venetian journal comparing his playing to that of Pugnani and Tartini, and contrasting his broad and noble style with Paganini's meretricious virtuosity. The embarrassment was all the more acute because Paganini was at that time in Venice. He attended Spohr's concert there on 18 October and two days later called on him to compliment him on it. Despite Spohr's earnest entreaties Paganini could not be prevailed upon to play and excused himself, according to Spohr's diary, by saying that his style was calculated to impress the masses, whereas if he were to play anything to a brother artist it must be in a different manner, for which he was not in the mood at present. Before leaving he promised to play to him if they met in Rome or Naples, but in the event their paths did not cross and they were not to meet again until 1830.

From Venice Spohr and his family journeyed on through Bologna to Florence, which he thought inferior to Dresden in every respect except its wealth of art treasures; these impressed him greatly. He particularly admired the great bronze doors to the Baptistry, remarking of the east door that 'in the whole world there is nothing more beautiful to be seen in the grouping, drawing perspective and purity of the work than these bas-reliefs'.[7] It is interesting to note that not just in music but in all matters of artistic judgement he maintained great independence of mind, for he observed in his diary, 'I never make use of a guide or book to find the objects worthy of attention in a city; I am averse to all dictation as to what I should admire.'[8] Musically Florence was disappointing, for his two concerts on 7 and 14 November, though well received, were too sparsely attended to bring him any profit.

Towards the end of November the family travelled on to Rome, where Spohr gave a concert on 18 December at which once more his *Gesangsszena* Concerto was greatly appreciated. Meyerbeer's arrival in Rome on 22 December brought Spohr news of the successful production of *Faust* in Prague and provided him with a comrade with whom he could exchange views on the operas they attended. Spohr's interest in Rossini's music is attested to by the considerable space which he devoted to it in his diary. The judgement of it at which he arrived was equivocal; he considered that 'he is by no means wanting in inventiveness and genius and, guided to the only correct way by Mozart's classic masterpieces, he might with these qualifications have easily become one of the most distinguished composers of vocal music of our day'. But as things stood Spohr suspected that Rossini, with his emphasis on coloratura and 'flowery song' (as Meyerbeer christened it),[9] was set on a course which would 'make a clearance of all *real* song, which is already very scarce in Italy, and in which the despicable horde of imitators, who here as well as in Germany pursue their pitiful calling, are doing their best to assist him'.[10]

Spohr's intention had been to go south to Naples in early January to be present at the opening of the new San Carlo Theatre on the 12th, but his plans were frustrated when Emily and Ida caught scarlet fever. To while away his enforced idleness during their convalescence he amused himself by inventing puzzle canons and began work on the *Quatuor brillant* in E which was later to be published as op. 43. By 20 January, however, the girls were fit enough to undertake the arduous and (on account of bandits) dangerous journey to Naples, where they arrived five days later.

Naples, despite its relative lack of fine buildings, seemed to Spohr one of the most beautiful and fascinating cities in the world, though he was forcibly struck here, as in Rome, by the juxtaposition of ostentatious wealth and abject poverty. The family spent the days pleasantly in walks and excursions; Spohr with his accustomed energy climbed Vesuvius, and venturing recklessly right up to the edge of its active crater, narrowly avoided disaster. Together they made more leisurely trips to the surrounding islands and to sights of archeological interest. While in Naples itself he and Dorette attended operas and concerts, of which Spohr as usual recorded his critical opinions. They also attended private musical parties where he played his Vienna quartets and quintets. In view of the high cost of hiring one of the theatres, Spohr decided to arrange his public concert, on 10 March, in the assembly rooms of the San Carlo Theatre. He considered this his best performance of the tour, and it certainly elicited the enthusiastic response of a local critic, who drew attention particularly to the vocal quality of his playing, saying:

Signor Luigi Spohr's first concert was very successful. Spohr is an excellent composer and perfect violinist . . . he surpassed the reputation which had preceded him. His method is excellent, his style expansive, his manner grand, melodious and full of expression. He knows the true beauties of art, which consist not in overcoming technical difficulties but in rendering instrumental music like vocal music.[11]

Shortly after this concert he received a proposal that he should accept the co-directorship (with Crescentini) of the Naples Conservatory. After discussion with Dorette and negotiations with the relevant government minister, he accepted the post in principle, but after long delays learned that because of problems with government finance the scheme had been abandoned. By this stage their savings were at a very low ebb, for receipts from concerts in Italy fell far short of what they had come to expect in Germany, and they made immediate preparations to travel northwards. They left Naples on 29 March, spent a few days in Rome, where they were able to hear Allegri's 'Miserere' in the Sistine Chapel, then pressed on as quickly as possible, leaving Italy by the Simplon Pass on 4 May 1817.

In Switzerland they found the population suffering from a severe shortage of food, in consequence of which prices were high and people had little inclination for concert-going. As a result the few concerts they were able to give brought in very little, and in Geneva they were forced to swallow their pride and request a loan from Pastor Gerlach, whose friendship they had gained in the previous year. In Freiburg, Karlsruhe, Wiesbaden and Ems receipts from their concerts were also meagre, and it was not until they arrived in Aachen in August that they earned enough from three well-attended concerts to repay their debt to Gerlach. Since the season was unpropitious for further concert-giving they remained in Aachen for several weeks, enjoying a pleasant respite from constant travelling.

During the latter part of their stay in Switzerland, Spohr had been able to finish the *quatuor brillant* which he had begun in Rome. The quartet reverts to the three-movement format of the op. 11 *Quatuor brillant*, and the first Allegro is, unusually, in *A B A* form. The whole composition contains hardly a trace of Spohr's characteristic dreamy melancholy, reflecting, perhaps, his intense enjoyment of his travels. The thematic material of the first movement shows signs of a new quality which suggests the melodic style of the young Wagner, and which was to become more pronounced in Spohr's next sets of quartets. Op. 43 is also notable for the first use of metronome marks in Spohr's works (he used the Rhein system at this time).

Another work which he began about this time and probably finished in Aachen was the set of male-voice part-songs op. 44. They are highly polished examples of the genre and enjoyed considerable popularity, but do not possess the directness and spontaneity of, for example, Weber's part-songs; like so much of Spohr's music the intricate treatment tended to limit its appeal to the dedicated amateur. The third song of the set, 'Kennt ihr das Land' (Brun), is interesting for the similarity of its opening to Spohr's earlier setting of Goethe's 'Kennst du das Land' (op. 37 no. 1); it hardly seems possible that this could have been unconscious. Both these new compositions were dispatched to the publisher Peters along with a number of other recently completed works, the payment for them being a welcome addition to his depleted purse.

Refreshed from their travels and with their financial position more secure, the Spohr family resumed their journey northwards into Holland. They gave concerts on the way in Cologne, Düsseldorf and Cleves, arriving in Amsterdam in October 1817. The Dutch were barely aware of the reputation which the Spohrs had achieved in Italy and Germany, but after their first concert at the German theatre in Amsterdam on 27 October, where Spohr played his *Gesangsszena* Concerto, a potpourri and, with Dorette, a piece for violin and harp (probably op. 118), a critic wrote:

We have *never* heard here a more spirited, expressive and also incidentally more perfect violinist. All kinds of execution are familiar to him, the grand and the brilliant as well as the charming and tender; his cantabile in particular surpasses that of all the other great artists we have heard here; also his staccato in one bow stroke is unique.[12]

After a second concert on 4 November they gave concerts in Rotterdam and the Hague, returning to Amsterdam to give two more concerts on 14 and 16 November.

It was Spohr's intention to proceed from Holland to England to take part in the London Philharmonic Society's season of concerts which began in February. In December 1816 he had received a letter from Ferdinand Ries, who was then living in London and was one of the directors of the Philharmonic Society, inviting him to take part in their concerts, and in October 1817 Ries had written again with more definite proposals, offering in the name of the Society a fee of 100 guineas for playing in their eight concerts plus a further 50 guineas for one of his compositions. However, at about the same time Spohr received another offer from a different quarter: an invitation from the management of the theatre in Frankfurt to accept the post of director of the opera and assume its duties as soon as possible. Though he had been travelling with little rest for nearly three years he was not immediately convinced that he should give up the touring which he so much enjoyed; he would have liked to continue his journey at least until the spring, and in addition the terms offered were not so good as those he had been given in Vienna. However, after discussion with Dorette it was decided that for the sake of the children, if nothing else, he should accept the Frankfurt post. His desire to mount a production of *Faust*, which he had not yet heard, undoubtedly made the decision easier for him.

VII

Kapellmeister in Frankfurt
1817–1820

Spohr was to spend less than two years in Frankfurt, but they were eventful
in several respects. Most importantly he was in a position to resume serious
composition. The period of his travels had been comparatively fallow after
the remarkably fertile two years in Vienna. Once settled into his duties in
Frankfurt, he returned enthusiastically to the business of composition, but
initially there was much else to occupy his attention. His position in the
Frankfurt opera house was very different from the one he had occupied in
the Theater an der Wien. In Vienna his responsibility had been solely for
the orchestra, and he had been required to direct the performances only in
the absence of the principal conductor, von Seyfried; in Frankfurt he was
both leader and director with sole responsibility for rehearsing the operas
and, along with Herr Ihlée (the director of the drama), sat *ex officio* on the
committee of the board of management which met weekly to decide the
programmes. Effectively, therefore, he was given a free hand in the artistic
direction of the opera. His first task was to raise standards of performance,
which had seriously deteriorated during the long illness of his predecessor
Schmitt. He began by infusing a new sense of discipline into his orchestra;
adopting the manner of directing to which they were accustomed, he used
his violin bow to give the time and joined in with his violin whenever it
seemed necessary to assist. It is apparent from his own account that one of
the main uses of the violin was to help the singers if they went astray, and
that it was largely at their request that he began in this way. Within a short
time, however, he had improved their reliability to such an extent that he was
able to dispense with the violin entirely and introduce the baton. By dint of
an intensive rehearsal schedule and the effectiveness of his conducting
method the quality of the orchestra was quickly transformed, though the
basic incapacity of several of the singers remained a stumbling block to first-
rate performances which Spohr was not able to overcome during his brief
period in Frankfurt. Nevertheless the company was soon strong enough for
him to consider putting on *Faust*, and one singer, the baritone Johann Nepomuk Schelble, was sufficiently good to prompt the composition of Faust's
additional aria 'Liebe ist die zarte Blüthe', in which the extraordinarily florid
coloratura testifies both to Schelbe's technique and the influence of Rossini

116

Ex. 86

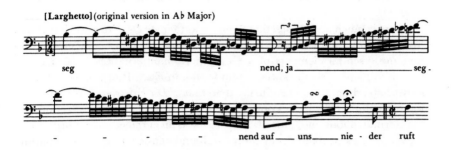

(though perhaps the Italian master would not have written such passages as ex. 86 for a baritone). When the production opened in March 1818 Schelble alone seems to have done justice to his role, for a reviewer observed:

The performance as a whole left much to be desired. Mme Friedel is not up to the part of Kunigunde; also Mme Hoffmann did not give enough to the part of Röschen. Hr Krönner had not the least of Mephistofeles about him, for he always looked thoroughly honest in it . . . Hr Höfler delivered his beautiful aria without any expression. Only Hr Schelble, who played Faust and sang extremely well, deserves praise! Instead of order on the stage disorder reigned supreme.[1]

It was probably a combination of these deficiencies and the unfamiliar complexities of the musical style that made the opera only moderately successful with the public at first, but, in a pattern which was frequently to be repeated, with Spohr's works, appreciation grew apace with greater familiarity and *Faust* remained in the repertoire of the Frankfurt opera until after Spohr's death more than forty years later. If the general public were slow to arrive at an appreciation of the opera, more cultivated listeners were not. The critic who found so much to cavil at in the performance was of an entirely different opinion about the work itself. He wrote:

An encouraging appearance in our theatre was the Romantic opera *Faust* by Spohr. When this national masterpiece was first produced on the Prague stage I was amazed to find no report of it in their newspapers. I am therefore induced to linger lovingly upon it, and the more so because of the great impact which the exquisite composition made on me. It is certainly a not too contentious truth that the province of Romanticism is the real homeland of opera; there is freedom on all sides, and art can unfold its powerful magic without constraint. It would not have been easy therefore to find a subject which entered more into the essential nature of opera than our German legend of Dr Faust, who in alliance with the highly poetical character of Satan again finds open to him his own Romantic kingdom which has no limits, but in which he must necessarily come to grief.

And after a long and detailed account of each number in the opera he concluded: 'From this it is easy to see that this excellent work possesses the high aesthetic values of a German artist; for its technical perfection Herr Spohr's universally known talent and deep knowledge of composition is sufficient warrant.'

There is much about *Faust* that seems to anticipate *Der Freischütz*. It is clear from Weber's comments about it and from those of other contemporaries that the essential elements of a German Romantic national opera were sought for, and to a substantial extent found, in *Faust*. If its success was less immediate, dramatic and enduring than that of *Der Freischütz*, it is nevertheless undeniable that Spohr's opera won by degrees a place in the affections of the German public and, indeed, that there was an enthusiastic minority who regarded it as a greater and more profound masterpiece. Comments in Zelter's report to Goethe on the 1829 Berlin production indicate the element of controversy that existed over the relative merits of Spohr and Weber as opera composers. He wrote that there was a conspicuous group of Spohr's partisans intent on adducing universally valid rules for all opera from the example of *Faust*, and that Weber seemed to be their prime target.[2] Allowing for all other differences between the two operas it is safe to say that the most important one was the nature of the music itself. Spohr possessed neither the desire nor, perhaps, the ability to embody in his music the German folk idiom which pervades *Der Freischütz*; where Weber's music made a direct appeal by its inspired simplicity of melody and its powerfully direct use of harmony and orchestral colour, Spohr's 'deep knowledge of composition', which led him to the subtleties and complexities that so amazed Zelter (see above, p. 78), blunted his opera's impact on the less musically cultivated listeners. In this respect the *AMZ* review of the 1829 Berlin performance is instructive; it referred to the 'extraordinarily lively interest of the hearers', but added that 'the opera appeared, however, to be very clearly comprehensible more to the connoisseurs of music than to the majority'.[3]

While he was preparing for the production of *Faust* Spohr had already begun looking for a libretto for a new opera. A suitable subject came to hand with the story of *Der Schwarze Jäger* (The Black Huntsman), from Apel's collection of supernatural tales, and with the help of Georg Döring, Spohr started to sketch the plot of the opera. This story was the same one which Kind had turned into *Der Freischütz* and upon which Weber was at that time working. When Spohr discovered that Weber had already completed the first act of an opera on the same subject he abandoned work on his version, though he had already started composing the music. But though Spohr had assumed that *Der Freischütz* would be finished first, it did not in fact appear until after he had completed the opera upon which he subsequently began to work. Recalling the circumstances later he stated: 'I have not regretted that I abandoned the materials of Apel's story, for with my music, which is not adapted to please the multitude and excite popular enthusiasm, I should never have met with the success that *Der Freischütz* obtained'.[4]

Though much of his spare time had been taken up with planning this opera Spohr was nevertheless able to produce the three String Quartets op. 45 during 1818. Plans for these had been in his mind for some time. On 28 July 1817 he had written to Peters: 'In order to please you and all those for whom my pieces are too difficult I promise you that my next three string quartets, which I intend to write as soon as I have the leisure, will be so easy that we can explicitly dedicate them to amateurs'.[5] In fact, the op. 45 quartets, which were finished almost exactly a year later, are not noticeably easier than any of the others (excepting the *quatuors brillants*). Spohr was well pleased with the results of his efforts, though, and wrote to Peters on 30 July 1818: 'Since I set considerable store by them and place them on a level with the instrumental compositions which are considered the best that I have so far produced, I believe it cannot be taken as vanity if my portrait, which collectors of musical portraits have long desired to have, is engraved on the title page.'[6]

The new quartets received their first public performances in a series of chamber concerts which Spohr instituted during the winter of 1818/19 in the Rothes Haus in Frankfurt. In January 1819 the *AMZ* reported: 'Spohr played quartets by Mozart, Haydn, Beethoven, Spohr, Fesca and Onslow in the weekly quartet meetings. Three new magnificent quartets by Spohr received great applause; they will soon be published by Peters in Leipzig'.[7] (They appeared in print some time before Easter 1819.) The first of the set, in C major, had fired the imagination of popular German Romantic novelist Jean Paul Richter when he heard it at a soirée at Schelbe's shortly after its completion, and he told Spohr of the poetical fantasies to which it had given rise in his mind.

The first two quartets of the set are undoubtedly the best; in the third Spohr reverted to a much more concertante style, and in the first movement the first violin has several lengthy semiquaver passages which at the speed specified by Spohr's metronome markings are extremely difficult. Op. 45 no. 1 is somewhat uneven in quality but contains much excellent writing and has some highly effective moments. The Finale is given an attractive 'alpine' quality by its main theme (ex. 87), but the finest movement of the quartet is

Ex. 87

the Andante grazioso in A flat. It begins with a simple theme which once again stresses Spohr's kinship with Schubert (ex. 88); the similarity is strengthened by the transition to E major for the middle section (ex. 89). In

Ex. 88

Ex. 89

op. 45 no. 2 in E minor Spohr comes closest to writing in a genuine quartet idiom. All four movements are fine, but again the slow movement is the gem of the whole. A particularly effective idea in this Larghetto is the combination of a cantabile theme in 2/4 with staccato semiquaver figurations in 12/8 (ex. 90). Overall there is a rich vein of melody running through the op. 45 quartets; the motivic treatment so prominent in the Vienna chamber works, though still important, is a much less dominant factor here, with Spohr concentrating on the construction of more varied and flexible melodies. Whereas in his earlier works a melody which does not fall into the regular

Ex. 90

eight-bar patterns is relatively rare, in op. 45 melodies extending beyond eight bars are the rule rather than the exception, giving the style a more lyrical flow and less Classical feeling. The opening of op. 45 no. 2 is a good example of this tendency (ex. 91).

Ex. 91

When Spohr abandoned his work on *Der Schwarze Jäger* he did not give up the idea of writing another opera for the Frankfurt stage. While composing the op. 45 Quartets he had already begun to cast about for a subject and finally decided on the familiar story of Beauty and the Beast. This had already been used as a subject for an opera by Grétry in his *Zémire et Azor* of 1771, of which Spohr retained affectionate memories from his childhood, but since it was no longer in the German repertoire there seemed no objection to his making use of the story again. Ihlée undertook to prepare a libretto from Marmontel's original: changing its four acts into two, he retained all the characters and situations, making what was essentially a straightforward translation. The familiar story may be briefly summarised. During a storm Sander and his servant, Ali, find themselves in a magic garden. They are welcomed by invisible spirits and plied with food and drink. By plucking a rose, they rouse the wrath of the garden's chief occupant, Prince Azor, who has been transformed into a monster for his vanity. Only the selfless love of a pure maiden can return him to his former condition. Sander's youngest daughter, Zemire, goes voluntarily to the garden in an attempt to break the spell. She is shocked at first by Azor's appearance, but feels first pity, then love. When she expresses the wish to return home to visit her family Azor gives her a magic ring, without which it is said she cannot return to the garden. Her sisters steal the ring, but she is nevertheless miraculously transported back. Ultimately the fairy who had placed the enchantment on Azor in the first place appears to release it, and with the union of Azor and Zemire everything ends happily.

The characters in the opera are more or less stock figures. The servant, Ali, with his greed and cowardice fills the traditional buffo role, appearing here for the last time in any of Spohr's operas. Ali's musical and spiritual affinity with Papageno is obvious in his Romanze (no. 3) (ex. 92). Zemire is

Ex. 92

the typical pure maiden, Azor the repentant sinner redeemed by love, Sander the well-intentioned doting father, the other daughters are jealous sisters. The nature of this material made *Zemire und Azor* a very different opera from *Faust*, despite their common supernatural element; it is an altogether lighter piece – engaging rather than gripping. As a critic observed after its first performance, it stood in relation to *Faust* as 'a charming picture by the colourful and gracious Correggio to the mighty creations of the bold and profound Michelangelo. Here the melodies emerge clearly and comprehensibly clothed in the tenderest harmony, while in *Faust* the predominance of a dark power, which triumphs in its conflict with the Pure, only allows the characterisation of the clashing principals.'[8]

Of all Spohr's operas *Zemire und Azor* contains, perhaps, the most appealing music; there is scarcely a number which fails to charm by its melodic freshness, rich (but not cloying) harmony, and delicate orchestral treatment.

The popularity of individual items in the concert hall and in publications during the decades after its composition was tremendous, and the Romanze 'Rose wie bist du' (no. 8) (known in England as 'Rose softly blooming') became Spohr's most popular operatic piece. In respect of its large number of set pieces the opera is more conventional than *Faust*, but despite the exceptionally florid vocal writing for Azor, Zemire and the two sisters (which Spohr himself confessed was influenced by Rossini's popularity) the individuality of his style is equally pronounced, and his use of off-stage chorus, chromatic harmony and colourful orchestration imparts a sense of genuinely Romantic fantasy to the opera, placing it in the tradition of Weber's *Oberon* and Mendelssohn's *A Midsummer Night's Dream* music.

Leitmotif does not play so important a part here as it had in *Faust*, but there is one true leitmotif which, though it only appears three times, has an important symbolic function. The motif is basically a single diminished chord resolving to a major triad, and it is played on each occasion by wind instruments, giving it a distinctive timbre (ex. 93). It is heard for the first

Ex. 93

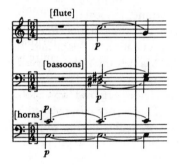

time in the entr'acte music (no. 10) played by an off-stage ensemble, just before Zemire's first transportation to the magic garden. It occurs a second time at the beginning of her recitative (no. 16) when despite the loss of the ring she is surprisingly returned to the garden; the chords are repeated as she sings the words 'Can I believe my eyes! Yes this is Azor's garden. What invisible power has brought me here in a flash?' The final appearance of the motif is in the melodrama at the beginning of the Finale, when the fairy (not referred to at all until this point) who was responsible for Azor's enchantment, at last reveals herself and explains to Zemire that it was she who had originally brought her to the garden and had done so again when the ring was lost. Thus it becomes clear that the motif had stood for her intervention. The use of a single progression in this way would seem to be unprecedented in opera, and anticipates by three years Weber's well-known use of the diminished chord as a symbol for Samiel in *Der Freischütz*.

The success of *Zemire und Azor* was considerable, and it was still performed in Germany until towards the end of the century.

In addition to his work on *Zemire und Azor* during the winter of 1818–19 Spohr composed a new sonata for violin and harp in G major (unpublished and so far untraceable) and occupied himself with a multiplicity of other activities. As well as giving quartet concerts, he conducted the first performances in Frankfurt of all eight of Beethoven's symphonies (the ninth was not yet written) at the *Museumsgesellschaft* concerts. He also devoted a considerable amount of time to instructing the violin pupils who had been attracted to Frankfurt by his residence there. Thus with the arrival of spring he felt greatly in need of a break from his labours and, obtaining eight days' leave of absence from his duties in the theatre, he joined four friends from Rudolstadt who intended making an expedition to a musical festival in Mannheim. With knapsacks on their backs, and two horns and a guitar between them, they hiked their way as far as Heidelberg, enlivening the journey with part-songs and fanfares. This part of the excursion was a welcome return to old habits, but the next stage looked forward to a future pattern of events; for Spohr's celebrity was now such that his appearance in any German town, even in a private capacity, was an event of importance to local music-lovers. His arrival in Heidelberg soon became known and a deputation from the town's musical society came to his inn with an invitation to Spohr and his friends to join the society's boat when it left for Mannheim in the morning. On reaching their destination they were greeted by the festival committee, who had been informed of his presence on the Heidelberg boat, and Spohr was again treated with the greatest deference. This sort of thing was to be repeated with increasing frequency for the rest of his life, during which he was to be the recipient of innumerable deputations, honours, serenades and garlands.

The respect with which he was treated on his journey does not seem to have been shared by the management committee of the Frankfurt theatre. His relationship with the parsimonious and, in his eyes, philistine Frankfurt merchants who made up this committee had begun to deteriorate seriously. There could be no complaint about the artistic success of Spohr's direction of the opera, for whatever could be obtained by careful rehearsal and the appointment of good musicians to fill any vacancies Spohr was well able to obtain; on top of that his prestige as a composer lent additional lustre to a formerly undistinguished theatre. But the care with which he insisted on preparing each production did not please everyone. The committee of management, representing the shareholders of the theatre, was always concerned to minimise the financial deficit and increasingly grudged Spohr the amount of time he required for rehearsal. He was frequently obliged to defend his methods with the observation that badly rehearsed productions would simply lead to falling audiences and consequently greater losses. It is probable also that his choice of operas did not meet with the committee's wholehearted approval; like Weber at Prague his repertoire consisted predominantly of French and German works. After he had produced Rossini's *Tancredi* the chairman, Leers, frequently told him: 'This is an opera that pleases and attracts the public; you must bring out more of that kind.'[9] Matters finally came to a head when at a general shareholders' meeting Leers remarked that they did not require an eminent artist so much as an indefatigable workman who would devote all his time to the theatre. After this Spohr handed in his resignation to take effect from 30 September 1819. In his journal *Die Wage* Ludwig Börne castigated the shortsightedness of the penny-pinching attitude which had led to Spohr's departure, commenting caustically: 'By dismissing him we acknowledge before all the world that Spohr is a great artist . . . That we lose him is not the worst of it, the worst is that he loses nothing by leaving us. It is a curse on the soil of our homeland that it can bear nothing great, noble or beautiful.'[10]

It was certainly with a light heart that Spohr tendered his resignation. He had made many friends in Frankfurt, among them Wilhelm Speyer, with whom he was to keep up a lifelong correspondence, but the growing irritations of his position at the theatre had rekindled his quiescent *Wanderlust*. Dorette, however, who had given birth to a third daughter, Therese, on 29 July 1818, was undoubtedly sorry to be uprooted again after having enjoyed a stable home life for only two years.

A number of possibilities presented themselves for the future. Shortly after Spohr's imminent departure became known he received an offer, from the Intendant of the St Petersburg court opera, Count Narischkin, of the position of solo violin in the Imperial orchestra. Less secure, though more tempting, was the prospect offered by an engagement for the London Philharmonic Society's 1820 season. Ferdinand Ries wrote to him on 7 September 1819 with more generous terms than before, promising an honorarium of £250 in return for which he was to 'direct or play solo three or four times or play in the orchestra for all eight concerts . . . play in no public or private concerts until you have played in two of our Philharmonic concerts . . . leave the manuscript of one of your compositions, which we can choose, as the property of the Society'.[11] Spohr wrote to Speyer from Hamburg on 19 October saying that the Society had promised to do all in their power to make his visit 'lucrative and pleasant', adding: 'I have learned here from someone who has just come from London that the announcement of my coming has already filled their subscription list so that even now no one can get any more admission tickets at any price.'[12] This was doubtless an exaggeration, but it is certainly true that for the 1820 season the Society had its fullest subscription list ever.

After settling his affairs, Spohr and his family left Frankfurt in early September and travelled to his father's house in Gandersheim, where the three children were to remain while their parents were away in England. There they stayed for over a fortnight, giving a concert to about 150 of Carl Heinrich Spohr's friends and neighbours, and taking advantage of the fine weather to arrange an open-air celebration of his mother's birthday. They then began a triumphal progress through the major cities of North Germany, performing in Brunswick, Hamburg, Berlin, Dresden, Leipzig, Rudolstadt, Gotha and Kassel. In Berlin their concert received a glowing report, which especially praised Spohr's violin playing: 'His playing is masterly; fire, feeling, firm posture, expressive adagio, full tender tone, admirable skill in passages of octaves and tenths, double, triple and quadruple stopping, the lightness and accuracy of the leaps, and refined bowstroke, were all equally astonishing.'[13] They also made the acquaintance of E. T. A. Hoffmann, who wrote a short *Nachtgesang aus der Genovefa des Mahlers Müller* in Spohr's autograph book, and while they were there Spohr indicated his interest in the post of Hofkapellmeister which had become vacant with the departure of Bernhard Romberg. This possibility was removed, however, by the speedy appointment of Gasparo Spontini, whose opera *Fernand Cortez* had deeply impressed King Friedrich Wilhelm III when he heard it shortly before in Paris.

After returning briefly to Gandersheim for Christmas, Louis and Dorette Spohr set off on the first stage of their journey to London in early January 1820. They travelled through Bonn, Aachen, and Brussels to Lille, giving concerts on the way, but in Lille the news of the assassination of the Duc de Berry and the obligatory public mourning brought concert-giving to an end for the time being. Another royal death, that of King George III, also interfered with their plans. In consequence of this event the start of the Philharmonic concerts was to be delayed until 6 March. Spohr, therefore, prolonged his stay in Lille and enjoyed several days of pleasant music-making in private circles. On 23 February he set out for Calais and after a stormy crossing of the Channel arrived in London about a week before the first concert.

VIII

London, Paris and Dresden
1820–1822

The journeys to London and Paris were to be both an end and a beginning;
they were the last major excursions which Spohr undertook as a virtuoso,
but the beginning of associations which, especially in the case of London,
were to have important consequences for the future. For Dorette more than
for her husband this concert tour marked the end of a performing career,
since during it she made her last appearance with him as a harpist. After
1820 her increasing ill health, caused probably by the strain of child-bearing,
motherhood and excessive travelling, made further touring impossible, and
resulted in her giving up the harp entirely. Much as Spohr relished travel it
is doubtful whether he would have enjoyed touring without Dorette, but it
was not solely because of this that his virtuoso career was drawing to its close.
The inner tension between performing and composing had reached a high
pitch, and though he was never to lose his love of the violin – his activities as
a teacher and performer continued to within a few years of his death at the
age of seventy-five – from the early 1820s onwards his attention was shifted
far more towards composing and conducting.

Spohr could not have chosen a more propitious time to make his debut in
England. The climate of musical opinion was exactly right for him to make
an impact as both violinist and composer. He was able to take advantage of
an updraught of enthusiasm for instrumental display and a much more narrowly confined, though steadily increasing, interest in serious German
music. In 1819 the *Quarterly Musical Magazine* commented: 'The prominent
feature of the times appears to us to be that the performance of instrumental
music has made very rapid strides in the favour of the public.'[1] At the heart of
this development was the London Philharmonic Society, which had been
formed in 1813 by a group of professional musicians whose primary purpose
was to provide a regular opportunity for the performance of the instrumental works of the great German masters. It gave eight long concerts annually during the season, each of which as a rule included two symphonies, two
overtures, a concerto, a chamber work and an item or two of vocal music.
The exalted tastes of the Philharmonic Society were by no means universally
shared by the concert-going public of London, but that it satisfied a growing
need is borne out by the proliferation of other concert series in its wake. The

Professional Concerts began in 1816, followed in 1818 by the City Amateur Concerts, and these were joined in 1820 by another series of subscription concerts given in the new Argyll Rooms. All of these were primarily instrumental, and even the so-called Vocal Concerts increasingly included a substantial amount of instrumental music. In the field of composition Haydn and Mozart were accepted as the great modern masters; indeed, Mozart's influence was considered to have been 'able to change, if not to fix, the taste of a whole generation in the fine arts'.[2] Subsequent developments were more cautiously received, however, and Beethoven, though obviously relished by many of those who participated in or attended the Philharmonic concerts, was viewed with suspicion by others. The tame applause for Mozart's 'Jupiter' symphony and the enthusiasm of the audience for Beethoven's Fifth Symphony at a concert in 1820 elicited the comment from one journalist that it was 'only to be accounted for by this rage for extravagance'; while in connection with a quartet by Mayseder it was predicted that 'It is . . . probable that the taste for romancing will be pushed into yet stronger absurdity before the perverted judgement of the many will be brought back to truth.'[3] Another critic, writing for the more fashionable *London Magazine*, was of much the same opinion about Beethoven, commenting: 'We confess we are not so far gone in the extravagance of the present day, as to relish the unconnected vagaries which some admire in the works of Beethoven'; and reviewing the Seventh Symphony and one of his string quartets the critic continued: 'The first seemed to us crude, though forcible, and tiresome, though fanciful . . . Upon the merits of the quartet we agree entirely with the silent but sensible adjudication of a lady of rank, who slept profoundly from the beginning to the end of it.'[4]

With respect to the position of music in society it was generally agreed that it was rapidly rising in public estimation around 1820. The *London Magazine* remarked, in its first issue, that it was 'difficult . . . to decide whether music have not attained a rank and importance among our pursuits, that places it above the sister art of painting, and very nearly upon a level with poetry, in its immediate effects upon manners and happiness'. And it went on to say: 'Music is now, indeed, so universally cultivated, that scarcely a house can be found without a pianoforte or harp, and our streets are thronged by itinerant musicians, both vocal and instrumental, of no mean acquirements.'[5] While it is clear that much of this activity was at an artistic level far below that of the Philharmonic Society, there is, nevertheless, enough evidence to suggest that even at a relatively popular level there was a growing interest in and respect for serious German music. There were, for instance, the regular performances on the Apollonicon (a sort of mechanical organ) advertised in the *Morning Chronicle*, which along with more popular items included such pieces as Haydn's 'Surprise' Symphony and Mozart's overture *Le Nozze di Figaro*. On the other hand, in the highest

echelons of society music was usually regarded as no more than an obligatory social ornament, and though no expense was spared to employ the
finest musicians to perform in private soirées they were excluded from the
company and their performances were often virtually ignored in a way that
was to disgust Spohr. The musical press, too, was not slow to criticise these
affairs. The *Quarterly Musical Magazine* observed:

Of what are called the private concerts of the Metropolis we cannot refrain from saying a few words. They partake of the magnitude rather than the grandeur to which
everything is now brought, and by this circumstance their value as parties met for
musical gratification is almost annihilated . . . In such places, music is scarcely ever
heard and never felt.[6]

Musical tastes seem to have been determined much more by social status in
England than in Germany; the same critic, contrasting the Concerts of
Antient Music (with subscriptions at 8 guineas) and the Philharmonic Soci-
ety (with subscriptions at 4 guineas), commented:

the one is supported by the Patrician families, the other is maintained by professors of
music, their connections, and amateurs of less distinguished rank. This is a very curious fact for it serves to show with what scrupulous exactitude the distinctions of condition are kept up even against the attractions of the highest enjoyments art can
offer.[7]

This was not entirely fair, however, since of the 750 subscribers to the Philharmonic in 1820, 55 were titled.

During the five months which he spent in London, Spohr made a marked
impact as a violinist. He and Dorette appeared several times in violin and
harp duets (not, as he stated in his memoirs, only once), and Spohr alone
performed his concertos, potpourris and other violin music in a considerable
number of concerts other than the Philharmonic, ranging from the relatively
inexpensive oratorio concerts (mixed instrumental and vocal concerts given
in the theatres when dramatic performances were suspended during Lent) to
a soirée at the Duke of Hamilton's. There is no doubt that despite the 'galaxy
of concerto players'[8] in London at that time his performances aroused an
exceptional degree of interest; The *London Magazine* commented: 'The principal novelty and attraction of the present season have been the performances of Mr. Spohr on the violin. This gentleman is considered to equal, if
not to exceed, any player that has lately been heard in England.'[9] The *Quarterly Musical Magazine*, concurring in this view, stated: 'The playing of
Mr. Spohr, a celebrated violinist, has been the grand circumstance of attraction during the season.'[10] More detailed press reports of his playing were
remarkably in agreement. Reviewing his first appearance at the Philharmonic on 6 March, when he played his *Gesangsszena* Concerto, the *Morning
Chronicle* wrote:

Our expectations, though raised very high, were fully realized. He performed a Concerto 'in the dramatic style', which consisted of a kind of recitative, a slow air, and a quick movement in the manner of a scena. The composition, in itself, is full of melody and taste, and he imparted so much sentiment to it, that his violin, if it did not actually speak a language, 'discoursed most eloquent music', and was more passionate than half the singers we hear. This strength of feeling in Mr. Spohr's playing, and his better judgement, teaches him to place it in the foreground rather than to make execution the most conspicuous. Of the latter, however, he possesses an abundance.[11]

The Times expressed a similar judgement in its notice of the Argyll Concert at which he played one of his violin concertos (possibly the Seventh) on 18 April, commenting:

Mr. Spohr's execution, admirable as it is, forms the least of his merits. Mechanical difficulties may be mastered by application, with a common capacity; but the true genius is discovered in style and expression: in these, and in his performance of an Adagio, he has few competitors. His instrument can scarcely be said to want a voice and words to give it sentiment and passion, and his manner might be studied by our best singers with advantage to themselves and the public.[12]

Not every critic was unqualified in his praise. A writer in the Quarterly Musical Magazine, while agreeing with his colleagues in essentials, made a perceptive observation. He remarked:

A critic at Rome has said of this artist, that 'he was the greatest singer upon the violin ever heard', . . . the highest compliment perhaps that can be paid to an instrumentalist . . . His manner is totally without pretension; his tone fine, his intonation admirable, and his execution of the most finished order. But as all exceedingly minute polish is apt to diminish force, the impression upon some was that he wanted fire; but much of this objection vanishes upon frequent hearing.[13]

The following year, in a comparison of the three violinists Mori, Spohr and Kiesewetter, the Quarterly Musical Magazine reiterated its opinion of Spohr's style of playing, saying that in contrast to Mori, whose temperament 'disposed him towards all that was energetic, there were traces in his great contemporary Spohr's execution of a mind continually turning towards refinement and deserting strength for polish'.[14] In his Musical Recollections of the Last Half Century, J. B. Cox referred to the preceding passage and added from his own experience of Spohr's playing:

His delicacy was so exquisite that his force was diminished in comparison . . .

It was doubtless for this reason that Spohr was by far the least popular of the three violinists at this time before the public: for although he was undoubtedly in the very first rank of his profession and talent, especially as the founder of a purely legitimate school, the interest he excited was lower in degree than that which, both before and since, has frequently attended the performance of players considerably below the standard he himself reached . . . Spohr did not condescend to astonish the 'ears of the groundlings', and so lost the approbation which extreme cultivation and polish will never create, simply because they transcend the judgement of 'the million'.[15]

Whatever reservations there may have been about the wider appeal of

Spohr's style of violin playing, there is no question that he himself was well
satisfied with his degree of success; as he wrote to Speyer on the eve of his
departure from London, 'You see that we can be very pleased with the proceeds of our stay, since we have gained more than possibly any foreign artist
since Haydn. I have been more gladdened however by the applause that all
our public and private appearances have received and which particularly for
our own concert was so tumultuous.'[16] Viotti's compliments after his first
appearance had specially pleased him.

In one practical respect Spohr had a direct influence on London violinists.
The *Quarterly Musical Magazine* noted: 'there is a peculiarity in the fitting up
of his violin, the tailpiece being considerably shorter than those in general
use. This construction is said to give a quicker return of the string from the
finger-board, and to confer greater facility in execution.'[17] In his 27 March
letter to Speyer,* Spohr wrote: 'My change on the violin has turned out
excellent; the violinists here are already beginning to imitate it.'[18] More
important than this, however, was his influence on the method of directing
an orchestra. A great deal has been written about his supposed use of a baton
when conducting at the Philharmonic Society, and the erroneous account in
Spohr's memoirs of his use of this method at a public concert during the 1820
season has been shown by Arthur Jacobs to be the product of 'the failing
memory of an aging man'.[19] Jacobs' speculation about what actually did
occur can now be amplified by further evidence of which he was unaware,
and it is clear that though Spohr used a baton only at rehearsals, his example
of firm direction both in rehearsals and concerts was not without its effect on
London musicians. The first occasion on which he was asked to lead was a
Philharmonic trial night on 3 April (a sort of open rehearsal at which new
works were tried out in order to decide whether they should be included in a
concert), where among other things three of his own orchestral works were
played. It seems clear from his letter to Speyer of 17 April that he directed
from the score with a baton on this evening and that he adopted the same
method at the rehearsal for the concert which he was required to lead a week
later. He described the prevailing system of direction and his own actions to
Speyer in the following terms:

The manner of conducting at the theatres and concerts here is the most preposterous
which can be imagined. With two conductors figuring away, there is really not even
one. He who is styled 'conductor' in the bills, sits at the piano and plays from the
score, but neither marks time nor gives the tempi; this the 'leader' or first violinist
ought to do. As he has, however, merely a violin part before him, he cannot help the
orchestra, and therefore contents himself with playing his own part and allowing the
orchestra to get on as best it can. Artists here have perceived the defect of such an

---

* Several letters published in the *Musical World* in 1860 from the autographs (supplied by Anton
Schindler) contain passages missing from the text printed in *Wilhelm Speyer der Lieder-
componist*.

arrangement, and the impossibility of an orchestra of fifty or sixty persons ever achieving a good ensemble with it, before I spoke to them on the subject; but they do not dare to make an alteration, because what is once established here is regarded as sacred and inviolable, for, after all, with all his political freedom an Englishman is the most abject slave of etiquette. I conducted however at rehearsal in my old and usual manner from the score; and in the evening, when the 'conductor' is obliged to figure behind the piano, I knew the things so by heart that I was able to help the orchestra even without the score.[20]

His innovation was noted by a reviewer in the *Morning Chronicle*, who wrote of his leading the orchestra in a 'novel and superior manner'.[21] What he in fact did at the concert on 10 April was to use his violin bow like a baton. A detailed review in the *AMZ* makes this clear, though the author of the article does not seem to have agreed with Spohr that such means were necessary to achieve a good ensemble with the Philharmonic Orchestra. The article stated:

In directing Herr Spohr did not follow the method which has been observed hitherto by Cramer, Salomon, Viotti, Weichsel and others; that is, merely to give the tempo and then make sure that it is kept to, and for the rest of the time to play with the orchestra as leader; on the contrary, he played only occasionally and for the rest of the time he held his violin under his arm and gave the beat with motions of his bow, also he gave a sign whenever there was an entry of a new section to show where it should begin; this latter however, and also the 'shh' . . . when there was a *piano*, was certainly not necessary for such an orchestra, where at least the principal of each section is a concert artist, and certainly it was even unwelcome to many. Yet it is said that now some other leaders, who cannot match him in respect either of playing or of certainty in indicating the entry of each section to the right instrument, imitate him and, at least from time to time, also take the violin under the arm and wave the bow by itself. The custom prevailing here, however, of accompanists at the pianoforte (which they call conductors, like lightning conductors) who give the time by clapping their hands or making other gestures and who also direct, was rejected by Herr Spohr, and this was a good thing.[22]

Spohr's example was not an entirely beneficial one, for while it paved the way for Weber and Mendelssohn to conduct in England and encouraged the tentative efforts of such Englishmen as Sir George Smart and Sir Henry Bishop to use the baton, it also had other undesirable side effects. The fact that he had been forced by custom to direct from the violin on the night of the concert encouraged leaders to attempt to assume the direction of the orchestra from the front desk, even when there was also a conductor, thus delaying the emergence of absolute control by the conductor. A letter to *The Harmonicon* on the subject of leaders and conductors in 1833 described the antics of some leaders in caustic terms, saying:

the custom . . . is for the leader to leave off playing at certain intervals, and then, assuming what I presume he thinks a very elegant attitude, and commanding position, flourishing his bow backwards and forwards most heroically (so that, while this species of charlatanism is going on there are, in fact, two conductors and no leader!). I presume this is done either to catch the attention of the ladies, or to impress on the minds of the unthinking part of the audience an idea of his importance and zeal.

The editor of the journal specifically credited Spohr with having inspired such behaviour, observing: 'The practice of beating time with the bow was introduced into this country by M. Spohr, and he, being a great musician as well as leader, has been, of course, imitated.'[23]

It was, however, neither as violinist nor as conductor, but as a composer, that in the long run Spohr was to make his greatest impact on the English musical world. By performances of his orchestral works at the Philharmonic Concerts and at his own Benefit Concert, and probably also of chamber works in private soirées with leading London musicians, he kindled a spark of interest in his music which, fuelled during the 1820s by the introduction of his most recent works, resulted by the 1830s in a widely held opinion that he was the greatest of living composers and worthy to be classed among the great composers of all time.

The ignorance of Spohr's compositions which prevailed at the time of his arrival in 1820 was almost total. The only one of his works which seems to have been performed in England prior to that date was the overture *Alruna*, given at the Professional Concerts on 5 February 1816. Ries, who kept in touch with events and opinions in Germany, was aware of Spohr's reputation, as is shown by a comment in his letter of 21 October 1817: 'we hope you will let us hear your beautiful symphonies and overtures here'.[24] The other directors of the Philharmonic Society, however, were, according to Spohr's own account, so uncertain about his credentials as a composer that they were initially cautious about agreeing to allow him to perform his own compositions on the violin. (A Philharmonic Society regulation permitted only the performance of concertos by Mozart or Beethoven, or other works which the directors should select, in order to prevent soloists introducing unworthy music into the programmes.) Spohr's performances of his *Gesangsszena* Concerto at the first Philharmonic concert on 6 March and of his *Quatuor brillant* op. 43 at the second on 20 March cannot have failed to convince them that he was no mere stringer-together of scales and arpeggios. But it was at the trial night on 3 April that they were first able to hear his orchestral works. Up to this time compositions for the orchestra alone had constituted a very small part of Spohr's output; before 1819, apart from the overtures to his operas, there was only the Concert Overture op. 12 of 1807 and the Symphony op. 20 of 1811, but in readiness for his journey to London he had added to the list a new concert overture in F. This, together with the overture *Alruna* and the symphony, was played at the trial night, where the enthusiastic applause which they elicited impelled the directors to request the symphony for their next concert.

The Overture in F was not publicly performed, because of the pressure of other works, until the following season, after which it lay neglected in the Philharmonic library, receiving only one more performance in 1874. Spohr himself had not kept a copy of the score and could not even remember the beginning of it when he compiled his thematic catalogue. It is scored for the normal double wind with timpani and strings, but as an afterthought Spohr added three trombone parts. The overture is typical of Spohr's style at this period, with its skilful orchestration, intensive chromaticism and thematic integration. The Adagio molto introduction in F minor contains the germinal material of the whole work; this is then expanded and developed in the ensuing Allegro vivace in F major, which is cast in abbreviated sonata form (the recapitulation beginning with the second subject). The work concludes with a brief but effective coda.

The Overture in F seems like a flexing of muscles for a much more significant work which Spohr composed in three weeks at the beginning of his stay in London. This was his Second Symphony in D minor (op. 49). Nothing shows Spohr's desire to make his mark as a composer in London more strikingly than the composition of this symphony. It had, as he informed Speyer, been 'conceived and brought forth in a spirit of the greatest enthusiasm',[25] and on its completion he determined that he would make his debut as a composer in London with it. The parts were not copied in time for it to be played at the trial night on 3 April, but Spohr persuaded the directors nevertheless to include it, rather than the First Symphony, in the programme for the next concert. At the rehearsal and concert on 10 April, Spohr brought his firm and efficient method of direction to bear on the orchestra and, as he observed rather modestly to Speyer,

My symphony was consequently executed with more precision and nicety than I could expect after one rehearsal, and that rather a hurried one, and it is to this no doubt that I am indebted for the fact that it was received by the public with greater enthusiasm than any other orchestral composition during my stay here. The Scherzo was encored and applauded after its repetition even more than before. This successful result is doubly gratifying because it encourages me to hope that I have not yet regressed as a composer; for I dare not trust unconditionally my own opinion, according to which this symphony is the best thing I have done in the way of orchestral music, partly because one is always fondest of one's youngest children and partly because a man is only too unwilling to confess to himself that the creative power of his youth is on the decline.[26]

There are certainly no signs of declining powers in the D minor Symphony; it contains some of Spohr's finest and freshest orchestral writing. In the first movement there is a concentration of material similar to the Overture in F, but the ideas are more distinguished, the contrasts more striking and the form more extended.

All but one of the essential germs from which the first movement grows are stated within the first twenty-two bars. The first five bars contain three important motifs (ex. 94), the oboe in an expressive solo then contributes an important variant of these, before the strings alone state a new theme at bar 19 (ex. 95), which is typical of the Romantic melancholy quality so often alluded to by contemporaries. The music builds up by degrees to a strongly

Ex. 94

Ex. 95

dissonant minor ninth on the dominant at bar 44, sustained for four bars before resolving in the fifth, then after a marvellously effective passage with the string section in octaves (ex. 96) the music reaches a C pedal, in prepara-

Ex. 96

tion for the expected relative major, though the dissonant diminished harmony which accompanies it suggests F minor. Ultimately however, at bars
76–9 all expectations of F are dispelled by a passage which seems to arrive at
a 'second subject' in the 'wrong' key (ex. 97). The first phrase of the clarinet

Ex. 97

and bassoon theme is new, providing the final motif from which the movement is built, but the second phrase links the theme with the previous material. From here the music gradually makes its way to the relative major and a brilliant string passage developing *e*, combined with *d* in the wind, which drives the music purposefully towards the double bar. These ideas continue to be combined in a variety of ways in the development section (ex. 98) which, beginning with another characteristic mediant shift to A flat

Ex. 98

[wind] [clarinet]
[bassoon]
[violin I]
[viola]
[strings]
[cellos & basses 8va]

major, changes mode after a few bars to A flat minor, then modulates enharmonically through a number of keys. The descending whole tones in the bass at this point have a striking and prophetic effect (ex. 99). Spohr eventually arrives at dominant preparation for D minor, which utilises the music of the movement's opening bars, but slips at the last moment into D major for a magically transformed reappearance, *pianissimo*, of theme *d–e*. A powerful D minor coda concludes the movement.

The Larghetto second movement in B flat begins with a gently yearning theme, luxuriantly harmonised (ex. 100). Clarinets and bassoons are used in chorus to good effect, and towards the close of the section the cellos are freed from the basses and soar above the violas in a manner increasingly characteristic of Spohr's orchestration. At bar 32 trumpets and horns herald a new section in G minor, in which a rapid ascending flourish assumes prominence. This essentially stormy section is punctuated by a calmer passage in which the flourish is heard only as a distant murmur while the woodwind are given expressive *pianissimo* solos. After a further outburst building to a tremendous climax, the opening section of the movement is repeated in a slightly elaborated form.

The Scherzo is one of Spohr's best. Formally it is interesting in that the Trio is repeated, but with different orchestration, and its repetition leads

Ex. 99

Ex. 100

straight into an exciting coda. The Scherzo begins in a breathless *pianissimo* (ex. 101), the theme being taken over successively by solo bassoon, oboe and flute before the repeat. In the second section the music, which has never risen above *piano*, subsides again to *pianissimo* over a dominant pedal before finally crescendoing in an exuberant release of tension, *fortissimo* in D major,

Ex. 101

with trumpets and timpani entering for the first time. An abrupt return to
pianissimo and solos from clarinet and oboe lead to the double bar. The Trio
in D major is of an entirely different character, seeming to recall the Ländler
which Spohr must have come to know during his time in Vienna (ex. 102).

Ex. 102

The theme is stated by wind and timpani alone, and repeated by strings; the
same procedure being followed for the second section. In Trio 2, after the
repetition of the Scherzo, strings and wind combine to give a full-bodied
account of the theme. In the Coda a particularly fine effect is created by a
solo timpani passage accompanied by wind, which precedes the final outburst from the full orchestra (ex. 103).

Ex. 103

(Ex. 103 cont.)

The Finale, as in the First Symphony, is a more lightweight movement. Spohr, mindful perhaps of the frequently reiterated charge that his music was too often inclined to the elegiac, seems to have decided to send his listeners away in a good humour. The principal theme, with its warm harmonisation, has something of the amiable flow that is characteristic of later nineteenth-century D major symphonic finales (e.g. Brahms and Dvořák) (ex. 104). The second subject has a humorous quality (ex. 105) especially when its second phrase is later given to the horn. In this symphony Spohr showed his thorough mastery of the orchestra, which he handled almost like a large chamber ensemble. The texture is never misjudged, and the variety of timbres which he achieved is remarkable; in this respect the D minor Symphony is unsurpassed by any contemporary work.

When writing his memoirs, Spohr seems to have imagined that his works made more of an impact in England at this time than they actually did. He stated that after the first performance of his Second Symphony 'the next morning all the London newspapers contained reports respecting the new symphony that had been composed in their town, and vied with each other in their praise of it'.[27] At this period it was quite exceptional for a newspaper to review a concert the next day. In this case the only ones which seem to have mentioned the performance at all were the *Morning Chronicle* (almost a month later on 4 May) and the *Quarterly Musical Magazine*. The latter's review was certainly not enthusiastic, for it simply remarked that 'A symphony of Mr Spohr was well received but did not excite extraordinary sensation.'[28] The *Morning Chronicle*, on the other hand, though it had no one to vie with, was more impressed, and considered that

The third concert was, on the whole, a brilliant performance, and owed much of its éclat to a new symphony by Mr. Spohr, performed for the first time, which places him amongst instrumental composers of the highest class, being as remarkable for the elegance and vocality of its melody, and the consistency of its design, as for the

Ex. 104

Ex. 105

scientific knowledge which it exhibits throughout. The audience received it with an applause that must have gratified the author, and which will, we hope, incite him to similar efforts. [29]

In subsequent concerts Spohr was able to perform a wide range of his other instrumental compositions. He and Dorette appeared three times in violin and harp duets; he performed several of his violin concertos and, with

141

Nicholas Mori, his Concertante op. 48; the First Symphony, the Nonet, another string quartet and the overture *Alruna* were all also introduced to the public. At his Benefit Concert the Second Symphony was repeated and among other things he was able to include another new composition – a Potpourri on Irish themes for violin and orchestra (op. 59), which he had found time to compose during his stay.

A number of years were to elapse before the admiration which Spohr's compositions elicited among a few connoisseurs was to bear fruit in a more widespread popularity in England. More tangible and immediate was the financial harvest which his celebrity as a violinist allowed him to garner. He spent much of the time, when he was not engaged in concert-giving or composition, giving violin lessons. These he undertook simply for the money, which by German standards was very considerable, and he frankly admitted that there was little he could do for most of his uninspiring pupils, who in any case were primarily rich dilettantes and only came to him in order to say that they had been pupils of Spohr. But he was not a mercenary; on one occasion he refused a proffered payment of £5 from a collector who had asked him to give an opinion on his collection of violins, and where his pride was concerned, as in the matter of playing at private parties for money, financial considerations were firmly subordinated to his artistic self-esteem.

Spohr's straightforward and honourable character as well as his profound musicianship brought him many friends and admirers in the London musical world. With Ferdinand Ries there developed a friendship which lasted until Ries's death in 1838, while Sir George Smart, who had organised Spohr's Benefit Concert for him, visited Kassel in 1825 and remained a friend throughout his life. All in all Spohr could feel well satisfied with his visit to London. As the *Morning Chronicle* wrote after his Benefit Concert,

Mr. Spohr has added considerably to his fame by this visit to London, where he has found more real judges of musical merit than foreigners unacquainted with this country are inclined to believe. He is an artist who unites, in one person, the qualities of composer and performer, in a degree of perfection that is seldom equalled, and we trust that at some future period we may congratulate the musical public upon the return of Mr. Spohr to a metropolis where the more he is known the higher his talents will be appreciated.[30]

For Dorette the experience had been less satisfactory. Not only had she been separated from her children for almost six months, but also her health had deteriorated further from the strain of so much travelling and from her attempts to master the larger, more powerfully strung Erard double-action harp which she had acquired in London. Her success in adapting to the instrument is attested by references to her 'great ability' and 'highly finished performance',[31] but the effort took its toll. Spohr, fearing that she would suffer a third attack of 'nervous fever', persuaded her to give up the harp and to concentrate on the less strenuous piano. It was with understandable reluctance that she abandoned the instrument on which they had achieved such success together for fifteen years. To soften the blow Spohr immediately began work on a quintet for piano and wind (op. 52) for Dorette to take part in, and had already finished the first movement before they left London.

It had been Spohr's original intention to travel immediately to Paris, but as he wrote to Speyer on the eve of his departure from London, 'I would still very much like to go to Paris, but my wife's longing for the children is so great that she will not even be delayed for a fortnight.'[32] They therefore went straight to Gandersheim, where they were reunited with their family and spent the rest of the summer and autumn with Spohr's parents. Dorette quickly regained her health, and Spohr applied himself with renewed vigour to composition. He began by completing the quintet. It is his first composition in which the piano plays a leading role, and his writing for the instrument, though brilliant and effective, shows his lack of practical familiarity with the keyboard. Chopin, after playing the work in 1830, observed that it was 'most beautiful, but badly written for the piano. Everything he tried to write expressly for piano display is intolerably difficult and it is often impossible to work out a fingering.'[33] It is a testimony to Dorette's skill that she was able to perform the quintet sufficiently well to appear in public with it. When she performed it in Hildburghausen in the autumn of 1821, a reviewer wrote 'Mme Spohr, the formerly outstanding harpist, played it with the greatest precision and the tenderest expression, so that the wish that one might rather have heard her on the harp as formerly had to be suppressed.'[34] The quintet quickly gained admirers and was to be performed by many of the most notable pianists of the day, including, as well as Chopin, Moscheles, Mendelssohn and Liszt. Reviewing it after its appearance in print the *AMZ* commented: 'It is quite definitely one of the most beautiful of Spohr's works, and that is to say one of the most beautiful pieces of instrumental music of our day altogether.'[35] In the middle section of the Larghetto, Spohr adapted to the piano the highly ornamented style of violin writing which he used, for example, in the Adagio of the Seventh Violin Concerto. It is hardly surprising that Chopin should have responded to the beauty of such passages as the one in ex. 106. In order to perform the new quintet in Gandersheim, Spohr hastily arranged the wind parts for string quartet and subsequently published it in this version also, as op. 53.

His sojourn in Gandersheim was spent in a pleasant combination of work and relaxation. He took on a new pupil, Eduard Grund, and applied himself assiduously to composition, producing in a short while the Ninth Violin Concerto in D minor (op. 55), as well as arranging two of his earlier violin and harp pieces for violin and piano (the Potpourri op. 50 and the Grand Rondo op. 51), and contributing two four-part male-voice songs to the third volume of a series entitled *Liedertafel* which was published by Peters. In October, Spohr was invited to undertake the direction of a music festival in

Ex. 106

Quedlinburg, where he was able to give the first performance of his new violin concerto and the first German performance of his Second Symphony. The concerto and symphony were also repeated in November in Frankfurt, where they made a powerful impression. Besides praising the music, the local reviewer, who was familiar with Spohr's playing, commented that the modified tail-piece on his violin made a noticeable improvement in the tone, especially on the G string.

The Ninth Concerto, which is in the usual three movements, includes trombones in the scoring and is a more grandiose work than the Seventh Concerto. The Frankfurt reviewer, mistakenly believing that it had been written in England, felt that he could detect Handel's spirit in the colossal effect of its opening tutti. The entry of the solo is, however, unmistakably in Spohr's manner; the yearning melody, prefaced by a chromatic scale of almost three octaves, seems the very essence of his style. A beguiling second theme, which the critic noted that Spohr performed with his 'inimitable portamento',[36] provides an excellent contrast. The Adagio is another of Spohr's lyrical slow movements which seem almost like improvisation. The Finale, though not lacking in fireworks, does not quite sustain the height of the previous two movements. Its opening theme in double stops is a good example of the technical demands which Spohr made in his concertos (ex. 107).

Ex. 107

Paris was the only musically important European capital which Spohr had not yet visited, and it was thus with some degree of anxious anticipation that he arrived in the city on 7 December 1820. Here lived his childhood idol Cherubini, and here too was the home of the French school of violinists whose example had inspired him in his youth and whose present representatives, Baillot, Lafont, Kreutzer, Habeneck, Fontaine, Guerin and others, maintained its high reputation; even that doyen of violinists Viotti, whose approval of Spohr's playing at his first concert in London had so gratified him, was now in Paris. It therefore meant a great deal to him to prove himself in such company, and especially to uphold the honour of German music among the self-congratulatory and inward-looking French. It was almost inevitable that he should be, to some degree, disappointed with what he found, for his own artistic outlook was as dogmatic as that of the French. He recognised and admired the high technical standards of playing among French musicians, but found a glaring deficiency in taste and judgement. In the second of four open letters which he contributed to the *AMZ* on the state of music in Paris, he observed:

one seldom or never hears in the musical réunions here an earnest, well-digested piece of music, such as a quartet or quintet of our great masters; everyone produces his show-piece; you hear nothing but *airs variés*, *rondos favoris*, nocturnes, and the like trifles, and from the singers romances and little duets; and however incorrect and insipid all this may be, it never fails to evoke a response if it is executed really smoothly and sweetly. Poor in such pretty trifles, with my earnest German music, I am ill at ease in such musical parties, and feel frequently like a man who speaks to people who do not understand his language; for when the praise of any such auditors sometimes extends even from my playing to the composition itself, I cannot feel gratified by it since immediately afterwards he bestows the same admiration on the most trivial things. One blushes to be praised by such connoisseurs. It is just the same at the theatres; the masses, the leaders of fashion here, do not at all know how to distinguish the worst from the best; they hear *Le Jugement de Midas* with the same rapture that they hear *Les deux journées* or *Joseph*.* It requires no long residence here to adopt the frequently expressed opinion that the French are not a musical nation.[37]

* Operas by Grétry, Cherubini and Méhul respectively.

Despite his warm admiration for a number of French musicians, Spohr felt much less comfortable in Paris than in London. There was little interest in orchestral music, and far less interest in, and knowledge of, the music of the German masters. Nevertheless, he took pains to perform his chamber music at the numerous soirées to which he was invited, and was particularly keen to seek Cherubini's opinion of his quartets. According to Spohr's account, Cherubini showed great interest in his music. On first hearing the Quartet op. 45 no. 1 he requested Spohr to repeat the performance, on the grounds that in form and style the music was so foreign to him that he could not follow it properly. Spohr was afterwards told that, apart perhaps from having heard one of Haydn's quartets at Baillot's, Cherubini was quite unacquainted with German chamber music. After a second hearing of Spohr's quartet, Cherubini spoke highly of it, but still requested at the next soirée that it should be played a third time. Much the same thing happened with op. 45 no. 2, the beautiful Adagio of which he is reported to have called 'the finest I ever heard'.[38] He also praised the Quintet for piano and wind. This quintet made a strong impression in the salons of Paris, thanks partly to its being championed by Moscheles with members of Reicha's quintet. After hearing Moscheles play it, Dorette, unable to match his energy and style in the allegro movements, no longer had the courage to perform it during their stay. Though he played much in private, Spohr made only one public appearance, at which he was enthusiastically applauded. He wrote to Speyer on 16 January 1821 that 'after the first solo of the violin concerto, the jubilation and cries of bravo were so great that one did not hear a note of the second tutti. And the applause continued thus until the end!'[39] But his performance received a mixed reception in the press. Most of the critics began by praising the French violinists and making it clear that no foreigner could really hope to aspire to such heights. The *Courier des Spectacles* even had the temerity to say of Spohr: 'if he stays some time in Paris he could perfect his taste and then, returning, form that of the good Germans'.[40] Such patronising remarks irritated Spohr intensely – he remarked: 'if only the brave fellow knew what the good Germans think of the artistic taste of the French!'[41] – and in his letters to the *AMZ* he made scathing reference to the ignorance, vanity and venality of the Parisian press. He took the occasion too to point out that the taste of the French violinists, for all their technical skill, was not in his eyes wholly unexceptionable. He noted disapprovingly that they had universally acquired a peculiar mannerism of accenting the last note of a phrase even when it fell on a weak beat, and that none of them seemed able to play an Adagio with real feeling. It is certainly notable that whereas in all the other countries he had visited his superb performance of an Adagio had been singled out for special notice, the French, whose predilection was for brilliant Allegros, took no notice of it. The lack of appreciation for Spohr as a violinist in Paris is indicated by the recollection of Fétis, six years later, that

Spohr 'had little success as a violinist and did not delay his return to Germany'.[42] And discussing German violinists in general he remarked patronisingly: 'though the school of violin playing founded by Franz Benda has not produced violinists of the first class, though Eck, Fränzl, Maurer, Möser, Spohr and Bohrer are inferior to the grand artists of the Italian and French schools, they are certainly men of estimable talent'.[43]

Overall the visit to Paris was far less successful from both the financial and the artistic point of view than the visit to London. Whatever interest in Spohr's compositions may have been aroused among French musicians, it was not sufficient to lead, as in England, to more extensive popularity.

Spohr considered returning to London for the 1821 season, but as no firm proposals were forthcoming from the Philharmonic Society, he and Dorette made their way back to Germany, stopping for some days in Strasbourg, where he was pleased to find his chamber music more enthusiastically received than in Paris. Settling down with his family in Gandersheim once more, they resumed 'the pleasant active life of the previous summer'.[44] Eduard Grund returned for further instruction and in turn resumed the musical education of Spohr's children, which he had undertaken the year before. Spohr soon felt the urge to compose, and chose to attempt something which he had not previously essayed: a large-scale unaccompanied vocal work. On the way to Paris he had spent some time in Heidelberg, were he was greatly interested to hear rehearsals of sixteenth-century Italian church music by Anton Thibaut's choral society. Daily visits to Thibaut's library had allowed him to familiarise himself thoroughly with the style of the music, and now with leisure to compose again he decided to try to produce an *a cappella* mass for double chorus in ten parts, in which he aimed to combine the 'ancient style' of church music with all the resources of modern harmony. The result was chromatic music of such difficulty that his first attempt to have it sung, by the Leipzig choral society, was an utter failure and it was not until some years later, when the mass had been published in a somewhat simplified version by Peters, that he heard a satisfactory rendering of his conception by Zelter's *Singakademie* in Berlin. The passage in ex. 108 from the Gloria is an

Ex. 108

[Allegro vivace]

147

(Ex. 108 cont.)

example of the extreme keys into which he allowed himself to venture. The mass is difficult but certainly not impracticable. The use of five soloists and a small and a large five-part chorus enabled him to achieve a wide variety of textures, and he made ample use of the opportunity thus afforded.

Hermstedt interrupted the composition of the mass with an invitation to give a concert in Alexisbad, for which he also requested a new clarinet concerto. Spohr readily agreed and quickly produced his Third Clarinet Concerto in F minor (which remained in Hermstedt's hands and was not published in Spohr's lifetime), as well as arranging, for violin and piano, a potpourri on themes from Winter's *Opferfest* (op. 80) of 1811 so that he and Dorette should have something new to play. Another invitation to give a concert in Pyrmont also provided the family with an enjoyable excursion and replenished their purse. It was clear, however, that this sort of life could not continue indefinitely. The education of the children especially could not be neglected; Emilie (14) and Ida (12) showed promise of becoming gifted singers, so he decided to take steps to ensure suitable tuition for his daughters, and a stimulating musical atmosphere for himself and Dorette. He wrote to Speyer from Gandersheim in August 1821 saying: 'The plan for the next year is now definitely fixed. In three weeks I will have my children confirmed then I will go with the whole family to Dresden and settle myself there for one or one and a half years. After that I might have a strong desire to undertake a second journey to Italy.'[45] Through the agency of his former pupil Moritz Hauptmann, who was at that time living in Dresden, an apartment was obtained for the family in advance of their arrival, the services of the celebrated singing teacher Johann Aloys Miecksch were secured, and in October they moved to Dresden.

Once they were settled in their new home Spohr quickly made contact with his old acquaintances in Dresden, foremost among them being Weber, who had held the post of Kapellmeister there since 1817. Although both composers shared the aim of fostering a vigorous national opera which could successfully challenge the Italians on the German stage, and though Weber seems to have had a high regard for Spohr's abilities, Spohr, perhaps subconsciously jealous of Weber's success with *Der Freischütz*, did not reciprocate, as his observations on Weber's opera indicate. After its great success in Berlin and Vienna Weber had put *Der Freischütz* into rehearsal in Dresden and Spohr was thus able to hear it in November 1821. He recalled:

As up to that time I had not entertained a very high opinion of Weber's talent for composition, it may readily be imagined that I was not a little desirous of becoming acquainted with that opera, in order to ascertain thoroughly by what it had achieved such enthusiastic admiration in the two capitals of Germany . . . The nearer acquaintance with the opera certainly did not solve for me the riddle of its enormous success; and I could alone account for it by Weber's peculiar gift and capacity for writing for the masses. As I very well knew that this gift had been denied me by nature, it is difficult for me to explain how an unconquerable impulse should nevertheless have led me to attempt dramatic composition anew.[46]

Jessonda, the new opera on which Spohr was at that time about to embark, became a concrete statement of his artistic creed, standing in sharp contrast to *Der Freischütz*, and it was to achieve a degree of success that must have helped confirm Spohr in his beliefs. *Jessonda*, however, was at this time more than a year in the future, and while waiting for the completion of the libretto Spohr had returned to quartet composition. Within a short time of arriving in Dresden he was introduced by Weber to all the best musical circles and soon instituted regular quartet parties in his own house. Having performed all his old quartets and quintets he set to work to produce new ones, completing one in E flat major and another in A minor before the end of the year. These, together with a third in G major, completed at the beginning of 1822, were published by Peters in February 1822. The E flat Quartet is among the best of his works in this genre. The first movement is another good example of Spohr's great skill in manipulating material; he never loses sight of his initial ideas but sustains interest throughout by constantly showing them in a new light and by the mercurial quality of his modulations. In the Adagio (A flat) Spohr's noble singing style is uppermost and the movement has a sincerity and depth of feeling which cannot fail to impress the unprejudiced listener. The Scherzo in C minor makes a perfect contrast with the soulful Adagio, having both terseness and vigour, and the relaxed Ländler-like Trio in C major provides a splendid foil to the urgency of the Scherzo. The Rondo finale is on the same high level as the preceding movements and brings the quartet to a brilliant conclusion. Neither of the other two quartets of op. 58 rise to quite such sustained heights as this, but both contain some fine writing; the A minor especially, though more of a display piece for the first violin, has much melodic freshness and appeal, and a number of interesting features. In the first movement, unlike op. 58 no. 1, there is a clearly differentiated second theme which has an almost operatic cast, and is noticeably similar to the lyricism of early Wagner, in *Rienzi* for instance (ex. 109). (It is noteworthy that the quartet was written when Spohr was lodging next door to the eight-year-old Richard Wagner and his family.) The second move-

Ex. 109

ment is interesting for its unusual form; being a combination of slow movement and scherzo. It is entitled Andante con variazioni and consists of a
charmingly simple theme in F major (4/4), followed by two variations, a
codetta, a scherzo in A major (3/4) which is a free variation on the original
theme with the second half extended, concluding with another variation on
the theme in the original key and time, and a short coda. Spohr never abandoned the Classical forms which he had inherited from Mozart, but sought
increasingly to vary them. The final movement of this quartet is a Rondo
all'Espagnola, which, however, is more Spohrish than Spanish; the title is
justified only by the use of a bolero rhythm (as in the Alla spagnola finale of
the Sixth Violin Concerto, this is virtually the same as a polonaise rhythm)
and a few conventional 'Spanish' inflexions (ex. 110). Throughout this move-

Ex. 110

ment the first violin is given a brilliant part, somewhat at the expense of
interest in the other parts, though there are many characteristic and charming touches in the harmony such as the major/minor ambivalence in ex. 111.
Op. 58 no. 3 presents no features which call for comment.

Ex. 111

A visit from Weber in early December 1821 brought about a rapid alteration of Spohr's plans. Weber informed him that he had been offered the post
of Hofkapellmeister in Kassel, but that since he preferred to remain in Dresden he would willingly recommend Spohr for the position. The proposal was
alluring, and in view of Spohr's interest Weber wrote in his reply to Kassel:
'We have the celebrated Spohr within our walls . . . such a brilliant and
renowned artist whose honoured name cannot but awaken respect in all
quarters would certainly be an ornament to the Elector's opera.'[47] Within a
week Spohr received a letter from Kassel offering him the post and asking
him to name his terms. From Gotha too came the offer of a post (Spohr's successor there, Andreas Romberg, had died in November 1821): the Duchess,
who was sister to Elector Wilhelm II of Hesse-Kassel, had never quite reconciled herself to losing Spohr and was anxious to tempt him back, but the lack
of an opera company in Gotha was a strong disincentive to Spohr to return
there. On 2 January he informed Speyer:

At last things are decided and I therefore hasten to write to you. I have been negotiating with Gotha and Kassel at the same time about an engagement. But I have now
decided for Kassel and am engaged there from 1 January for life as Hofkapellmeister
and director of the opera with a salary of 2000 thalers and a yearly leave of absence of
two months. In a few days I am setting out from here and expect to arrive in Kassel
about the middle of the month.[48]

Spohr travelled to Kassel alone, for it had been decided that, in order to
minimise the disruption of his daughters' education, they and Dorette would
follow him in the spring. His journey took him through Leipzig, whence he
wrote to Dorette on 9 January, and Gotha. In Gotha he was once again
strongly pressed to reconsider taking up his old post there; the Duke and
Duchess both paid court to him and in a final bid to persuade him, Count
Salisch, the Intendant of the court orchestra, promised on his word of
honour as a Freemason that the offer would be kept open for six months in
case Spohr should find Kassel uncongenial. Perhaps with the deliberate
intention of pointing out the difference between the two cities, Count Salisch
cautioned him about the nature of the regime in Kassel; Spohr observed in a

letter which he wrote to Dorette just before leaving Gotha: 'He warned me to write nothing personal from Kassel. The post might not be trustworthy. I will therefore write little in my letters of the state of affairs which prevails there.'[49] That he genuinely believed Salisch's warning to be well founded is evidenced by the circumspection of his subsequent letters to Dorette and a number of cryptic references to matters that it would not have been convenient for his new employer to know about. In view of Spohr's well-developed liberal principles it may be doubted whether this was an auspicious beginning to his association with the city which was to be his home for the remainder of his life. Nevertheless, for good and ill he entered Kassel through the Leipzig gate on 14 January 1822.

IX

Hofkapellmeister in Kassel: operatic triumph
1822–1825

Kassel, capital of the Electorate of Hesse, was a city of about twenty thousand inhabitants. Edward Holmes, an English musician who visited it in 1826, observed:

Cassel, viewed from the road in the light of the setting sun, looks like a city of palaces in a fairy tale, 'with glistering spires and pinnacles adorned'. It is surrounded by fine bosky hills. Beautiful as the situation is, and cheap as is the expense of entertainment, there is no city in Germany in which I should less like to reside than Cassel; the military swarm in this place, and there is such an eternal manoeuvering and drumming going forward from morning to night, that the town is like one great barrack.[1]

The military presence that Holmes found so disturbing was a symptom of the political control which the new Elector Wilhelm II was determined to exercise. There were many among the inhabitants of Hesse who looked back to the time when Kassel was capital of the short-lived kingdom of Westphalia, under the rule of Napoleon's brother Jerome, as a golden age of liberty. Another English visitor to Kassel during the 1820s, Sir Arthur Brook Faulkner, noted:

Political writers there are none worth a farthing. The censorship is very strict – a snake ready to sting the unwary. The moment a man gives indications of political spirit, if he has any talents to make it effective – and some such have ventured into print – he has his choice either to be silent or to submit to the extremity of the law and the elector. He writes independently at the risk of expatriation. So that all journalists are the tools of power and slaves of sordid calculation . . . We surely cannot wonder that the manliest constitution of mind should droop under such a domineering régime; and though cordially detesting its author, yet are the people obliged (it cannot be said without a murmur) to bear with the best grace the weight of a chain which they see no prospect of being able to break.[2]

Such conditions could not be said to bode well for so liberal-minded a man as Spohr.

Wilhelm II had been active in reforming the administration of justice, police, forests etc., and by these actions had materially benefited the citizens of Kassel. At the same time, however, he alienated public opinion by his imperious behaviour towards individuals and by his unedifying personal life. He incurred considerable opprobrium by living openly with his mistress, Countess Hessenstein (a former milliner from Bonn whom he had elevated to the nobility), and since the Electress Auguste was a popular figure his estrangement from her was in itself ground for discontent. Compared with the oppressive governments of pre-revolutionary France with their *lettres de cachet* (arbitrary imprisonment without trial) or the many present-day regimes in which political murder is endemic, Hesse in the first half of the nineteenth century may seem an almost utopian state. Political freedom and liberty, however, were ideas which, springing from the Enlightenment of the eighteenth century, were a driving force in intellectual circles at this time and seemed far more important to many than mere material contentment. They were ideas which Spohr shared to a considerable degree, but in his case they were combined with a large measure of pragmatism. He took a keen interest in the political reform movement of the day, was prepared to make a stand on behalf of what he saw as essential human rights and dignity, and was active throughout his life in helping those less well off than himself; but he always believed that his first duty was to the ideals of his art. Distasteful as many aspects of the political system in Kassel were to him (and they became more distasteful with the passage of time), he was so much bound up with the fulfilment of musical aims that as long as these were unhindered it was possible for him to achieve a *modus vivendi* with a regime which he made little secret of deploring.

There can be no doubt that the Elector knew of his Hofkapellmeister's political opinions; his network of spies was too efficient for him to have been unaware of Spohr's association with other members of the Freemason community and participation in the Electress's circle, the so-called 'Augustenruhe', where conversation ranged freely from intellectual and artistic matters to serious political discussion. But the Elector, though no great lover of the arts – unlike his sister, Caroline Amalie, Duchess of Gotha – was extremely interested in and proud of his fine new court theatre, and keen to maintain standards of performance at the highest possible level. To this end he was willing to subsidise it heavily and to overlook the political views of an artist who could produce such fine results as Spohr. The rewards of this tolerance were that he possessed one of the finest opera companies in Germany and could enjoy the reflected glory of Spohr's growing reputation as one of the greatest living musicians.

For Spohr, the musical conditions in Kassel during his first eight years there were almost ideal. Already on 18 January 1822, only four days after his arrival, he wrote to Dorette in Dresden saying that he had quite made up his mind to forget about the proposals that had been made to him in Gotha. Six days later he again expressed his satisfaction with the way things were working out, writing: 'My sphere of activity is exactly like that in Frankfurt but without its unpleasantness, and I could not have found a more agreeable one in the whole of Germany',[3] for as he observed in his next letter, 'With my sphere of activity I am very happy. The artistic direction of the opera – distribution of roles, the decision about what should be studied and given, arrangement of rehearsals etc. – is wholly given over to me; also the management consults me about engagements.'[4] His first appearance in the theatre, to conduct Winter's *Opferfest* on 20 January, had been a notable success; he told Dorette how an improvement in the standard of the orchestra had been generally noted, that the audience had applauded the overture vigorously as well as the ensembles ('something unheard of here'), and that the Elector had complimented him after the performance.[5] A similar success attended his direction of the orchestra's third Subscription Concert of the season, which took place two days later, at which the Electress had also showered him with compliments. (The Elector was not present, since he never attended the same functions as his estranged consort.) His mood of euphoria was sustained by a surprise dinner given in his honour by the orchestra, at which he was greeted by trumpets and drums, and was the recipient among other things of a fulsome poem which ran: 'Long live the German master, the creator of noble works full of sweet charm and yet also full of giant strength, who disdains the false fame of tinkling sounds with which inferior art too often seeks the beautiful, whose name garlanded with fame has already for a long time traversed the world.'[6]

In the first few weeks Spohr's mind was full of plans to raise the standard of the Kassel musical establishment. During the tenure of its previous director, Benzon (dismissed for incompetence), there had been a significant decline in the quality of the orchestra and the opera, but Spohr could see their potential and he informed Dorette: 'I am convinced that if only four or five good artists were to be engaged our orchestra would soon become one of the best in Germany.'[7] Having gained the Elector's confidence by some notable initial improvements, he was in a strong position to get what he wanted, and thus secured his agreement to the engagement of 'seven outstanding artists'[8] as replacements for weaker members of the orchestra. Moritz Hauptmann and Ferdinand Spohr were included among the new musicians, as well as a number of first-rate wind players; the cello section had already been strengthened prior to Spohr's appointment by the engagement of Hasemann, who had been a member of his quartet in Frankfurt. With such a group of musicians under his command Spohr was rapidly able to make good his boast that he would raise the Kassel orchestra to a pre-eminent position. He was able to keep it at a high level throughout all the changes of the next thirty-five years, being particularly fortunate in having a constant supply of good violinists in the pupils who flocked to him from all over Europe (he insisted on participation in the orchestra as part of their training). Sir George Smart, visiting Kassel in 1825, noted in his diary that the orchestra consisted of '16 violins, 4 violas, 4 celli and 3 or 4 bassi',* and that 'Spohr beat time . . . he had a short stick.'[9] Sir Arthur Brook Faulkner, who visited Kas-

* For a complete list of the Kassel orchestra in 1823 see *AMZ*, xxi (1823), 505–6

sel four years after Smart, was astounded by the quality of the orchestra, observing after hearing a performance of Auber's *La Muette de Portici*:

[It] is got up under the direction of the renowned Spohr, an artist whose celebrity, both as violinist and composer, is too well and extensively known to require any 'weak witness of his fame'. In all my experience of operas I never remember hearing an instrumental piece go off so well as the overture, which I consider one of the prime morsels of the whole composition. The executive precision of the orchestra, which consisted of upwards of forty first-rate performers, makes all praise to halt behind it. The whole was moved and inspired as if by one soul and impulse . . . The sudden bursts of harmony sent forth from forty instruments, all mingling like the elements of light, and converging towards one grand impression, was an excitement which baffles any power of description that would paint it to the ear.[10]

The first of Spohr's own operas to be produced in Kassel was *Zemire und Azor*, given on 24 March 1822 with great success. Five days after this performance he wrote to Speyer:

On Sunday last my opera *Zemire und Azor* was given an excellent first performance and received by the public with great enthusiasm. After the performance I was called forward, a distinction which, so far as Kassel is concerned, has not happened to a composer before. The applause with which that piece was received, and which increased more and more towards the end, has to a certain extent consoled me for the unfavourable reception which the opera met with in Vienna and Munich. But I derived far more pleasure from the fact that the opera, which I had certainly not heard for a couple of years, pleased me myself who am a very severe critic of my former things. I am now convinced that this composition, like others of my works, needs to be performed very strictly and in the spirit of the work in order to please the non-connoisseur, but that by a negligent performance they can easily be so spoiled that even the connoisseur would be at a loss with them.[11]

Dorette had arrived in Kassel with the children in early March and was thus able to witness her husband's success. At first she appeared occasionally in public – at the second concert of the 1822/23 subscription series she played the op. 52 quintet – but she gradually withdrew from public performance and could then only share passively in his artistic triumphs, though she continued to be an astute critic and, perhaps more importantly for Spohr, their enduring love for one another provided a secure and stable basis for their lives. After sixteen years of marriage their letters show the continuing intensity of their love and mutual dependence. The importance of this for Spohr's happiness is indicated by the beginning of his second letter from Kassel, where he wrote: 'Dearest heart's-soul, How I long for you, how I love you and how terribly long the two months until your arrival will be';[12] and again on 7 February: 'Separated from you, my dear wife, I feel straight away how indispensable you are to me and how I cannot even be happy without you.'[13] On Dorette's part, her whole life was dependent on their relationship; she wrote from Dresden: 'My love for you is so great that I would sacrifice everything for you, even my life and what is more my happiness for the future with all its beautiful dreams and hopes.'[14] It is clear from their correspondence as a whole that these were not merely conventional endearments.

Once the family were reunited in Kassel there was nothing to mar Spohr's contentment. Certain now that they would stay in Kassel for some years, they sought a permanent home in the attractive wooded suburbs of the city, but in the meanwhile settled down happily in a rented house in the Schöne Aussicht which, in accord with its name, had a fine outlook. Domestic bliss and professional satisfaction coincided to provide an ideal atmosphere for creative work, and in the spring of 1822 Spohr began work on the new opera which had been in his mind for some time. He had conceived the idea for *Jessonda* on a rainy day in Paris in 1821 when, to while away the time, he borrowed Antoine Lemièrre's drama *La Veuve de Malabar* (1770) from his landlady. Seeing its potential for an opera plot he purchased it from her, and having sketched out a rough scenario during the following summer passed it on to Eduard Gehe, a literary amateur in Dresden, to be worked into a libretto. Spohr and Gehe were not the first to adapt Lemièrre's story; it had first appeared in Germany as a play, translated and arranged by Carl Martin Plümicke in 1781 as *Lanassa*, and incidental music had been composed to this version by Johann André. The story had then been set as an opera by Christian Kalkbrenner, and a continuation of it by Johann Nepomuk Komareck, *Marie von Montalban oder Lanassas zweiter Teil* (1792), was adapted as a libretto by Carl Reger and set to music by Peter von Winter. In Italy Simon Mayr produced a version of *Lanassa* in 1817, shortly after Spohr had met him there. In Gehe's version the name of the heroine was changed from Lanassa to Jessonda, and the story (which differs from Lemièrre's and from Spohr's scenario to a considerable extent) was as follows:

Act I begins with a ceremony of mourning for the Rajah of Goa. It is made clear that his young widow, Jessonda, is to be burned on his funeral pyre. Two characters are introduced in this scene: the ruthless High Priest, Dandau, and a young priest, Nadori, who abhors the priesthood of which he is, through no choice of his own, a member. Towards the end of the scene a messenger arrives to say that a Portuguese army has landed and is advancing on the city. The second scene takes place in Jessonda's apartments. In conversation with her sister, Amazili, it is revealed that she was married to the old Rajah against her will, having been torn from her real love, a Portuguese general. Nadori, who has been sent to deliver the ritual message of death, falters when he sees the beauty of the sisters and falls immediately in love with Amazili. He vows to help save Jessonda.

Act II opens in the Portuguese camp, with warlike exercises in progress. The general of the army, Tristan d'Achuna, is portrayed as a high-minded man (the campaign is to avenge Portuguese traders treacherously murdered by the natives) sorrowing for his true love, who had mysteriously disappeared with her whole family from her home on the Ganges some years earlier. He has agreed to a truce with the Indians so that they can carry out what he believes to be harmless religious ceremonies. The Bayaderes (female votaries) bring Jessonda to the sacred stream for purification. Nadori renews his vow to help and decides to inform the Portuguese commander of the true purpose of the ceremonies. Tristan comes to investigate, and he and Jessonda recognise each other as the lost lover whom they had believed they would never see again, but before Tristan can take action to save her, Dandau arrives on the scene and reminds him that he had given his word of honour not to impede the ceremonies. After a tense confrontation, Jessonda is taken back to the city.

At the beginning of Act III, Tristan is in despair, bound by his word and thus unable to save Jessonda from her fate, but Nadori arrives to tell him that Dandau has himself broken the truce by attacking the Portuguese ships. Released from his oath, Tristan orders an attack, and Nadori volunteers to guide them through a secret passage into the city. Meanwhile during the preparations for the sacrifice a storm is raging, at the height of which a colossal image of Brahma is struck by lightning and destroyed. This is taken as a sign that the god is angry over Jessonda's perfidy, and arrangements are made to expedite the sacrifice. However, the Portuguese manage to storm the city in time, and the opera ends with the joyful unions of Tristan with Jessonda and Nadori with Amazili.

Overall it may reasonably be maintained that Gehe, notwithstanding inflated versification, produced one of the best German opera librettos of the period. Inspired both by the dramatic possibilities of the libretto and by his aspirations for the future of German opera, Spohr worked on the score between March and December 1822 with exceptional care. As he informed Speyer in January 1823,

I have recently been so much engaged on a new opera that I have somewhat neglected everything else. It is now ready, and I am very glad to have completed such an important work. If I expect more from this opera than from the earlier ones it is because of my greater experience and the inspiration I felt in the work on every number of the successful libretto. In order to devote myself to the work only in my hours of inspiration, I have allowed myself much more time with this than with all the former ones.[15]

Jessonda differs considerably in several respects from Spohr's earlier operas, most significantly in its extensive use of chorus and ballet, and in the replacement of spoken dialogue by recitative. His new approach was carefully thought out, and in many ways *Jessonda* was intended as a manifesto to German composers. He made his ideas explicit in an article entitled 'Aufruf an deutsche Componisten' (Appeal to German Composers), which appeared in the *AMZ* shortly before the première of *Jessonda*. The article began: 'The long-expected moment seems at last to have arrived, when the German public, cloyed with the insipid sweetness of the new Italian music, longs for what is of real and intrinsic value.' He believed that much depended on finding a libretto 'which shall at the same time please the mind endowed with taste and that which is uncultivated', and was emphatic about the composer's responsibility to the dignity of his art, saying: 'If we have been happy enough to obtain such a subject, we should no longer speculate on mere theatrical effects, as several of the modern composers do; but we ought to follow the bent of our feelings, and compose music of a true dramatic character adapted in every respect to the subject in tone, style and character.' Furthermore, he stressed the importance of the orchestra and, suggesting that the spoken dialogue should be replaced by continuous music, he observed: 'If the critic reject the opera as a work of art and call it monstrous, it is the sudden transition from speech to song that justifies him in so terming it.' But he felt that the adoption of continuous music had implications for the character of the story, which should be poetical but uncomplicated; he did not wish to set to music 'dialogues on the common occurrences of life, of which our operas contain such abundant examples'. In a footnote to his article Spohr added:

The opera *Jessonda*, which I lately composed, possesses (at least so I flatter myself) all these requisites. In its representation, I shall shortly be able to obtain a convincing proof of whether the theory I have laid down above will hold good in practice, and if through an imposing display of pageantry (consisting of groups of dancing Bayaderes, warlike dances, processions of priests, a religious sacrifice etc.), the multitude will find attraction at the same time that the more cultivated will be pleased by the music and by the action itself.[16]

A notable feature of *Jessonda* is its combination of flexibility and formality. As *The Harmonicon* observed shortly after the opera's publication in 1824, 'In this, as in his other works, Spohr, treading closely in the footsteps of Mozart, has proved that dramatic music may be brought into regular forms without injury either to truth of expression, or theatrical effect.'[17] On the one hand Spohr creates extensive scene-complexes – Act I has only one break, for the change of scene; Act II is continuous (only Amazili and Nadori's Duet, no. 18, does not link musically into the next number); Act III, though there is one change of scene, is musically continuous, the two scenes being linked by a sustained note on the horn – on the other hand the individual constituents of these complexes are a succession of formal structures (though almost invariably open-ended), bound together by recitative. The recitative varies between what is essentially secco and a kind of dramatic arioso, but these two types of recitative are not clearly separated; even in the 'secco', which is accompanied only by strings, metrical sections are frequently interspersed, and the lyrical quality of the vocal writing throughout gives them a melodic character quite unlike the traditional secco recitative of Italian opera. Spohr's handling of the recitative in *Jessonda* is closely related to his treatment of the scena in his earlier operas, but he achieved a far greater dramatic intensity in parts of this work, most strikingly in the recitatives preceding Jessonda's arias in the first and third acts, Nadori's in the second, and Tristan's 'vision' at the beginning of the third. The latter has more than a passing affinity with Tannhäuser's, and elsewhere there are a number of remarkable foreshadowings of Wagner (who conducted *Jessonda* on many occasions). One example is the opening of the second scene of Act I (ex. 112);

Ex. 112

another is the delivery of the message of death at the beginning of the first Finale, where the repeated rhythm of crotchet, quaver rest and three triplet semiquavers on the timpani is the same as that used by Wagner when Brünnhilde warns Siegmund of his approaching death in the second act of *Die Walküre*; and there are also general similarities between Spohr's fine first Finale and the scene in the last act of *Siegfried* where the hero wakes Brünnhilde from her trance.

The set-pieces of the opera which are enclosed in the framework of recitative comprise, in addition to the three finales, six arias, three duets, a Terzett and three extensive scenes with chorus and ballet. The latter, which consist of the introductions to Acts I and II and the scene of the destruction of the image (no. 26) in Act III, have no parallel in Spohr's earlier operas. Perhaps he was influenced by what he had seen at the Paris Opéra in 1821 as well as by the possibilities for lavish productions which the Kassel theatre offered after its reconstitution in 1821. The contrast between the dark and sombre quality of the Rajah's obsequies in Act I and the bright and exciting military exercises in the Portuguese camp at the beginning of Act II is highly effective. The scene with the night-time ceremonies, storm and destruction of Brahma's image in Act III is one of the high points of the opera; here, as in *Faust*, Spohr made telling use of off-stage chorus from within the temple. The second Finale, with its confrontation between the Indian and Portuguese armies, also utilised massed choral effects.

The arias and duets are more conventional and offer few unexpected features. All but four of them have the traditional slow and fast sections, though Jessonda's first aria (no. 7) reverses the usual order for the purpose of portraying her resignation to her fate, and the key scheme is unusual – the Agitato being in E minor and the concluding Larghetto in A flat major. Tristan's aria in G minor (no. 12) is similar to Ali's G minor aria in *Zemire und Azor*, both being in polacca rhythm, and many of the melodic phrases, modulations and rhythmic patterns elsewhere are reminiscent of earlier works. The arias and duets are nevertheless highly attractive music, and their contemporary popularity is attested by the frequency of their appearance (especially nos. 12, 15 and 18) in concert programmes during the first half of the nineteenth century.

In *Jessonda* Spohr used reminiscence and motif, but without their having so central a role as in *Faust*. The only true leitmotif is the phrase (ex. 113)

Ex. 113

[Allegro maestoso]

used to represent Tristan's oath; it plays an important part in the second Finale when Dandau reminds him of it, and also dominates the beginning of Act III, where Tristan dwells on the evil consequence of his oath. In addition there are a number of well-judged uses of thematic and motivic reminiscence. A curiosity is the use of a phrase identical with the 'love' motif from *Faust* at the point in the first Finale where Nadori is overcome by Amazili's beauty – presumably an unconscious association of ideas, since this is a typically 'Spohrish' phrase.

Timbre, tonality and rhythm play an important part in distinguishing the Indians and Portuguese. Trombones and the key of E flat are closely associated with the Brahmins; each appearance of Dandau and the Brahmins is accompanied by trombones, which are not otherwise used except at the very end of the Finale, where the key of E flat is also taken over for the first time by the Portuguese, doubtless to underline their victory (and also to end the opera in the tonality with which it began). The tonal characterisation of the Portuguese is not so clear, but D major, the principal tonality at the beginning of Act II, seems consciously to be used in opposition to E flat; thus Tristan's and Jessonda's recognition duet in the second Finale is in D major and is interrupted on the arrival of Dandau by an abrupt modulation to E flat and the introduction of trombones. Other things associated with the Indians are the 6/8 metre in which all the Bayaderes' music is written, and the use of cymbals, triangle etc. to accompany their dances. Overall the orchestration in *Jessonda* is masterly; the use of divided violas without violins in the Larghetto of Dandau's and Nadori's duet (no. 3) gives it an appropriately sombre character, and throughout the opera the wind instruments are deployed with Spohr's accustomed sensitivity. One of the many examples of imaginative orchestration may be cited to illustrate his feeling for orchestral colour: ex. 114 with its low flutes, clarinets and horn perfectly conveys a sense of foreboding as the two Bayaderes attempt to array Jessonda for the sacrifice.

Ex. 114

It is evident that Spohr saw *Jessonda* as the embodiment of his theories, and it is equally evident, from the reception which the opera met with throughout Germany, that he was right in feeling he had produced a work that was ripe for its time and for the mood of his compatriots. *Jessonda* was in many ways as much of a milestone in German opera as Weber's *Der Freischütz*. It may not have obtained the distinction of having its tunes whistled in the streets, but its influence on musicians and musical cognoscenti was profound. Its impact at the time is attested in Frau von Bawr's *Geschichte der Musik für Freunde und Verehrer dieser Kunst* (1825), where, discussing opera, she observed:

After Weber comes Spohr: indeed, through his opera *Jessonda* he has successfully wrestled for the palm with the composer of *Der Freischütz* even in northern Germany. Earlier Spohr was known as a greater violinist and instrumental composer, though he had also produced the operas *Faust* and *Zemire und Azor*, which despite many excellences, were not generally known.[18]

The extraordinary reception which *Jessonda* gained at its first performance in Leipzig in 1824 was remembered as late as 1884, when the *Musical Times* recalled:

After the charming duet between Nadori and Amazili in the second act, an excited enthusiast in the boxes rose and made a speech, demanding three times three cheers for the true 'master of German art', which were duly given, with deafening flourishes of drums and trumpets, forming a scene which has only once since (at Bayreuth in 1876) seen its parallel. [19]

Following the opera's success in Leipzig it was produced by Guhr in June 1824 at Frankfurt and in 1825, at Spontini's invitation, under Spohr's baton, in Berlin, where it achieved a similar triumph. By the end of the decade it was firmly established in the repertoires of almost all the theatres in Germany and remained a repertoire piece until the First World War. Among *Jessonda's* notable interpreters later in the century were Wagner, von Bülow, Mahler and Richard Strauss, while Brahms was numbered among its ardent admirers; he once exclaimed after a performance of *Jessonda* in Vienna (probably during the 1880s): 'I find the opera magnificent. But, of course, I saw and learned to love it in my early days, and it affects me in the same way as my other youthful enthusiasms do. *Jessonda* captured my heart and I shall feel the same about it for the rest of my life.'[20]

The success of *Jessonda* more than any other single event, perhaps, confirmed Spohr as one of Germany's leading composers. By the end of the decade there were few in Germany or England who would have disputed his claim to be recognised as the greatest of all living composers, for those who might be thought to have rivalled or surpassed him were all dead before 1830. Weber survived the première of Jessonda by less than three years; Beethoven followed him to the grave a year later, and Schubert, whose works were just beginning to attract notice in the musical world, died the year after that. Spohr stood head and shoulders above those who were left. But it was not just *Jessonda* and the successful compositions which followed during the next ten years that validated Spohr's claim to pre-eminence; having long been accepted as the greatest of German violinists and a composer of distinction, he was now also able to establish himself as a great conductor and musical reformer. Having brought the standard of his orchestra and opera to a lustre which was inferior to none, Spohr began a vigorous policy of introducing new operas to the repertoire. Between 1822 and 1832 more than forty new operas were introduced to Kassel. These included Weber's *Freischütz* (1822), Lindpaintner's *Sulmona* and Rossini's *La Gazza Ladra* (1823), Weber's *Euryanthe* and Méhul's last opera *Valentine de Milan* (1824), Conradin Kreutzer's *Libussa* as well as two of Auber's earlier works and his own *Der Berggeist* (1825), Boieldieu's *La Dame Blanche*, Auber's *Le concert à la Cour* and Sacchini's *Oedipus auf Colonos* (1826), Weber's *Oberon*, Auber's *Le Maçon* and Spohr's own *Pietro von Abano* (1827), Lindpaintner's *Der Vampyr*, Rossini's *Le Siège de Corinthe* and Meyerbeer's *Il Crociato* (1828), Auber's *La Muette de Portici* (1829), Spohr's own *Der Alchymist* (1830), Ferdinand Ries' *Die Räuberbraut*, Auber's *Fra Diavolo* and Rossini's *Guillaume Tell* (1831). As the above list indicates, there was nothing one-sided in Spohr's choice of works. The encouragement of German composers was balanced by a keen awareness of other contemporary developments, and Spohr's well-known critical opinion of Rossini did not prevent him from bringing his operas to the stage. He recognised the worthwhile qualities even in works which he could not wholeheartedly admire.

A similar eclecticism is shown in Spohr's choice of works for the orchestra's subscription concerts. Over the next thirty years he initiated the Kassel public into the beauties of many works by Haydn, Mozart and Beethoven hitherto unknown to them, as well as introducing the works of his younger contemporaries such as Mendelssohn, Schumann and Schubert, and even Liszt and Berlioz. In addition to directing the opera and the subscription concerts Spohr enriched the musical life of Kassel by instituting, within a few months of his arrival in 1822, a St Cecilia Society which gave a number of choral concerts each year. As a result of the formation of this society he was able to take an active part in the revival of Bach's music, in which he had been interested for a number of years (he had owned the autograph of Bach's Two- and Three-part Inventions since his time in Gotha), but it also had the effect of stimulating his own desire to write choral music. His first composition for the society was a modest enough effort, a *Hymne an die heilige Cäcilie* (later published as op. 97) for chorus, soprano solo and organ, which he wrote for performance on 22 November 1823, when the soprano solo was taken by his daughter Emilie. It was not to be long, however, before his quiescent interest in oratorio was reawakened, leading to the production of a succession of works which in their own field were to have as great an effect on his reputation as *Jessonda*.

Apart from the *Hymne*, 1823 saw the composition of a scena and aria, 'Tu m'abandonnai ingrato' (op. 71), which greatly impressed Edward Holmes when he heard it during his visit in 1826, a *quatuor brillant* in A major (op. 68), and two potpourris on themes from *Jessonda* (op. 66 for violin and orchestra and op. 64 for violin, cello and orchestra). The most substantial and interesting of the works composed in 1823, however, was the Double Quartet in D minor op. 65, which he wrote during March and April. On 4 April he wrote to Speyer:

I have already completed three movements of a double quartet. This is a wholly new kind of instrumental work, which, so far as I know, I am the first to attempt. It is most like a piece for double chorus, for the two quartets who co-operate here work against one another in about the same proportion as the two choirs do. I am very eager to hear the effect and am consequently hastening to finish.[21]

The double quartet was given for the first time in the house of Spohr's friend Otto von der Malsburg, whose music room was the largest of those in which his quartet circle's meetings took place, and was soon afterwards published by Peters.

Spohr was not correct in believing himself to have been the first composer to attempt the genre; in 1804 Albrechtsberger had published a set of 'Trois Sonates à deux choeurs, savoir deux Violons, Alto et Basse du premier, et deux violons, Alto et Basse du deuxième Choeur', each of which consists of an adagio and a fugue. Spohr, however, derived the idea from Andreas Romberg (who may possibly have known Albrechtsberger's sonatas), who had written two movements, a first Allegro and a Minuet and Trio, of a projected double quartet. At their last meeting before Romberg's death the problems and possibilities of such a work had been discussed, and Spohr, who readily responded to a musical challenge, had at length carried it out.

In his three subsequent double quartets, Spohr was to aim for greater equality between the two quartets; in op. 65 he treated them essentially like concertino and ripieno. There are some passages in which they answer one another, but in general the second quartet plays an accompanying role to the brilliant concerto-like writing of the first (Spohr's pupil Hubert Ries even performed the work in Berlin in 1834 arranged as a concerto for string quartet and orchestra), though the two quartets sometimes join forces for emphasis. As in so many of Spohr's compositions the first movement is based almost entirely on material from the opening theme, which falls into two parts – a vigorous unison opening and a more lyrical continuation (ex. 115). The second subject is a major-mode version of this theme and the codetta sees another transformation of it. In the development, after a bold modulation from A to D flat major, he introduces a new theme which is accompanied by figures derived from the opening of the main theme. The Scherzo in G minor makes very effective use of a contrast between a staccato and legato phrase, while the G major Trio is like a gently lilting siciliano in which the second quartet accompanies solos by the members of the first quartet, with an ostinato rhythm. An interesting touch is the return of the Trio material, in G minor, after the repetition of the Scherzo, to form a coda. The Scherzo is followed by a simple Larghetto, which could appropriately be called 'Song without Words' (having a close affinity with the style Mendelssohn was to adopt in a number of his *Lieder ohne Worte*). In the Finale – an Allegro molto in D major – there is a formal peculiarity found in a number of Spohr's other sonata movements, in that recapitulation begins with the second-subject material.

The D minor Double Quartet awakened great interest when it became known, and was widely regarded as having added another branch to the already impressive laurel wreath which, in the imagery of the day, encircled Spohr's ample brow. A reviewer of the first Vienna performance at one of Schuppanzigh's quartet concerts described it as 'a work of art which by itself would suggest the place of honour for its composer among the most excellent masters, if it were not that each of his works bears the stamp of the highest

Ex. 115

mastery'.[22] G. W. Fink, reviewing it in 1828, made the decisive judgement: 'Adequate perusal and attentive listening to the present work of art has been sufficient to convince us that it is the best of Spohr's works in every respect which he has yet produced.'[23] And the Viennese *Allgemeiner Musikalischer Anzeiger*, in an enthusiastic article on Spohr's music in general, commented: 'To lavish yet more praise on this double quartet, upon which universal opinion – *vox populi, vox Dei* – has already plainly and unequivocally pronounced would be like carrying coals to Newcastle' (literally: owls to Athens).[24]

Spohr began the year 1824 in the best of spirits. His musical activities were flourishing, and his domestic life in the charming new house, where they had gathered their first harvest of fruit and vegetables in the autumn, was idyllic. He wrote to Speyer on 6 January:

We have begun the New Year healthy and happy, and live in our new property very contentedly and free from any care. I also continue to be very satisfied with my work; our music becomes continually better and will soon be able to rank with the best. In our grand concerts in the theatre this year the symphonies in particular were almost perfectly executed and thus aroused the public's warmest interest. Also there is brisk competition among our soloists to see who can produce the greatest excellence. I have formed a quartet circle jointly with two cultured art-loving families, in which this kind of music is performed with the greatest possible perfection. After the music we remain together until eleven or twelve o'clock and converse only about artistic matters. In this manner we have also played in the New Year.[25]

After returning from the triumphant performance of *Jessonda* in Leipzig, Spohr settled down to work on a set of three violin duets (op. 67), the first he had composed since 1816, and completed them during March and April 1824. His renewed teaching activities and the outstanding abilities of his pupils, among whom at that time were Ferdinand David and Friedrich Pacius, were doubtless responsible for this re-awakened interest. These duets are far from being mere teaching pieces, however, for he once more showed his sensitivity to instrumental sonorities and his deep understanding of the violin. They are less taxing than the op. 39 set, but no less effective.

While working on these duets Spohr received a request from the Elector to compose a new opera for performance as part of the festivities to be held in celebration of the marriage of his daughter, Marie, to Duke Bernhard Erich of Saxe-Meiningen in March 1825. After the success of *Jessonda* Spohr was far from unwilling to undertake the task. He decided upon using Carl August Musäus' 'Wie Rübezahl zu seinem Namen Kam', which had appeared in his *Volksmärchen der Deutschen* (1782–7), as a basis for the plot – the same story which he had requested the ill-fated Körner to make into a libretto for him in 1812. For his librettist on this occasion he turned, not unnaturally, to Eduard Gehe, and sent him a draft plan with the order of scenes to work from. The resulting libretto, however, did not come up to his expectations; as he observed to Speyer, Gehe 'made such a monstrosity of it that I sent him his payment but straightaway laid the work aside'.[26] He then asked Georg Döring, with whom he had collaborated over the abortive *Der schwarze Jäger* in Frankfurt six years earlier, to produce a libretto for him. He believed that one reason for the unsatisfactoriness of Gehe's version was the adherence to rhyme and metre, so he stipulated that Döring should avoid them altogether, and he felt subsequently that the resulting version had 'gained infinitely in truth and character' and that it was 'on the whole very amusing'.[27] Had there not been such urgency to begin work on the music Spohr might perhaps have taken a more critical attitude towards the material; with hindsight he later recognised its weakness. In fact, of all the librettos of Spohr's mature operas, that of *Der Berggeist* is by far the most unsatisfactory.

The scenario is as follows: Beneath the mountain the earth gnomes are seen digging for treasure. Troll, a man who has become a gnome, tells his fellow spirits and their ruler, the Berggeist, about the joys of human love. The Berggeist, hearing this, determines to discover the nature of love by kidnapping a mortal woman. The next scene takes place above ground, where the wedding of Alma and Oskar is in preparation. Ludmilla, Alma's maid, warns the other servants to avoid a certain spot in the mountains where the gnomes are supposed to have power. Then follows a duet between the bride and bridegroom. Alma's father, Prince Domoslav, joins them and after a trio all except Alma, who wishes to have a few moments alone, proceed to church for the wedding. The Berggeist and attendant gnomes interrupt Alma's aria, and despite the reappearance of Oskar, whom the Berggeist fixes to the spot by magic, the terrified Alma is dragged off and all attempts at rescue are frustrated by a supernaturally raised storm. The second act begins once again in the subterranean domain, where the Berggeist attempts to win Alma's love and, to please her, allows her to summon the spirits of her earthly friends. Troll flirts with the spirit of Ludmilla, but finding that as a wraith she is incapable of love, decides to return to earth to capture the real thing. This he accomplishes, as Domoslav reports to Oskar in a brief scene. The rest of the act takes place below in preparation for the Berggeist's union with Alma. In Act III Ludmilla is brought beneath the mountain by Troll, where she soon begins to plot her and Alma's escape. She promises Troll that if he helps them she will be his. The Berggeist is implausibly duped into counting the flowers he has raised to please Alma, and while he is thus engaged Troll, Alma and Ludmilla make their escape. Reunited with Oskar they think themselves safe, but the Berggeist overtakes them. However, after a confrontation, the Berggeist agrees that human love is not for him, blesses the pair and returns to his realm with Troll.

Whether such feeble material could ever have been made the basis of an effective Romantic opera libretto is a moot point. Other composers of the period certainly thought that it could, for the story was used by Franz Tuczek (1801), Weber (1805), Wilhelm Würfel (1824), Lindpaintner (1830) and Christian Gottlieb Müller (1840), though none of these operas enjoyed any more success than *Der Berggeist*. But whether or not they could have made something of it, it was certainly not in tune with Spohr's musical temperament. In Spohr's version a number of substantial alterations were made to Musäus' original at the composer's request. Most importantly he changed the Rübezahl, a comic buffoon-like character in Musäus' tale, into the more powerful and serious Berggeist,* but in doing so he fell into the absurdity of

---

* See the letters of Döring to Spohr of 22 March, 3 and 12 April, and 5 December, in the Murhardsche Bibliothek der Stadt Kassel und Landesbibliothek.

taking an essentially grotesque and humorous story too seriously, ending up with something which was neither a comic fantasy nor a credible drama. Döring did nothing to alleviate the problem. His delineation of character is stiff and conventional, and he was unable to give any sort of dramatic coherence to his heterogeneous material.

In contrast to the feebleness and conventionality of the libretto, the musical treatment of the opera is of great interest for in *Der Berggeist* Spohr travelled considerably further along the road towards 'music drama' which he had taken with *Jessonda*. This opera is likewise through-composed, but Spohr dispensed entirely with 'numbers', constructing it instead in 'scenes', these being built up into extensive complexes with long stretches of unbroken action. There is far less 'secco' recitative than in *Jessonda*, and while the constituent elements of traditional opera – aria, ensemble, accompagnato scena, etc. – are still recognisable, these are almost invariably open-ended; thus, though much of the music of these portions is as attractive as that of *Zemire und Azor* and *Jessonda*, little could be extracted for use in the concert hall.

The most powerful parts of the opera are the sections where Spohr dispensed with conventional forms entirely, and through a mixture of chorus, aria and recitative, combined with bold orchestral and harmonic effects, achieved a genuine dramatic pace. This style is used much more intensively here than in his earlier operas; the sorts of static set pieces such as he had employed at the beginnings of the first and second acts of *Jessonda* are avoided in *Der Berggeist* (though the opportunity for ballet and scenic effects provided by the Berggeist's attempts to entertain Alma in Act II are not passed over). A good example of Spohr's flexible use of harmony and texture in dramatic arioso is the Berggeist's first attempt to woo Alma at the beginning of Act II, in the section beginning 'Dein Anblick hat der Liebe Flamme in meinem Innern angefacht', with its characteristic alternation between A major/minor and F major. The two final scenes of the first act may be taken as illustrative of the sort or large-scale structures which are typical of the opera. Scene 6 begins with a short Larghetto (E flat 12/8) played by the orchestra while Alma, who at her own request has been left alone for a while, dwells on her first meeting with Oskar. She expresses her thoughts in short passages of recitative which are separated by renewed sections of larghetto. After an increase in tempo, a motif from the gnomes' music in the Introduction to Act I makes a brief appearance in the orchestra, giving a hint of their as yet unsuspected proximity. Alma takes up the Larghetto theme at tempo primo and sings of her love for Oskar; this, however, is interrupted by another appearance of the gnome theme and a subdued off-stage chorus. The tempo presses forward more urgently, and Alma experiences nameless feelings of disquiet. The chorus ceases, her anxiety subsides and the Larghetto is resumed, but only briefly; the gnomes renew their chorus, the music speeds up to allegro agitato and modulates to E flat minor as the gnomes finally make their presence apparent to Alma. A climax is reached when the Berggeist himself appears and in a dramatic recitative makes clear his intention of abducting Alma. After a confrontation between Alma and the Berggeist, accompanied by declamatory interjections from the chorus, a new climax is reached at the beginning of scene 7 (Allegro molto, C minor) with the arrival of Oskar in response to Alma's cries for help. The Berggeist's motif (first heard in the overture and used on several occasions later in the opera to accompany his appearance or the threat of his appearance) now begins to play a part in the musical texture. Domoslav and his retainers also arrive, but all are rendered impotent to help Alma by the Berggeist's power. Another stringendo leads to an Alla breve, and the act drives to a powerful conclusion as Alma is carried off. At no point in these scenes does musical logic take precedence over the dramatic exigencies of the situation, and the same is true of many other scenes in the opera.

There is much effective dramatic music in *Der Berggeist*, which, had it been composed to a more suitable libretto, would doubtless have provided a worthy successor to *Jessonda*. As it was, the discrepancy between the Romantic conception of the music and the absurdity of the libretto inevitably condemned the opera to failure.

At its première in Kassel on 24 March 1824, *Der Berggeist* was rapturously received, and Speyer, who had come over for the occasion, wrote a glowing review for the *AMZ*, in which he gave weight to Spohr's own views on the superiority of German over Italian music, saying at one point: 'It seems to us a cheering sign that in recent times the excellent dramatic compositions of the truly German Spohr have found the most joyful acceptance in all places which had not, through proximity to Italy, or because of local conditions, developed a taste for well-polished trivialities and titillating sentimentality.'[28] In Leipzig, where it was brought out in September of the same year, it also had an enthusiastic reception and the composer was again cheered by the audience to the accompaniment of flourishes of trumpets and drums. Spohr described his reception as 'the most flattering I have ever yet experienced' and, overwhelmed by the occasion, convinced himself that 'this music from beginning to end is genuinely dramatic'.[29] He did not perceive that the applause was more a tribute to the composer of *Jessonda* than an endorsement of *Der Berggeist*. A reviewer of the Leipzig performance was not so blinded by the brilliance of the occasion nor, like Speyer and Spohr himself, anxious to be a propagandist for German opera, and while finding much to admire he noted soberly that it 'found applause, but not so universally as *Jessonda*'.[30]

When Sir George Smart visited Kassel in 1825 he spent an evening at Spohr's house playing through the newly printed vocal score of *Der Berggeist* with Spohr, his wife and daughters singing the various roles. He noted in his diary: 'I had a tight job with the music which appears fine but is very difficult',[31] and he also remarked that Spohr intended sending the score to a theatre in London; but *Der Berggeist* was never produced there, though the duet 'O calma o bella' was performed at the Philharmonic Society in 1830 and 1831, and parts of the opera found their way into a conglomerate production entitled *Der Alchymist* (see p. 206 below) at Covent Garden in 1832. In fact following the Leipzig production its only subsequent staging outside Kassel seems to have been at Prague in 1837, and it never became a repertoire piece.

After the busy time occasioned by the preparations for the Princess Marie's wedding (for which Spohr had also composed a Torch Dance for the Hessian Army's fifty-three trumpeters and two pairs of kettledrums, and a Festival March into which, at the Elector's request, he introduced the German folk song 'Und als der Grossvater die Grossmutter nahm'), he was once more able to apply himself to composition. In response to a commission from Count Brühl, Intendant of the Berlin Hoftheater, he composed incidental music to accompany a production of *Macbeth*, consisting of an overture and seven numbers (op. 75). The overture opens with an atmospheric Andante grave and contains some felicitous ideas in the following Allegro appassionato, particularly when an expected cadence into D major is frustrated by the brass, whose stern *fortissimo* unison B flat heralds E flat minor and the music of the opening. However, the undistinguished subject material causes the work to flag, and neither the overture nor the rest of the music seems quite to capture the mood of Shakespeare's play. It is in many ways too polished; as Zelter perspicaciously observed to Goethe, in a letter describing the production, 'The composer (Kapellmeister Spohr from Kassel) is a clever man, and were there not so many good details then the whole might have been better'.[32]

A far more significant and successful work than the *Macbeth* music was the Eleventh Violin Concerto in G major (op. 70), which he composed during the summer of 1825 after his return from a family visit to the Speyers in Offenbach. It is planned on an expansive scale and is impressive both for the lyrical quality of its themes and for the unity of the whole work. The first movement opens with twenty-two bars of symphonic Adagio and then, dispensing with the customary orchestral tutti, the soloist enters after only seven bars of the Allegro vivace with an assertive theme. The second main theme is a genuinely Romantic one, which unfolds in an almost improvisatory manner over a recollection in the orchestra of the opening idea of the movement (ex. 116). The second movement, an Adagio in E minor, is another fine example of Spohr's sensitively ornamented cantabile, though it also contains some highly effective passages of violin figuration quite unlike anything in the earlier concertos. The Rondo (Allegretto), with which the concerto concludes, suffers somewhat from rhythmic squareness, a fault to which Spohr is not infrequently prone; however, like the rest of the concerto

Ex. 116

(Ex. 116 cont.)

it contains an abundance of brilliant idiomatic writing and appealing melodic ideas. Overall, much of the thematic material, together with the richly chromatic harmonic treatment which it receives, seems to presage the later Romantic violin concertos of Wieniavski, Bruch, and even Brahms and Tchaikovsky.

Spohr gave the first performance of the concerto in a concert in Leipzig during his visit there to conduct *Der Berggeist*. With all his other duties and activities since moving to Kassel he had tended to neglect his violin playing during the spring and summer, only taking it up again seriously when his winter quartet meetings came round (see *WS* p. 80). It was thus with some trepidation that he appeared before the Leipzig public again as a violinist, remarking, 'I had often been heard in Leipzig in my best period and expectation was very high.' Notwithstanding the many rehearsals and other distractions therefore, he ensured that he found time every day during his stay for a couple of hours' practice, and in the event his performance of the new concerto had a gratifying reception. According to his own account written shortly after the concert, 'The enthusiasm grew from movement to movement so that because of the applause no one heard a note of all the short tuttis in the Rondo.'[33] In connection with Spohr's violin playing at about this time it is interesting to note that Edward Holmes wrote after visiting Kassel some twelve months later: 'It may be said . . . that though he plays less now than formerly, being much engaged in composition, his taste seems, if possible, heightened.'[34]

X

Oratorio and opera: success and failure
1825–1830

Shortly before Spohr's visit to Leipzig for the première of *Der Berggeist* in 1825 Friedrich Rochlitz, whose glowing review of his playing and compositions twenty-one years earlier had launched him on his career, wrote to him with the proposition that he should set to music an oratorio text which he had compiled. Spohr eagerly seized upon the idea, and not simply because he was inspired by the concept of writing an oratorio; his reasons were rather more calculated. As he explained to Speyer,

From the enclosed letter from Rochlitz you will see what I intend as a major task for next winter. The reasons why I have decided on this are as follows: (1) In order to give my operas time for further dissemination, I ought not to write a new one immediately; also I will exhaust and repeat myself if I always tackle the same genre of composition. (2) If I had not promised to compose Rochlitz's really excellent text immediately I would probably have lost it, and (3) I have the inclination and I hope the talent to write in the style specified in the letter, and finally, now is the right time, when there are so many choral societies and musical festivals, to come forward with such a work.[1]

He began the composition of the oratorio immediately on his return from Leipzig, towards the end of September, and had finished the first part in time to give a performance of it with piano accompaniment at the St Cecilia Day concert in Kassel. Hauptmann wrote to his friend Hauser after this performance: 'The music is very fine; it begins rather tamely, but you do not feel this afterwards, when he has warmed to his subject.'[2] Spohr himself, writing to Speyer, mentioned that he had noticed the deep impression the performance had made on performers and listeners alike, and continued:

The observation was of the greatest importance to me, for it convinced me that I had found the right style for this work. That is, I have taken pains to be really simple, reverent and true in expression, and have carefully avoided all affectations, pomposities and difficulties. The advantage is: straightforward practicability for amateur societies, for whom the work is principally intended, and through that an easier apprehension of my ideas by the general public.[3]

By February 1826 he had finished the whole oratorio, which was given its first complete performance on Good Friday in Kassel. Spohr wrote that 'The effect was, though I say it myself, extraordinary. Never have I derived such satisfaction from the performance of one of my major works.'[4]

Die letzten Dinge is a remarkably original conception – Hauptmann thought it 'only too modern'. On a formal level Spohr's treatment is in many ways analogous with his approach to opera, but in some respects it is clear that Rochlitz's ideas on the musical treatment of the work, as set out in his correspondence with Spohr, were not without influence on its final form. The extensive overture and the long orchestral introduction to the second part as well as the orchestral postlude to 'Gefallen ist Babylon' (no. 18) were directly in line with Rochlitz's suggestion in his letter of 18 July 1825, where, after making specific recommendations, he continued:

You will easily see, by the way, that I have left scope for the most perfect orchestral music – which after all is the finest achievement of our music – to stand on its own (thus also allowing the depiction of those innermost feelings that are beyond words) which has never been the case before in vocal music; and you, who along with Beethoven are without a doubt the greatest master of this genre, will assuredly produce the most excellent effects with it.[5]

In a subsequent letter of 1 November, which accompanied some additional text that Spohr had requested in order to make the work a more satisfactory length, Rochlitz made suggestions about the treatment of the new items, most of which Spohr seems to have accepted. Spohr followed his recommendation that 'Sei mir nicht schrecklich' (no. 15) should be a duet. He was also influenced by Rochlitz's detailed ideas about the setting of 'So ihr mich' (no. 16); this, Rochlitz argued, should be written in the 'old Roman church style' with 'all the voices in semibreves and minims, in unison', with an accompaniment in staccato crotchets (giving the example of the opening of Spohr's own overture to *Jessonda*) or in counterpoint. Spohr adopted the second idea, writing a fugue in E minor for the orchestra (also used as the middle section of the introductory Sinfonia to Part II) with unison voices. It is possible also that Rochlitz was responsible for Spohr's use of alternating quartet and chorus – an effect much admired by contemporaries – for though he did not adopt it for 'Und siehe ein Lamm' (no. 5) as Rochlitz advised, he did use it with great effect for 'Selig sind die Todten' (no. 19), which was almost certainly composed after 1 November, and for 'Heil! der Erbarmer' (no. 12), which may well have been composed after receipt of the letter.

The most immediately striking feature of *Die letzten Dinge* is its unity. As in his operas, Spohr used the repetition of musical material as a unifying device. A particularly prominent idea is the cadential figure in ex. 117, which first appears in the Andante grave of the overture and seems always to have a 'holy' connotation. Spohr's association of this cadence with the church is indicated by its appearance in the cathedral scene in *Faust* (without the chromatic inflection in the final bar) (ex. 118). This association was carried over into subsequent works, for the final bar of the same cadence is to be found with a similar connotation in his next oratorio, *Des Heilands letzte Stunden*, and

Ex. 117

[Andante grave]
[woodwind]

pp

Ex. 118

[Andante]

p

in the Seventh Symphony, *Irdisches und Göttliches im Menschenleben*. It does, however, also appear in other works where no such association can have been intended and is symptomatic of his increasingly unreflective reliance on stock cadential formulae. Spohr also aimed at unity in the overall structure of the oratorio. As in *Der Berggeist* he sought to avoid a mere succession of separate numbers. There are few items which could satisfactorily be extracted for individual performance, and no self-contained solos. Apart from the duet 'Sei mir nicht schrecklich', *Die letzten Dinge* contains no formal numbers for the soloists; they are used either for sections of arioso-like recitative, or for solo or ensemble passages in the choruses. The majority of numbers are directly linked to one another by musical means, and even where one number ends with a sense of finality, the beginning of the next usually indicates that an *attacca* is intended, as for instance nos. 10 and 11 where, after a firm E major ending to the chorus, the following recitative begins tentatively in the same key, and after a four-bar stringendo it arrives at F major (the key of the number). This sort of abrupt juxtaposition of keys is a typical feature of the work and undoubtedly accounts for much of the fascination which it exerted on contemporaries, for it imparted an unprecedented kind of expressiveness to the music. No composer before Spohr had used modulation and chromatic alteration so intensively to illustrate the nuances of his text. The constant modulation and harmonic colouring which in his instrumental music often seemed like mere caprice was given palpable significance when allied to the emotional implications of the words. This relationship of harmony and meaning is already clearly apparent in Spohr's earlier setting of words, in his Lieder opp. 37 and 41 and in *Faust* as well as in his later operas, but in *Die letzten Dinge* he brought it to a new level of intensity. Sometimes, indeed, there seems an almost aimless quality to his modulations; a typical example of his tonal wandering is the solo section 'Siehe er kommt' in the first chorus, which, beginning and ending in F major, goes through C minor, B flat major, E flat major, E flat minor, B major, G minor, B flat major and D minor in twenty-nine bars. On the whole, though, the harmony is closely related to the text (as in ex. 119),

Ex. 119

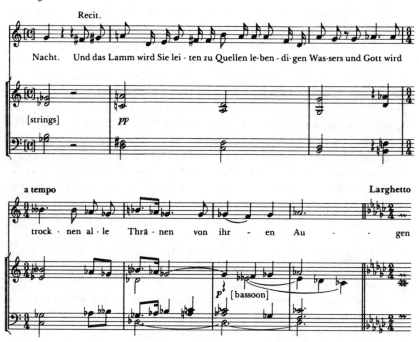

and Spohr achieves a high degree of expressiveness which must have been particularly telling to an audience whose ears had not been schooled by later developments. Innumerable contemporary accounts from the 1820s and 1830s testify unequivocally that this was precisely the effect it did have.

The success of *Die letzten Dinge* was tremendous. Spohr had been correct to speculate that the time was ripe for oratorio, and he had accurately matched his music to the taste of the day. In May 1826 when he directed it at the Rhenish Music Festival at Düsseldorf it was received with such enthusiasm that the festival had to be prolonged by a day so that it could be performed for a second time. A selection from the oratorio in piano arrangement, which Spohr hastened to publish, was quickly sold out, and the full vocal score was then issued by Simrock. After that the work rapidly gained a very wide circulation in Germany and further increased Spohr's already high reputation.

The oratorio's impact in England, after its first performance at the Norwich Festival of 1830, was even more profound, for it was able to do what *Jessonda* could never have done in England, transforming Spohr virtually overnight from an instrumental composer who was an object of admiration only among connoisseurs and professional musicians into an almost universally acknowledged master of the first rank. The effect of *The Last Judgement* (as it was entitled in England) on English opinion will be dealt with more fully in a later chapter.

After the effort and challenge of composing *Die letzten Dinge* Spohr returned to the more familiar field of chamber music, and in April 1826 composed his B minor String Quintet (op. 69). Between July and September he completed a set of six Lieder (op. 72), and in the months of August, November and December he wrote one each of a set of three string quartets (op. 74). Coming freshly to chamber music again after a gap of three years and stimulated by writing for quintet, which he had not done for more than ten years, Spohr's inventiveness was at a high level in the B minor String Quintet. The fine, dramatic first movement is, like that of the D minor Double Quartet, dominated by the material of its opening theme. The Scherzo, one of Spohr's most vigorous, is more diatonic than usual and has an almost Beethovenian directness; the Trio is wholly in Spohr's own idiom. There is a simple but masterly transition from Scherzo to Trio (ex. 120), and the whole movement is among the best of its kind. The Adagio which follows is at the same high level as the preceding movements; its last twelve bars, with their hesitant syncopations and ambiguous harmony, are quintessential Spohr (ex. 121). A barcarolle-like Allegretto concludes the quintet; the initial mood (ex. 122) is sustained at a low dynamic (with only two brief crescendos to *forte*) for more than sixty bars, creating a marvellous sense of suspended animation. Although the semiquaver figurations on which the next section is based are conventional and somewhat mechanical (ex. 123), and the movement does not quite sustain its early promise, the final section is highly effective. The quintet certainly does not deserve its current neglect.

None of the op. 74 quartets seems quite to match the overall quality of the B minor Quintet, though individual movements are fine. The Allegro vivace of op. 74 no. 1 in A minor may be numbered among the best of his quartet first movements; it makes very cogent use of a terse figure which begins the movement (ex. 124). The presence of this figure is also felt during the contrasted second subject (ex. 125). Another of its many forms presages the lamentations of the Nibelungen in Wagner's *Das Rheingold* (ex. 126). The other movements of this quartet do not rise to the same heights; the Finale in particular, with its undistinguished, even trivial, theme which harks back to Rode (ex. 127), is very disappointing. No movement of op. 74 no. 2 in B flat falls to this level, and the work is written in a more balanced quartet style, but only the dreamy Larghetto, in G minor, rises above the merely work-

Ex. 120

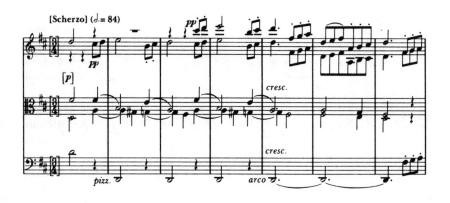

Ex. 121

Ex. 122

Ex. 123

Ex. 124

Ex. 125

Ex. 126

Ex. 127

manlike. An interesting feature of this quartet is that there is no minuet or
scherzo, the middle two movements being the Larghetto and an Allegretto
con variazioni in 2/4. Op. 74 no. 3 in D minor is the best of the set as a whole,
though here too the stereotyped treatment of the sonata-form movements
and the reliance on stock violin figurations such as ex. 128 are undeniable

Ex. 128

weaknesses. Spohr pertinaciously adopted the same procedure in the exposition sections of the first movements of almost all his chamber works – first subject, passagework, second subject, more passagework leading to a heavily emphasised cadence, codetta – and with the passage of time, as his harmonic and melodic mannerisms became more pronounced and inflexible, this led (with some notable exceptions) to monotony and staleness. This is especially true of chamber works in which the violin dominates, where it often seems as if his fingers rather than his mind determine the contours of the music.

The six Lieder op. 72, on their smaller scale, are far more successful, all of them possessing considerable charm and expressiveness within the limits of Spohr's essentially lyrical nature. All but the first song are through-composed, and Spohr again shows his sensitivity to the details of the text. In no. 2, 'Schifferlied der Wasserfee' (Tiecke), there is a characteristic passage where his chromaticism seems not gratuitous but essential to the expression (ex. 129). Many similar instances could be cited from these Lieder. The piano writing is more idiomatic than in the previous sets and, though it still does not always quite suit the conformation of the hand, there is a wider range of textures and sonorities. A nice touch is in the final song, 'Schlaflied' (Tieck), when, just before the text mentions the singing of birds, the piano anticipates it and continues periodically to imitate birdsong. Spohr's cadential mannerisms are as prominent as ever in these Lieder; the suspended dominant thirteenth occurs in four of the six, while another old favourite is to be found in no. 4 (ex. 130).

The New Year of 1827 brought with it the desire once again to write an opera. *Der Berggeist's* lack of success doubtless rankled with Spohr. He realised that the weak libretto was in a large measure to blame and thus eagerly siezed upon the chance of what seemed to him an excellent adaptation of Tieck's novel *Pietro von Abano* by the young Kassel lawyer and poet Carl Pfeiffer. Pfeiffer initially offered the libretto to Carl Friedrich Curschmann, a twenty-three-year-old musician who had come to Kassel as Spohr's pupil, but when Curschmann enthusiastically showed Spohr the libretto and told him of his plan to write an opera, Spohr talked him out of the project, probably on the grounds that it was too ambitious for him. Whether Spohr's motive in dissuading Curschmann was an entirely disinterested one is impossible to determine; it is clear that he was greatly impressed by the libretto. But, whatever the case, an arrangement was quickly arrived at between Spohr, Curschmann and Pfeiffer, and after a few alterations had been made to the libretto Spohr started work on it in February 1827 and wrote to Speyer saying, 'never have I begun a task with such ardour'.[6]

The story (considerably modified from Tieck) is set in medieval Padua. Antonio, a Florentine nobleman, has just returned to Padua to claim his bride Cäcilie, the daughter of the Podesta of Padua and his wife, Eudoxia. His joy at returning is turned to despair when a funeral procession

Ex. 129

Ohn' Sorgen nur wei·ter, wie hei·ter der Mor – gen! fliess

Bächlein, fahr Schifflein ohn' Sor – gen nur wei – ter, be · geg – net doch

al   les   wie Schick sal ver · hangt;

Ex. 130

(a) [Allegretto]

wen - den

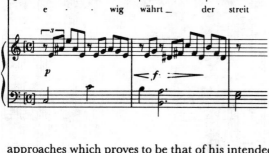

(b) [Allegro agitato]

e - wig währt _ der streit

approaches which proves to be that of his intended bride. While the Podesta and Eudoxia are attempting to comfort him, they are interrupted by the merriment of a band of students hailing the skills of their teacher Pietro von Abano. Pietro himself appears and apologises for the unseemly behaviour of his students, after which the procession goes on its way. It then transpires that Pietro, whose amorous advances Cäcilie had refused, plans to obtain her corpse and bring it back to a semblance of life, by sorcery, in order to satisfy his lust. The next scene finds Antonio wandering forlornly in a forest, where he comes upon Rosa, Cäcilie's twin sister, who has been kidnapped by bandits. At first he mistakes her for Cäcilie, but she explains the position and they are just about to escape when the bandits return. Despite Antonio's heroic efforts to cut his way through them, they overpower him and he is left for dead. The final scene of the first act takes place in Pietro's house, where the sorcerer, with the aid of his servant, Beresinth, and a chorus of invisible spirits, attempts to reanimate Cäcilie's corpse. In this he is successful but Cäcilie, realising the horror of her position, falls into a swoon. The next act begins with Eudoxia and her husband, who tells her that Antonio has found Rosa but was wounded in the attempt to rescue her and is now being taken

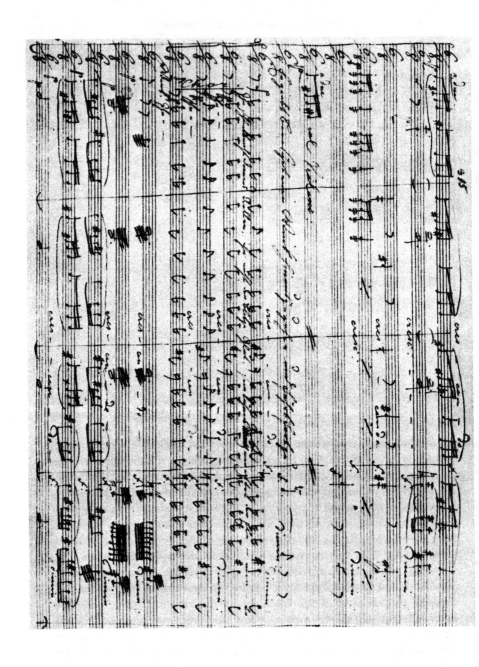

care of in Pietro's house (they are still unaware of Pietro's depravity). The Podesta determines to go with a troop of soldiers to free Rosa from the robbers. Meanwhile, in Pietro's house, the sorcerer is watching over the body of the slumbering Cäcilie. He leaves her still sleeping, and Antonio, who has been wandering about the house, stumbles upon her. She wakes and tells him how her soul was suddenly hindered from going to Heaven and is suspended between life and death by Pietro's sorcery. She cuts short Antonio's protestations of love and tells him sadly that she must be restored to death and that for this to be accomplished she must be taken to the cathedral where a priest's benediction will be able to release her soul. Antonio agrees, unwillingly, to comply with her wishes. Back in the Podesta's house Eudoxia anxiously awaits the return of Rosa; then both Rosa and Antonio return with the Podesta, accompanied by a crowd of rejoicing people. Antonio feels that Cäcilie wishes him to allow Rosa to replace her in his affections, and the two pledge their love for one another. Then, remembering his promise to Cäcilie, he hurries off to fulfil it. The final scene takes place in the cathedral, where Pietro is about to be consecrated Rector of the University. Antonio brings in the reanimated Cäcilie, who sinks down at the altar praying fervently and ultimately expires. He explains to the assembled people about Pietro's crime, and they hasten to put the sorcerer to death. The opera closes with a prayer and the betrothal of Antonio and Rosa.

Spohr finished the score of *Pietro von Abano* in August 1827, and the first performance took place in the Kassel Hoftheater on 13 October. It became clear immediately, however, that certain features of the story were likely to prove an obstacle to its general acceptance. There were elements in it which were too strong for the tastes of the day; the audience in Kassel seems to have found the opera both fascinating and repellent. Spohr described the second performance to Speyer, who had been over in Kassel for the première:

It went excellently this time without any error. A real deadly silence from beginning to end showed the active involvement of every listener. However, there was rousing applause only a few times and at the end of the opera; but the most gripping moments went without any such thing. The alterations and cuts worked very well, and I hold that the opera, its content and the treatment, is the best thing of its kind in the last twenty years. My friends are of the same opinion; but the ladies find several scenes too horrible.[7]

Spohr was far from willing to make concessions to what he saw as narrow-mindedness on the part of the public and continued to have the highest hopes for the opera's prospects. It met, however, with little more success than *Der Berggeist*, for the objections proved stronger than he had anticipated. In Frankfurt, where it was staged shortly afterwards, substantial changes were made to satisfy the objections of the Catholic authorities to the cathedral scene in which a bishop was included (though only as a speaking part). Spontini, who was Spohr's guest in Kassel at the time of the second performance of the opera, asked for the score to be sent to Berlin, but Count Brühl was unwilling to allow it to be staged as it stood and wrote to Spohr with the request that he should make substantial changes. He objected in particular to the explicit sexuality of the story, writing: 'certain things can be told and read but not presented on stage . . . where, however, as in *Pietro von Abano*, carnal lust is aroused for a corpse which has been briefly restored to an appearance of life by the magic of a disgraceful man, it can only awaken the greatest abhorrence'.[8] Spohr refused to be persuaded that his opera contained anything to which a reasonable person should take exception and replied to Count Brühl saying that the repertoire of the Berlin Hoftheater contained operas which by the application of the same criteria must be considered equally doubtful, but which did not seem to cause offence, and added: 'The opera was found to be gripping and full of suspense, more so than is common with opera, but not embarrassing or offensive'; and he refused to alter it as requested, saying, 'I would have to give myself much strenuous time and effort to change a work which would rest unknown on the shelf while the most barren products from abroad make their way easily across all the German stage.' That he felt discouraged in his attempts to encourage a school of German opera is obvious from these remarks. It is small wonder that he should have been annoyed to see performances of *Pietro von Abano* prevented by the apparent prudery of his fellow countrymen, especially since it contains much that is musically first-rate. The quality of the opera was perceived by Meyerbeer, who wrote to Spohr after he had borrowed the score from the publisher Schlesinger:

I cannot conclude without thanking you for the pleasure which the perusal of your masterpiece *Pietro von Abano*, which Herr Schlesinger lent me, has afforded me, and I am happy to be able to say that in particular the Finale of the first act (though only two characters are furnished by the poet), the scene between Antonio and the half-lifeless Cäcilie in the second act, and the ingenious manner in which the stringed instruments, half *con sordini* and half *senza sordini*, shadow forth the dialogue between the living Antonio and the spirit-like Cäcilie, the imposing Finale of the second act, and besides these, numerous other features of splendid dramatic invention, excellent declamation, novel and picturesque instrumentation and harmony have truly charmed me and excited in me the most ardent desire to be present at a performance of your masterpiece.[9]

Despite the return to spoken dialogue in *Pietro von Abano* (apparently adopted because prevailing religious scruples obliged Spohr to make the bishop a speaking part), the attempt to achieve dramatic truth through greater continuity of action and motivic reminiscence is pursued as intensively here as in *Der Berggeist*. Spohr still clung, however, to the the traditional forms of recitative and aria, though, as in his previous two operas, these are mostly linked to what precedes and follows. He assiduously welded the numbers into scene-complexes; thus there are only two breaks for dialogue in the first act and three in the second. These extended scenes are constructed with great skill; the opening section (nos. 1–6), with its juxtaposition of solos and ensembles with a chorus of priests and a chorus of students, is particularly striking; while the first Finale (no. 10), where Pietro, Beresinth and a chorus of invisible spirits resurrect Cäcilie, is a worthy companion to Weber's Wolf's Glen scene, creating a sense of horror far more convincingly than the witches' scene in *Faust*. (It is noteworthy that Spohr seems to have associated the key of B minor with witchcraft and sorcery, for the witches' music in *Faust* and *Macbeth* as well as much of this Finale are all in that key, which is relatively uncommon in Spohr's music.) During the incantation Spohr uses a motif from the Larghetto introduction to the overture; this again appears, evocatively, in no. 14 as Cäcilie reveals Pietro's sorcery to Antonio. Motif and reminiscence are also used effectively elsewhere in the opera. As in Spohr's earlier dramatic works, the orchestra plays an important part, and he again brought his sure feeling for colour into play. The scene in Act II (no. 14) which Meyerbeer mentioned, where half the strings are muted, is only one example among many. The low flutes doubling violas in the 'resurrection' scene is another.

Much of the music of the opera, especially where Spohr abandoned strict forms, is very powerful, and none of it is disappointingly weak; but the continuing reliance on the old formal conventions for many arias and ensembles contrasts uncomfortably with the freer sections, and the predominance of Spohr's harmonic and melodic mannerisms are undoubtedly drawbacks to the opera's overall impact. These factors contributed as much, perhaps, as the unpalatable subject matter of the opera to its failure.

In July 1827, while Spohr was working on *Pietro von Abano*, Moritz Hauptmann, who was also writing an opera, bemoaned his own inability to work in a concentrated manner, and observed: 'Spohr is certainly to be envied; he can sit down quietly every morning and do his quantum of composition for the day.'[10] For Spohr composition seems almost to have been as much a necessity of life as eating and sleeping. Writing music, though, was in no way a routine task for him; he may often have had an external reason for beginning a particular type of composition, but he did not write simply to fulfil a commission or to have something to send to a publisher. Once he had decided what he was going to compose he threw himself into the task with immense enthusiasm, having no thought for anything but the work in hand. Frequently at the beginning of a new project he would write to one or another of his friends saying something to the effect that he had never begun a work with such ardour. Once the work was completed and launched on its way it seems quickly to have been pushed to the back of his mind by his absorption in the next composition. As a result he was able more easily to bear the disappointment if it did not succeed as well as he had hoped. There was thus little opportunity for him to brood over the realisation that *Pietro von Abano* was unlikely to fulfil his expectations.

In December 1827 he occupied himself with the composition of a second double quartet (op. 87) in E flat. In it he sought to get closer to the double-chorus style which he had aimed at in the First Double Quartet, and felt satisfied that he had done so. Hauptmann, who heard it at a rehearsal for one of the Kassel Subscription Concerts shortly after its completion, was of the opinion, however, that good though it was, it did not quite equal the first. He wrote:

Fine as it is, I prefer the first; it has more originality and freshness. Spohr's second attempt in a new genre is like a lake or pool which owes its formation to the fresh springs of his first inspiration: it is exquisitely clear and the banks are lovely, but the mighty rush of the original stream is lovelier still.[11]

The image was a well-chosen one in this instance, for the E flat Double Quartet is altogether gentler and more genial than the D minor. The first movement begins, like its predecessor, with a passage in unison, but with a theme which is the antithesis of the bold opening of the D minor (ex. 131). Thereafter the movement flows amiably on its way, and Spohr freely indulges his delight in enharmonic modulation with enchanting effect. The Menuetto has a determined march-like quality (reminiscent of the String Quartet op. 29 no. 2), contradicted by the relaxed Trio in which the first violin and viola of the first quartet disport themselves in ingratiating arabesques: the coda fragments the material of the Menuetto and fades into silence. The Larghetto con moto which follows is a movement of great beauty and depth, containing some very effective instrumentation, in particular the passages of syncopated demi-semiquavers which pervade the middle of the movement and give a breathless quality to the closing section (ex. 132). The allegretto Finale is one of Spohr's liveliest and most captivating: it has a Bohemian flavour which at times calls to mind Smetana and Dvořák. Much use is made of the rhythm introduced by the second quartet (ex. 133), while an idea initially allotted to the first quartet as a melodic counterpart to this rhythm is developed to provide a lilting *pianissimo* theme in the dominant.

When this double quartet was performed in Vienna in November 1828, a reviewer observed: 'It is an exquisite work, wholly worthy of its celebrated creator; it is so intelligible, clear and melodious that all present were enraptured by it.'[12]

In February 1828 Spohr returned to symphonic writing after an interval of eight years, completing his Third Symphony in C minor (op. 78) by the middle of March, in time for it to be given its première in Kassel on Easter day in a concert which also included a 'Miserere' by Leo and Beethoven's Ninth Symphony. The Third Symphony is a fresh and vital work. In the orchestration a far greater opulence of sound is apparent than in the Second Symphony; while the handling of the individual wind instruments is as sensitive

Ex. 131

as before, there is no longer the impression that he was writing as if for a
large chamber ensemble, and the strings are on the whole used much more
homogeneously. In the Finale some of the string writing presents technical
difficulties, although the effect is not especially virtuosic: only in the Scherzo
are the first and second violins treated in an overtly soloistic manner, with
Spohr's own mastery of the violin reflected in precipitous leaps (ex. 134).
With respect both to form and melodic content Spohr explored new avenues
in symphonic writing in this work. An Andante grave introduction to the

Ex. 132

Ex. 133

Ex. 134

first movement begins the work with that grand, noble, yearning sentiment
which had become indelibly associated with Spohr's name in the minds of
his contemporaries. After a series of characteristic chromatic progressions
over an A flat pedal, a reiterated melodic phrase gives birth to the main
theme of the Allegro. Despite its regular sixteen-bar construction, this
theme has a genuinely Romantic quality, imparted both by its colourful harmony and by the way in which, because of the increased movement at the
ends of the phrases, it seems to ebb and flow while at the same time always
surging forward (ex. 135). In contrast to the first two symphonies, where

Ex. 135

previously stated ideas are continuously developed in the bridge passages, the Third Symphony introduces new material at this point. When the second subject in the relative major is reached, however, the theme announced by clarinet proves to be almost identical with the first subject but after eight bars is differently continued in a playful passage that acts as a foil to the tensions of the earlier part of the movement (ex. 136). The other interesting fea-

Ex. 136

ture of the first movement is its middle section where, instead of the expected development, the music of the Andante grave reappears, elaborated and modified to fit the 6/8 allegro tempo. (A similar idea had been tried in the Octet op. 32 of 1815.) The overall tonal scheme of the movement is conventional, though, as might be expected, there is no lack of distant keys; for example, the move to B major/C flat major, in the bridge passage of the exposition, which finally resolves itself as a Neapolitan of B flat, or the shift to F sharp minor at the beginning of the coda, whence the tonic is reached via twenty-three bars of ingenious and effective chromatic progressions. The slow movement,* a Larghetto in F major 9/8 which begins with a long-drawn-out melody of a dreamy sentimental nature, was particularly admired by contemporaries. A novel effect is created by the use of unison violins, violas and cellos, accompanied by piquant chords from the rest of the orchestra, for the statement of the second subject (ex. 137). In order to repeat the device at a convenient pitch in the recapitulation, Spohr engineers its return in D flat, modifying the end of the theme so that it modulates to F major.

---

* In common with Spohr's other larghetto movements it should be taken at a slow tempo, probably c. ♪120, not (as on the only available modern recording) c. ♩. 76. Unfortunately, though Spohr gave metronome markings for the other three movements he omitted to do so for this movement.

Ex. 137

The Scherzo (C minor 6/4) is more restless than playful and never quite attains a climax. In the Trio (C major) the wind instruments cavort capriciously with charming effect.

Spohr clearly intended the Finale to play a different role from those of his earlier symphonies. Here he rejected the idea of a lightweight pendant to the work (as he was also to do in all his subsequent symphonies) in favour of a final movement which would balance the first. His handling of sonata form in these two movements, though, is quite different.* He again shows his liking for economy of thematic material, for almost everything in the movement derives from one of four motifs which are contained in the first theme (ex. 138a). The second subject (ex. 138b) is constructed from a combination of these, and has a humorous, almost operatic overture quality, especially when it returns with violins and cellos exchanging material. As in the first movement there is no conventional development; instead Spohr produced a fugue based on the main theme (ex. 138c), but the effectiveness of this section is somewhat marred by the predictable regularity of the subject's eleven entries at precise four-bar intervals. Overall, though, the Third Symphony is an eminently successful work which deservedly won and maintained a place in the repertoire throughout the nineteenth century.

In the middle of his work on the symphony, Spohr received an invitation to direct *Die letzten Dinge* at a music festival at Halberstadt in the coming June. So that he would also have something new to perform there he wrote, during May, a twelfth violin concerto (entitled Concertino) in A minor (op. 79). In this work he reverted to a form somewhat similar to his *Gesangsszena* Concerto of 1816. The first movement, marked Andante grave, begins with a seventeen-bar orchestral introduction after which the solo violin initiates a dramatic recitative-fantasia punctuated at intervals by orchestral reminis-

* Tovey's remark in his article on 'Sonata Form' in the *Encyclopaedia Britannica* – 'The masterly scheme (there is only one) of Spohr is (as Schumann remarked) not so easy to imitate as it looks; but it is the prototype of most pseudo-classical works up to the present day' – indicates that he knew very little of Spohr's music.

Ex. 138

cences of the introductory section. This leads without a break into the second movement, an expressive Larghetto con moto, which is interesting for its alternation between 12/8, 9/8, 6/8 and 3/8, and for the coherence of its thematic material. The Larghetto con moto is also linked with the movement that follows it, a lively polonaise in which the technical resources of the violin are displayed in bold leaps and dizzying roulades.

The high spirits which pervade the finales of the Double Quartet in E flat, the Third Symphony and the Concertino may be taken as symbolic of Spohr's state of mind at this period. Notwithstanding the reverses which had beset his last two operas, he had every reason for satisfaction both in his personal life and in his works. The mutual love between him and Dorette remained as strong as ever, and they shared the joy of watching their youngest daughter, Therese, growing up into an affectionate and lovable girl. The two elder daughters had married: Ida in 1825 to an architect, Johann Heinrich Wolff, and Emilie in 1827 to a manufacturer, Wilhelm Zahn; but since both husbands were natives of Kassel the family remained close knit. Spohr's only regret was that neither of his elder daughters seemed likely now to fulfil the musical aspirations which he had had for them. The continuing growth of his reputation must also have conduced to his contentment. Invitations to conduct his own works were more numerous than he could accept, and wherever he went he was treated with honour and deference. Academic honour also came his way with the award of a doctorate from the University of Marburg on 28 July 1827. Though Spohr was not a vain man he was undoubtedly gratified by the evidence of the esteem in which he was held. Equally important for his sense of well-being was the real satisfaction which he continued to derive from his musical activities in Kassel. Writing to Friedrich Rochlitz in July 1828, shortly after his return from the Halberstadt Music Festival, he remarked:

My work in my post is so much to my taste that I could not match it in any other German city. This is because our theatre has no Hofintendant who interferes more or less everywhere in the artistic direction. On the contrary, here the opera is wholly given over to me, and the General Director of our theatre, who understands nothing about music, reposes the greatest confidence in me. Also it is satisfying to me to have raised our opera, if not to the best, at least to one of the most excellent in Germany, though I admit that this is a result less of my merit than of the fortunate chance which has brought together so many outstanding singers. With singers such as Mesdames Heinefetter, Schweitzer and Roland and Messrs Wild, Eichberger, Föppel and Sieber, one can already do something excellent. With every new production I come more and more to the conviction that opera is not given anywhere with more precision on stage and in the orchestra than here. This is acknowledged by the Prince and the public, and already the former has often given proof of his satisfaction with my efforts. In this respect there remains nothing for me to desire but that Kassel were a bigger city and our public ten times as great as it is. [13]

In this optimistic frame of mind Spohr set to work in August 1828 to compose a fourth clarinet concerto, which Hermstedt had requested for performance at a festival in which they were both to take part in July 1829 at Nordhausen. Unlike the Concertino op. 79, the Fourth Clarinet Concerto is a full-scale work in the conventional three movements. The first movement has a predominantly serious tone which carries over into the declamatory Larghetto, but Spohr was unable to prevent his ebullience breaking out in the brilliant Rondo à l'espagnole which concludes the concerto.

Between October 1828 and February 1829 he composed another set of three string quartets (op. 82). The first of these, in E minor, is a very uneven work; its outer movements are close to the *quatuors brillants* in style. The gently brooding Andantino second movement is on a much higher plane than the rest of the quartet; the closing section of its main theme has analogies (ex. 139) with Brahms' similar use of tonic pedal passages in codetta sections, for instance the Andante of his Violin Sonata op. 100. Op. 82 no. 2 in G major is a much more evenly balanced quartet, both in the quality of its movements and the equality of its part-writing. The first movement, an amiable lilting Allegro in 6/8, makes great play with a rising semitone appoggiatura which is prominent in its main theme (ex. 140). The second subject derives from this theme, but Spohr imbues it with an entirely different character (ex. 141). The development section begins with it, and here he casts it in a form that again brings Wagner to mind (ex. 142). The slow movement, in B minor, is one of Spohr's most beautiful, having a finely sustained continuity of mood.

Ex. 139

Ex. 140

Ex. 141

Ex. 142

Instead of a minuet or scherzo, the next movement is a lively Alla polacca. The Finale is a witty, bustling Allegro, full of off-beat accents. As a whole this quartet is among Spohr's best. Op. 82 no. 3 in A minor, while not quite achieving the consistency of no. 2, is an attractive work with a number of interesting features. A certain similarity between part of the first theme and King Mark's motif from Wagner's *Tristan und Isolde* is noticeable. The coda of the first movement provides an excellent example of Spohr's increasing liking for surprising the listener with a distant modulation just before the end of a movement (ex. 143). The Andante which follows is unusual for its rhyth-

Ex. 143

(Ex. 143 cont.)

mic irregularity: the main theme is written with an alternation of 4/8 and
3/8, while the middle section and coda remain in 3/8 (ex. 144). The Scherzo
is excellent, the finest movement of the quartet. The Finale slips too easily
into a display piece for the first violin. It begins with a twenty-four-bar

Ex. 144

Andante

Andante in which the first theme of the ensuing Allegro is introduced; then, instead of a development section Spohr repeats a version of the Andante. It is noteworthy that the main idea on which the movement is based is identical to the 'love' motif from *Faust*.

The quartets were well received by contemporary reviewers. A critic in the *Berliner Allgemeine Musikalische Zeitung* was most impressed by no. 3, asserting that it belonged with 'the most beautiful modern compositions in this genre'.[14] A reviewer in the *AMZ* waxed poetic about many aspects of these quartets and specially admired the second, but found things to criticise too. He considered the last movement of no. 3 'more full of artifice than art' and took exception to the use of the familiar main theme which he recognised from *Jessonda* and from some of Weber's works. He concluded with the exclamation 'And yet again a church-cadence! [*Kirchenschluss*]';[15] charges of repetitiveness in Spohr's music were to occur with greater frequency in the succeeding decades.

The enthusiastic acclaim with which *Die letzten Dinge* was being greeted throughout Germany impelled Spohr once more towards religious music. Here at any rate he was achieving a success which had eluded him on the operatic stage since *Jessonda*. Thus from March to May 1829 he worked at a setting of Mahlmann's 'Vater Unser'. The text is a poetic meditation on the Lord's Prayer, which Spohr set for four soloists, chorus and orchestra. The cantata consists of nine numbers, the majority of which are linked to one another; there is no recitative. As in *Die letzten Dinge*, telling use is made of the soloists as a quartet in alternation with the chorus, and where solos occur they do not constitute complete numbers. The sonority of the choral and orchestral writing as well as the harmonic idiom call to mind Brahms' *Deutsches Requiem* on more than one occasion. Spohr gave a performance of his 'Vater Unser' with piano accompaniment at the St Cecilia Day concert in Kassel in November 1828 and repeated it with orchestra in the winter Subscription Concerts. When published shortly afterwards by Schlesinger it rapidly gained a wide circulation among German choral societies, and then, after the success of *The Last Judgement* at Norwich in 1830, made its way to England where it was performed for the first time in London by the Vocal Society in April 1836.

During August 1829, after returning from the Nordhausen festival, Spohr composed a new *quatuor brillant* in E flat (op. 83), a three-movement work which, apart from the curious fact that he yet again included an Alla Polacca, is of no special interest. He was then irresistibly drawn back to the idea of writing opera. For a librettist he turned once more to Pfeiffer and suggested as a basis for the plot a story entitled 'The Student of Salamanca', by the American writer Washington Irving – part of a collection of tales published under the title *Bracebridge Hall* in 1822. Spohr, having read a German translation which appeared in 1823, had already considered the story for a possible libretto in 1825, as his correspondence with Döring over *Der Berggeist* indicates,[16] but the fortuitous appearance of *Pietro von Abano* had caused him to shelve the project. Now that he had decided to essay another opera his mind reverted to this earlier idea. He and Pfeiffer worked closely together over the first draft of the scenario; Pfeiffer filled the right-hand sides of the pages leaving the left for Spohr's comments and amendments. Then Pfeiffer, working under the pseudonym 'Fr. Georg Schmidt' because of the Elector's disapproval of government officials engaging publicly in literary activities, produced a libretto which has been described as one of the best German Romantic opera books.[17] *Der Alchymist*, as the opera was called, contains an abundance of the exotic elements so beloved by Romantic musicians. The curtain rises on a ruined Moorish castle, which is occupied by the eponymous alchemist, Felix de Vasquez, and his daughter Inez. A band of gypsies (given a much more pervasive role than in Irving) arrive outside, and one of their number, Paola (not identified by Irving, but portrayed by Pfeiffer as a dispossessed Moorish princess), sings of her faithless lover. Inez appears at a window and, unaware of the gypsies, sings of her lover Alonzo (called Antonio by Irving). She is courted also, however, by Don Ramiro (Don Ambrosio de Loxa in Irving), who hires the gypsies to sing a bolero under her window. But Inez spurns his blandishments and he vows vengeance. Meanwhile the alchemist's experiments result in an explosion and Alonzo, by rescuing him from the ensuing conflagration, wins his esteem. Act II opens with a scene between Paola and Ramiro, who it transpires is her fickle lover, and she upbraids him about his designs on Inez. In the next scene Alonzo and Inez come upon the gypsy encampment where they are provided with an entertainment. Paola tries to warn them that they are in danger, but in vain, for the gypsies, who are in Ramiro's pay, take them prisoner. When Vasquez comes in search of his daughter he is arrested by the officers of the Inquisition, to whom he has been denounced by Ramiro. The final act opens with Vasquez in prison. The second scene takes place in Ramiro's palace, where music and dancing are being provided to distract Inez. Inez is informed by Paola that her father is awaiting execution, and she entreats Ramiro to secure his release. In the final scene Vasquez is being led to execution when Alonzo, who has escaped, arrives saying that he will prove the old man's innocence and obtain a pardon from the judges. When he has departed, Inez, who has also escaped, rushes in, hotly pursued by Ramiro, who tells the onlookers that she is his mad sister. As Inez tries to commit suicide Alonzo reappears with the pardon and in a duel defeats Ramiro; as, however, Ramiro is only wounded, he is taken away by Paola who hopes to make an honest man of him. Everyone else joins in a general rejoicing.

The music of the opera is dominated by the Spanish setting. *Singspiel* and *opéra comique* had frequently contained similar exotic elements as had

Spohr's own operas *Zemire und Azor* and *Jessonda*; Méhul's *Joseph* (1807), Spontini's *Fernand Cortez* (1809), Cherubini's *Les Abencerages* (1813), Auber's *La Muette de Portici* (1827), and Rossini's *Guillaume Tell* (1829) all make effective use of foreign colour in their music, but in *Der Alchymist* Spohr took pains to sustain the exoticism throughout the opera. To this end he used orchestral colour (harp, triangle, castanettes and tambourines, as well as unusual sonorities from the normal orchestral instruments), rhythm and harmony. The C minor overture – perhaps the finest of Spohr's operatic overtures – already establishes the Spanish atmosphere. After an Adagio introduction where the alchemist's motif is introduced, a stringendo leads into the Allegro, and a theme based on Spanish dance rhythms constitutes the first subject (ex. 145); the second subject, beginning unusually in E flat minor,

Ex. 145

continues to employ a similar rhythm (ex. 146). For a while this section slips into the expected E flat major, but shortly returns to E flat minor; these major/minor alternations are characteristic of the opera and help to intensify its 'foreignness' (ex. 147). Triplet semiquaver flourishes and bolero rhythms, reminiscent of Spohr's alla Spagnola movements from the Sixth Violin Concerto of 1809 onwards, are freely used throughout the opera; the Fandango in the ball scene (no. 19) begins with an almost exact transcription of the first sixty bars of the all' Espagnola Finale of the String Quartet op. 58 no. 2 (exx. 110–11).

As in *Pietro von Abano*, Spohr again used spoken dialogue, but it is reduced to a minimum and is virtually dispensable. (Why he should have used it at

Ex. 146

Ex. 147

all is not clear, since there were no religious scruples to be met here.) Out-
wardly *Der Alchymist* resembles *Pietro von Abano* in other respects. The opera is
divided into 'numbers', but these are built into scene-complexes. The forms
used for the individual components of these complexes are interesting.
Spohr had become progressively less satisfied with the conventional recitative and aria, recognising that it held up the action too much, and that its
predictability made for monotony. Thus in *Der Alchymist* there is only one
number that follows the conventional pattern (no. 5); in all the other solo
and ensemble numbers Spohr either used variants of the recitative and aria
or adopted simpler, song-like structures such as Romanze, Ariette and
Duettino as well as melodrama and *scena con coro*. In two numbers (9 and 18)
he used a version of the two-part aria in which the sections are separated by
recitative; no. 9 contains two contrasted Allegro sections with the key
scheme A flat - E minor, and no. 18 an Allegro agitato in G minor followed
by a Larghetto con moto in A flat which contains one of the few examples of
coloratura in this opera. The vocal writing, in general, is more in the style of
Spohr's Lieder.

Spohr began the composition of *Der Alchymist* in October 1829 and completed it by April of the following year. Its first performance took place to celebrate the Elector's birthday on 28 July 1830, when it was enthusiastically received. In September Spohr wrote to Count Redern, Count Brühl's successor as Intendant of the Berlin Hoftheater: 'in the four performances which the opera was given before the departure of Herr Wild, my expectation that it would please the public more than my earlier operas was confirmed, and so I may well hope for a wide circulation for it if it has previously enjoyed a good reception in Berlin'.[18] A month later he informed Speyer that the Count had promised to put it on in the new year and added, 'if he keeps his word I shall go there to direct it'.[19] Spohr's hopes, however, were once again to be disappointed, for the Count did not keep his word and the only city to stage *Der Alchymist* besides Kassel was Prague, a city where admiration for Spohr's works was exceptionally strong. A London production at the Theatre Royal, Drury Lane in 1832, though billed as Spohr's *Der Alchymist* had little to do with that opera, being a hotch-potch of items cobbled together from six of his stage works by that notorious bowdleriser of operas Sir Henry Bishop.

Intrinsic reasons for the failure of *Der Alchymist* are not so easy to find as they are for its two predecessors *Der Berggeist* and *Pietro von Abano*. The libretto is by no means contemptible, while the music has an undeniable freshness and charm, and contains strong dramatic moments. It seems likely that the failure was less a result of the opera's own shortcomings than of a general trend. Spohr's operas were, on the whole, considered to be music for the connoisseur rather than for the generality of opera-goers. *Zemire und Azor* was perhaps the most genuinely popular, with its almost Rossinian lightness and brilliance; but *Faust* and *Jessonda*, though deeply admired by many German musicians, had established their place in the repertoire almost as much by the fact that, in the upsurge of patriotic fervour which followed the defeat of Napoleon, the German public needed to acclaim great German art-works as by the genuine admiration which they elicited from an influential portion of their hearers. Weber's *Der Freischütz* succeeded, as Spohr recognised, because it answered both the need of the German nation and the taste of the audience for easily assimilable music; that *Jessonda* should have attained and retained for more than half a century an almost equal success was perhaps surprising. However, the wave of enthusiasm on the crest of which these works had ridden was losing its impetus during the 1820s as the bulk of the public increasingly returned their allegiance to the less demanding products of the French and Italian schools. Weber discovered how flimsy were the foundations on which German opera rested when in *Euryanthe* he eschewed the popular elements that had contributed largely to the success of *Der Freischütz* and consequently produced a work which failed to arouse public enthusiasm. Both Spohr (who had scant regard for *Der Freischütz*) and

Schubert (who admired it) felt, however, that *Euryanthe* was in fact a less satisfactory opera than its predecessor. Weber's final stage work, *Oberon*, was left in an unsatisfactory form by his early death, and whether the course of German opera might have been changed had he lived is an unanswerable question. Spohr had neither the inclination nor Weber's ability to write for the masses and could only continue to produce works which, from the musical point of view, inspired opera audiences with more respect than enthusiasm. Fétis' attitude to Spohr's operas, expounded in an article in the *Revue Musicale* in 1827, probably embodied not only the insular French view, but also reflected the attitude of a large proportion of German opera audiences. Having devoted his attention to Weber, Fétis observed that next to him Spohr was the most distinguished German composer of the present generation, but remarked of his operas:

these works enjoy a brilliant reputation in Germany, though they are almost entirely devoid of melody; the harmony is besides so tormented, and the modulations are so numerous, that they cause the listener more fatigue than pleasure. The faults with which I have just reproached Spohr are those of the whole of the present German school. It seems that all the composers believe themselves dishonoured if they write simple and natural melodies.[20]

A similar though more respectful view of Spohr was shared by some German critics, instances of which are to be found with increasing frequency during the 1830s. A representative example may be taken from a review of the Prague production of *Der Alchymist* of 1838, which commented: 'The music is, and one would not expect it to be otherwise from a master like Spohr, written in an exemplary and correct manner, but presents on the whole more erudition than inspiration and fantasy.'[21] This was not, however, a majority view among German critics, especially during the 1820s and 1830s, but it may well have been shared by the majority of theatre managements either as a matter of taste or of financial prudence. If German opera led to poor attendance figures, questions of artistic integrity and patriotism must generally take second place. A review of the vocal score of *Der Alchymist* which appeared in 1832 firmly laid the blame for the lack of success which was the fate of most German operas on the shoulders of unimaginative management and an uncultured public, saying:

We hasten with the advertisement of this opera all the more since we hope not only to gratify many friends of the very esteemed tone-poet by it, but also thereby, at least to a certain extent, to remedy an injustice by which German opera composers are all too often afflicted by German theatres. It is unfortunately almost always the rule that German works by really first-rate men are allowed to sleep peacefully for years while even very trivial foreign rubbish is fearlessly preferred to them. This is now also to be seen with *Der Alchymist* . . .

After further complaints about the bad management of theatres, the critic continued:

When the magic wand of good will and the Aaron-staff sprout on the altar of patriotism, then and only then will things improve. Until this inner spring we will and must possess ourselves in patience. All those who are of our mind, however, can create a pleasant climate in their own fortunate greenhouses. That at least is a refuge! Under such conditions, though, things look very gloomy to a reviewer of German opera.[22]

Part of the problem was that there was not enough good German opera being written to sustain a national movement; Weber and Spohr alone were considered first-rate composers. Marschner with his three most successful operas, *Der Vampyr* (1828), *Der Templer und die Jüdin* (1829), and *Hans Heiling* (1833), was unable to throw sufficient weight into the balance to restore the fortunes of German opera. It was apparent to acute observers in the late 1820s that the high hopes which the success of *Der Freischütz* and *Jessonda* had engendered at the beginning of the decade had come to nought. As Moritz Hauptmann wrote to Franz Hauser, speculating on the choice of an opera for the Elector of Hesse's birthday celebrations in 1828,

I suppose we must have recourse to some foreign work; between you and me, *Il Crociato* most likely. One's first feeling is disapproval; I know mine was; but where are we to find anything *new* in this country? Lindpaintner, Marschner, Aloys Schmitt? Even supposing the Italian opera were inferior to ours, I should prefer it as not being German, for I had rather not parade our poverty.[23]

Hauptmann excepted Spohr from this general charge against German opera composers, stressing however that he was the only exception.

XI

Revolution and bereavement
1830–1836

In both a real and a symbolic sense *Der Alchymist* marked another turning point in Spohr's life. When it became clear that the opera had failed to hold the stage he effectively gave up the attempt to achieve further operatic success (his final opera, *Die Kreuzfahrer*, was fourteen years in the future). The disappointments embodied in the failure of *Der Alchymist* were a harbinger of less congenial times. At the end of 1830, however, the storm clouds were still beyond the horizon and Spohr could give free rein to his naturally optimistic nature, for not only could he cherish hopes that *Der Alchymist* would gain widespread acceptance, but he could also believe that a new and better political era was about to dawn for Germany. On 27 July, the day before the première of *Der Alchymist* in Kassel, the revolution which was rapidly to topple the repressive regime of Charles X broke out in Paris. The French example gave rise to a general resurgence of the reforming spirit in Austria, Prussia and many others of the German states. In Kassel, during the Elector's absence in Karlsbad (whence it was rumoured that he was attempting to obtain the elevation of his mistress, Countess Reichenbach, to the rank of princess), rioting broke out on the evening of 6 September over the price of bread. This was contained by the military with the assistance of the middle classes, but tension remained high. The Elector returned to his capital on September 12 and a few days later, unable to rely on his troops, assented reluctantly to the summoning of the Estates, which had not met since 1815, and to the drawing up of a new constitution for Hesse.

There could be no doubt where Spohr's sympathies lay. In November he wrote enthusiastically to Speyer:

During the tremendous events of the last few weeks I have often thought of you and wished that I could talk to you about them. I read in the papers that you too have assumed the dress of a hero and put yourself at the head of the Offenbach citizens' guard! I have to be content to show my patriotism through artistic accomplishments. First we celebrated the summoning of the Estates with a festive performance in the theatre; then with the court orchestra I gave the Bürgermeister Schaumburg, whose eloquence is to thank for this joyful event, a solemn serenade; and finally, for the opening of the Diet, put on a grand musical performance in church with both choral societies and everyone in Kassel who can scrape or blow.[1]

Early in January the Electress returned to Kassel where a public reconciliation with her husband took place, and on 9 January 1831 the new constitution was promulgated. That evening the event was celebrated by a festive performance of *Jessonda*, preceded by a play specially written for the occasion by Niemeyer, for which Spohr had composed a hymn, 'Hesse's song of joy on the establishment of its constitution'. The Elector and Electress did not remain together for long, however, for the next day Countess Reichenbach returned secretly to the palace at Wilhelmshöhe and the Elector immediately went to visit her. When this became known in the town a mob gathered, threatening to drive her out by force. The news that she had left was greeted with widespread satisfaction, but shortly afterwards the Elector took up residence with her in Hanau. From there he still attempted to make his authority felt, at least on the members of his Hofkapelle. In order to save money he decided to close down the Hoftheater and dismiss all the musicians since he was not able to benefit from the performances. To this effect an order was dispatched to Kassel, instructing that those without contracts were to be immediately dismissed while others, even those with contracts for life, were to be offered two months' salary, and the Elector had added in his own handwriting that it was to be 'that or nothing'. The theatre Intendant Feige raised strong objections to the implementation of the order and the Elector was forced to send a second, less extreme, document which accepted that the theatre should not close, but required financial retrenchment; it contradictorily stated, however, that all the provisions of the first order were to be complied with. Hauptmann complained: 'thus the theatre was still to be continued while every member of the company, with or without contract, was to be sent about his business! It gives one a headache to try and make any sense out of all this; mere crazy malice, nothing more nor less.'[2] In the event the company kept their jobs, though because of the departure of the Guards to Luxembourg a number of wind players were lost to the orchestra. The Elector was described by Hauptmann at this juncture as 'getting stupider and more venomous than ever', and it is clear that he acquiesced with reluctance in the limitations which his subjects were imposing on his authority.

In spite of the Elector's reluctance, the process of reform continued and Spohr made no secret of his political views. On 16 May 1831 Hauptmann wrote to Hauser:

Do you ever manage to see an account of the proceedings of our Diet? They are quite in the orthodox parliamentary style, with their Hear! Hear! Bravo! Laughter, etc. We have some really good speakers amongst them. About 200 tickets of admission are given to strangers. Spohr goes very often – he is a great 'Liberal'. *Excelsior* is the motto. *Brauskopf* must cave in – which is generally the way with this much extolled Liberalism.[3]

Spohr's own letters are quite without Hauptmann's cynical tone. In June 1831 he wrote to Speyer:

Apart from the plight of our theatre, everything goes pretty well in Hesse, and liberal ideas are spreading just as in the rest of Europe, but even more so here. The throng of people who want to attend the deliberations of the Estates is tremendous, and one is lucky to get an entrance ticket once in a week. What is discussed there, as is the case with most of the great questions of the day, is then further discussed in our reading museum where a kind of political club has been formed, and since the members of the Estates are honorary members of it, these discussions are not without influence on the official debates.[4]

Six months later he was still full of optimism about the political situation and the long-term consequences of the reforming movement. In December he observed:

In Hesse, Baden, Brunswick, Saxony etc. etc. things have definitely become very much better and will become better still, and even though there are occasions when selfishness, particularly among the privileged classes, is blatant, nonetheless we can see an awakening of public-spiritedness and patriotism which latterly we would certainly not have thought possible. We should not, I admit, look for it among the Frankfurt money-grabbers, who are too much influenced by the federal Diet mentality. But outside Frankfurt, even in Prussia and Austria, it is obvious that a wholly new spirit has awakened which the federal alliance will never again be able to stifle.[5]

The times were certainly not free of serious worries for Spohr, though, for the state of the Hoftheater continued to give cause for anxiety. In August 1831 he wrote to Marschner that 'it vegetates with continually empty houses and daily accumulates a greater mass of debts which Heaven knows who will pay'.[6] And in December he wrote to his friend Anton Streicher in Vienna:

Our theatre, once if not the best at any rate one of the best in all Germany, will close at least temporarily next Easter and thereby make a considerable number of people unemployed just after we had prevented its closure immediately following the glorious revolution. But they cannot take anything from those of us with life contracts, since in a constitutional state the laws of employment cannot be destroyed by peremptory order, as the Elector discovered to his disgust.[7]

In his personal life, too, 1831 was not propitious. The year had begun auspiciously with the celebration of his Silver Wedding on 2 February, when family and friends gathered to give him and Dorette a surprise party, but had then been clouded by a series of personal losses. On 4 February his daughter Ida lost a three-month-old child, but a much more crushing blow was the death of his brother Ferdinand on 9 March after a short illness. Their relationship had been a close one ever since Spohr, at the age of fifteen, had assumed responsibility for his education. Ferdinand had played under his brother's direction at the Theater an der Wien; he was one of Spohr's first appointments to the Kassel orchestra, and a regular member, as violinist, of his quartet. Spohr possessed too much self-control to parade his grief, but its extent may be gauged from Hauptmann's comment: 'We often used to tell Spohr, half in jest and half in earnest, that everything went too well with him, and that a little trouble is part and parcel of our lives. No lack of that now! It is easy enough to preach in that fashion, but when troubles do come, one feels so sorry – so very sorry.'[8] A third blow followed in July 1831, when his friend and collaborator Carl Pfeiffer died suddenly while bathing in the river Fulda.

All these disruptions to the usually smooth routine of Spohr's life were hardly conducive to the detachment of mind he required for composing. It is no surprise to find that the eighteen months following the completion of *Der Alchymist* were a lean period. His only compositions were a short piece of introductory music to Ehlers' *Siege of Missolunghi*, and the Festive Hymn which he wrote for the proclamation of the constitution. He did, however, complete a labour which had been in his mind for several years, upon which he could work without the intensity of creative concentration that was denied to him by the excitement of the times. This was his *Violinschule*, a plan for which he had already proposed to the publisher Haslinger in March 1827, but which, because of the pressure of other commitments, he made no further progress with at that time. He took up the idea again in September 1830, writing to his friend Adolf Hesse that he had begun work on it with little enthusiasm, and only because he had been pressed to undertake such a task for some considerable time, but confessed that having started he was beginning to become absorbed in it, particularly in the working out of the studies. On 28 October 1831, in another letter to Hesse, he mentioned that it was completed.

The *Violinschule* covers every aspect of violin playing as Spohr practised it, from the most basic elements to the most advanced techniques, and contains sixty-six studies specially composed to provide material for practice at every stage. A final section on 'Delivery, or style of performance' deals with the manner of performing concertos, quartets and sonatas, and playing in an orchestra. However, Spohr's rigid artistic creed excluded from the true canon of violin playing a number of techniques which were then gaining currency and have since become standard weapons in the violinist's armoury. The techniques employed by Paganini and his imitators, which opened up a whole range of new possibilities for the instrument, were anathema to Spohr. After hearing him play during a visit to Kassel in June 1830 Spohr had written: 'In his compositions and performance there is a strange mixture of the highest genius, childishness and tastelessness, so that one feels alternately attracted and repelled.'[9] With respect to harmonics, for instance, having stated that only the natural harmonics at the quarter-, third- and half-way points of the string should be used, he appended a footnote saying:

The abovementioned harmonics, as not materially differing in sound from the natural notes, have at all times been used in conjunction with the latter by all good violinists. All others, however, and particularly the so-called artificial harmonics, must be rejected as useless, because they so totally differ from the natural notes of the instrument. It is indeed a degradation of this noble instrument to play whole melodies in such childish heterogeneous sounds. Despite the great sensation created by the celebrated Paganini in recent times by the revival of the ancient and wholly forgotten harmonic playing and by his eminent perfection therein, however alluring such an example may be, I must nevertheless seriously advise all young violinists not to lose their time in such a pursuit, to the neglect of that which is more important.[10]

The other area in which Spohr's technique is most significantly different from that which later gained currency is bowing. He excludes all springing bowings; his normal manner of performing passages which would later have been played with a springing bow, in the middle or lower half, seems to have been as a détaché at the point, or, for special effect the staccato, which was a number of sharply detached notes taken in a single up – or more rarely down – bow, using only the upper half of the bow and without its leaving the string. He remarks of this stroke that 'The ability for it must be to a certain extent innate; for experience proves that frequently the most distinguished violinists, notwithstanding their utmost exertions, can never attain it, whilst greatly inferior performers acquire it without the slightest trouble.'[11] His own mastery of this stroke, and his use of it in his compositions, led to its being generally known as the 'Spohr staccato'. In his approach to bowing, he was largely following in the traditions of the French and Mannheim schools, and it was through them that he had early acquired his strong aversion to springing bowing (see diaries of 1803). Spohr's authority in this matter weighed heavily on many violinists of the succeeding generation. Joseph Joachim, uncertain about the propriety of springing bowings in classical compositions, asked Mendelssohn's advice and received the recommendation: 'Always use it, my boy, where it is suitable, or where it sounds well.'[12] In his rejection of springing bowings Spohr was, in fact, at odds with the direction in which violin technique was developing; one of his most influential pupils, Ferdinand David, includes two forms of springing bowings in his *Violinschule*, and the English violinist, Henry Holmes, to whom Spohr dedicated his last three violin duets, supplements the section on bowing in his edition of Spohr's *Violinschule* with directions for practising springing bowings. It seems probable, though, that Mendelssohn, whose admiration for Spohr's execution of the staccato is on record (see below, pp. 231–3), intended the principal theme of the last movement of his violin concerto op. 64 to be played with this staccato, for Joachim reports that 'he [Mendelssohn] never wished the theme to be rendered with the "flying" staccato but rather with a light pointed note, short and piquant. The "flying" bow-stroke appeared to him to be too light and flaky. To many, the way of execution desired will prove difficult.'[13] In other respects, too, such as vibrato (which Spohr in common with most of his contemporaries regarded as an ornament to be used with discretion) and methods of fingering, his technique differed significantly from later nineteenth- and twentieth-century violinists.

Despite its conservative features, the *Violinschule* remained a classic for almost a century, appearing in numerous foreign editions and being constantly reprinted. At the time of its first publication the *Wiener Theater-Zeitung* observed in the course of a long article:

It required the penetrating and searching mind of a Spohr, who surpasses in complete scientific culture the authors of every existing school, to condense in systematic order so important a branch of art, which has been two centuries in acquiring shape . . . The world-famed master, Spohr, has by this excellent work alone ensured an undying celebrity, and thereby added but a new and beautiful leaf to the laurel wreath that encircles his brows. [14]

And more than seventy years later, in the Joachim–Moser *Violinschule*, Andreas Moser paid tribute to Spohr's influence on the development of violin playing and observed that 'as an executive artist Spohr was undoubtedly one of the greatest masters that ever lived'. [15]

In November 1831 Spohr returned to composition with the first of a set of three string quartets op. 84. The first movement of this work in D minor has an unrelieved seriousness which may reflect the personal sorrow he had recently experienced. Its themes are more austere than is usual with Spohr, and the suppression of the customary elegiac or lyrical element is notable. The development section has a rare purposefulness, building up by degrees from an uneasy calm to a stormy climax. Though the rest of the quartet does not sustain this level of excellence the other movements have grace and charm; the larghetto second movement looks back, contrastingly, to the detached poise of a previous age of certainty, being imbued with an almost eighteenth-century elegance. The Scherzo again introduces a more serious element which, however, is relieved by the graceful Trio. The Finale, in D major, is the exact antithesis of the first movement, for it is all high spirits and, uncharacteristically for Spohr, is never once checked by lyrical episodes; this may perhaps be taken as symbolic of his continuing optimism and his sense that the world, despite all contra-indications, was becoming a better place to live in.

The other two quartets of op. 84, in A flat major and B minor, neither of which contain anything exceptional or unexpected, followed in January and March 1832.

In the meanwhile a new complexion had entered into the political situation in Hesse. On 30 September 1831 the Elector Wilhelm II, who did not intend returning to Kassel, had agreed to requests that he should appoint his son Prince Friedrich Wilhelm as co-regent while he himself remained absent from the capital. The new regime began well enough, for the liberal tide was still flowing strongly. Towards Spohr the Prince behaved courteously and considerately, but the Elector kept his son short of funds and by the spring of 1832 financial considerations had led the Prince to order the closure of the Hoftheater for an indefinite period. All those without contracts were dismissed; this included all but three of the singers. The orchestra were almost all protected by their contracts from such arbitrary treatment, but pressure was brought to bear on them to resign their posts for a lump sum to be agreed with each individual separately. They were all summoned to attend a meeting at which Spohr, as head of the musical establishment, was asked first to reply to the proposal. He firmly declined to waive his legal rights and announced his intention of maintaining them in the courts if necessary. The rest of the orchestra followed suit, and only one oboe player, who had failed to have his contract made out at the time of his appointment, was lost. The musicians may have assured their positions, but there was no preventing the closure of the theatre, for the inability of the Prince and the unwillingness of anyone else to find the necessary funds was incontrovertible.

Spohr was thus left with few official duties to perform and during April and May 1832 occupied himself principally in composing three psalm settings for unaccompanied double chorus and soloists (op. 85). For his texts he used Moses Mendelssohn's translations of Psalms 8, 23 and 130, 'Unendlicher, Gott unser Herr', 'Gott ist mein Hirt' and 'Aus der Tiefe ruf' ich Gott zu dir'. His settings are a distinguished contribution to the small repertoire of nineteenth-century unaccompanied German religious choral music; Spohr displays his sensitive aural imagination in the wide range of sonorities which he obtains by combining and contrasting his three four-part groups. Psalms 8 and 130 conclude with fine fugues; in relation to this it is interesting that in his *Erinnerung an Felix Mendelssohn Bartholdy* Robert Schumann noted: 'To my question "Who writes the best fugues among living composers?" Mendelssohn answered unhesitatingly "*Spohr*".'[16]

It is possible that Spohr's choice of Psalm 130, 'Out of the deep have I called unto Thee O Lord', was a deliberate response to the troubles of the times, for by Easter 1832 it was becoming increasingly obvious that the tide had turned against the reformers throughout Europe. Russia had crushed the Polish revolution and refugees were flooding into Kassel, bringing with them disillusionment and disease. Spohr was particularly worried lest Dorette, whose delicate health became ever more disturbing, might fall victim to cholera. Nevertheless he was not despondent; he had lost much of his euphoric optimism about the prospects for liberalism but did not yet appreciate the strength of the forces for reaction. Despite Prince Friedrich Wilhelm's appointment of the ultra-conservative Ludwig Hassenpflug as his chief minister, Spohr seems not to have been fully aware of the extent of the Prince's determination to negate the reforms, though it was to be brought home to him over the next few years. In October 1832 he wrote to Speyer that 'Because of the great interest which I took and still constantly take in the political regeneration of Germany, the recent reverses have annoyed me too much to allow me to become totally engrossed in creative work.'[17] But a month later he could write: 'With all the worries of recent time I am nevertheless glad to have lived through them. A completely new spirit has been awakened in Germany and we may yet, with luck, see the fruits of it.'[18]

In spite of his avowed lack of concentration Spohr had managed to complete a major work during the summer of 1832 – his Fourth Symphony, *Die Weihe der Töne*. He began it in July while holidaying with Dorette in Neundorf, where his doctor considered that the warm sulphur springs might be efficacious in curing a stiff knee he had acquired while skating during the previous winter. The treatment cured his lameness, and the relaxed atmosphere lifted his spirits; musical friends from nearby Hanover came with their instruments, and a musical party was organised at which Spohr's op. 84 string quartets were played. Amid these congenial surroundings his creative urge was re-kindled. Having with him a posthumously published volume of Carl Pfeiffer's poems, he toyed with the idea of setting one of them, *Die Weihe der Töne*, as a cantata in memory of his friend, but on reflection decided to use the poem as the programmatic basis of an instrumental work which he entitled *Die Weihe der Töne, characteristisches Tongemälde in Form einer Sinfonie*.* The work is in four movements, but their form and content are considerably modified by the scheme of the poem. The first movement, which illustrates the first two of the poem's nine verses, is the closest of the four to a conventional symphonic movement. A Largo introduction, in which an important motto phrase (ex. 148) is introduced,

Ex. 148

evokes the 'deep silence of nature before the creation of sound', described in verse 1. This leads to a sonata-form Allegro, whose first theme – a seamless lyrical melody – grows out of the motto phrase after ten bars of dominant minor ninth (ex. 149). Though the large-scale sectional and tonal structure is entirely what might be expected from Spohr, the detail with which it is filled is closely related to the imagery of the second verse of the poem and is not conventionally symphonic; contrast rather than the intricate interweaving of a few ideas, in which Spohr usually indulged, is the distinguishing feature of the movement. At bar 63 of the Allegro the violins begin a semiquaver figuration which is unbroken for fifty-eight bars (clearly to be identified with the rustling breezes described by the poet), and when the music has arrived at the dominant in bar 81 the string section provides a gently undulating harmonic background to imitations of birdsong, for more

---

* Known in England as *The Power of Sound*, or *The Consecration of Sound*.

Ex. 149

than forty bars, from flutes, oboe, clarinet and horns (ex. 150). Shortly before the close of the exposition chromatic semiquaver rumblings in the bass herald the storm which functions as a development section, the developmental

Ex. 150

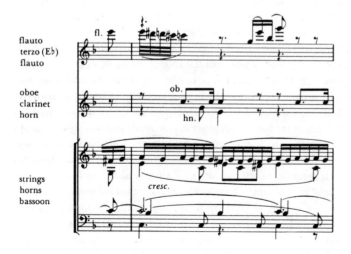

(Ex. 150 cont.)

quality being maintained by the presence of the motto phrase. Recapitulation is regular, and the distant echoes of the storm are heard once again, *pianissimo*, in the coda.

The second movement illustrates verses 3 to 5, which deal with the role of music as lullaby, dance tune and serenade. Spohr chose to give each of these ideas its own melody in a different time; thus the Lullaby is in 3/8, the Dance in 2/8 and the Serenade in 9/16. After all these themes have made their appearance they are ingeniously combined (ex. 151). In this Andantino Spohr reduces the orchestra, omitting flauto terzo (in E flat), oboes, trumpets, trombones and timpani, and uses a solo cello for the Serenade.

In the following movement Spohr makes his own addition to Pfeiffer's scheme in verses 6 and 7; these deal with the role of music to inspire courage in war and to give thanks for victory. Spohr chose to treat this as a military march followed by a thanksgiving chorale prelude, and in order to justify a contrasting Trio section in the March he adopted a narrative approach. The first section, 'Departure for battle', suggests the departing army, by a gradual diminuendo from *fortissimo*, fading into a middle section representing the anxious 'Feelings of those left behind' (this element is absent from the poem). Finally the March returns, quietly at first as if from a distance, but rising in a crescendo to a jubilant climax. The chorale prelude that follows is based on an *Ambrosianischer Lobgesang*, played by flutes, oboes, horns and trumpets while the rest of the orchestra weaves contrapuntal textures round it.

Another chorale prelude, this time using the funeral chorale 'Begrabst den Leib', begins the final movement with a Larghetto depicting the burial of the dead. This leads into an Allegretto, subtitled 'Consolation in tears', whose

Ex. 151

(Ex. 151 cont.)

opening theme has a close similarity to the consolatory theme in the last movement of Tchaikovsky's 'Pathétique' (ex. 152). The movement is subdued throughout and ends, as did the first movement, with horns and timpani alone.

Ex. 152

The similarity between Spohr's intentions in this work and Berlioz's in the *Symphonie Fantastique* (written in 1830, but almost certainly unknown to Spohr before the publication of Schumann's article on it in the *NZfM* in 1835) is a close one; both composers stipulated that the programme/poem should be distributed or read to the audience before the performance, and both allowed the programme to dictate significant modifications to the conventional symphonic form. But the end products are quite different. Spohr does not, like Berlioz, create startling new orchestral sonorities; his orchestration, though, is beautifully calculated for richness, exquisite balance and a perfect blend of sounds – it contrasts with Berlioz's like a béarnaise sauce with a vinaigrette. The same is true of the musical style, for despite the unusual external features of *Die Weihe der Töne* the melodic and harmonic idiom is absolutely characteristic of its composer.

The symphony immediately gained wide acceptance in Germany as a masterpiece. Schumann, though he had reservations about the poem's suitability, qualified his criticism with the comment: 'it must however be understood that no attack is intended on what is in other respects a musical masterwork'.[19] Hauptmann was more blunt about his objections to the programmatic intentions in the symphony, and suspected that it was evidence of Spohr's waning creativity, observing: 'It is questionable whether he was attracted by any vital interest in it; he wanted some spur, some incitement to compose; the old spontaneity begins to fail him. If music has to be forced this way what is Art but a milch cow?'[20] There was a good deal of similar objection to Spohr's use of a programme from more conservative musicians both in Germany and in England (where it was given for the first time at the Philharmonic Concert of 23 February 1835), but from the start the symphony had many enthusiastic admirers and by the 1840s had become established as one of its composer's *chefs-d'oeuvre*; even in France, where Spohr's music made far less impact, it was published by Richault as *La naissance de la Musique* and was the only one of Spohr's symphonies to be performed by the Conservatoire orchestra.

Die Weihe der Töne was completed towards the beginning of October 1832 and received its first performance in Kassel on 4 November as part of a series of concerts which, by order of Prince Friedrich Wilhelm, were being given every Sunday in place of theatrical performances, to raise money for the Hoftheater. The concert at which the new symphony was given was well attended, but the others attracted only sparse audiences, for there was widespread resentment that the receipts from these concerts were being diverted from the fund for the relief of widows and orphans of musicians to which they had been applied at Spohr's suggestion since 1826.

The situation in Kassel remained an uncongenial one for the members of the Hofkapelle, and even more so for those citizens whose livelihoods depended upon the theatre but who had been employed without contract. This was very much on Spohr's mind when, speculating about a possible date for the reopening of the theatre, he wrote: 'If only so many people had not been deprived of a living we might wait for it calmly; but humanity demands that we should try to achieve it as soon as possible.'[21] His own position was not threatened and, indeed, the Prince had appointed him to membership of the three-man board of directors for the Hoftheater, which at least gave him the opportunity to take a direct part in drawing up proposals for re-establishing the theatre on a sound financial basis. Money remained the primary obstacle to its reopening. A scheme put before the Estates, which would have required a subsidy from them, was rejected, and various other ideas which were transmitted to the Prince failed to gain acceptance. Spohr was ultimately forced to pin his hopes on the belief that the Prince and his entourage would find the long winter's evenings so tedious without a theatre that they would be goaded into devising a method of raising the necessary funds. But he admitted to Speyer in November 1832 that though the Prince very much wanted to have a 'really brilliant theatre', he could not find any way of achieving it while the Elector still had his hands firmly on the purse strings. Spohr recognised that in this matter the Prince was not to be blamed, but there were already indications that he was not going to be an easy master to work for. In early October 1832 Spohr had begun rehearsals of J. S. Bach's St Matthew Passion, which he hoped to perform publicly later that month, but all applications to the Prince for the necessary permission were fruitless, and the project had to be abandoned at the last minute. (He was at last able to perform it the following year, and repeated it subsequently on a number of occasions.)

Apart from the pleasant relief of a family reunion in Gandersheim for the Golden Wedding of Spohr's parents on 26 November, the winter of 1832/33 was perhaps the bleakest that Spohr had experienced since coming to Kassel. Even the chamber-music gatherings which had been such a feature of previous winters, and were to remain a source of great pleasure to him in future years, took place only once or twice during this winter. Hauptmann complained that the only opportunity to hear chamber music had been a series of quartet concerts mounted by Wiele and Hasemann, but that 'from the first they gave us an overdose of late Beethoven and though they themselves raved about the beauty of it, it hastened the collapse of the whole enterprise'.[22] At one of the few quartet parties which did meet at Spohr's house his new Double Quartet in E minor (op. 87), with which he had been occupied during the months of December and January, was played. As in the case of the String Quartet op. 84 no. 1, the first movement of this double quartet seems to embody a mood appropriate to the external circumstances, but there is much more of restless agitation and passionate urgency than of bleak austerity in the first movement of the double quartet, and the lyrical element so characteristic of Spohr's style is given far greater scope. In the variation movement which follows Spohr allowed full play to his own virtuosity as a violinist, but without destroying the special double-chorus character of the medium. The Scherzo and Finale are on the same high level; in the latter, piquant use is made of a quaver triplet rhythm (possibly intended to be played with a *fouetté* (whipped) bowing at the point); it is used to particularly good effect in conjunction with viola and cello pizzicatos in a sequence of suspensions (ex. 153) and at the very end of the movement.

With the approach of spring, prospects for a revival of musical life in Kassel began to brighten. The tedium of the winter had produced its desired effect on the Prince and his court; funds had somehow been found, and Spohr was instructed to travel to Meiningen to attempt to engage a travelling opera company, directed by Bethmann from Berlin, which was under contract there at that time. Duke Erich, the Prince's brother-in-law, was persuaded to release the company early, and their services were secured for Kassel for the months of March, April and May. The Hoftheater was reopened with a performance of *Der Freischütz*, and within a short time Spohr was able to reintroduce to the repertoire many of the operas which it had formerly contained. In November 1833 the theatre was officially reopened with

Ex. 153

its own company once again and by degrees was re-established on a more secure footing. The conditions under which it was obliged to function were not, however, such as to allow a return to the former brilliant productions. Financial security was guaranteed only within the restraints of a strict budget. In 1835 a correspondent from Kassel observed: 'Our opera company is now in its second year since the "theatre catastrophe" and pursues a troubled course, i.e. it is always aiming for greater stability and security. And indeed in this process of development one sees many signs of improvement, though its present condition is always dependent upon the changing situation.'[23] Despite this continuing degree of instability and the financial constraints, Spohr was able to resume his efforts on behalf of new music. In 1834 he introduced Marschner's *Hans Heiling*, J. C. Lobe's *Der Zauberblick oder die Fürstin von Granada*, Meyerbeer's *Robert le Diable* and Hérold's *Zampa*. But the prospects for a flowering of German opera were now even less favourable than they had seemed just prior to the political upheavals of the previous few years. Marschner was able to add little to what Spohr and Weber had already achieved, Lortzing was essentially too lightweight, Wagner's *Die Feen* (1833) gave no indication of the works which were to begin to transform the situation ten years later; others, such as Lobe, were unable to contribute anything of lasting significance, while Meyerbeer could hardly by that stage be regarded as a genuinely German composer. Weber had criticised Meyerbeer's pandering to Italian taste in 1820,[24] and his music had since been tailored more in the French fashion. Spohr did not find Meyerbeer's music entirely palatable; referring to *Robert le Diable* he noted that it contained 'wholly splendid numbers but also very many trivialities and plagiarisms'.[25]

The national aspirations which looked for expression in a truly German opera during the previous two decades had been realised in only a handful of works; *Faust, Jessonda, Der Freischütz, Euryanthe* and to a lesser extent *Zemire und Azor* and *Oberon*. Of older works, Mozart's great operas and Beethoven's *Fidelio* retained the place of honour, while a few others such as Weigl's *Schweitzerfamilie* and Winter's *Opferfest* managed to retain a toe-hold in the repertoire for a few more years. But until Wagner began to find his own distinctive voice, German opera was essentially to be a spent force. The new operas which occupied the Kassel stage in the latter part of the 1830s were almost entirely by non-Germans: such composers as Auber, Halévy, Adam, Bellini and Donizetti. Spohr had little enthusiasm for much of this music but there was no viable alternative.

In his direction of the opera Spohr was as active as ever during the 1830s. A report in 1838 noted that he 'steers and directs the opera with youthful energy, strength and perseverance'[26] (he was then fifty-four), but a great deal of the optimistic enthusiasm for his operatic endeavours which fills so much of his correspondence during the 1820s had evaporated. No amount of exertion on his part could overcome the financial obstacles to a full recovery of the theatre's former glory. In 1838 it was observed that 'genuine novelties have not appeared in the opera repertoire, but merely "newly studied" works, some of these being pieces which those who can still remember the golden days of our opera have previously seen much better done'.[27] The following year it was pointed out that the lack of a ballet and a sufficiently large chorus and the generally overriding desire to minimise expenditure were severely limiting factors on the choice and adequate presentation of large-scale operas.

The disappointments which beset Spohr's musical activities in Kassel during the 1830s were paralleled in his life with even greater intensity, for a series of personal misfortunes were to descend upon him with a force which might have crushed a less self-disciplined person. In 1833, however, it seemed that life was resuming its former pattern. His musical duties in Kassel settled into at least a semblance of normality, and he was able again to undertake conducting engagements elsewhere. In June he travelled to Halberstadt to share with Friedrich Schneider the direction of the Sixth Elbe Music Festival, where, apart from his 'Vater Unser' and the duet 'Schönes Mädchen' from *Jessonda*, he performed a concertante for two violins and orchestra in B minor (op. 88) which he had composed the previous April. The performance of this new composition was considered by the *AMZ* critic to have 'aroused the greatest sensation of the concert', and he felt that it displayed 'such a masterly and noble strain of melody that it must be considered as one of Spohr's most beautiful works'.[28] It seems probable, though, that much of this enthusiasm was engendered rather by Spohr's performance than by the intrinsic merits of the composition itself, for despite some undeniable beauties the concertante as a whole is so deeply infused with the individuality of Spohr's musical style that it lacks individuality in its own right. There is once again more than a hint of the unreflective dependence on well-worn phrases and formulae, which, however original when Spohr had first employed them, led increasingly, with their constant recurrence in his works, to the charge of mannerism.

The pleasant excursion to Halberstadt was followed by a holiday in Marienbad, where it was hoped that bathing and drinking the waters would restore Dorette's ever weakening constitution. While they were there, Spohr composed a waltz 'à la Strauss' for the local musical society's orchestra, subsequently published as *Erinnerung an Marienbad* (op. 89). He later came to the conclusion that it was lacking in the freshness of Strauss's and Lanner's waltzes, but he was perhaps in this instance too severe on himself. It is certainly a trifle, but a charming and highly polished one. The English critic of the *Musical World* aptly summed up its qualities when he wrote:

Here is a stinging reproof to Herrn Strauss, Lanner, Labitzsky and all such gentry! here is music to which ladies may dance and musicians listen with equal delight . . . the whole is, like all Spohr's small pieces of handicraft, the perfection of graceful beauty. The pianoforte arrangement is from one of the most exquisitely finished orchestral scores on a small scale we have ever seen.[29]

Returning from Marienbad with renewed hope of Dorette's recovery, Spohr plunged energetically once more into the old routine of teaching, conducting and composing. A letter from Speyer provided the impulse for creative work during August and September 1833. Speyer had written to inform him that the Frankfurt *Liederkranz* had just given an excellent performance of his male-voice part-songs op. 44, adding that 'the enthusiasm which these caused gave rise to the desire to have several choruses from you', and in relaying the society's request Speyer trusted that 'on account of our friendship you will not refuse me'.[30] The resulting six *Vierstimmige Gesänge* op. 90 were despatched in manuscript to Frankfurt in October and after publication achieved a wide circulation in Germany among the rapidly proliferating *Männergesangvereine* which assumed importance as centres of political and national aspirations during the period of reaction which set in after the collapse of the reforming movements.

As part of the returning pattern of normality, the regular chamber music meetings were reinstituted in the winter of 1833/34, and Spohr was thus prompted to write something new for them. The resulting work was a string quintet in A minor (op. 91), which he finished in February 1834. It cannot, however, be numbered among his most successful works. Like the op. 88 concertante, it contains beautiful passages and is written with his accustomed skill, but overall there is a marked lack of freshness, while the tendency to fall into familiar formulae and the paucity of distinctive material are again particularly noticeable.

Plans for a much larger work had meanwhile been germinating in his mind. While passing through Leipzig on their return from Marienbad in July 1833, the Spohrs had called on Friedrich Rochlitz, who took the opportunity to offer him the text of another oratorio. This was a treatment of the passion which he had originally published under the title *Das Ende der Gerechten* in 1806. It had been set to music by Schicht in 1806, but obtained no lasting popularity outside Leipzig. Having ascertained that Mendelssohn, to whom Rochlitz had also proposed his text, did not intend to proceed with it (he was just beginning work on *St Paul*), Spohr began work on the oratorio, renamed *Des Heilands letzte Stunden*, in the spring of 1834.

Despite the constant anxiety occasioned by Dorette's relapse into debility which the winter brought with it, and the interruption of another visit to Marienbad in the summer of 1834, Spohr made rapid progress on the composition, spurred on by his wife's constant interest. By the beginning of November the bulk of the oratorio was complete and Dorette was able to accompany him to a meeting of the *Cäcilienverein* early in the month at which the finished portion was tried through with piano accompaniment. On the way home Dorette spoke to him 'with accustomed perspicacity on its details'.[31] Less than a fortnight later she was dead. The date of her death, 20 November, is inscribed in Spohr's handwriting on the score of *Des Heilands letzte Stunden*, at which, by Dorette's expressed wish, he had continued to work up to the last, whenever he was not attending her bedside.

Spohr was utterly devastated by Dorette's death. For almost thirty years she had been an essential element in his life, as companion, lover and critic. As he wrote to Speyer on 30 January 1835,

You have known my incomparable wife long enough to understand the full extent of my loss! She was so bound up with my whole existence that I do not know how to come to terms with the new situation, for there was no business and no pleasure in which she did not take part; thus whatever I begin to do I always miss her.[32]

After the initial grief had diminished somewhat, Spohr attempted to distract himself by working on the orchestration for the completed portion of the oratorio and about New Year had regained his self-possession sufficiently to compose the remaining numbers, though, as he informed Speyer, 'the effect on me of having to compose something for the first time which I could not play to her cannot be described! This sorrow, this feeling of desolation, ah, it is an inconsolable condition'.[33] Nevertheless, the resumption of creative work was also therapeutic, for on 10 January he had written to Rochlitz: 'you will already have heard of the irreparable loss which I have sustained. The dreadful time which followed and the feeling of desolation prevented me from working for a long time, but in this [*Des Heilands letzte Stunden*] I first found consolation and reassurance'.[34]

The finished oratorio was premièred at Easter 1835 in Kassel, and made a deep impression. Spohr's friends confirmed his own opinion that it was the finest thing he had composed, and his former pupil Friedrich Nebelthau wrote a highly appreciative review of the work in the *AMZ*, where he compared it with Bach's St Matthew Passion, commenting: '[it] gives the German nation a new monument to its ancestral artistic fame'.[35] Hauptmann, however, expressed a less uncritical view in a letter to Hauser, where he wrote: 'much of it is very good and it is written with more freedom than is usual with Spohr. It is sure to be very effective. There is plenty of sentimentality, that we must admit, and I allow that it is our own fault; sentiment is the inseparable individuality of the age and of the individuals reflecting it.' But after hearing the performance he observed: 'Our oratorio went off brilliantly. Spohr surpasses his fellow-composers in the finish of his work as a *whole*; so true and genuine is his artistic instinct, that he will not tolerate a passage unless it blends harmoniously with the whole'.[36]

The spiritual influence of Bach's St Matthew Passion on Spohr's oratorio is unmistakable, and in one respect led to a serious disagreement between Spohr and Rochlitz. In January 1835 Rochlitz sent the composer a number of suggestions about the musical treatment of the work, including one that the words of Jesus should not be delivered by a solo voice, but should be given to a male-voice choir 'in the manner of the ancient Church'. Spohr, who by that time had virtually finished the oratorio, replied to Rochlitz on 10 January saying that it was too late to make substantial changes and that, in any case, with respect to giving Christ's words to a soloist, 'our pious forefathers had no hesitation about it so I cannot see why we should have any scruples'. Rochlitz protested vehemently against Spohr's unwillingness to make any alterations, and. Spohr countered by specifically citing Bach's Passion as a justification. The dispute continued by post into February, and Spohr continually refused to be swayed by what, as Hauptmann reported, he regarded as 'cant and hypocrisy'.[37] Spohr solicited Mendelssohn's opinion of the matter and was supported in his stance by the reply: 'I think that what a sincere musician writes with devotion and from the heart will certainly not be a profanation, whether it is for solo, chorus or anything else.'[38] In the end Spohr had his way, and Rochlitz was forced, reluctantly, to accept the *fait accompli*, though not before he had indignantly returned unopened the copy of the score which Spohr sent him.

Spohr's interest in Bach and his contemporaries is apparent in the musical style of the oratorio at a number of points in the work. The overture, a sombre fugue with a curious time signature (ex. 154), is interrupted three

Ex. 154

times by a section in 3/2, later to be sung to the words 'Er war der Christ, der Sohn des Hochgelobten'; Judas' solo (no. 4) has a running bass throughout, giving the impression of a continuo part (ex. 155); the chorus no. 24 has a Handelian quality, reminiscent of 'Thou shalt break them' from *Messiah* (ex. 156); while in the final chorus, a chorale prelude, Bach is again to the fore (ex. 157). None of this sounds merely like imitation, however, for the whole work is thoroughly suffused with Spohr's individuality of harmony and melody, which in some respects tends towards mannerism. Hauptmann complained: 'It is a matter of surprise to me that Spohr should be able to write an Oratorio that lasts three hours without a single new tone or harmonic progression . . . i.e. one that does not immediately suggest its author. It must be intentional, else I cannot conceive why we get that everlasting

Ex. 155

Ex. 156

Ex. 157

cadence of his* repeated perhaps 30 times over'.[39] On the other hand there is also much effective use of chromaticism which, especially in conjunction with the fine orchestration, is highly expressive. (Many passages which seem crude or ineffective in the vocal score make quite a different impression in performance – see p. 254 below for a contemporary opinion on this point.) At times, though, the music seems to lapse into sentimentality – for instance Mary's 'aria' no. 27, which with its horn, harp, violin and cello obbligato parts is redolent of the drawing room and is somewhat cloying. But there are many numbers of considerable power, such as several of the crowd choruses (nos. 17, 21 and 32). In no. 32 where the veil of the Temple is rent, Spohr calls for six timpani tuned to A flat, A, D, G, B, and C and uses double rolls to

---

* Hauptmann quotes Spohr's characteristic use of the dominant thirteenth (see for instance ex. 130a).

reinforce the tempest. No. 17 is a good example of the dramatic flair which is evident throughout much of the work; it begins surprisingly on a dissonance, interrupting Joseph of Arimathea's recitative 'Auch mir erschien er ein Prophet des Herrn' ('To me he seemed a prophet of the Lord') (ex. 158).

Ex. 158

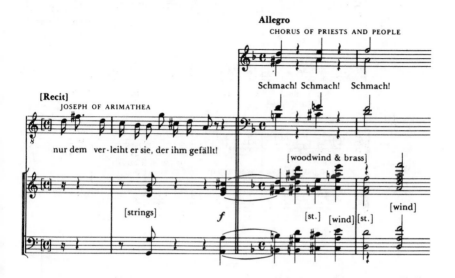

After a violent section there is a sudden *piano* and poco ritenuto where the people call 'Kaiphas, Kaiphas, rede' ('Caiaphas, Caiaphas, judgement'); then follows a fugato to the words 'Wir sind Abraham's Samen' ('We are Abraham's children'), which aptly conveys the self-satisfied dogmatism of the priests and people; this leads back into the violent first section, and the chorus concludes in the same open-ended way that it had begun with the return of the call for judgement, and Caiaphas's response (ex. 159).

Taken as a whole *Des Heilands letzte Stunden* must be regarded as one of the finest nineteenth-century oratorios; it may well be deemed to be not inferior to Mendelssohn's *Elijah* in either its dramatic impact or the quality of its music, and may certainly lay claim to being the finest nineteenth-century treatment of the Passion.

In the early months of 1835 Spohr's inclination to compose gradually revived. In May he wrote a new concertino for violin and orchestra in E major (op. 92); he took it with him on his summer holiday, and during a short stay in Düsseldorf played it with Mendelssohn who accompanied him from the score. According to Spohr's own account, a characteristic up-bow staccato so fascinated Mendelssohn that he several times asked him to repeat

1830–1836

Ex. 159

chorus

orchestra

232

(Ex. 159 cont.)

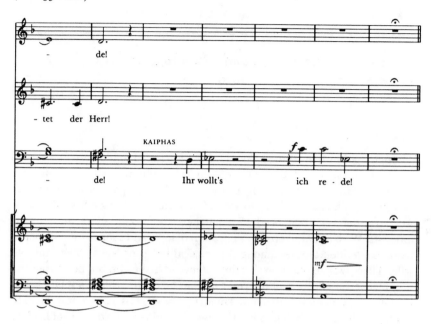

it, exclaiming to his sister, Fanny: 'See, this is the famous Spohrish staccato, which no violinist can play like him.'[40] From Düsseldorf he travelled on, accompanied by his seventeen-year-old daughter Therese and his sister-in-law Minchen Scheidler, to Zandford in the Netherlands, where he hoped to derive benefit from sea bathing. Their stay was blessed with fine weather, and Spohr, who had always been a keen and vigorous swimmer, greatly enjoyed the bathing. In addition the party was flatteringly entertained by the music-lovers of Amsterdam, who mounted a concert of Spohr's music in his honour. The recuperative benefits of all these pleasures, however, were almost entirely negated by the sudden and unexpected death of Minchen Scheidler. This tragedy reopened all the old wounds for Spohr and his daughter, and they returned despondently to the intensified loneliness of Spohr's house in Kassel.

XII

Remarriage and returning stability
1836-1839

Though Spohr often seemed aloof and self-possessed to his contemporaries, his temperament did not incline him to a solitary and self-sufficient existence. Having recovered from the immediate impact of his grief over Dorette's death and the shock so soon afterwards of Minchen Scheidler's, he soon felt the very real need of a partner who would share his musical interests. With a characteristic application of logic and sound common sense he began to look around among the musical ladies of Kassel for a suitable wife. There was no question this time of love at first sight, but he considered that by careful selection of the right woman he could achieve a relationship in which companionship might ripen into love. His choice was quickly made; it fell upon Marianne Pfeiffer, twenty-eight-year-old sister of his late friend Carl Pfeiffer, whose piano playing and general enthusiasm for music had attracted his attention at rehearsals of the *Cäcilienverein*. Self-conscious about the disparity in their ages, he proposed in writing in September 1835 and to his great joy was accepted. At Spohr's request the wedding was expedited as much as possible and took place on 3 January 1836.

From Spohr's personal point of view the marriage was a great success. He reported to Speyer a month after the wedding:

Since the 3rd of January I have again been living in my old accustomed domestic manner and feel once again very happy. My wife has such refined taste for the nobler things in music and such eminent skill in sight-reading that through her I have been able to get to know much music for violin and piano which was previously unknown to me.[1]

Marianne also familiarised him with much of the piano repertoire. As he wrote again to Speyer in December 1836, 'It makes me very happy that so much and such good music-making takes place in my house, for my wife makes great progress and has now acquired the elegance in performance which is indispensable to the newest piano compositions of Mendelssohn, Chopin etc.'[2] But a crucial difference from his first marriage was that whereas Dorette, who had been an equal partner in his early artistic triumphs, had offered Spohr criticism as well as encouragement, Marianne almost inevitably offered him only adulation.

During the summer vacation of 1836, accompanied by Marianne and

Therese, Spohr made a leisurely progress through Eisenach, Gotha, Erfurt and Leipzig, visiting old friends and receiving enthusiastic musical tributes from his many admirers. Travelling on to Dresden they met up with the Kleinwächter family, whom Spohr had been friendly with for more than thirty years, and also Adolph Hesse, whom he had known since 1828. Together they made an idyllic journey in glorious weather through parts of Switzerland, which Spohr was to commemorate in a duo concertant for violin and piano (op. 96) entitled *Nachklänge einer Reise nach Dresde und in die Sächsische Schweitz* (Reminiscences of a Journey to Dresden and in German Switzerland), usually referred to by Spohr as his *Reisesonate*. After returning to Dresden and parting from their companions, Spohr and his family went on to Brunswick to visit his brothers and attend a music festival there. Almost immediately after arriving back in Kassel they set out again to Paderborn, where a former pupil of Spohr's, Gerke, was to direct a performance of *Des Heilands letzte Stunden*. From this extra excursion they returned, thoroughly gratified, to Kassel.

The ever-increasing respect in which Spohr was held in the musical world was in marked contrast to the way in which he was constantly subject to petty annoyances from the Electoral Prince in Kassel. These were in character with the growing repressiveness of Chief Minister Hassenpflug's reactionary regime, but were also indicative of Prince Friedrich Wilhelm's desire to give vent to his irritation against a man who made no secret of his liberal sympathies and dislike of authoritarian government. The Prince's smallmindedness was shown in his refusal to grant permission for Marianne Pfeiffer to marry Spohr (permission was required by the Electorate's law, since she was the daughter of an official) until the last minute. Despite the efforts of Spohr's friend Otto von der Malsburg, who, as Oberhofmarschall should have made out the requisite document, permission was not forthcoming until Marianne had waived all her claims to a future pension. Spohr considered, probably with justification, that this obstructiveness was largely a result of the liberal activities of Marianne's father, Oberapellationsgerichtsrat Dr Burkhard Wilhelm Pfeiffer, in the 1831 Diet, where he had been instrumental in securing a substantial cut in Hessian military expenditure. It is equally possible that direct resentment against Spohr also played its part in this incident. A further example of the Prince's obstructiveness occurred in 1837 when he frustrated Spohr's plan to hold a music festival at which he proposed performing Mendelssohn's *St Paul* and some of his own music at Whitsuntide. The Prince raised so many objections in matters of detail that in the end Spohr had no choice but to cancel the festival and bear a considerable proportion of the financial loss himself. Irritations between Spohr and his employer continued with another incident in the summer of 1837, when Spohr, having accepted an invitation to go to Prague to conduct a revival of his opera *Der Berggeist* at the beginning of his vacation, did not receive his formal written leave of absence at the proper time. A personal approach to the Prince at the opera on the night before his proposed departure elicited only an indistinct answer in which the Prince merely made the self-evident observation that the permission had not been made out. Despite this Spohr, accompanied by Marianne and Therese, left Kassel early the following morning, hastening their journey to the border in case an attempt might be made to prevent them leaving the Electorate.

After a successful production of *Der Berggeist* in Prague, during breaks in the rehearsal period for which Spohr had enjoyed long swimming excursions in the Moldau, they travelled on to Vienna and spent a pleasantly relaxing fortnight there. From Vienna they journeyed on to Salzburg, where Spohr made a pilgrimage to Mozart's birthplace and paid a visit to his widow, Constanze. In Munich, which they next visited, Spohr found to his embarrassment that the Electoral Prince was also there, but on meeting him only a brief allusion was made to the unauthorised departure, and there the matter ended.

The following year, however, Spohr again experienced a delay in obtaining the official permission for his statutory holiday at the usual time. In this case the circumstances made the Prince's attitude not only capricious but also heartless, for Spohr had just suffered another shattering personal loss. His nineteen-year-old daughter Therese died on 3 June 1838 from an attack of the 'nervous fever' which had killed Dorette. He wrote to Speyer in despair on 6 June: 'Today I write to you with a broken heart, for this afternoon I bury my good Therese, your godchild. Ten days ago in blooming health, she has now been dead for three days . . . words cannot convey what I have lost in this good talented child. She was the perfect image of her late, unforgettable mother.'[3] Spohr's friends in Kassel mourned with him. Hauptmann wrote to Hauser: 'She was such a bright, sweet creature, there is universal mourning in Cassel for her loss. My grief for her father is beyond words. Spohr will stand a great deal, but this is a fearful blank; the old days were the happiest after all, and Therese was the last relic of that time.'[4]

After a delay of eight days in obtaining his leave of absence, Spohr and Marianne were able to get away from the painful memories which Kassel held for them. They travelled to Karlsbad where, in company with Adolph Hesse, they spent their time in walking and music-making, and slowly recovered their composure. On their return to Kassel via Leipzig, Spohr made the acquaintance of Schumann who, according to Marianne, 'though in other respects exceedingly quiet and reserved evinced his admiration for Spohr with great warmth'.[5]

Perhaps surprisingly, the shock of Therese's death did not cause a significant hiatus in Spohr's compositional activity. The productive period which had begun with his marriage continued unchecked. The conformation of Spohr's output during these years is essentially different from that of the preceding decade, one immediately noticeable feature being that song composition played a much greater role. Between 1836 and 1839 he wrote some forty Lieder and duets. These fall into several categories. About half of them are straightforward songs for solo voice with piano accompaniment; five, however, have an accompaniment for piano duet, while six (op. 103) are for soprano with piano and clarinet. There are also a number of duets for two sopranos and for soprano and tenor with piano accompaniments. All but seven of these songs were published in sets – op. 94 (six songs for alto or baritone, completed in January 1836), op. 139 (five songs, three of which date from 1836 and the other two from 1842 and 1845; the set was published in 1848), op. 101 (six songs from 1836 and 1837, three of which have piano-duet accompaniments), op. 103 (October to December 1837), op. 105 (six songs for soprano or tenor, February to July 1838), and two sets of three duets opp. 107 and 108 (November and December 1838). Many of these songs are charac-terised by the mannerisms of harmony and melody that had by now become inseparably linked with Spohr's name; as Rellstab remarked in a review of opp. 103 and 105, 'It is not difficult to find the weakness of Spohr's songs: one can show that the master repeats himself, that he remains true to his old manner, to certain forms and phrases especially loved by him to the point of boredom.'[6] Similar criticisms of Spohr's music were prevalent both in Germany and Britain at this time; an Edinburgh critic, for example, made much the same sort of remarks about *Die Weihe der Töne* after its first perform-ance there in 1837, but he tempered his animadversions with a significant rider, commenting:

That Spohr is deficient in *invention*, or the power of creating new phrases, modula-tions, and progressions of harmony, is unquestionable, otherwise he would not so fre-quently and glaringly repeat himself. His phrases, modulations, and progressions, in the present work are to be found in many of his compositions already before the public, yet these are ever so beautiful, so delicate and so delicious, that we are con-strained to yield ourselves up to their influence.[7]

Similar remarks are legion; *The Analyst* said of the Third Symphony: 'With all his mannerism and self-repetitions Spohr ever and anon makes so direct an appeal to one's sympathies that we feel disposed to throw all his egotism into the background.'[8] It is certainly true that despite their mannerism, many of the songs written at this period are highly attractive. The op. 103 set especially contains much fine writing, and the use of the clarinet in all its registers is masterly, as is the wide variety of textures achieved from the three performers. Amid many beauties, one passage from no. 6 may be cited; here the imaginative accelerating-trill effect in the clarinet conduces to a splendid climax (ex. 160). Clearly Spohr was not unaware of the constrictions of his musical style and though he could not break out of his mannerist's straight-jacket he sought increasingly to attain variety by unusual combinations and external stimuli, hence the songs with duet accompaniment. He also sought

Ex. 160

to vary the textures of his piano accompaniment more widely, probably as a result of Marianne's piano playing. Good examples of this can be found in op. 94 no. 6, 'Sonntag und Montag', where he uses drone effects and stark two-part writing to create a rustic effect (ex. 161); in op. 105 no. 5, 'Des Mädchens Klage', with its Chopinesque piano part (ex. 162); and others.

The chamber works from these years are fewer than formerly and on the whole disappointing in quality. The *quatuor brillant* op. 93, composed in September 1835, is unremarkable; Schumann noted that 'Forms, modulations, and melodic phrases were Spohr's often-heard ones',[9] though he

Ex. 161

Ex. 162

observed approvingly that in sheer technical polish the work was masterly. A fifth string quintet in G minor (op. 106) has more musical interest, and is written with greater regard to a fair distribution of interest among the instruments. The first two movements, Allegro moderato and Larghetto, are skilfully written as usual, but are little more than compilations of Spohrish phrases and modulations cast in the customary forms. The Scherzo is the best movement; Spohr gives it vitality by abrupt changes from 3/4 to 2/4. Scherzo and Trio are repeated, and in the concluding bar of the coda the first violin and cello play harmonics, anticipating the Finale, where harmonics figure prominently. Curiously, Spohr indicates the use of harmonics which he had frowned upon in his *Violinschule* (i.e. at the lower end of the string). The modern notation of harmonics had not evolved at that time, so Spohr indicated the actual pitch of the sound in small notes (ex. 163).

Ex. 163

All the other chamber works of the years 1836 to 1839 were for violin and piano, consisting of three duos concertants (opp. 95, 96 and 112) composed in quick succession between March 1836 and March 1837, and a Rondeau alla spagnuola (op. 111) of April 1839. The duos are large-scale four-movement works in which both violin and piano are, as the title suggests, given parts of equal prominence and considerable virtuosity. This was Spohr's first essay in virtuoso piano writing since the Quintet of 1820, and he was not entirely at ease with it. A more serious drawback, however, is that the increasing intricacy of the harmonic idiom which he had developed during the 1820s and 1830s, coupled with a paucity of strong or distinctive melodic ideas in opp. 95 and 112, makes these works somewhat faded and monotonous in comparison with his earlier works. The *Reisesonate* op. 96 is by far the most successful of the group, having a freshness that the others lack; its thematic material is bolder and its contrasts more striking. Spohr explained the scheme of the work as follows:

In the first movement I endeavoured to describe the love of travel, and in the second the journey itself, by introducing the postillion's horn calls customary in Saxony and the neighbouring part of Prussia as the principal idea of the Scherzo, played by the violin on the G string in a horn-like manner, worked out with striking modulations on the piano, and then in the Trio I depicted a daydream such as one so willingly yet unconsciously surrenders to in the carriage! The subsequent Adagio represents a scene in the Catholic court chapel of Dresden, beginning with an organ prelude on the piano alone; after this the violin plays the intonation of the priest at the altar, after which follow the responses of the choristers in the same tones and modulations as they are given in Catholic churches, including the one in Dresden. This is followed by an aria for castrato, in which the violinist must imitate the tone and style of that kind of singing. The last movement describes in a Rondo the journey through Saxon Switzerland, endeavouring to recall in places the grand beauties of nature and in other places the merry Bohemian music which one hears echoing from almost every rocky glen; a task which in such compressed limits could of course only imperfectly be realised.[10]

Spohr's interest in programme music continued strongly during these years; Hauptmann seems to have been right in thinking that Spohr increasingly needed the stimulus of a programme to fan his creative spark into flame. The *Reisesonate* was followed in November 1836 by a *Phantasie* in the form of a concert overture, on Raupach's tragedy *Die Tochter der Luft*. Schumann remarked of this work, when it was performed at the Gewandhaus in 1837, that 'his well-known originality was more than ever prominent; while in his elegiac violins, his sighing clarinets, we recognised once more the noble, suffering Spohr'.[11] Spohr himself was not wholly satisfied with the *Phantasie*, and the following year extensively reworked it as the first movement of his Fifth Symphony, which he composed in response to a request from the directors of the Vienna Concerts Spirituels, made during his visit there that summer. This symphony is undoubtedly the best of Spohr's major works from this period and may justly rank among his best works from any period. It begins with an Andante introduction whose opening theme plays an important part in the first and last movements (ex. 164). The themes of the exposition section of the first Allegro have a freedom of phrase structure and rhythmic irregularity unusual for Spohr, and (as in the first movement of the *Reisesonate*) one is at times reminded of Schumann. The halting

Ex. 164

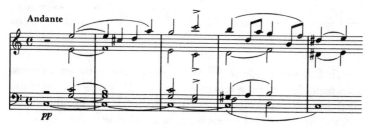

rhythms of the second subject as well as the piquancy of the orchestration are effective, and an abrupt change from 9/8 to 3/4 towards the end of the section makes a strong impact. Spohr forswore a conventional development; instead he transformed the theme from the introduction into a long rhapsodic melody. The melody – spun out to more than forty bars – is initially stated by the oboe (ex. 165), then taken over by the strings while the woodwind

Ex. 165

accompany it with fragments of the first subject in a manner strikingly reminiscent of Tchaikovsky. The Larghetto in A flat is one of Spohr's most beautiful orchestral slow movements; it has a remarkable quality of sustained concentration. The rich wind writing and the tendency of strings to exploit their lower registers, together with the use of three trombones (extremely rare in symphonic slow movements at that time), give it a warm Romantic colouring. A melodic figure from the middle section pervades the recapitulation of the first section, which is punctuated by languid horn calls that seem to fade into the distance at the close. The Scherzo takes up the horn-call idea, but in a quite different mood, for the opening phrase on the horn seems designed to wake the listener from his reverie. A delightful Trio in D flat provides a charming contrast to the exuberant C major Scherzo, and an exciting coda rounds off the movement. In the Presto Finale three themes vie with one another for supremacy. The first subject contains two contrasting ideas, and in the development Spohr constructs a fugato on the second of these themes, employing the first of them as a counterpoint. The second subject is a version of the theme first heard at the opening of the work, thus giving a sense of unity to the symphony (ex. 166). The coda builds

Ex. 166

up to a triumphal climax, made all the more exhilarating by the use of trombones and horns in their highest registers.

It is clear that Spohr was consciously trying to break new ground in this symphony, for writing to Adolf Hesse on 27 September 1837 informing him

that the score was completed, he remarked: 'I believe that I have introduced
many new effects as well as much that is unusual in the orchestration, and
am very keyed up to the first rehearsal.'[12] At its première in Vienna on 1
March 1838 it was rapturously received by audience and critics alike. The
Allgemeine Theaterzeitung observed enthusiastically:

It is again a work that speaks its own master's praise in eloquent language; a pure
whole, containing everything within itself, cast in a perfect mould. The introduction
. . . breathes a cheerful repose which gradually assumes an impassioned character
and prepares the listener for the transition to the Allegro . . . which replete with treasures of harmony bears in itself the germ of an imposing effect . . . The second movement . . . is a conglomeration of deep feeling, warm fantasy, expressive melody
etc.; here again every note speaks to the heart with irresistible force . . . The Scherzo
. . . opens boldly with fresh courage in life; the sharp rhythms, the restless and continuous competition of wind and stringed instruments, the impetuous bursts of tonic
power as opposed to the soft, clear flowing cantilena of the Trio, – all this effected in
so original a way as to defy expression in words . . . For the presto Finale, the poet of
sound appears to have husbanded as much as possible the sum total of his creative
powers . . . None of the innumerable beauties went unnoticed, each movement
received the deserved tribute to his mastery; indeed the richly fantastic Scherzo was
so universally electrifying that it had to be repeated. [13]

Curiously, while the Fifth Symphony retained its popularity in Germany for
several decades, in England it was badly received and hardly ever performed; Chorley referred to it as 'the notoriously driest and least interesting'
of Spohr's symphonies. [14]

The only orchestral work of 1838 was an overture to a musical play, *Der
Matrose*, adapted from the French by Birnbaum, for which Spohr also wrote
a song, 'Der Sturmwind braut' (the remainder of the music was composed by
Hauptmann, Baldewein and Grenzebach). In February 1839 he wrote
another concertino for violin and orchestra, op. 110, to which he gave the
title *Sonst und Jetzt* (Then and Now). The impulse to compose this work seems
to have come directly from a visit to Kassel by Ole Bull in January 1839,
when he gave two concerts and took part in one of Spohr's quartet evenings.
As he had been with Paganini, Spohr was both fascinated and repelled by
Ole Bull's playing. He praised his bow control and the certainty of his left
hand, but felt that he sacrificed the nobility of the instrument too much to
showy effects designed merely to impress the general public and particularly
deprecated the weak tone of the lower strings, necessitated by the thinness of
the strings required to execute artificial harmonics effectively. After Bull's
departure Spohr decided to embody his feelings about the changing style of
violin playing in music. *Sonst und Jetzt* consists of two contrasting sections, a
Tempo di Menuett antico (*Sonst*) and a tarantella-like Vivace in 2/4 (*Jetzt*).
The Menuett displays the noble, singing qualities of the violin in an expansive movement; this is interrupted by the Vivace in which technical
fireworks are dominant. The Menuett reasserts itself briefly, but is dismissed
again by the Vivace which concludes the Concertino.

The idea which lay behind *Sonst und Jetzt*, of contrasting different styles and periods, led Spohr to a further essay in the same direction. In July and August 1839 he explored the concept more fully in his *Historische Symphonie* (Historical Symphony) op. 116, subtitled 'in the style and taste of four different periods'. Its programme was as follows: 'Largo grave, Allegro moderato, Pastorale – Bach and Handel period 1720; Adagio (Larghetto) – Haydn and Mozart period 1780; Scherzo – Beethoven period 1810; Finale, Allegro vivace – the most modern period 1840.' The different movements are not accurate stylistic imitations, though the intentions are made clear by the use of characteristic stylistic devices or direct allusions to the music of the composers concerned. Thus Bach is represented by an introductory Largo and a fugue, Handel by a Pastorale (having a perceptible kinship with 'He shall feed his flocks' from *Messiah*); Mozart is recognisable as the model for the second movement by the employment of a phrase from the slow movement of his Symphony no. 39, while in the Scherzo Spohr went one better than Beethoven by beginning with a solo for three timpani. The Finale puzzled many contemporaries; it is essentially a trivial movement with noisy orchestration, including triangle, side drum, cymbals, etc., and was clearly intended as a satire on everything Spohr disliked about modern music. After the Symphony's first London performance on 6 April 1840 the critic of the *Musical World* observed:

The intention of the Finale was evidently overlooked by the audience, who hissed it for what they, probably, deemed its essential unworthiness. Judging from its clamour, its redundance of leaps from one scale to another, and its looseness of construction, we presume Spohr intended to satirize the present French and Italian schools of instrumental writing; and if so, he has succeeded admirably. The audience, however, did not see the joke, and consequently treated that as earnest which the composer could only have meant as a severe, but not unfair, piece of ridicule.[15]

The Atlas had a slightly different interpretation of the hostile reception of the last movement, mischievously wondering whether it had been hissed either 'because the joke was not appreciated, or because any persons in the room endured a sense of personal ridicule'.[16]

The symphony did not gain many admirers. Mendelssohn, in a diplomatic response to Spohr's request for his opinion,* stated that he felt Spohr should have portrayed the modern period with an example of his own style, observing: 'For the sake of the greater effect of the whole work, I would rather have had a greater instrumental piece in freer form, somewhat like the overture to *Faust* or so many of your magnificent, spirited overtures in its place.' Schumann, on the other hand, felt that Spohr had not really escaped from the confines of his own style at any point in the work, commenting in a review:

* The draft of his letter to Spohr, in the Deneke collection (Bodleian Library, Oxford), is full of alterations, showing the care he took in framing his criticisms.

He remains the master as we have always known him and loved him. In fact these forms to which he is not accustomed bring out his individuality even more strongly, just as one with a particularly characteristic bearing reveals himself most clearly when he assumes a disguise. Once, Napoleon went to a masked ball; he had been there hardly a moment before he . . . clasped his arms together. Like a bush fire the cry spread throughout the hall: "the Emperor". Similarly, when this symphony was played one could hear from every corner of the hall the sound "Spohr" and again "Spohr".[17]

Leaving aside the question of the musical worth of the *Historische Symphonie*, it has considerable interest as possibly the earliest serious nineteenth-century attempt at a species of pastiche that was to be essayed by such composers as Tchaikovsky and Stravinsky, while the satire of the Finale antic-ipates Nielsen's lampoon of modern techniques in his Sixth Symphony. The *Historische Symphonie*'s inception was rooted not only in Spohr's dissatisfaction with the most recent musical trends, but also in the developing interest in what were known as Historical Concerts at which a range of works from the seventeenth century to the nineteenth century would be performed. The earliest composers to have retained a significant place continuously in the instrumental repertoire up to 1839 had been Haydn and Mozart, but in the 1820s and 1830s the music of earlier composers was gradually being redis-covered and performed. Historical Concerts were given at the Leipzig Gewandhaus, and shortly prior to Spohr's composition of his *Historische Symphonie* he and Hauptmann had been in correspondence with Speyer over possible items for such a concert in Frankfurt.

If the *Historische Symphonie* was, strictly speaking, a failure, Spohr had little more success with his sacred music at this time. Between 1836 and 1838 he composed three choral works, none of which attained widespread popu-larity; a setting of Psalm 24 for soloists and chorus with piano accompani-ment, which he did not publish (if he had felt it worthy of publication he would probably have orchestrated the accompaniment); a *Hymne* (Cantata), 'Gott du bist gross' op. 98, for soloists, chorus and orchestra; and a setting of Klopstock's 'Vater Unser' for double male-voice chorus with accompaniment for wind instruments. The 'Vater Unser', composed in January 1838 and orchestrated in March, originated from a request from Speyer in October 1837 for a new work to be performed in a festival which was to be held to raise money for a *Mozartstiftung* (a fund to further the study of promising young musicians). 'Gott du bist gross' was composed in October 1836. It is, as usual, a highly polished piece of work, well proportioned and expertly scored, but is again so strongly tinged with Spohr's mannerisms that the listener is constantly reminded of *Die letzten Dinge*, *Des Heilands letzte Stunden* and the 'Vater Unser' of 1829. After its first performance in England, at the Royal Academy of Music on 23 April 1839, a hostile but perceptive critic wrote:

Louis Spohr has taken up his real position in Germany amongst living composers; he has been injudiciously exalted in England, but every new production of his pen assists the artist and the amateur in forming a right opinion of the extent of his genius and acquirements. He has the mechanism but not the poetical temperament; if he could have united these qualities of art and nature, he would be not only the greatest musician living, but the greatest that ever lived. As it is he is certainly inferior to such men as Cherubini and Mendelssohn; men by no means accustomed to walk up and down a very small room habited in a strait waistcoat. [18]

This critic's view of Spohr's position, however, was by no means universally accepted in England, and, as events were to show, far from Spohr's reputation declining in England, it was yet to reach its highest peak.

XIII

Renewed ties with England
1839–1842

The last twenty years of Spohr's life were to be strongly coloured by a closer association with England. Between 1839 and 1853 he made five visits during which he conducted and played his own music, and was an object of veneration to musicians, press and public. Spohr's impact on English music both before and during the period of Mendelssohn's popularity was very much stronger than has generally been recognised. In the nineteen years which had elapsed since his visit of 1820 his music had steadily gained a firm place alongside the works of Mozart and Beethoven in the programmes of concerts which had any pretensions to seriousness. But Spohr was not without his critics, and his reputation had been a subject of considerable controversy in the musical press.

The decade following Spohr's 1820 visit had seen a gradually increasing dissemination of his music in England. Several works, including the overtures op. 12, *Alruna* and *Jessonda*, and the First Symphony were published in English editions for chamber ensemble. These seem to have enjoyed a degree of popularity among amateurs; the overture to *Alruna* certainly went through more than one edition and when performed at the Philharmonic concert of 19 May 1823 *The Harmonicon* observed; 'Spohr's overture to "Alruna" is one of the best productions of this excellent composer: if he proceeds as he has begun, – and he has plenty of time before him, according to the usual chances – he will become one of the greatest musical ornaments of Germany.'[1] Between 1825 and 1828 there were at least fifteen separate English publications of selections from the operas *Faust* and *Jessonda*, though these received a mixed reception from the reviewers. A typical attitude was expressed in a review of 'The Admired Airs in Spohr's Celebrated Opera Faust' which appeared in *The Repository of Arts* in 1826. There the critic observed:

The specimens of Spohr's Dr. Faustus, selected and carefully adapted by Mr. Griesbach, fully confirm our opinion of this author's style. There is everywhere abundance of thought and musical science, and no lack of strong modulation; all is very good music: but we are not ashamed to confess it, the pleasing tunes of even Kauer and Dittersdorf, countrymen of Mr. S. much inferior to him in the scale of compositorial gradation, possess more attractions for us according to our *present* relish. What changes time may effect in our taste we will not answer for.[2]

In England, as in France, there was a strong feeling at this time that Spohr's works were more calculated to appeal to the professional musician or connoisseur than to the average concert-goer (though in England this was considered less damning than in France); thus in 1824, after a performance of the Second Symphony at a Philharmonic concert, *The Harmonicon* wrote:

Amongst the living composers of orchestral music, Spohr stands very high; his science, his knowledge of the powers of various instruments, his elegant taste and indefatigable industry in revising his compositions, and in giving the highest finish to them, altogether imparts a charm to his productions which, if it be not felt and admitted by the multitude, is enjoyed and acknowledged by the connoisseurs; and the grand test of his merit is, that the more he is heard, the more he is admired. His works certainly are much elaborated, and it requires no slight knowledge of the art to be enabled to appreciate them. This is particularly the case with the symphony performed at the fourth concert, which does not unfold all its beauties to the uninstructed hearer, but to skilful judges, – or at least the majority of them, – it affords high intellectual pleasure.[3]

Nevertheless some critics were more difficult to convince. Of the overture to *Faust* one wrote in 1828: 'The overture to Faust is obscure; it has not yet unfolded itself to our understanding: we hear very good judges assert that it is full of meaning – that the genius of the composer is there manifest in all its power. We therefore still continue to suspend our judgement under the hope that we may yet become enlightened.'[4] In addition there was a considerable number of critics who were less fair-minded than this, such as the one who said of the *Faust* overture, 'we are compelled to say of this overture, that it is a most tiresome, dreary, uninteresting mass of crudity and chromaticism, destitute of melody, and with not one feature of originality.'[5] On the whole, though, the feeling that as Spohr's music became more familiar it would be more widely appreciated seems to have predominated. Thus, after a performance of the overture to *Der Berggeist*, a critic in *The Athenaeum* (probably John Ella), wrote in 1830: 'The overture of Spohr is a splendid composition. We are warm admirers of this author because we are well acquainted with his music: when he is more heard and better known, we are quite sure that the general feeling among our amateurs will be equally in his favour.'[6]

It is difficult to assess how much of Spohr's music was available in England in German editions during the 1820s, but the amount was probably considerable, and, as the following passage from *The Atlas* shows, imported music was much in demand among serious amateurs. The critic (Edward Holmes) observed:

English music principally finds a market among young ladies who have a morning to waste in *shopping*, and who are attracted by a title, an ornamental frontispiece or dedication, to place in their portfolio the novelty of which is forgotten before the week is out. What a noble prospect for a composer! The foreign music shops, which from a small beginning a few years ago, have increased so wonderfully, and are now thriving well, have shown how incompetent were existing native publications to satisfy the good taste of the country; and there is a large body of amateurs, who, from one year's end to another, scarcely ever purchase an English piece. Weber's appearance in this country, the success of his operas, the favour of German instrumental music, the manner in which the quartetts, quintetts, etc., of Beethoven, Spohr etc., are performed in private parties show the progress of a taste for music of a high character.[7]

This passage also demonstrates some of the changes which were taking place in the cultural climate of England during the third decade of the century. An increasing seriousness of taste was becoming apparent throughout the artistic spectrum as a corollary to the increasing economic and political power of the middle class. The Reform Bill of 1832 and the development of artistic tastes which rejected Regency frivolity and aristocratic domination were products of similar forces; the technical precision and seriousness of purpose in Spohr's music was mingled with a Romantic feeling which aptly matched the temper of this trend. Whatever else might be said about it there was a feeling that Spohr's music was 'sound', that he was, as Edward Holmes wrote, 'a composer over whom none ever retrograded in taste'.[8]

It would be too easy to imagine, however, that such developments of taste were accepted meekly by everyone. Holmes recognised that the majority must be brought into line by the cognoscenti and that what was deemed good for them might not always be palatable at first. When in 1831 a Philharmonic concert included three items by Spohr, he wrote:

For ourselves there was not a note that we would have changed; but, we fear, the interests of such music as Spohr's demand that it should be rather insinuated by degrees – carefully and discreetly – than thrust boldly forward, to stand upon its own merits; for we have evidence that a great many of the subscribers are not yet sufficiently advanced in taste to comprehend it, and these hearers only require rather *too much* on one occasion to be impatient at the sight of the author's name in the bills; consequently, the repetition of the practice will only harden their prejudice. We throw out this hint as a prudential measure, for we hold that the more unanimous the feeling of pleasure at the end of a movement, the more beneficial the effect upon art; because the directors gain credit with the audience, which will enable them in time to fashion their taste as they please.[9]

Clearly therefore in 1831 Spohr was highly respected by many serious and influential musicians, and was gaining increasing regard from important sections of the musical press. In its review of the 1830 season, *The Harmonicon* could comment that the Philharmonic concerts had 'brought forward some new things of great merit, by Spohr chiefly'.[10] Yet his music had so far failed to obtain widespread popular favour. But by that time events had already taken place that were to lead to his gaining, by the early 1840s, the generally accepted position in England of the greatest composer of the age.

These events were the performances of his oratorio *Die letzten Dinge* (*The Last Judgement*) at the Norwich Festival of 1830 and his opera *Zemire und Azor* (*Azor and Zemira*) at Covent Garden in 1831. Reviewing *Die letzten Dinge* in 1829, Edward Holmes had written prophetically in *The Atlas*:

We doubt whether . . . any composer now living possesses the same knowledge of the secret affinities between matters of the external world and the invisible world of music or whether any can find utterance for human passion in music than Spohr. In this he is like Mozart. We again recommend this oratorio to the notice of directors of musical festivals as a good subject well set, calculated to please every person of imagination and taste, and peculiarly adapted to gain fame in this country.[11]

Edward Taylor, looking back in 1843 on the progress of Spohr's reputation in England, remarked that in the 1820s his music had encountered the prejudice that 'a professed fiddler' could not be a fine composer, and pointed out that this opinion had encouraged even the participants in the first performance of *The Last Judgement* to view the enterprise with misgivings. But, as he went on to say,

It was diligently prepared and carefully rehearsed: the day of performance came – and there was but one opinion. It bore down all opposition – subdued every prejudice; musicians of all schools – foreign, English, ancient, modern – all yielded their willing homage to the genius of its author: Vaughan and Knyvett, Braham, Stockhausen, were united and equal encomiasts. Perhaps the most emphatic testimony of its power was given by Malibran, whom it completely subdued, and who was obliged, sobbing and almost hysterical, to quit the orchestra. 'I thought' she said to the person who now records her words, 'that I had been too practised a stager to make such a fool of myself before an audience: but I had yet to learn the full power of music upon the heart – I have now felt it all.'[12]

Taylor's description of the oratorio's impact is hardly too extravagant; critical opinion at the time was almost unanimous in its praise. *The Harmonicon* wrote:

The Last Judgement . . . we consider as one of the greatest musical productions of the age. It would be presumptuous in us, having heard it but once, were we to attempt a minute detail of all the beauties of this elaborate work, in which is embodied every passion, sentiment and feeling, and however elevated the name of Spohr may justly be as a composer of the highest class of instrumental music, this sublime oratorio will add immensely to his reputation and henceforth his name will be inserted in the list of those authors whose studies, efforts and genius have been most conspicuously successful in this the noblest branch of art.[13]

The effect of such enthusiastic recommendation can be seen in the appearance of a vocal score of the work from Novello in 1831, followed closely by orchestral parts, and in the large number of performances it received over the next few years. In 1830 it was performed at Norwich and Liverpool; in 1831, at the Philharmonic Society (the only time an oratorio was ever given at those concerts), and again in London at Vaughan's benefit, as well as at Dublin, Derby, Oxford and Manchester; in 1832, at Gloucester; in 1833, at Worcester and again at Liverpool; in 1834, at Hereford; in 1835, at Cambridge and York; in 1836, at the Royal Academy of Music and the Sacred Harmonic Society in London, and again at Manchester and Worcester. No doubt there were other less important performances which did not leave their marks in the national press. The durability of the oratorio's success is

attested by Sir Frederick Gore Ouseley in a footnote to the English translation of Naumann's *History of Music* (1884), where he remarked that 'In
England it has been very frequently performed, and still in great measure
retains its original popularity.'[14]

In the wake of the stir caused by *The Last Judgement* a performance was
mounted at Covent Garden of *Azor and Zemira*. It is clear from an abundance
of evidence that the production aroused a very high level of interest among
serious musicians. A volume was published containing the complete music
of the opera, *The Harmonicon* published a substantial number of extracts from
it in its musical supplement for 1831, and at least five other publishers issued
selections (including a set of quadrilles based on the opera). The *Morning
Chronicle*, reviewing the first night, concluded: 'G. Penson gave out the opera
for Thursday and Saturday, without any expression of dissent, and with very
warm applause. We saw in the house many musical professors of eminence,
both native and foreign, all interested for the success of imported Spohr.'[15]
The Times noted that 'the opera was exceedingly well received by a very
crowded audience',[16] while later during its run *The Atlas* observed: 'The
musical professors so abundant here on the first night have sent their pupils
and friends by dozens – the boxes are full, there is a good independent pit,
and no want of *encores*: let, therefore, Spohr's compositions and Covent
Garden flourish together.'[17] There was, however, a degree of ambivalence
towards the opera. To many, the seriousness of Spohr's style was less acceptable in opera than in oratorio. The dichotomy between the major part of the
musical public, whose predilections were for light and undemanding music,
and the smaller but influential portion who were the arbiters of cultivated
taste is apparent in some reviews. There is perhaps a hint in the following
passage from The *Morning Chronicle* that the critic was not wholeheartedly in
support of the musical Germanophiles. He wrote:

Sir George Smart . . . has laid the town under no little obligation to him for making
it better acquainted with the excellencies of one of the greatest and most original
composers of modern times. To call him great and original in these days, is almost, in
other words, to say that Spohr is German. We do not pretend to say that the music of
Spohr is calculated to be as popular in this country as that of Rossini, from the very
circumstance that it has greater depth and power of genius; but the German has not
the gaiety and brilliancy of fancy of the Italian, which captivates at once, and
requires little trouble to be understood.[18]

And he went on to remark that the 'airs . . . sometimes want melody' – a comment which prompted Edward Holmes to come forward with a 'Defence of
Spohr', couched in a heavily sarcastic vein. He observed:

A charge of want of melody has been brought against Spohr . . . about as justly as if
we should say of the Rev. Mr Irving that he wanted words, or of one like the memorable Daniel Lambert that he wanted fat. Melody in the sense of the objectors means
something like 'Meet me by Moonlight' or 'Come where the Aspens Quiver'; and
embraces all such successions of harmonious sounds as may be ground by a street

organ, and brought home to the ears without difficulty . . . They listen to Spohr in the buckles and ruffles of their grandfathers. It is hard upon the cause of good music that a fine work should suffer from the pique or spleen of writers who do not understand it. The composer affronts them by his invention and contrivance; a new harmony is like a knock in the face; the modulation becomes puzzling – the critic confused and resentful, and so makes up his mind to say 'this man has no melody'. It is sufficient that the opinion will be deemed well-founded by the common rout of hearers – the numbers on the side of the writer will secure him from the ill effects of the laughter of the better sort.[19]

Notwithstanding the 'numbers on the side of the writer', neither *Azor and Zemira* nor *Der Alchymist* (or rather a hotch-potch of items from various of Spohr's operas arranged under that title by Henry Bishop), which was given at Drury Lane in 1832, achieved lasting success. As a writer in *The Analyst* remarked in 1839, *Azor and Zemira*

did not receive that patronage from the public due to its merits; while the theatre itself was not benefited by the experiment. A total revolution must take place in the whole European taste for vocal music, which even in the recesses of Germany, is fast welcoming the modern Italian school, before the opera music of Spohr becomes what might be called the stock property of the theatres.[20]

And in a more pungent style a contributor to the *Musical World* had made much the same point in 1837, saying:

The 'Azor and Zemira' and the 'Alchymist' were, on their production on the London stage severally well supported and performed; but the music which suits the refined voluptuousness of the drawing-room, goes no way in meeting the broad stirring passions which agitate the pit and galleries of Covent Garden or Drury Lane: . . . Jessonda, Alma, Inez, Cecilia, and Kunegunda, may wail themselves into hysterics, syncopes, or convulsions, without arousing the sympathies of John Bull; and lucky will they be if they can but muzzle the deep growl of his ill-smothered indignation.[21]

In the concert hall, however, there was a steady increase of performances. The number of serious concert-giving organisations in London proliferated rapidly during the 1830s, and by the end of the decade Spohr's orchestral, chamber and vocal music had become a regular feature with all of them. Important new works such as the Fourth Symphony (*Die Weihe der Töne*) and the oratorio *Des Heilands letzte Stunden* were introduced almost immediately on their appearance. The symphony was hailed by *The Athenaeum* as a work 'which is entitled to the first rank in compositions of the highest order',[22] and by *The Spectator* as 'one of the highest flights of musical poetry that imagination has conceived or genius accomplished'.[23] And all the other critics, though differing in their opinions about the propriety of its programmatic intentions, were more or less in agreement that it should be regarded as a work of major significance. *Des Heilands letzte Stunden* (known in England at first as *The Crucifixion* and later as *Calvary*) was very well received by those critics who reviewed its first performance in London at the Vocal Concerts on 27 March 1837. The *Morning Chronicle* concluded its review:

At present we can only add that this performance of it produced a strong impression on a numerous and very musical audience. When performed (as it will be) at our great festivals, it will be found not to yield in sublimity of conception, richness of imagination, profound feeling, and command of all the resources of the art, to any existing production of the sacred musical drama. [24]

The Times concurred, concluding: 'We are much mistaken if this sublime oratorio do not, at the approaching festivals, command a first place in the attention of the public already prepared for the enjoyment of it by "The Last Judgement".'[25]

In view of such sanguine hopes it is perhaps surprising to discover not only that the oratorio was not given at any of the provincial festivals during the succeeding two seasons, but also that even its success at Norwich in 1839 failed to establish it in the repertoire. But the reasons for this were almost entirely connected with English notions on the religious impropriety of treating the subject of Christ's passion and death in music – notions the strength of which was to be shown at the time of Spohr's 1839 visit.

Despite the interest in and enthusiasm for Spohr's work which had grown up during the 1830s there was, on the eve of his 1839 visit, a marked division of opinion among critics as to whether his claim to be considered as one of the really great composers was well founded, and whether or not his music had already passed the peak of its popularity. As his apologists became more vocal and his works figured more largely in concert programmes, so his detractors began to adopt a more strident tone. Even some of the more partial critics reacted against the extreme adulation with which many musicians viewed his music. As the critic of the *Morning Chronicle* observed in 1836, 'Spohr is a great man; but few are so great that they cannot be overrated and assuredly Spohr is not one of them.'[26] Looking back in 1840, H. F. Chorley commented on

the vicissitudes through which the composer's reputation has passed among us, and the violent partizanship of which it has been the object. By some he has been extolled to the seventh heaven, as surpassing Mozart, Weber, and Beethoven, in right of sweet melodies, rich harmonies, and magnificent conceptions – by others, degraded to the level of those respectable, but most wearisome persons, who produce a multitude of carefully-executed works, upon the liberal allowance of half an idea. [27]

The news that he was to come to Norwich to direct his oratorio in 1839 caused one correspondent to write to the *Musical World*:

I perceive . . . that Spohr is to come over for the purpose of presiding at his own oratorio. Poor fellow! they will make a great stalking-horse of him. He should have come here ten years ago when his music was, to a certain extent, popular. His constant repetitions of himself in his later publications have made the public lukewarm, if not indifferent to his real merits. [28]

In the event, however, Spohr's visit was both personally and musically a triumph and was vastly to reinforce English respect and admiration for him.

In early September 1839 Spohr, accompanied by Marianne and Caroline von der Malsburg, arrived in England and stayed for a few days in Edward Taylor's London house, cementing a lifelong friendship, before travelling on to Norwich for the festival. Press interest in the visit had increased greatly during the week before the festival and continued at a high level throughout. Spohr's personal direction of his own music was a revelation to many who had not previously appreciated its beauties to the full. A constant complaint of Spohr's protagonists in the preceding decade had been that his works could not be properly appreciated while they were so often mutilated in performance; now under their composer's firm direction difficulties were vanquished and obscurities banished. After he had conducted his overture to *Faust* at the evening concert on 19 September *The Times* observed:

Spohr . . . conducted his overture to *Faust*, and we may be said never to have heard it to such perfection before, although one of the stock pieces of the Philharmonic. This is one of the many advantages which the presence of a great foreign writer confers on an English orchestra. It was so when Weber visited England. He gave his most popular overture a new reading: and the same remark applies in this case, for the leading instrumentalists of the Philharmonic band, holding the same positions in the Norwich orchestra, will permanently profit by the advantage thus thrown in their way. And we may remark here, that we never witnessed anything like the same degree of enthusiasm as the London performers display. They have usually to perform a prescribed routine of duty, deriving little or no interest from novelty and therefore occasioning a very limited degree of excitement. Here they are acting under the strongest feeling of that kind; for no event could be so pregnant with interest to English instrumentalists as the presence of Spohr. [29]

And summing up the whole festival the *Morning Chronicle* wrote:

Its most remarkable feature – a feature, indeed, which will make the Norwich Festival of 1839 an era in the annals of music – was the production of Spohr's great work under the personal direction of its author. The performance on this occasion has enlightened many (and ourselves, we confess, among the number) as to the character of Spohr's sacred music. We have long possessed Mr Taylor's excellent edition of the work, and have heard it on a small scale in London, but we were not enabled by these means to form any adequate notion of its effect when performed by an immense vocal and instrumental orchestra, and with the precision derived from long and diligent preparation. From the extraordinary fulness of the score and the complication of the parts, we have imagined that the harmony, in many places was confused and cumbrous; from the heaps of flats and sharps which met the eye – the crowds of dissonant combinations – the chromatic chords, and unusual intervals given to the voices, we had supposed that many passages were harsh and rugged, if not absolutely impracticable; and from the paucity of songs, the want of duets, and the absence of other means usually employed to give lightness and variety to works of this nature, we had concluded that it was deficient in melody, and would be heavy and fatiguing in performance. All these opinions entertained by us in common with many other more competent judges, we find were very erroneous. Spohr's harmonies, full, complex, and chromatic as they are, require only to be clearly performed to be understood; his vocal intervals, though excessively difficult in execution, are smooth in effect; and, notwithstanding the small number of regular airs, there is no want of melody, for in every concerted movement, and every chorus, the most exquisite strains flow from every part of the orchestra. The listeners are carried away by the full tide of feeling, which rises at the very opening and never subsides till the last faint notes of the conclusion die away upon the ear, leaving us, as it were, spellbound and in a trance, the influence of which was evinced by the dead silence which pervaded the immense assembly in St Andrew's Hall after the sounds from the orchestra were hushed.[30]

The emotional impact of the oratorio was tremendous. As in the case of Malibran and *The Last Judgement*, it was not only the audience who were overwhelmed. According to one reporter: 'One of the principal singers, a lady whose exemplary life, as well as her distinguished talents, render her an honour to her profession, declared today that the strength of her emotions sometimes almost overwhelmed her, and rendered her nearly unable to proceed.'[31]

Spohr also performed as a violinist at two of the evening concerts, playing his newly composed Concertino *Sonst und Jetzt*, and, with his English former pupil Henry Blagrove, the Concertante op. 48. *The Times* remarked of his violin playing:

There is a charm in his violin, when employed in the execution of his own music, which no other performer can impart. Many professional men from all parts of the kingdom were congregated in the hall, and it is an evening which they will not readily forget. We institute no comparison between Spohr and the other great violinists; he stands alone in his view of the character and resources of his instrument; they have their excellencies, he has his; but it may be safely affirmed that those who have not heard him have left one chapter of the violin school unread.[32]

Overall the enthusiasm of his reception was remarkable, even in a country so prone to lionise great men as England. The audience on his first appearance welcomed him with 'loud and reiterated cheers',[33] and he quickly won the admiration of the musicians too. The *Musical World* noted: 'In his manner of directing an orchestra he is a model; blending firmness with good temper and exacting the utmost accuracy from every performer, without ever by word, look, or gesture, wounding the feelings of any. He is, consequently, idolised by the members of the orchestra, who strain every nerve to please him.'[34] The effect of this visit on the development of Spohr's reputation in England was, therefore, profound. Almost overnight the carping of hostile critics was quelled and a greater tone of admiration and respect adopted towards him in the vast majority of the press. A correspondent to the *Morning Chronicle*, appealing for Spohr to be induced to come to London, reflected the high level of enthusiasm which was generated by his appearance at Norwich, when he wrote:

The greatest living musician is now among us – a genius inferior only to his own exalted countrymen Handel, Beethoven, and Mozart; as a profound scholar, a finished artist, a grand master of the depth of harmony, the equal, if not the superior of either of them. Could the admirers of Handel, Mozart or Beethoven, bring either from his grave to preside at an oratorio, with what delight and enthusiasm would he not be welcomed and gazed upon! And is their great living rival to return home unheeded and unheard except by the affluent gentry of Norwich?[35]

Spohr returned to Germany profoundly impressed by the warmth of his reception. According to his wife he considered this and his subsequent visits to England as the 'most brilliant period of his active life'. An immediate consequence of the visit was the composition of a new oratorio. During a coach ride between London and Norwich, Edward Taylor had secured Spohr's agreement to write a work for the 1842 Norwich Festival to Taylor's own text, on the biblical story of Belshazzar's defeat by Cyrus and the liberation of the Jews from Babylonian captivity. Before the end of 1839 the text of *The Fall of Babylon* had been sent to Kassel and translated into German as *Der Fall Babylons* (for Spohr was too uncertain of his understanding of English to undertake to set the original). He began work on the music in December 1839, completed it in piano score by October 1840, and performed it in this form on St Cecilia's Day in Kassel. The orchestration was finished by December 1840. Taylor then had the (doubtless galling) task of retranslating the text into English; as he remarked in his edition of the work: 'The German translator having in most of the pieces altered the original meter, the present libretto is of necessity conformed to his version, and even the metrical errors are unavoidably retained. Of the original poem, little more in fact remains than the sense and the scheme.'

The oratorio is in two parts. Part I establishes the situation, introducing the Jews and Persians along with their leaders, Daniel and Cyrus. It is divided into five scenes in much the same way that Spohr had adopted in his operas. Part II takes place entirely in a room of the palace in Babylon and begins by introducing Belshazzar and his court. It contains the dramatic high points of the writing on the wall and the capture of the city by the Persian army.

Whereas Bach had been Spohr's spiritual predecessor in *Des Heilands letzte Stunden*, *Der Fall Babylons* belongs more to the genre of Old Testament dramatic oratorio exemplified by Handel's *Saul*, *Judas Maccabaeus*, *Samson*, etc., and adopted by Mendelssohn in *Elijah*. The music, though, owes far less to direct Baroque influences than does *Des Heilands letzte Stunden*. There are the usual fugues, but none of them has any sort of deliberately archaic feeling. The recourse to chromaticism is even greater in this oratorio than in the previous two, and in some places it seems far more aimless, weakening the impact of the music rather than imparting greater expressiveness. In spite of some fine numbers and many individual beauties, *Der Fall Babylons* is, as a whole, weaker than either *Die letzten Dinge* or *Des Heilands letzte Stunden*. It begins well with an impressive overture into which themes from the work are interwoven, and an expressive chorus of lament for the Jews (which clearly made a strong appeal to S. S. Wesley, since he utilised its opening bars for the

beginning of his own anthem 'Cast me not away' (1848); his works abound
with direct plagiarisms from Spohr). After a recitative and aria for Daniel,
the scene concludes with an unusually lively fugue (ex. 167). The next scene,
set in the Persian camp, includes an aria with chorus (no. 7) which has an
almost vulgar jauntiness and a very definite operatic flavour (ex. 168), as

Ex. 167

Ex. 168

does the chorus of soldiers (no. 11) in the penultimate scene of the first part.
The final chorus of Part I is notable for the vigour of its unison chorus opening. Part II begins rather lamely with a far too genteel portrayal of Babylonian revels (ex. 169), though there is some skilful double-chorus writing. The

Ex. 169

scene of the writing on the wall (no. 23), and the storming of the city by the
Persians, however, have greater dramatic impact. Despite attractive music in
the subsequent numbers, and especially a rousing final chorus, the oratorio
flags somewhat after this point, for there is no further drama and the text
admits only of moralising and celebration.

Notwithstanding the weaknesses which are apparent in retrospect, *Der Fall Babylons* made a very powerful impact at the time of its appearance. After its first performance at Norwich in 1842 it created a level of enthusiasm that caused the *Morning Herald* to observe: 'that such interest should be excited in a provincial town upon the performance of a new musical work is, perhaps, a circumstance unequalled in the annals of music'.[36] The critics vied with one another in their praise of the work. The *Morning Chronicle's* account is typical; there it was asserted that 'The genius of Spohr has this day achieved its greatest triumph in England', and it concluded:

Its music is characterised by all the greatness of Spohr's genius, and by his peculiarities of manner; but the traits of genius, as well as the peculiarities of manner, I must reserve till another opportunity; and in the meantime I shall only venture to say that the *Fall of Babylon* is the greatest work of its class that has appeared since the days of Handel.[37]

That this sort of feeling was general among the participating musicians is made clear by the report in *The Times*:

It was curious to observe the conduct of the London performers, whose habit is usually to hasten from the orchestra at the last bar of a performance. This morning congratulations were passing all around, as if for the achievement of some great triumph; every countenance was lighted up with pleasure, and they lingered in the orchestra to give vent to the feeling of gratification and pride which everyone felt who took part in the performance.[38]

German reviews were hardly less enthusiastic, and indeed a writer in the *AMZ* hazarded the opinion that Spohr's mannerisms were less pronounced in this work than in many of his more recent productions.[39] In both Germany and England, however, the initial enthusiasm had waned within a few years, a contributory factor to this being the huge popularity of Mendelssohn's *Elijah* (1845), and the sagacity of an unattributed remark reported with relish by H. F. Chorley in 1842 was borne out: 'It has been violently overpraised, it will be unjustly abused and then quietly forgotten.'[40]

Apart from a male-voice part-song written in February for the dedication of Schill's Hospital in Brunswick, *Der Fall Babylons* occupied the whole of Spohr's creative attention during 1840, but he was much involved in other active projects as usual. In the spring he revived his early opera *Der Zweikampf mit der Geliebten* in Kassel and derived much nostalgic pleasure from it. Then at the beginning of June, having obtained the requisite leave of absence with unwonted ease, he assumed the direction of the Lower Rhine Music Festival at Aachen. His enjoyment of this excursion was only slightly marred by a disagreement with Anton Schindler, who criticised the tempos in Spohr's performance of Beethoven's Seventh Symphony, forgetting, perhaps, that Spohr had played in the second performance in Vienna under Beethoven's direction in 1814. After a brief return to Kassel, Spohr set out with Marianne for Hamburg, to fulfil an invitation to direct *Jessonda*; he stopped on the way at Gandersheim, where he saw his mother, who was dangerously ill, for the last time, and gave her great pleasure by a performance with Marianne of some of his compositions. In Hamburg the production of *Jessonda* was highly successful, among the more cultivated part of the audience at any rate. The critic of the *Hamburger Zeitung* took the opportunity to contrast the solid musical worth of *Jessonda* with the more popular but, in the critic's eyes, less worthy music of the Italian operas, which had just finished their season there. He wrote:

The lovers of music in Hamburg celebrated on Sunday a real music festival in the theatre; they were not only enabled to express aloud their recognition of the German master, but they had the opportunity also of drawing a comparison between *Jessonda* and *Lucrezia Borgia*. In *Jessonda* all is tender yearning and sweet hope, the golden age of fond first love: in *Lucrezia Borgia*, hyena-like cunning in the poison envenomed breast; nothing of love's purity, love's grosser passion alone; the music is in the same relationship.[41]

The partizanship of serious music critics in favour of German music and Spohr in particular continued strongly in both Germany and England at this date. In London, where *Faust* and *Jessonda* had both been staged for the first time in 1840 by a visiting German company, a similar contrast was drawn by a number of critics between the merits of German and Italian opera. The production of *Faust* at the Prince's Theatre elicited cool notices from many of the fashionable critics whose allegiance was primarily to Italian opera, but such attitudes called forth a spirited defence in the *Musical World* where the critic (probably Edward Holmes), echoing a similar defence of *Azor and Zemira* nine years earlier, launched into a hard-hitting attack on his critical colleagues:

The Newspaper critics have stumbled on a puzzler at last for their 'talented pens'. Spohr's *Faust*, clearly enough, does not sit comfortably on their stomachs, and yet they are somewhat scrupulous about avowing their distaste for the dose. Some of the products of this antagonist-action are rather amusing. In some quarters we hear of *Faust* as 'deficient in melody', but yet possessing a great deal of 'harmony'; – in others, it is represented as very 'scientific, but not pleasing'; and much more fiddle-faddle of a like tendency, plainly showing that the critics have got into shoal water where they will probably remain until the next tide of Donizetti, or some similar deliverance shall float them off.[42]

Perhaps chastened by the onslaughts of the *Musical World*, or perhaps genuinely more impressed by the music, the vast majority of critics gave *Jessonda* a much warmer reception. *The Spectator* felt that it 'must be placed on the same level with Don Juan, Fidelio and Euryanthe',[43] while the *Morning Chronicle* asserted that '*Jessonda* is not surpassed by any opera that we know, and it is equalled by very few.'[44] *The Britannia* remarked: 'We must give it our unqualified praise; it is a tissue of the most lovely melodies and delicious combinations of harmony we ever heard.'[45] *The Times* too could not find a single criticism to make and concluded:

It is difficult to convey even a remote idea of this very elaborate and recondite composition . . . the instrumentation is wonderful . . . so profuse is the composer of his ideas, that the stage and the orchestra seem two resources and it is hard to listen duly to the one without passing over the other too lightly. It is not a work to be heard once, to tickle the ear for a moment, but it must be studied again and again, and still it will be exhaustless . . . Far different from Marschner's opera played the night before, and, standing by it in majestic contrast, it does not strike and animate, but it absorbs, gradually arrests, and then grasps the mind, which follows the composer as a leader to some unknown region.[46]

The attitude of French critics towards Spohr's operas and to his music in general was very different. When *Faust* had been given for the first time in Paris in 1830 considerable interest had been aroused in advance of the production; as Fétis observed, 'The majority of French musicians had attended the performance of last Tuesday [20 April] with ardour, desirous to know, at last, the dramatic composer who in Germany occupies the premier position since the death of C. M. von Weber.' But after demolishing the libretto he remarked: 'only very powerful music could prevail against the disadvantages of such a story; unfortunately I am compelled to say that that of *Faust* is not what is needed; it has not justified the high reputation of its author, and I have difficulty in persuading myself that it is the work about which I have read so many eulogies'.[47] And of the same performance another critic opined that the opera was, 'in general, arid and tormented'.[48] French opinion of Spohr did not improve during the twelve years that elapsed between the Paris premières of *Faust* and *Jessonda*. The carping reception which *Jessonda* met with in April 1842 contrasted sharply with the enthusiasm it had elicited in London two years earlier. Henri Blanchard, after describing Spohr as 'one of the most knowledgeable harmonists in Germany', remarked that 'It would truly be necessary to be an artist and a professional to be pleased by a hearing of Spohr's calculated rather than inspired music.'[49] *Le Ménestrel* made a similar judgement, commenting: 'It is, one might say, well-made music, but cold, monotonous and also tedious; one finds in it a bass aria, a soprano duet and a soprano aria which possess estimable qualities; but inspiration is absent, it has no life in it.'[50] Nor did Berlioz find much to admire, beginning his highly critical review with the observation that 'The score of Jessonda enjoys a certain reputation in Germany; it is not, however, it seems, the best of Spohr's works. The Parisian public found it in general to be dull, without character, lacking in élan, in contrasts, in variety, in fresh, grand or brilliant ideas, that which gives life to music and especially to dramatic music.'[51] As a corollary to this, Spohr's own view* of Berlioz's *Benvenuto Cellini*, which he heard in London in 1853, shows that this lack of sympathy was reciprocal, and provides a palpable instance of the ever-present chasm between German and French taste which remained a perpetual barrier to Spohr's acceptance in France.

* See below p. 327.

XIV

'The great Spohr – the immortal while yet living'
1841–1843

The years 1841 to 1843 were full of fruitful experiment in composition for Spohr, and culminated in another triumphal visit to England. He passed the first half of 1841 quietly attending to his duties in Kassel and composing. Between January and June he wrote a fantasia on themes from *Der Alchymist* for violin and piano and a setting of Psalm 128 for chorus, soloists and organ (orchestrated the following April) to an English text for Broadley's collection, which Mendelssohn and Moscheles also contributed to. But the most important work from this period was a trio concertant for violin, cello and piano. This was composed in response to a suggestion by the publisher Julius Schuberth, with whom Spohr had stayed in Hamburg the previous summer. The piano trio was a genre which Spohr had not previously attempted and, like his earlier first essays in a new medium, he brought a notable freshness of approach to it. As had been the case with the duos concertants for violin and piano of 1836–7, he wrote three trios in quick succession in May 1841, March–April 1842 and September–October 1842, (opp. 119, 123 and 124).

His treatment of the medium is highly individual. Many contemporary reviews made the point that his approach differed considerably from anything that had gone before. *The Atlas*, for instance, observed of op. 119:

As in every other species of composition, Spohr has undertaken and treated this pianoforte trio in a manner entirely his own. As elsewhere, he may reproduce himself, but he imitates no-one beside. Through all the details of its construction, even to the manner of using the instruments in combination, it has no parallel in the trios of Beethoven, Hummel, Mendelssohn, or any other writer. Almost the first characteristic that strikes the eye is its immense and continuous intricacy . . . Its harmonic march is so complicated, its parts so intervolved, and its plan so little capable of the kind of analysis to which ordinary or even extraordinary space limits us, that anything permitted us beyond general remark would do but scant justice to the composition. [1]

And another English critic thought it 'One of the very best and completest efforts of its composer'. [2] In Germany the trios received an equally good press. Their freshness and inventiveness was commented on by a number of critics; it was noted of op. 123 that 'Spohr has not appeared so young and hearty for a long time', [3] and of op. 124 that 'he presents through his vigorous activity much youthful talent'. [4] This freshness is particularly evident in the scherzos of all three trios. In op. 119 syncopated rhythms in the piano part give the music an almost jazzy effect (ex. 170). (The thirds doubled at the octave are characteristic of Spohr's piano writing in these works.) The

Ex. 170

Scherzo of op. 123 is notable for the way Spohr combines the material of the sharply contrasting Trio section with that of the Scherzo on its repetition (ex. 171). Spohr's example here may have been directly responsible for Men-

Ex. 171

(Ex. 171 cont.)

delssohn's adoption of a similar procedure in the Scherzo of his C minor
Trio op. 66 (dedicated to Spohr). Thematic interlinking is further continued
in op. 123 with the relationship of the Finale's second subject to the Scherzo
(ex. 172). Thematic or motivic relationships between movements are increasingly to be found in Spohr's later works; in op. 119, for instance, a version of
the main theme of the slow movement reappears in the development section
of the Finale, recalling Schubert's E flat Trio, which Spohr may well have

Ex. 172

known. (This sort of cross-relationship had been explored much more intensively by Mendelssohn – in his early A minor String Quartet op. 13 (1827), for example – though thematic links between movements are almost entirely absent in Mendelssohns's later works.)

Spohr's trios contain abundant examples of individual and imaginative treatment of the instruments. The piano often does not have the real bass of the harmony – something hardly to be met with in earlier trios – and this is frequently done with the intention of creating unusual sonorities. In this respect the opening of the Larghetto of op. 123 is striking, where, for the first twenty-six bars, the cello and violin parts are, with the exception of a few notes, below the piano part; until the violin enters in bar 13 the cello is consistently more than two octaves below the piano (ex. 173). Another typical example of Spohr's feeling for sonority is the beginning of the first movement of op. 124 (ex. 174). The cello is occasionally used in its very highest register, as in the Variations from the same trio (ex. 175); and the extremes of the piano keyboard are not neglected.

Technically the trios present exceptional difficulties for all three players; they are certainly more taxing for the strings than almost any other nineteenth-century trios and must have been far beyond the abilities of the

Ex. 173

(Ex. 173 cont.)

average amateur. This was remarked by contemporary reviewers, as was the point that, in view of their intricacy, a performance of the utmost nicety was required to reveal adequately their musical qualities; a sloppy rendering would render these qualities virtually imperceptible. Counselling amateurs to approach the music with 'an artist-like feeling of enthusiasm', J. W. Davison said, with reference to op. 119:

Thus approached and thus rendered, we cannot hesitate to say, that the result will be fully up to their expectations, will wholly satisfy their most zealous imaginings. In

Ex. 174

Ex. 175

any case, were this trio less of a masterpiece than it assuredly is, being the first effort of its kind from the pen of so great a composer as Spohr, it is indisputably an object of very general interest among all true worshippers of music, professional or amateur, one and all of whom, if our admonition be accepted will not lose a moment in obtaining it.[5]

In the hands of such interpreters as Joachim and Halle, the trios remained in the repertoire until the end of the century, after which, with the bulk of Spohr's music, they languished in neglectful obscurity.

Between the composition of the First and Second Piano Trios, in August and September 1841, Spohr wrote another major work; his Seventh Symphony. His enthusiasm to tackle a large-scale orchestral work had been roused by the enjoyment of his summer vacation of 1841, when he and Marianne had travelled to Switzerland via Stuttgart and the tiny state of Hechingen. Prince Friedrich Wilhelm Konstantin of Hohenzollern-Hechingen, of whose ardent and genuine love of music Berlioz has left a vivid account in his *Mémoires*,[6] had several times written to Spohr expressing his enthusiasm for his music. Marianne described in a long letter home how throughout Spohr's visit to Hechingen the Prince paid him the most flattering attention, and how during a specially arranged performance of his Fifth Symphony by the court orchestra 'the Prince evinced feelings of delight such as we had never yet witnessed, he could scarcely control himself; held Spohr constantly by the arm or hand, and not only whispered to him his admiration at every passage, but frequently gave expression to his feelings aloud'.[7] In Lucerne they were honoured guests at a performance of *Des Heilands letzte Stunden* and derived great pleasure from the natural beauties of the region. Refreshed and inspired by his journey, Spohr told his wife as they returned by carriage from the Lucerne festival that he felt a very powerful impulse to write a substantial orchestral work, possibly some new and extended form of symphony. Marianne replied half jokingly that perhaps since he had written double quartets he should try to write a double symphony for two orchestras. Spohr seized upon the idea, but decided that he must give the two orchestras some programmatic significance. After considering and rejecting a number of schemes he finally decided to illustrate the warring principles of good and evil in the human heart, entitling the work *Irdisches und Göttliches im Menschenleben* (op. 121). A small orchestra of eleven solo players (flute, oboe, clarinet, bassoon, two horns, two violins, viola, cello and bass) is associated with the spiritual side of man's nature, while a full orchestra appears to be identified with blind urges and uncontrolled passions.

In the layout of its movements as well as its orchestration, the symphony is unusual. The programmatic scheme of the work determined its formal characteristics. Spohr chose to treat his theme in three main sections, which he headed 'The child's world' (*Kinderwelt*), 'The age of passions' (*Zeit der Leidenschaften*), and 'The final victory of the godly' (*Endlicher Sieg des Gött-*

lichen), each prefaced by a four-line verse. The first movement begins with an Adagio which is dominated by the small orchestra, and continues with an Allegretto in 2/4 whose themes have an appropriate childlike simplicity. Here too the small orchestra is dominant, though there are passages of skilful interplay between the two groups. The second movement is far weightier; three trombones, two clarino trumpets and timpani are added to the second orchestra, which now assumes a more assertive role. First there is a Larghetto in F minor creating a mood of foreboding; then at bar 17 the metre changes from 4/4 to 12/8 and the tonality to a A flat; there ensues, over a pizzicato bass, a love duet in Spohr's operatic style between the clarinet and bassoon of the first orchestra. The stringendo effect created by this change of metre is continued with a genuine stringendo into the Allegro moderato at bar 41 which constitutes the bulk of the movement. A semiquaver figure in the bass acts as a motivic link between the sections, assuming ever more menacing connotations with the addition of dramatic crescendos from the horns. The Allegro moderato is based principally on three themes and a number of motifs. The first main theme is turbulent and passionate, the second yearning and the third martial (recalling the march from *Die Weihe der Töne*); this is clearly intended to represent the warlike in man's nature. After a recapitulation of material the movement ends with a powerful coda in F minor. The third and final movement is in two unequal sections, a Presto in C minor of 309 bars and a concluding Adagio of 50 bars, which follows without a break. The Presto, in 6/4, begins with a statement of an unruly and violent theme by the second orchestra, into which are interspersed snatches of a calmer theme in long note-values by the first orchestra. The general pattern of the Presto is that the calming voice of the small orchestra becomes gradually more insistent and its material more connected, building up to a statement of a thirty-six-bar theme in C flat major at bar 106. The second orchestra's vigour decreases so that by this point the roles of the two orchestras are reversed, with the first orchestra's theme punctuated by ever-weakening outbursts from the second. There are several resurgences of energy from the second orchestra, however, before the first finally gains the ascendant. The concluding Adagio begins with both orchestras in concord in a sort of apotheosis whose opening has a resemblance to the Dresden Amen (ex. 176).

The symphony was very well received by reviewers in Germany. Schumann in particular wrote a wholly enthusiastic review, concluding:

The deep mind of the master now opens itself in the whole of its rich fulness, and speaks to us in the noblest sounds. In an expressive horn solo the composer depicts the laughing rose-time of childhood in the most unaffected manner as if it came accompanied with godly blessings, full of gay, innocent games, so harmless, so cheerful and undisturbed; all is full of variegated dreams as is a happy life of childhood, and mixed with this are the earnest but mild and affectionate smiles of the great

Ex. 176

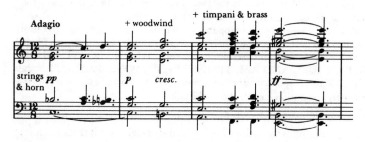

master who, by a magical image, has depicted with a joyous melancholy his own childhood – there is indeed in this movement so much heartiness, so much purity of emotion, it wells up with such force from the soul's depths, that through it the creator must become dear and valuable to us . . . The second movement . . . is full of unrest and thoughtfulness, it sounds so troubled, so enticing, so treacherous and yet so full of longing desire – one feels that man has lost himself, that wild passions rage through him and that he eagerly hunts after idle desires which do not satisfy, cannot content him . . . The last movement . . . depicts mankind still imprisoned in the path of error; the better voice becomes louder and more pressing, till the inward warning sounds again triumphantly, and idle endeavour and struggle find an end in sweet and holy peace. An intention develops itself in music as in poetry; in these compositions of Spohr it dictates itself in the noblest and most emphatic way; therefore honour to the great German master.[8]

In England there was more scepticism about the validity of illustrating such metaphysical ideas as this in music. The writer of an article on 'Musical Composition and Performance in Europe' which appeared in the *Foreign and Colonial Quarterly Review* was speaking for many of his fellow countrymen when he maintained:

Ries, Lachner, Lindpaintner, Marschner, and a tribe of meritorious elaborators . . . have been too often led into noisy or fragmentary mysticism when they aimed at sublimity . . . The baneful effect of these *strainings* in place of natural efforts, has even reached a master as substantive and worthy as Spohr. Seduced by the popularity which he imagined Romanticism was gaining, and too mistrustful to commit the genuine creations of his own thought and fancy to futurity, he has been led of late to attempt the rhapsodical, the descriptive and the mysterious in composition, as if he had been impelled towards it by his demon.[9]

But the Seventh Symphony had its staunch supporters in the press, and it had been to oppose objections similar to the above that J. W. Davison concluded a long article, filled with more flights of fancy than the work itself, with an astonishing attack on those whom he considered unable to appreciate the symphony's deeper meaning, saying:

Such are the melancholy impressions to which I am subject under the influence of this, in my opinion, fine musical poem, the masterpiece of one of the greatest musicians that the world has produced – the artistic triumph of the illustrious Spohr, which I fear has been but little understood in this country – and I anticipate for a long period must remain so. When the *critics of the day* have resigned their pens, and have ceased to deal out delusions as monstrous as unmeaning – as absurd, as unartistic – as unpoetical, as commonplace – as flippant, as shallow – as meagre and invention-less, as erroneous and besotted – when their places are taken by wiser men, and better musicians, and truer poets, and sounder thinkers, WHEN ARTISTS SHALL DISCOURSE OF ART, AND AMATEURS LISTEN WITH RESPECT – then *and not till then*, will the deep meaning of such metaphysical works as this symphony of Spohr be properly communicated to the multitude.[10]

Davison's fears were well founded, for, despite the wholehearted enthusiasm of a few, the symphony was seldom performed in England after its première at the Philharmonic Society on 30 May 1842. In Germany it fared better, but there too it had fallen out of the repertoire within a few years of Spohr's death.

A visit to Kassel by Liszt in November and a concert to commemorate the fiftieth anniversary of Mozart's death in December brought the year 1841 to a satisfactory conclusion, and 1842 began pleasantly with a visit from William Sterndale Bennett. Spohr received him with great kindness (some of his piano pieces were well known in Kassel) and, according to Bennett's account, treated him as though he were his son. Of their first meeting on 5 January, Bennett wrote in his journal:

Since dinner have paid my visit to Spohr, who has always been represented to me as a cold haughty person, but whom, I am proud to say, I found quite the reverse . . .; he received me very kindly; talked with him about his new Symphony which we are to have at Philharmonic this next season, and other matters . . . Tomorrow I shall hear under his direction 'The Templar and the Jewess' of Marschner, though, as he told me, he wished me to hear 'Fidelio' which he was to have given, but in consequence of the illness of one of the singers [was] postponed; he received the message to this effect while I was with him, and the coolness with which these Germans take these matters perfectly astonishes an Englishman, at least it does me. Now I only want to see Cherubini, and I shall know the only three great men left in our Art, viz. Spohr, Mendelssohn and Cherubini.

Three days later after attending a music party at the von Malsburgs' house he wrote to his future wife, Mary Wood: 'Spohr was there and got up one of his double Quartetts for me to hear, he also played one of his single Quartetts. I never heard such playing in my life. He is now nearly sixty years old, but has the greatest energy.'[11]

1842 and the first part of 1843 was on the whole a period of vexation and disappointments for Spohr, though productive of a number of compositions, including, besides the Second and Third Piano Trios, several Lieder, six mixed-voice part-songs op. 120, a concert overture 'im ernsten Styl' op. 126, a piano sonata op. 125 (dedicated to Mendelssohn), and a set of six 'Lieder ohne Worte' for violin and piano op. 127 (alternatively titled *Elegisch und Humoristisch*). Spohr informed Speyer in January 1843 that in the concert overture he had attempted 'a new form, or rather a new style'; [12] it does not seem, however, to indicate new departures in style, though it has a good deal of vigorous writing in it and, like *Die Töchter der Luft*, is more symphonic in character and scope than the earlier operatic overtures. Indeed, the connection with *Die Töchter der Luft* is more than superficial, and stylistically the work has much in common with the Fifth Symphony. Apart from the trios, perhaps the most interesting of this group of compositions is the piano sonata. As with the trios, the impulse for its composition came largely from publishers' promptings, and though it cannot be classed among Spohr's finest works, it contains some extremely attractive music. The opening bars proclaim its authorship without a shadow of doubt to those familiar with Spohr's idiom (ex. 177). Another typically Spohrish touch occurs with a remote modulation towards the end of the first movement (ex. 178), and

Ex. 177

Ex. 178

among other characteristic passages is a beautifully managed enharmonic modulation in the Romanze (ex. 179). Mendelssohn inevitably wrote an appreciative letter of thanks for the dedication, but Spohr received many spontaneous letters from other pianists. An extract from one of these is interesting as an example of the genuine enthusiasm his music was capable of eliciting at this time; this letter came from Seyler, cantor at Gran Cathedral in Hungary, who wrote:

Times innumerable, in the hours when my duties permit me some relaxation, do I charm myself at the piano with that sonata you dedicated to Herr Mendelssohn-

Ex. 179

[Romanza]

Bartholdy. Carried away by the magic of its tones I now take up the pen on behalf of all pianists of feeling who may not always have the opportunity to be enchanted by your larger compositions, to render you the warmest thanks for this beautiful work . . . I would moreover earnestly entreat you to let me know whether we pianists may encourage the hope of having such another composition, with which with two hands alone we may discourse with the world-famed German hero of musical science?[13]

During the early part of 1842 Spohr began to experience the return of a liver complaint from which he had suffered intermittently for the past few years. This however was alleviated by the summer vacation in Karlsbad, where he underwent a strict regimen of bathing and taking the waters.

On his return home he was deeply saddened to learn that Moritz Hauptmann was leaving Kassel to take up the cantorship of the *Thomasschule* in Leipzig. Hauptmann had been one of Spohr's closest friends and associates over a period of more than thirty years. There is no doubt about Spohr's warm and constant affection for him, though Hauptmann's letters reveal that he did not always wholly reciprocate. Hauptmann was frustrated by the unrewarding routine of his duties in Kassel, which already he described in 1830 as: 'Rehearsal from 9 am to 12.30, then a game of billiards for an hour with Spohr, then dinner, with the prospect of a dead-alive afternoon. From 3 to 6, fifths and octaves, from 6 to 10 *William Tell*, then to bed; and next morning the same old story over again.'[14] This frustration expressed itself in his letters in occasional almost spiteful outbursts against Spohr, whose outward composure he often found it difficult to penetrate. Thus he complained in 1838:

Spohr's circle is narrow and very limited; it isn't his nature to converse; he has his say, and then there's no more to be said; it's law for all time. He talks about 'interesting harmonic progressions' just as he did 25 years ago; it used to interest me then, but I don't care a straw for it now, except in connection with other matters, and even then it's superfluous.[15]

In spite of these passing irritations Hauptmann retained a large measure of affection and admiration for Spohr. Spohr consoled himself for the loss of his old friend with the knowledge that Hauptmann was going to take up a position worthier of his talents. There was no such element of consolation in the other disappointment that Spohr had to endure in the autumn of 1842 – the Electoral Prince's refusal of permission for him to go to Norwich in September to conduct *The Fall of Babylon*. When the Prince's refusal became known moves were instituted through the British Embassy in Frankfurt to persuade him to relent, and when these foundered the Duke of Cambridge wrote a personal letter to the Prince in the most pressing terms. Finally, when this too had failed, the citizens of Norwich sent an enormous signed petition which, however, met with an equal lack of success. The English press were loud in their condemnation of 'Him of Hesse',[16] as *The Athenaeum* contemptuously called him. Even *Punch* indulged in a touch of satire on the subject, remarking: 'The Elector of Hesse-Cassel – magnanimous potentate! – would not suffer Spohr to visit Norwich, to preside at the performance of his *Fall of Babylon*. The Elector has, with proper spirit, followed up this measure with a decree that, upon pain of death, no nightingale is to listen to its own music within his vast dominions'.[17]

Spohr derived some consolation from newspaper reports of the oratorio's tremendous success, which were sent to him from England, but the incident made him once more acutely conscious and resentful of the restrictions on his freedom which his tenure of the Kassel post entailed. His exasperation with the repressive regime in Kassel was expressed in a letter to Speyer in January 1843 where he wrote: 'Ernst has passed through here without stopping. I very much regret not having heard him, though I cannot blame anyone for bypassing Kassel, since the Prince and the police vie with one another in putting as many difficulties as possible in the way of foreign artists. This is in many respects a horrible resting place.'[18] These feelings were reinforced in the following spring when the Prince threw obstacles (which, however, were eventually overcome) in the way of his Easter performance of Bach's St Matthew Passion. It was only consideration for the sorrow that would be caused to his wife and her family by his permanent departure from Kassel that prevented Spohr from leaving at this juncture, for early in 1843 he was offered the vacant directorship of the Prague Conservatory. He wrote to Hauptmann saying:

I am so weary of all the vexations I meet with here that even at my time of life I could almost make up my mind to leave this place if my wife were not so attached to her family and would not be unhappy away from her friends; . . . Such a field for action and a residence in musical Prague would suit me well.

Hauptmann replied urging him to accept the post and to leave 'good, beautiful but oppressed Kassel for majestic Prague'.[19] But by the time he received Hauptmann's letter his mind was fully made up and he had already declined the offer. Had Spohr been gifted with prescience he might, perhaps, have acted differently, for these were far from the last annoyances and obstructions that he was obliged to endure in Kassel.

For the time being, though, his artistic direction, of the opera at any rate, was largely untrammelled. He was able therefore to mount a production of Wagner's Der fliegende Holländer in May 1843. Spohr was still seeking eagerly for the way forward in German opera and on reading the libretto of Wagner's opera had immediately been fired with enthusiasm for the work, regretting that he himself had not 'met with a similar and as good a one to set to music ten years before'.[20] After getting to know the music he set out his view of it in a letter to Lueder, inviting him to Kassel for the coming performance:

This work, though somewhat approaching the new Romantic music à la Berlioz, and although it has given me immense work on account of its extreme difficulty, interests me nevertheless in the highest degree, for it is written apparently with true inspiration – and unlike so much of the modern opera music, does not display in every bar a striving after effect, or effort to please. There is a great deal of the fanciful in it; a noble conception throughout, it is well written for the singer; enormously difficult it is true, and somewhat overcharged in the instrumentation, but full of new effects, and it will certainly, when it comes to be performed in the greater space of a theatre, be thoroughly clear and intelligible. The theatre rehearsals begin at the end of this week, and I very much want to see how the fantastic subject and the still more fantastic music will come off en scène. I think I am so far correct in my judgement, when I consider Wagner as the most gifted of all our dramatic composers of the present time. In this work at least his aspirations are noble, and that pleases me at a time when all depends on creating a sensation, or in effecting the merest eartickling.[21]

After a successful performance on Whit Monday 1843, Wagner, who fearing a fiasco had not come to Kassel, wrote to Spohr to thank him for the care he had taken in the opera's preparation, exclaiming at one point in his letter:

I see that a lucky star has risen over me, since I have gained the sympathy of a man from whom an indulgent notice only would have been sufficient fame for me:– but to see him take the most decisive and crowning measures on my behalf is a piece of good fortune which assuredly distinguishes me above many, and which really for the first time fills me with a sentiment of pride such as hitherto no applause of the public could have awakened in me. [22]

With the advent of his summer vacation Spohr made preparations for another journey to England. As compensation for his being unable to direct *The Fall of Babylon* at Norwich, Edward Taylor had made arrangements for him to conduct it in London in July 1843. The Philharmonic Society too, at their directors' meeting on 29 January, had decided to make him the offer of an engagement, which he gladly accepted. The news of his impending arrival gave rise to a high level of anticipation in the press, very different from the lukewarm interest which had been shown prior to his 1839 visit. The success of that visit and the triumph of *The Fall of Babylon* at Norwich had caused an upsurge of interest in Spohr and his works, together with a recognition of his pre-eminent position in the musical world. Something of the flavour of the enthusiasm which he was capable of generating can be seen from J. W. Davison's account in the *Musical Examiner* of his feelings on first seeing Spohr on 26 June, the evening of his arrival in London, at a *conversazione* given by Sterndale Bennett. He wrote:

Spohr has come among us. What associations does this honoured name awake in the bosom of every true artist! Spohr – the great Spohr – the composer of the *Power of Sound* and *The Last Judgement*, is in England – in London – in the midst of us all . . . Spohr whom we have hitherto regarded as a dream – as an ideal being – as something intangible, wrapped in a cloud, and visible only to the mind's eye, which pierces all obscurity – he, Spohr sat before us. [23]

A more rational appraisal was given in the *Musical World*, where it was observed that Spohr was

a witness to his own admittance into the realms of classical immortality. His writings take their station among the master-pieces of Bach, Handel, Gluck, Haydn, Mozart, Beethoven, Weber and Cherubini. They have long enjoyed that distinction and nothing can now remove them from the rock upon which they are fixed . . . their influence will survive until art is on its death-bed. [24]

On 27 June Spohr attended a meeting of the aristocratic Catch Club and on 29 June of the Melodists, where he could enjoy the fine English part-singing which he so much admired. From the very first day of the visit he was given hardly a moment to himself, being constantly invited as guest of honour to 'musical entertainments and dinner parties . . . at the majority of which he himself took an active share in the performances'. [25] Perhaps the most extraordinary event of this kind was a gargantuan musical entertainment given to an invited audience of some fifty people on 2 July by Mr Alsager, city editor of *The Times*. This consisted entirely of Spohr's compositions, beginning at 2.00 pm with the First Double Quartet, the Quintet for piano and wind (with Moscheles as pianist), the Second Double Quartet, and the Nonet. Then followed a 'Déjeuner à la fourchette' at 5.00 pm and a 'second act' at 7.00 pm, consisting of a String Quintet, the Octet and the Third Double Quartet. This remarkable tribute was, in Marianne's words, 'in every respect successful, and got up with princely magnificence, [and] must have been the more gratifying to Spohr, when he saw how the company listened until late in the evening with admirable perseverance and rapt attention to his music without showing the least signs of weariness'.[26] At the Philharmonic Society on 3 July he conducted his overture *Der Alchymist*, his Symphony *Die Weihe der Töne* and a duet from *Jessonda*, and played his Concertino in E major (op. 92). The *Morning Chronicle* noted that 'the crowded room contained almost everyone at all distinguished in the musical world. The utmost curiosity was felt to see the illustrious veteran who now stands foremost among living musicians'.[27] The newspapers were loud in their praise of the symphony and were at one in agreement that it must be considered as a very great work, despite a few reservations in matters of detail, especially about its programmatic intentions. The *Morning Chronicle*, for instance, remarked: 'next time we shall throw away its programme and ode to sound, and enjoy its beauties as a musical composition'.[28] *The Spectator* disagreed, saying: 'we are not disposed with our brother of The Chronicle to burn the ode next time we hear the sinfonia. To a work of this sort such a key is absolutely necessary'; and this critic concluded his review after a detailed analysis, with the comment: 'Such is a faint and feeble outline of this great work which, if not pregnant with poetry of the highest order, we have yet to learn what poetry is'.[29] In an article in the *Examiner* (reprinted a few weeks later in the *Musical World*), J. W. Davison wrote ecstatically about the work, beginning with the assertion: 'This symphony may be considered as one of the noblest creations of the human mind. The intention is deep and metaphysical, and the execution of that intention masterly and splendid.' He went on to say of the first Allegro:

There are moments when we could think it the finest thing in all music, and at all times, as a matter of mere instrumentation we must pronounce it matchless. Then its subject – so heavenly, so appropriate for the infancy of sound – how charmingly it colours the entire movement, what freshness it throws over it . . . All this is as perfect as anything we know – nothing more fresh or lovely ever came from the pen of mortal – nothing!

After further effusions about the next movement, he referred to the March as being 'next to the *finale* of the C minor of Beethoven the most exhilarating thing in the whole range of music'. The Trio he liked less, but the return of the March and the ensuing Song of Thanksgiving was able to 'restore us to the seventh heaven of music. The prayer for the dead, and the consoling beauty of the *finale* are beyond all praise. The only reproach to this last movement is its brevity.'[30]

The result of this sort of advocacy was the acceptance in England of *Die Weihe der Töne* as Spohr's orchestral masterpiece. It was soon even included in the classical part of Louis Jullien's Promenade Concerts, where, with the price of admission at one shilling, it must have become familiar to many more people than could ever have heard it at the concerts of the Philharmonic or the Societa Armonica, where the tickets for each concert cost ten shillings and sixpence.

One reason for the tremendous impression which *Die Weihe der Töne* made on this occasion was the excellence of the performance; never before had it been given without blemish in England. When it had last been performed at the Philharmonic, in 1838, the orchestra had broken down completely in the second movement. Under Spohr's own direction all the problems which had bedevilled earlier performances were vanquished. Chorley, in spite of his coolness towards Spohr's music, commented in *The Athenaeum*:

As a conductor, his command of his forces remains without a drawback, as all felt who remembered former Philharmonic essays at the symphony in question. He absolutely brought the players to a pianissimo, hitherto as fabulous a thing among them as the Unicorn; thus imparting to the first allegro an exquisite and fanciful delicacy, without which one half of its import is lost.[31]

A similar testimony to his conducting was given in the *Morning Chronicle* after the performance of *The Fall of Babylon* on 21 July, where it was observed:

Without apparent effort – without gesticulation, without bustle – he has the art of conveying his meaning to every member of the orchestra in a manner which is hardly to be mistaken. No performer who attends to such a conductor can ever be at a loss. But, unfortunately, such conductors are few; the common fashion being to flourish a great deal when everything is going smoothly, and the moment a difficulty occurs to leave the band to shift for itself.[32]

There was a good deal of disapproval of exaggerated conducting among more conservative English musicians, as is indicated by an entry in Sir George Smart's diary of the Bonn festival of 1845 where he remarked on 'a new cantata by Liszt – conducted (with plenty of twisting of the person) by himself'.[33]

A week after Spohr's first appearance at the Philharmonic Society an extra concert conducted by him was given by royal command. This was the first time a reigning monarch had attended a Philharmonic Concert, and it is evident from the flattering attention which Queen Victoria and Prince Albert paid to Spohr during the interval that they too accepted his pre-eminence in the world of music. The performance of *The Fall of Babylon* at Hanover Square on 7 July, for which the Philharmonic orchestra had offered its services free of charge, was not so successful. It had been badly advertised, and *The Atlas* complained:

We have heard several amateurs and professors of distinction complain that they knew of the occurrence only through its notice in the morning papers of the following day; and if such be the general complaint, we wonder not that the greatest musician of Europe should have the mortification of directing one of his finest works in the presence of less than three hundred persons. We trust that this is the true explanation of the matter; for, otherwise, there is a stain on the musical taste of the London public which scarcely any time can efface.[34]

Another reason, however, also lay behind the bad attendance; that was the odium into which Edward Taylor had fallen with his musical colleagues. The *Morning Post* observed that 'It was pretty well known that Mr. E. Taylor was the director of the arrangements. This fact kept away a large number who would not, like some of the elder professors we recognised in the room, distinguish a German Spohr from a Norwich Taylor.'[35] The same reason had kept many young musicians away from a dinner given on 4 July in Spohr's honour by members of the musical profession. The critic of *The Britannia* commented on this event in the following terms:

It was remarked that, with the exception of Sterndale Bennett, the professors were all of the old school, and that the rising talent of England did not, by its presence, assist in the testimonial to Spohr. As this matter has given rise to much conversation, it may be as well to explain the reason why the attendance was not larger than it was. It has been the misfortune of Spohr to be closely connected in this country with Professor Taylor of Gresham College. It has been frequently observed that men of little or no talent themselves possess a sufficient quantum of impudence to obtain a reputation, such as it is, by associating themselves as the toadies and hangers-on of genius.[36]

The *Musical World* was broadly of the same opinion, considering that

amid all the delight which the presence of Dr Spohr has excited, and all the triumphs, public and private, the great German has obtained, one black spot has almost poisoned the hilarity of his visit to England – one blotch has scurvied the otherwise spotlessness of his welcome – viz. his connection with a certain professor; . . . It is disgraceful that the most illustrious musician of Europe, a great and good man, stricken in years, and crowned with glory, should be thus made a mere prop for the tottering reputation of as thorough a harlequin as ever spat upon literature.[37]*

Spohr himself appears not to have been aware of the nature of Taylor's alleged offences and, if he was, cannot have believed the charges to be warranted, for none of this controversy seems to have disturbed their good relationship.

On 12 July, Spohr and Marianne set out on a week's tour of southern England and Wales accompanied by Taylor, who was doubtless glad to escape the jealousies and backbiting of the capital. They returned to London in time for Spohr to direct the final rehearsal for a second performance of *The Fall of Babylon*, which had been hastily arranged by the Sacred Harmonic Society at Exeter Hall to compensate for the poor attendance at Hanover Square. The contrast between the two performances could not have been greater. The *Morning Chronicle* referred to the 'most crowded audience we

* The roots of Taylor's unpopularity and the immediate cause of the virulent hostility towards him are too complex to be entered into here. For further explanation see the author's D. Phil. thesis, 'The Popularity and Influence of Spohr in England' (Oxford 1980), Appendix A.

have ever seen assembled in Exeter Hall'. The hall, which seated more than three thousand, 'was literally crammed to the very utmost; it seemed as though a single person more could not have stood within its walls'.[38] The *Musical World* felt that the performance 'must be regarded, to speak entirely without hyperbole, as a great national event . . . for it has called forth a demonstration of popular enthusiasm, such as had been rarely manifest upon any occasion, political or civil in this country', and went on to exclaim rapturously:

Spohr – the great Spohr – the immortal while yet living, founder of a new feeling, if not of a new school in music, – Spohr, the mighty master, who has stamped upon the hearts of his contemporaries that impression to which we are rarely susceptible but through the medium of an age's authority, the comprehension of a man's merits – Spohr, whose name conveys more to the minds of those who feel its import than any words can signify, has been acknowledged by the *people* in a manner that does them, no less than him, the highest and the proudest honour.[39]

The performance was accompanied by 'tumultuous cheering that from time to time burst from the audience', and at the end of the oratorio, 'the people, at a loss to find a new and further way of expressing their rapture, demonstrated it more prominently by mounting upon the benches'.[40] According to the *Musical Examiner* the performance gave rise to 'an enthusiasm so unrestrainable that in our lives we cannot recall its parallel'.[41]

The Times summed up the evening and the whole visit more calmly, but with an equal conviction of Spohr's greatness, saying:

With this performance the visit of Dr. Spohr to London has terminated – a visit which will be a memorable one to the musical profession, and by all true lovers of art will be long adverted to with deep interest. No man living has indeed more genuine claims on their gratitude, or has done more for the art as himself. Nothing is more striking in him than the great variety as well as the excellence of his productions. In his . . . compositions are to be found numerous examples which will live so long as music occupies the rank of an art and must circulate all over the civilised world.[42]

Spohr's departure, the day after the Exeter Hall performance, was marked by tokens of esteem similar to those which had attended him throughout his visit. According to his wife's account he was 'painfully moved' by his departure, but was not given time to brood, for he was besieged by a constant stream of well-wishers, while the many requests for his autograph 'kept him occupied at his writing table up to the time of his departure'. On the steamer he had barely remarked jokingly 'There is now indeed scarcely a lover of music in England who has not my autograph', when a boat drew alongside carrying several gentlemen and numerous albums, which had arrived too late; so he spent the rest of the journey down to Gravesend writing in them.

There is no doubt that, despite the lowering clouds of the Taylor affair, Spohr's visit had been a triumph, and may be seen as marking the high point of his popularity in England. From almost every quarter he had been 'acknowledged as one of those immortal minds who shed undying glory upon their art'.[43] The general level of the reverence accorded to him was such that it seems an almost incredible tribute to pay to a living musician. An important element in this reverence, given the prevailing moral climate, was the impression which he made as a man. Those who saw his detached self-possession as coldness or haughtiness (such as Chorley) were very much in a minority. The predominant opinion was that expressed in the translator's preface to Spohr's *Autobiography* (1865):

Modest and unassuming at the commencement of his career, Spohr continued so till the end, notwithstanding the celebrity he achieved and the high position to which he attained. The praises showered upon him neither turned his brain nor puffed him up with pride; and he has left us an example of high morality, great amiability, and bright domestic virtues, too rare alas! among artists and men of genius.

That this view was already prevalent in 1843 is shown by the perceptive account of his character and evocative description of his appearance given in an article in *The Atlas* at the time of his visit:

Throughout his long life, Spohr has been guided but by two principles, a conviction of the importance of his mission as an artist, and a determination to work it out to the uttermost. Musical history may, perhaps, tell of a career more dazzling in its progress, and more imposing in its results than his, but it can boast of none more conscientious, more unblemished, more truly devoted to one object. He has never once sold his birthright for a mess of the world's pottage; he has never once flinched from the grand but toilsome path of the artist, to court a temporary popularity; he has never wilfully written a note that he would wish to recall. Of pride or personal affectation he has not a grain. His mere appearance defies all suspicion of it. Look at his fine benevolent face, his noble expansive forehead – is vanity, or worldly cunning, or a solitary unworthy feeling there? Observe his demeanour, nay even his dress, his simple, unartificial manner, his ponderous and unstudied step, his quaint old-fashioned coat, that mocks all change of fashion with the length and squareness of its tails, his dear old scratch-wig that, despite its oddity, we would not for worlds have changed for the most luxuriant crop of curls – is there a trace of aught save sturdiness of mind and simplicity of character? True, these are but trifles; but they mark the man. And now see the result of so pure and earnest a life as his. He is reaping his reward. Enemies he has none; and the coldest of his admirers are constrained to confess his genius and his sincerity of purpose, while those who really comprehend his works, and *know the man*, not more fervently adore his art than venerate his character.[44]

The visit and its aftermath produced a tremendous amount of discussion of Spohr's true place in the musical pantheon, and the point was frequently made that he must be seen as occupying an unquestionable position in the line of great composers. According to the *Morning Post*, Dr Horsley had said in his speech at the Greenwich dinner that 'His reputation ranked with the greatest genius of the present day and would take its position with that of past ages, with Bach, with Handel, Haydn, Mozart and Beethoven, and other great men.'[45] Much the same point was made in the *Musical World* the following year when, in discussing the appointment to the Edinburgh chair of music, it asserted; 'A GREAT musician is the rarest accident of nature. Add one to this list who can:– Handel – Bach – Gluck – Haydn, Mozart, Beethoven, Cherubini, Weber, Spohr, Mendelssohn. From the beginning of music we find ten *great* musicians – which shows the infinite nature of art, and the immense difficulty of encompassing its mysteries.'[46]

In the eyes of most critics only Mendelssohn, of other living musicians, could be placed on the same level as Spohr; opinions differed as to which should be given precedence over the other, but in print at least few were prepared to make too positive a judgement, and most were content simply to accept them both as the unchallengeable bearers of the sacred torch of legitimate composition.

Occasionally Mendelssohn was referred to in terms such as 'the most distinguished composer of the age',[47] as was the case in *The Maestro* in 1844. The writer was almost certainly Gruneisen, who seems never to have warmed to Spohr's music, but whose idolisation of Mendelssohn is shown by an editorial in the same journal.[48] But equally this sort of comment can be found applied to Spohr, as is shown by passages already quoted. An example of a direct comparison from this period, in which a case is argued for Mendelssohn's superiority, is a long letter to the editor of the *Musical World* by G. French Flowers. He maintained of Spohr that 'though he may not rank with the greatest masters . . . yet, in my opinion, he comes immediately after Cherubini and Mendelssohn'; and he continued:

Allowing that Spohr has equal genius with Mendelssohn, yet his works do not present such a variety of artistical points, and noble designs as are found in the writings of the latter composer. The characteristic of Spohr's harmonies (which are full of grace and beauty), consists chiefly in the discreet and varied use he makes of the chromatic scales, in his frequent modulations, particularly into minor modes, which must always create the softest emotions whenever they are heard; were his strength equal in producing astonishing plots and bold designs, then, perhaps, he might be placed before Mendelssohn; this composer, however, surpasses Spohr in this respect and his harmonies being more *diatonic* must necessarily give his music a more majestic and bold effect.

It should be noted that French Flowers rated Cherubini higher than either of them, but nevertheless he fully endorsed the high position which each of them held in the ranks of great composers, saying: 'It is not unworthy of remark that Cherubini, Mendelssohn and Spohr have each formed a school of music peculiar to himself, and no composer can claim so high a ground in the truly original, poetic and scientific styles which characterise their splendid compositions.'[49] In passing it may be observed that his very high estimation of Cherubini was somewhat eccentric and would not have received general concurrence; the *Musical Examiner* remarked that while Cherubini was often cited as a great composer, little of his music was familiar to the author (probably Davison), and that in frequent conversations with Mendelssohn on the subject of the great composers Cherubini had never been mentioned.[50]

Whenever a direct comparison was made between Spohr and Mendelssohn at this time it was invariably couched in the most respectful terms towards both of them, and nineteenth-century regard for seniority generally induced writers to award Spohr the palm. Thus the *Standard* commented that Spohr 'may now, without injustice to the junior master, Mendelssohn, be recognised as the first instrumental composer of the day'.[51] *The Atlas*, in the enthusiasm engendered by Spohr's visit, canvassed a similar opinion at greater length and with a revealing analysis of the state of musical composition in Europe, saying that it was

undeniably true that so few are they whose fame will endure after the manner of the great departed, that in Germany, France, and Italy combined, not more than six could be found who could visit us with claim on our affection. We say *six* as including the debatable celebrities of the continent; our own unflinching opinion is, that of all the continental musicians now living, there are but two whose works are destined to survive the vacillations of taste, and to combat unscathed with the assaults of time. And if these men be really so few, let us the more rejoice that one of them has come among us. Spohr – we will not give him the conventional 'M', nor his own proper 'Herr', nor his academical 'Doctor', – Spohr – whose works have incessantly enraptured us, have borne us with him in one hour through a long existence of passionate delight, have made us, nothing loth, weep with him or exult with him as he would, have taught us the dignity of music, and bid us reverence it as one of the few evidences of its own immortality which the soul of man is empowered to leave behind it on earth. Spohr – the illustrious, the high-purposed, the single-minded Spohr – is among us breathing our air, walking our streets, eating with us, talking with us, and asking of us a welcome. Let it not be charged against us, that in thus seeking especially to commemorate his sojourn among us, we would unjustly exalt him above his great compatriot Mendelssohn. Far from it. We trust we have heart large enough for all worthy music, and for all its worthy creators. But we look on Mendelssohn as one who has grown up in our own era, – as one whose fame, though established, is not completed – as one who, young and with time before him, shall, at the consummation of his labours, belong to the temples of the next generation. Spohr is now old; his fame has been ripening and ripe for near forty years. We regard him as the last remnant of that glorious band of moderns, which, beginning with Haydn, has proudly dubbed Germany the greatest musical country of the world. With him that era terminates; with Mendelssohn, distinguished by characters totally different from this last, but reviving much of the spirit of the penultimate, begins a new period of art, and, we trust and believe, one no less brilliant than any of its precursors. We think of Spohr, then, as of one already and surely canonized to immortality. We hail his presence as we should that of Haydn, or Mozart, or Beethoven.[52]

Writing from the Bonn Festival two years later Davison was similarly careful, in placing Spohr on the highest pedestal, to pre-empt the charge of unjustly exalting him above Mendelssohn, commenting:

Spohr fully deserves all the honours paid to him – his years, his experience, and his genius make him the acknowledged representative of German music at the present time. After Mozart came Beethoven – after Beethoven, Weber – after Weber comes

Spohr, and to him, should he survive him, will succeed Mendelssohn. It is fit that in art, as in other matters of import, priority of years, when accompanied by proportionate worth, should have due weight - and I am not making any comparison between Spohr and Mendelssohn when I honour the dignity that sits so gracefully upon age.[53]

Nevertheless, comments can occasionally be found which indicate a clear preference for Mendelssohn in specific fields of composition, especially that of oratorio after the production of *Elijah* in 1845; thus the *Musical World*, in a discussion of oratorio, remarked: 'Spohr, the only possible rival of Mendelssohn, though his oratorios abound in beautiful melodies, delightfully harmonised and instrumented, does not sustain that *upward* flight, which is the first quality we look for in such important efforts.'[54] Chorley agreed broadly with this verdict on Spohr as a vocal writer, but even he, little as he relished Spohr's music, confessed that 'As a writer for stringed instruments, Dr. Spohr is admirable - as a symphonist, too, he shares honours with Mendelssohn.'[55]

Mendelssohn, though widely idolised, was not above criticism, and *The Spectator* complained in 1846, as others had complained of Spohr, that 'Repetition, and forms in danger of becoming hackneyed abound too much in this master';[56] but taking all the available evidence into consideration, it seems that the public utterances of music critics on the supremacy of Spohr, or his equality with Mendelssohn, were somewhat at odds with general opinion or in some cases even perhaps with their own private feelings. It is clear that the open press discussion of their respective merits which took place in England in the 1850s was already taking place on a private level in the 1840s; this impression is certainly gained from a letter which Mendelssohn wrote to Charlotte Moscheles in 1841, where he expressed his regret at being set up as a rival to Spohr. He wrote in reply to a letter from her:

The only thing I regret in your charming letter is that you should have countenanced the strange attempts at making comparisons between Spohr and myself, or the petty cock-fights in which, for some inconceivable reason and much to my regret, we have been pitted against each other in England. I never had the slightest idea of such competition or rivalry. You may laugh at me, or possibly be vexed at my taking up such a silly matter so seriously. But there is something serious at the bottom of it; and this pretended antagonism, imagined by Heaven knows whom, can in no way serve either of us, but must rather be detrimental to both. Besides, never could I appear as the opponent of a master of Spohr's standing, whose greatness is so firmly established; for, even as a boy I had the greatest esteem for him in every respect, and, with my riper years, this feeling has in no way been weakened.[57]

Despite the rather pointless wrangling over which of the two was the greater composer, it is clear that when all was said and done there was no doubt that both must be placed in the top rank. Some, like Davison, would have admitted that they once thought Spohr 'the greatest composer the world ever produced, - or nearly so';[58] but the commonly accepted view was that he must be placed lower, but only just lower, than the three great masters of German music. Particular compositions, however, were often cited as being on the same level as theirs; for instance, the *Morning Post* referred in 1844 to 'the magnificent "Weihe der Töne", a symphony which, with his second (in D minor) ranks justly with the instrumental triumphs of Beethoven and Mozart'.[59] A writer in the *Quarterly Review* expressed it neatly when he observed:

It has been cleverly said by Reichardt that Haydn built himself a lovely villa, Mozart erected a stately palace over it, but Beethoven raised a tower on top of that, and whosoever should venture to build higher would break his neck. There is no fear of such temerity at present. Weber, Spohr and Mendelssohn have each added a porch in their various styles of beauty, but otherwise there are no signs of further structure.[60]

Indeed, including the 'debatable celebrities of the continent', there seemed to be very little competition. Chorley, in a review of the works of A. F. Lindblad, commented:

Few, we apprehend, will deny that musical creation in Europe is in a state of suspense, if not of exhaustion. The schools of Italy, Germany and France have no-one to show younger than Mendelssohn – Rossini continues capriciously silent – Meyerbeer, in the prime of his renown, cautiously or coquettishly reserved – Spohr wastes his strength in vain efforts to achieve the picturesque and dramatic – and Auber, if still piquant, is piquant by repetition rather then variety.[61]

Of the composers Chorley mentioned, only Spohr and Mendelssohn could be considered to be in the true Classical tradition. Among young English critics and composers the feeling that the only true standard could be set by German music was still strong. The force with which this view was expressed, as well as the natural inclination to accept it among professional musicians, and the fact that it was easy to maintain the *moral* superiority of German music over Italian and French music, made it difficult for opponents of the view to voice their opinions without circumspection; to question it would almost have been tantamount to questioning the existence of God.

Other German composers who might have presented a challenge to the position of Spohr and Mendelssohn in the hierarchy of great composers were hardly known in England. Schubert had not yet assumed his place in the musical pantheon, being effectively represented in England only by a few songs; his C major Symphony was ridiculed by the Philharmonic orchestra and his works scathingly attacked in the *Musical World* in 1844. Schumann, who might have been considered a living rival, fared little better until Clara Schumann popularised his music in the 1860s. Chorley was a particularly vehement critic of his compositions; as late as 1856 he remarked: 'ours are days when taste must be carefully watched, and the works of Dr. Schumann (with some trifling exceptions) are too pretending to be endured'.[62] Of non-German composers who might have been considered, Chopin, though admired, could not, in view of his restricted output, be considered a great composer, and Berlioz made little impact until the 1850s, when despite a degree of popularity he was still regarded as something of an eccentric. Composers who primarily wrote opera were considered to be outside the pale by most of the musical intelligentsia, the only important exception being Cherubini, whose operas were, in any case, seldom performed in England.

Very similar attitudes towards Spohr were prevalent in Germany during the 1840s, though there was a much greater awareness of the achievements of other composers apart from Mendelssohn, such as Schubert, Schumann, Liszt, Wagner, Gade and a host of lesser lights; thus while still respected as the Nestor of German composers, Spohr no longer seemed to be the standard-bearer of musical progress. His lessons had been learned and he did not appear to have anything more of value to contribute to the musical developments of the day. His primacy, however, was almost invariably insisted on, even by those who were sharply critical of his more recent music, and this was to remain the case until his death. As late as 1854 Hans von Bülow could castigate 'the sublime impropriety of the pretension with which Kapellmeister Lindpaintner now represents himself as the Altmeister of the departing epoch, forgetting that Spohr alone can bear this honour'.[63] The combination of respect with the recognition that Spohr already belonged to an era that was past is clearly shown in an article in the *NZfM* in 1842 entitled 'The State of Modern German Music' which, surveying developments during the previous generation, stated:

After Beethoven's death there was no one who could come into his inheritance and take over his role (for the greatest talent of the time, Franz Schubert, soon followed him). But his example made a powerful effect, especially on the younger composers, whose idol he was . . . The most celebrated composer of that time, Spohr, wrapped in his enclosed individuality, remained untouched by all these phenomena, but Mendelssohn Bartholdy seized upon the movement and direction of their spirit and with his shrewd talent placed himself at the head of the new endeavours.[64]

XV

An operatic finale
1843–1847

The successful performance of Wagner's *Der fliegende Holländer* at Kassel in May 1843 had given Spohr new hope for the future of German opera; after the lean years of the 1830s he now saw in Wagner a composer of genius pursuing similar aims to those for which he himself had so strenuously striven in the 1820s. It seems probable that this, together with the boost to his spirits which his triumphal reception in England had given, impelled him once more to attempt an opera. However much Spohr might have persuaded himself that the failure of his last four operas to hold the stage was more a comment on the operatic climate in Germany than upon his compositions, the fact remained that they represented a great deal of frustrated effort for him. But he had never entirely given up the idea of returning to opera; and when the Kassel Hoftheater was re-established after its closure, he wrote in a letter of 6 June 1833: 'I have the desire once again to attempt a comic opera, if I can find a good libretto; but that is a difficult problem.' As his correspondence shows, he was offered many opera librettos in the intervening years, but the problem remained a difficult one, and the following ten years had seen a shift of interest towards symphony, oratorio, and church music. Now between September 1843 and May 1844 Spohr wrote his last opera, *Die Kreuzfahrer*.

For this opera Spohr decided to prepare his own libretto with the assistance of his wife. He chose as a basis August von Kotzebue's drama *Die Kreuzfahrer* (1803), reducing the original five acts to three but retaining the essential elements of the story virtually unchanged. Act I opens in the crusaders' camp, where Balduin, who had been thought dead, is welcomed back after escaping from a long captivity among the Saracens through the aid of his friend, the papal legate Adhemar. Enquiring after his betrothed, Emma, whom he had left in Germany, he receives no positive news, and is callously told that she is probably married or dead. The scene ends with the departure of the crusaders on hearing that one of their number, Bohemund, has captured an Emir's daughter, leaving Balduin and Adhemar to lament the lack of moral seriousness among the younger crusaders. The next scene takes place in the courtyard of a convent where wounded crusaders are treated. Emma had come to the Holy Land in search of Balduin; having

286

heard that he is dead, however, she determines to enter the convent rather than return home, despite being warned of the strict rule that living entombment awaits any nun who breaks her vows by speaking to or unveiling herself before men. In the following scene the Abbess, Cölestine, reveals her hatred for Emma, on account of having herself taken the veil after being crossed in love by Emma's father. The act concludes in the crusaders' camp where the Emir's daughter, Fatima, is being harassed by her captors, who are attempting to remove her yashmak. Balduin chivalrously comes to her aid, and when Bohemund refuses the Emir's offer of a ransom unless he turns Christian, Balduin undertakes to act as his champion in a combat with Bohemund. Balduin is victorious, though wounded, and the Emir departs after thanking him profusely. Act II begins with a short scene between Balduin, Fatima and the Emir, in which the latter gives Balduin a ring and vows to help him if he should ever be in need. The location then shifts back to the convent, where Emma, now admitted as a nun, is detailed to dress Balduin's wounds. When his helmet is removed she recognises him and faints in his arms. She is discovered thus by the Abbess and nuns. Balduin is ejected, and the Abbess, deaf to Emma's explanations, is determined to exact the penalty of entombment. The Portress of the convent offers to help Emma escape and contrives to admit Balduin through a secret passage, but before they can make good their escape they are captured by the soldiers who guard the convent. Emma is again imprisoned and Balduin again ejected, threatening vengeance which the Abbess scorns. Act III finds Balduin in despair outside the convent. His appeals for help to the soldiers guarding it are in vain, but then the Emir arrives with his troops and undertakes to assault the building. The final scene takes place inside the convent church where preparations are being made for Emma's entombment, and a funeral service is being performed. As she is being walled up trumpets sound announcing the Saracen attack and she is saved from her fate. At this point the legate Adhemar returns and decrees that because of her betrothal Emma was not really a nun; thus the Abbess retires in confusion, and everything ends happily with the lovers united.

The story has many parallels with Spontini's *La Vestale*; the condemnation of the heroine to death for violation of a religious prohibition, last-minute deliverance by a *deus ex machina* (in Spontini the lightning of the gods: in Spohr the Saracens), and the consequent reunion of the lovers, are common to both. It seems probable that rather than attempting to emulate Wagner's *Der fliegende Holländer* Spohr was trying to produce a German equivalent to the French *grand opéra* of Spontini and Meyerbeer which still occupied a prominent place on the German stage; in other words, in *Die Kreuzfahrer* he was again responding to the impulses which had helped to produce *Jessonda* more than twenty years earlier. Not only do both these works have a pseudo-historical subject, eschewing the supernatural element which pervades five of his other operas, but also there are close analogies in the formal structure. Both are through-composed and have numbered recitatives, solos and ensembles which are welded into scene-complexes, and in both, choruses of soldiers and a religious ceremony play an important part, though in the details of the treatment there are considerable differences. Instead of an overture, *Die Kreuzfahrer* has a brief orchestral prelude leading into a soldiers' chorus. The bulk of the action and drama is carried on in a fluid mixture of 'secco' recitative and arioso (ex. 180), and while musically this is essentially similar to the technique used in *Jessonda*, here it represents a much larger proportion of the work, and the arioso sections are more pervasive. Another important difference is that the set pieces are on a smaller scale and more flexible in structure; pursuing the path he had followed in *Der Alchymist*, Spohr sought to avoid interrupting the action by long and elaborate formal arias. All the solos and ensembles in *Die Kreuzfahrer* are formally simple and fairly brief or, as in the case of the duet no. 22, where Emma and Cölestine

Ex. 180

(Ex. 180 cont.)

ist das Opfer ih - rer Lie - be, jetzt sind wir gleich! sie büs - se, sie ent -

ritard. diminuendo _ _ _ _ _ *(Emma tritt auf)*

sa - ge, so bleib ich fer - ner Mut - ter ihr. Tritt na - her

Recit.

Kind. Sei oh-ne Furcht: der Büs-sen den verzeiht die Kir-che

sing together only at the very end, they are more like sections from a finale. A prominent characteristic of the whole opera which sets it apart from his earlier operas is the avoidance of melismata of more than two (or very occasionally three) notes, and of vocal display in general. The orchestra is larger than before, containing, in addition to the usual four horns and three trombones, an ophicleide, bass drum, side drum, low-pitched bell and organ. With his customary sensitivity to the handling of instruments, Spohr makes effective use of these resources to heighten the dramatic effect. The bell and organ contribute to the impact of the well-managed dramatic moment in Act III when Balduin, waiting impotently outside the convent, hears from within the beginning of the ceremony which accompanies Emma's entombment. Such moments, though, do not invest the work with vitality as a whole; Spohr's mannerisms are evident throughout, and the melodic invention is far less fresh and spontaneous than in his previous stage works. The novelties are cosmetic and soon wear thin, revealing the well-worn physiognomy which lies beneath.

The first performance of *Die Kreuzfahrer* took place on 1 January 1845 in the Kassel Hoftheater, where it was given an enthusiastic reception. Spohr wrote to Adolf Hesse:

That my opera should have made so deep and lasting an impression on the public, the minority of whom are musically educated, I ascribe to the truthful character of my music, which aims only to represent the situation perfectly, and discards all the flimsy parade of modern opera, such as florid instrumental solos and noisy effects. In addition I was exceedingly pleased that the singers, who did not find in their parts any of the usual things for gaining the applause of the crowd, nevertheless showed at every rehearsal a greater interest in it, and a zeal to study such as I never previously observed in them. But the result shows, too, that this style of song, which is so apt for all and gives an opportunity of displaying the best notes and the degree of feeling and expression of which each is capable, is a very grateful one; for our singers were never so applauded, and after the second performance they were all called for together onto the stage.[1]

Considerable interest in Spohr's new opera was shown outside Kassel. It was staged within a year in Berlin (at Meyerbeer's instigation) and later in Brunswick and Detmold, while Mendelssohn arranged a concert performance of Act III at the Leipzig Gewandhaus (conducted by Gade). In Dresden the score was retained for some time before being sent back to Spohr without explanation for its rejection, and when he had written a strongly worded letter of complaint for this treatment, he was told that it could not be staged because of religious objections to the libretto. The same grounds seem also to have prevented its performance in Catholic cities such as Munich and Vienna where the libretto had been sent for perusal. The Berlin performance, which the composer himself directed, was eminently successful; as the *AMZ* remarked: 'The success was outstanding, and at the end of the performance, the composer was tempestuously called for.'[2] This production elicited almost universally appreciative reviews. Rellstab wrote a long notice in the *Vossische Zeitung*, in which he commented:

We have to speak of an artistic event that will occupy one of the most prominent and honourable positions in the history of our stage – the first performance of Louis Spohr's new opera *Die Kreuzfahrer*. The merits of the master have already made themselves so prominently conspicuous, and the worth of that which we possess in him is so fully acknowledged, that it is not necessary even to speak of the character of his music, nor of its effects on the development of art in the present day . . . What we had to expect as a whole everybody knew who is familiar with the artistic direction of Spohr's genius – and who does not know it? That we should hear a work that might be ranked with the noblest of the kind to which the composer has adhered throughout his whole life was to be expected. But we frankly confess we had not dared to hope for so much freshness, so many instances of fiery power, as the now more than sexagenarian master actually gives us! Throughout the whole he is the same we have long known; but in many circumstances of the detail he presents us with numerous gifts of new and finished excellence – also of frequent brilliancy. His muse has never addressed herself to the crowd; she never sought to seduce by coquettish and alluring advances; her language, her movements have alone been animated by a noble spiritual inspiration and sought to win the heart by purity and dignity.[3]

There is, however, the feeling in this review, and even more so in others, that the opera had achieved little more than a *succès d'estime* – that the warmth of the public and the press was rather a tribute of respect and admiration for the composer than for this particular work. Another critic was specific on this point when, after many appreciative observations, he remarked:

We content ourselves here with the comment that in every respect we regard Spohr as a greater instrumental and oratorio composer than opera composer, and that this last opera appears to show no progress in comparison with *Faust* and *Jessonda*. To put it bluntly: this new opera is far poorer in melodic invention than those earlier ones, and the well-known manner of the master predominates in it far more than in any of his earlier works.[4]

That Spohr did not deceive himself on this point is evident from a letter which he wrote to Wagner on 11 February 1845, saying:

I am entirely of your opinion with respect to the abortive efforts of present-day German opera composers. I fear, however, that you expect too much from what I may have been able to achieve in contrast to them. For I well know that in this art form experience and technical knowledge are less able to replace youthful imagination than in any other.

In external matters Spohr's life continued along a smooth and predictable path during the mid 1840s. A constant stream of minor irritations from the authorities in Kassel contrasted strongly with the reverence and enthusiasm which greeted him elsewhere. His summer vacation in 1844 began with a trip to Paris, undertaken partly so that Marianne could see the city, partly to visit the international exhibition of industry, and partly also to renew his acquaintance with French musicians. He was treated with respect in Paris and spent an enjoyable time in the company of Habeneck, Penseron,

Halévy, Auber, Berlioz, Adam and others. As a mark of honour the Société des Concerts, reassembled almost to a man from various parts of the country, gave him under Habeneck's direction a private performance of Beethoven's 'Pastoral' Symphony on 14 June in the Conservatoire, prior to which Spohr himself rehearsed them in his *Die Weihe der Töne*, which, according to the *Revue Musicale*, was 'performed with religious care and of which all the beauties were keenly felt'.[5] The following day, as he was about to leave Paris, a deputation from the Société des Concerts presented him with a silver medal commemorating the founding of the Society. The attitude of the French, however, was very different from that of the English, as the reception of *Jessonda* in 1843 had shown. Certainly the visit to Paris was of a much more private nature than his visit to London the previous year, but that fact in itself is symptomatic of the difference. There was no great interest in Spohr's music among the public, the press, or even the majority of Parisian musicians.

A visit to Brunswick in September was more typical of the sort of reception which Spohr had customarily received. A music festival was held in his honour, the high point of which was his own direction of *Der Fall Babylons* in the church of St Aegidius where he had been baptised sixty years before. The festival, which also included a performance of his Fifth Symphony, was accompanied by numerous events in honour of the composer, among them a cantata of welcome composed and conducted by his old hiking companion Albert Methfessel. Spohr's only regret was that his father, who had died the previous year, could not be present to see his son's triumph.

An invitation from New York to conduct a music festival there in 1845, which Spohr received towards the end of the year, stated that he had been unanimously selected by a general meeting of the Music Society 'as the first of all living composers and directors of music'.[6] It was a tempting prospect for someone who loved travel as much as Spohr, and especially since his daughter Emilie was now living in New York with her husband and child, but on consideration of the time that the journey would take, and the short stay that this would allow, he declined the invitation. This decision was also doubtless connected with his interest in the success of *Die Kreuzfahrer*, and the possibility of directing it in one of the major German cities. In the event, however, he was almost prevented from conducting its first performance in Berlin in July 1845, for during a festival in his honour organised by his former pupil August Pott in Oldenburg in June he was overcome by severe abdominal pains and, after an agonising night during which he imagined that every moment would be his last, was advised by the doctor who attended him to cancel all his other engagements for the summer and spend the rest of his vacation in Karlsbad to restore his health by taking the waters. Thus he wrote to Bremen, where he was to have directed *Jessonda*, and to Berlin announcing his inability to fulfil the engagements. As it turned out, he felt so much recovered after a week in Karlsbad and was so anxious to direct the Berlin première of *Die Kreuzfahrer*, that he shortened his cure and arrived in Berlin in time to take the final rehearsals. While in Berlin Spohr was once more the recipient of numerous tributes. Perhaps the most signal honour was an invitation to dine with King Friedrich Wilhelm IV, conveyed to him by no less a person than the distinguished scientist and explorer Alexander von Humboldt. Equally gratifying was a surprise visit, on the eve of his departure, from the whole of the Berlin Royal Orchestra with Meyerbeer and Taubert at their head, to present him with a finely wrought golden laurel wreath, after which Meyerbeer made a speech thanking Spohr 'for all the great and beautiful things which, in his enthusiastic love of true German art, he had hitherto created, and especially for this his excellent work *Die Kreuzfahrer*'.[7] Spohr's stay in Berlin also had its private pleasures. He was hospitably entertained in the house of the sculptor Professor Wichmann and took part in musical parties with his usual zeal. A writer in the *AMZ* recorded how Meyerbeer and Adolf Hesse had spoken to him 'with admiration about the masterly performance of the celebrated veteran'. He then went on to give his own impression of Spohr's playing:

Thanks to Hesse, I later had the pleasure of hearing the master. It was in the early morning and, apart from Spohr's wife, who is as cultured as she is unassuming, no one was present but the two of us, Hesse and I. It hung by a hair, or rather by a G string, whether I should again miss hearing him; luckily the loose G string was able to be tightened, for it is well known that a virtuoso string player will not let himself be heard on a new unplayed string. Spohr then played. The first thing I heard him play was a breathtaking scale passage in B major, from low B to the one three octaves above. This passage was *ex ungue leonem*, and one knew whom one had before one. Frau Spohr sat down at the piano and we then heard three Lieder ohne Worte for violin and piano [presumably from op. 127] . . . we were particularly enchanted by a delicious Andante in A major [this must be either Andante in E minor or Adagio in A minor] which showed the composer and the virtuoso in an inimitably beautiful light, so that it was difficult to say which of the two should bear off the prize. To say anything new or specific about Spohr's playing should be as impossible as it is superfluous, since everything that can be said about it has already been written by the most gifted minds. We will only say this: in order to appreciate Spohr's compositions, not only those for the violin, one must hear him perform them himself. There is nothing at all effeminate or sentimental in his playing – rather something manly and serious; and the elegiac element which admittedly suffuses his compositions seems to become through his performance deeply thoughtful, noble and beautiful. Frau Spohr played the by no means easy piano part with accuracy and admirable discretion.[8]

This description of Spohr's performance of his own music is particularly interesting in view of the charges of sentimentality and effeminacy which were so often levelled at it at a later period; much indeed depends on the manner of performance of Spohr's music.

Within a short time of returning to Kassel, Spohr was once again on the move – this time to Bonn, where he was to share with Liszt the direction of the festival which accompanied the unveiling of the Beethoven monument. Spohr conducted, among other things, the *Missa Solemnis* and the Ninth Symphony. Both he and Liszt were the recipients of extravagant tributes; even before the rehearsal of the *Missa Solemnis* he was, as Sir George Smart noted in his diary, saluted by trumpets and drums from the orchestra.[9] Smart later commented acidly that 'there was rather too much Drumming and Trumpeting to Spohr and Liszt . . . for the Festival was in honour of Beethoven *not* of Spohr and Liszt'.[10] However, he was greatly impressed by the performance of the Ninth Symphony, observing that it 'went famously; . . . I never heard this Sinfonia so well performed before.'[11] Smart's diary indicates that Spohr's health was not fully recovered, for at another point, under the heading 'Persons I saw at Rehearsal', he wrote: 'Spohr and his wife, he took us into the Gallery that we might hear better, he came up there during Liszt's Cantata, he went away after 2 thirds of it being tired with conducting and so hot that he had his wife's shawl put over his Great Coat – he does not seem strong.'[12]

Spohr's health continued to be variable throughout the succeeding winter, and, writing to Speyer in March 1846, he declined an invitation to stay with him in Frankfurt during the summer vacation, mentioning that he had also refused an invitation to direct his oratorios in London, since he regarded the continuance of his cure in Karlsbad as a priority; but he added that should his health be sufficiently restored he intended to travel to London the following season and would visit Frankfurt on the return journey. By the summer of 1846, however, it seems that Spohr's health was considerably improved, for Hauptmann wrote to Speyer later in the year:

We had the pleasure of seeing Spohr here; he stopped off in Leipzig for six days on his journey to Karlsbad. We found him fresher and more vigorous than when we left him four years ago in Kassel. He made a great deal of music, at all times of day; he was continually of the most amiable cheerfulness and was not to be exhausted, less so than many younger men. In many ways he is a real rock, which one can lean upon.[13]

One of his reasons for visiting Leipzig was to make the personal acquaintance of Wagner. This was accomplished to the mutual satisfaction of both men. In a letter home Marianne wrote:

We were most pleased with Wagner, who seems every time more and more amiable, and whose intellectual culture on every variety of subject is really wonderful. Among other things he gave expression to his sentiments on political matters with a warmth and depth of interest that quite surprised us, and pleased us of course the more from the great liberal feeling he displayed.[14]

Wagner himself recalled the meeting in *Mein Leben*:

This meeting with him did not leave me unimpressed. He was a tall, stately man, distinguished in appearance, and of a serious and calm temperament. He gave me to understand, in a touching, almost apologetic manner, that the essence of his education and of his aversion to the new tendencies in music had its origin in the first impression he had received on hearing, as a very young boy, Mozart's *Zauberflöte*, a work which was quite new at that time and which had a great influence on his whole life. Regarding my libretto for *Lohengrin*, which I had left behind for him to read, and the general impression which my personal acquaintance had made on him, he expressed himself with almost surprising warmth to my brother-in-law, Hermann Brockhaus, at whose house we had been invited to dine, and where during the meal the conversation was most animated. Besides this we had met at real musical evenings at the conductor Hauptmann's as well as at Mendelssohn's, on which occasions I heard the master take the violin in one of his own quartets. It was precisely in these circles that I was impressed by the touching and venerable dignity of his absolutely calm demeanour.[15]

The quartet performed at Mendelssohn's music party was the recently completed op. 132, and Marianne described how Mendelssohn and Wagner 'read from the score with countenances expressive of their delight'. Marianne also commented on Mendelssohn's 'unmistakable attachment to and esteem for Spohr' – a feeling which was certainly mutual, for Hauptmann had observed several years earlier that Spohr was 'very devoted to Felix'.[16]

The rest of their stay in Leipzig was enlivened by more private and public performances. The pupils of the Thomasschule under Hauptmann's direction sang Spohr's psalm for double choir 'Aus der Tiefe' (op. 85 no. 3) as well as his favourite Bach motet, 'Ich lasse dich nicht'. On the following day the Gewandhaus orchestra gave a surprise extra concert consisting entirely of Spohr's works, in which the fifteen-year-old Joachim played one of Spohr's violin concertos to the composer's great satisfaction, and the evening concluded with *Die Weihe der Töne*, with Spohr, at Mendelssohn's request, conducting the last two movements. On the final evening of his stay a private music party took place at which Mendelssohn played the piano in Spohr's First Trio (op. 119) and the viola in his Third Double Quartet (op. 87). The following morning the Spohrs left by train for Karlsbad, and Mendelssohn ran alongside the carriage to bid them farewell as they drew out of the station. This was to be their last meeting, and Mendelssohn's death the following year was a sad blow to Spohr, from both a personal and an artistic viewpoint. He wrote to Hauptmann, on receiving the news in November 1847: 'What might Mendelssohn in the full maturity of his genius not have written, had fate permitted him a longer life! For his delicate frame the mental exertion was too great and therefore destructive! His loss to art is much to be lamented, for he was the most gifted of living composers, and his efforts in art were of the noblest!'[17]

In Karlsbad, Spohr was able to hear Ernst, who had travelled so precipitately through Kassel in 1843, give a concert, with Spohr's *Gesangsszena* included in the programme. According to Marianne, he played with 'great care and expression, but not entirely accurately'.[18] Spohr enjoyed the benefits of the relaxing routine to which the patients at the baths were subject, and despite the injunction against prolonged mental exertion he gave way to the impulse to compose, writing the last movement of a piano trio in B flat (op. 133) which he had begun in Kassel in May. He always referred thereafter to this movement as *der Sprudelsatz* (the bubble movement) in memory of the benefits he had derived from the Karlsbad springs. Stopping off to visit his old pupil Eduard Grund in Meiningen on the return journey to Kassel, Spohr was able to try out the newly completed trio at a specially arranged music party, and seems to have been fully satisfied with the results of his labours.

The trio is not, however, despite some attractive writing, as convincing a work as its three predecessors; its first movement in particular suffers from one of Spohr's cardinal defects – rhythmic monotony – a problem which few nineteenth-century composers entirely avoided. Trochaic rhythm is stubbornly conspicuous throughout this 9/8 movement, to the point where, except in the hands of the most sensitive performers, it becomes irritatingly obtrusive. The Menuetto has an air of restrained elegance, but the constant stream of semiquaver triplets in the Trio section give it a rather fussy effect. The two final movements are more successful. At the beginning of the Poco adagio Spohr establishes a reverential mood which is complemented rather than disturbed by passages of a more declamatory nature (ex. 181). The Finale is spirited, giving promise of the freshness Spohr was to recapture in the few fine works he was still to write.

With all its shortcomings, the trio seems to have been very well received, and in England the *Musical World* even went so far as to say, after its performance at one of Lindsay Sloper's soirées in March 1848,

The first movement over, a murmur of praise and favourable criticism ran through the audience. According to all, Spohr had newly imbibed the waters of rejuvenescence. The *minuetto* evidences the peculiarities of Spohr's genius, but is hardly so much as the *allegro*, a spontaneous inspiration. It presents some highly effective passages for the pianoforte, which were interpreted by Mr Sloper in a masterly manner. The *adagio* is an exquisite movement, the subject clear and elegant, and varied in the most charming manner possible; the dialoguing of the violin and violoncello is managed with the happiest effect. The entire movement is in every way worthy of Spohr's genius in its loftiest moments. The last movement, Presto, is as bright and fleeting as a flash of lightning. We shall have occasion by-and-by to speak more largely of this work; at present we can hardly allude to it impartially, so deeply were we impressed with it on a first hearing. The trio gave the most intense delight to all present, and there was but one opinion expressed as to its merits.[19]

During the two years between the completion of *Die Kreuzfahrer* and the B flat Piano Trio, Spohr had composed a number of substantial works. Despite a strenuous round of other activities and his variable state of health, he had written a violin concerto, a concerto for string quartet and orchestra, a string quartet, a string quintet, a piano quintet and a setting of Psalm 84 for soloists, chorus and orchestra. To some extent, though, all of these works show signs of creative exhaustion. As in *Die Kreuzfahrer*, the technical skill is

Ex. 181

always apparent, but the feeling that the composer is constantly working over the same well-dug ground is inescapable, notwithstanding passages and even whole movements in which he found genuine inspiration.

The Violin Concerto in E minor op. 128 (completed in November 1844) was to be Spohr's last work in a field in which he had proved himself a master more than thirty years earlier. His violin concertos were widely considered the finest examples of the genre from the whole of the century up to that time, especially nos. 7, 8, 9, and 11. The Beethoven Violin Concerto was little known and little regarded until Joachim championed it, and even the subsequent popularity of Mendelssohn's E minor Violin Concerto (1845) did not succeed, in the opinion of many, in ousting Spohr's concertos from their preeminent position. As one reviewer remarked in 1850, after a performance of the Mendelssohn Concerto by Ernst,

> it was a musical treat of the highest order. But when we find this concerto placed, by Mendelssohn's fanatical worshippers, above all other compositions of its class, and those of Spohr in particular, we can only say that such indiscriminate eulogy is merely injurious to its object . . . The violin has rarely been the instrument of a great composer; Spohr is the only musician of our day who can be classed on the one hand with Mozart and on the other with Viotti; and the concertos composed by the author of Jessonda stand quite alone and unrivalled. Independently of their grandeur and beauty of conception, they have, even in the midst of difficulties, that graceful flow and smoothness which can be obtained only by a profound knowledge of the fingerboard, and a command of all the delicacies of the bow. [20]

But there would have been general agreement that Spohr's later concertos and concertinos did not reach the peaks his earlier works had scaled. In op. 128 he reverted to a full-length concerto form, but could not recapture the fire and inspiration which had animated the works composed before 1824. Spohr himself performed the new concerto (dedicated to his former pupil August Pott) during his visit to Pott in Oldenburg in the summer of 1845. It was received and reviewed enthusiastically, though in the long run it failed to gain any widespread popularity, and clearly the warmth of its reception was rather a tribute of respect and affection for the composer than an endorsement of the work itself. The Concerto for String Quartet and Orchestra in A minor (op. 131) was composed almost a year later, between October and December 1845. The idea was probably derived from the double quartet (perhaps directly suggested by his pupil Hubert Ries's arrangement of op. 65 for quartet and orchestra). To some extent the overall effect of the work suffers from the subordinate role allotted to the orchestra, and his treatment of the solo and tutti groups is far less subtle than in the Seventh Symphony. There are no formal or stylistic surprises, and indeed much of the time the reliance on well-worn formulae is only too apparent; but the work has, nevertheless, many attractive qualities. As a contemporary critic remarked:

> Though age has somewhat circumscribed the flights of fancy, and phrases and harmonies in the well-known Spohrish manner ring out, yet is the flight always stronger and higher, the style altogether nobler, and this late work of the celebrated composer does not lack the many charms which his earlier works contain in so rich a quantity. [21]

The three chamber works are all flawed by unsatisfactory movements, and by a general reliance on the usual stock of melodic and harmonic formulae; in the first movement of the E minor String Quintet op. 129 (February to March 1845), for instance, Spohr virtually quotes a declamatory passage from the Larghetto of his E minor Piano Trio op. 119 (ex. 182). Similar examples are legion. Elsewhere the thematic material is often merely undistin-

Ex. 182

(a) Piano Trio op. 119

[Larghetto]

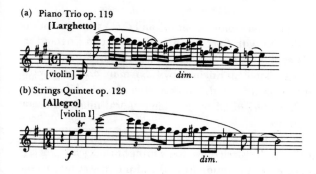

(b) Strings Quintet op. 129

[Allegro]

[violin I]

guished and the rhythmic pulse lacking in variety, the first movement of the
Piano Quintet op. 130 (August to September 1845) being a glaring example
of both these blemishes. In this movement Spohr seems even more than usual
to be preoccupied to the point of stubbornness with a few nondescript ideas;
it is permeated by a semiquaver figuration relieved only for a short time by
an equally uninteresting second-subject theme of a march-like character
which has dozens of close relatives in Spohr's earlier works. The slow movements are more successful than the first movements, in which the failure to
develop the material convincingly is a serious drawback. The Adagio of
op. 130 has a finely sustained dreaminess and contains passages of real beauty,
while that of the String Quartet op. 132 (February 1846) is deeply expressive
(ex. 183). The Adagio of op. 129 is marred by a disappointing middle section.

Ex. 183

[Adagio]

The scherzos (in opp. 129 and 130 they are placed second) are not so vital as
those of earlier works, suffering again from the repetition of familiar
material; that of op. 130, for instance, harks back to those of the op. 123 and
op. 124 piano trios. The Scherzo of op. 129 is interesting in having two Trios
using the same music but in different keys (A and F) and a final altered

Scherzo section. The finales of all three works are vigorous and attractive, but also offer nothing new.

The setting of Psalm 84 for four soloists, chorus and orchestra, consisting of four numbers, was written with Spohr's impending visit to England in mind. The chorus with soprano solo 'How lovely are thy dwellings' (no. 1) was published almost immediately in England by J. Surman, and achieved a considerable degree of popularity, but the work as a whole, which is replete with the mannerisms characteristic of Spohr's later choral music, did not gain a place in the repertoire.

On his return to Kassel from his summer vacation of 1846, Spohr was subject to another instance of small-mindedness from Prince Friedrich Wilhelm. In Karlsbad he had received an invitation from the Landgrave von Fürstenberg to visit Vienna in November 1846 to direct *Der Fall Babylons*, but despite an application for Spohr's leave of absence signed by Metternich the Prince once again refused permission, and the performances had to be deferred indefinitely. In total contrast to this treatment was the Prince's behaviour the following January, when the whole of Kassel celebrated the twenty-fifth anniversary of Spohr's appointment. Spohr wrote to Speyer:

Though the universal, I ought to say hearty, sympathy of my fellow citizens of all classes was very gratifying to me, the celebration overall had many painful moments and I was heartily glad when it was all over. What surprised me most was that the Prince took so much interest in it and overwhelmed me with courtesy, and I am eager to see whether his wholly altered behaviour towards me will last.[22]

The festivities, public and private, continued for three days, from the 20th to the 22nd of January, and Spohr was showered with honours. The Prince had already bestowed the Hessian Order of the Lion on him some years before (according to Hauptmann, in a fit of pique against the theatre Intendant Feige, who did not have the order); now he denominated him *Generalmusikdirector* with the entrée at court; The King of Prussia sent the Order of the Red Eagle third class, the chief magistrate of Kassel presented him with the freedom of the city, and numerous societies conferred honorary membership on him.

An account of this anniversary was prepared by Dr Friedrich Oetker (translator of *Der Fall Babylons*) and published, the proceeds being devoted to charity. Otker also proposed to publish an account of Spohr's life, and for this purpose asked Spohr to make notes; the biography was never written, but this stimulus provided the occasion for Spohr's beginning his *Lebenserinnerungen*, for once he started to recall his past life he became enthralled with the idea of setting down his experiences in a connected narrative. He continued to work intermittently on his reminiscences over the next ten years. In the early months of 1847, however, he was impelled more towards composition. By March he had completed a companion volume of pieces for violin and piano to the Lieder ohne Worte op. 127; a Barcarole written in 1845 was the starting point for the set of *Salonstücke* op. 135, and it was followed up between December 1846 and March 1847 by a Scherzo, a Sarabande, a Siciliano, an Air varié and a Mazurka.

A more substantial and important composition followed these charming trifles: his fourth and last double quartet, op. 136 in G minor. A notable feature of this work is that the two quartets are treated much more equally than in the three earlier double quartets, and a more telling use is made of the antiphonal possibilities of the ensemble. There is no sense here that one quartet is the concertino and the other the ripieno, and it is inconceivable that it could lend itself, like op. 65, to arrangement as a quartet concerto. In its treatment of the medium op. 136 is certainly the most subtle of the double quartets, and while it is not perhaps equal in spontaneity of inspiration to its precursors, it is far fresher and more imaginative than the chamber works of the preceding few years. The first movement is permeated by Spohr's familiar vein of lyrical melancholy, established in the first few bars. A tenderly hesitant second subject (ex. 184) provides material for much of the effective development section. Rhythmic vitality is imparted by some arresting changes of time from 6/8 to 3/4. In the slow movement, echo effects between the two quartets are evocatively employed, and these, together with cello pizzicatos accompanying expressive, sustained harmonies help create a movement of considerable beauty. The Scherzo also utilises the medium's possibilities for answering phrases, with melodic material being constantly tossed from one quartet to the other; it has a determined, almost aggressive character nicely complemented by the genial Trio. The Finale sustains the high quality of the previous movements, having an irresistible forward drive

Ex. 184

(Ex 184 cont.)

which is intensified rather than weakened by the second subject in 6/4, where a feeling of pent-up energy is generated.

In the summer of 1847 Spohr was able to make his deferred journey to England. J. W. Davison had reported, after a conversation with Spohr at Bonn in 1845, that his 'enthusiasm for England and the English is unbounded';[23] he had certainly made many good friends among English musicians. Accompanied by Marianne and her sister, he stayed with Edward Taylor at his house in Regent Square and enjoyed reunions with the Horsley and Benedict families as well as meeting many other friends. On the whole, his visit to England was a much less public affair than the previous one. Spohr's only public appearance, other than to conduct the Sacred Harmonic Society in his oratorios and the newly composed 84th Psalm, was at the Beethoven Quartet Society where, at a meeting entitled 'Homage to Spohr', consisting entirely of his works, he took the first violin part in his E minor Double Quartet. On that occasion the *Musical World* noted that 'his playing electrified all present'.[24] Even this event, however, was a semi-private one, and the wider public had no opportunity to hear him.

Attention was largely focused on the performance of his oratorios. The original intention had been to give all three of them, but religious objections to *Calvary* were still strong enough to interfere with this plan, and in the event it was found expedient to substitute a second performance of *The Fall of Babylon*. As had been the case in 1843, the majority of the press and the large audiences which came to hear his music at Exeter Hall were highly enthusiastic. All the critics, however, were agreed in placing *The Fall of Baby-*

lon lower than *The Last Judgement*, but opinion differed as to how much lower. After the first performance of *The Fall of Babylon* on 9 July the *Daily News* averred:

'The Fall of Babylon' is a great work which could be equalled by no living musician save only Mendelssohn; but it is not we think equal to Spohr's own previous oratorios 'The Last Judgement', and 'The Crucifixion'.[25]

This critic found it too secular in parts and commented of the 'handwriting on the wall' scene that it was 'like all attempts of the kind (Handel's included) a total failure'. But he nevertheless concluded, 'These, however, are the blemishes of a noble work, which contains beauties of the highest order.' The *Morning Post* declined to specify its reservations about the work because of the excitement caused by Spohr's presence and 'the great personal respect in which he was held alike by the performers and the audience'.[26] In fact, many reviews avoided going into details about the composition, clearly for similar reasons. However, articles in the *Illustrated London News* and the *Morning Chronicle*, probably both by Gruneisen, and in *The Athenaeum* by Chorley dilated at some length on what they saw as the weaknesses of the oratorio. The former repeated the old charge which he levelled at Spohr's compositions in general, saying in the *Morning Chronicle*:

After several hearings we see no reason to change our opinions as to the merit of this work. It is the production of a man of great learning; but it is not to our minds an inspiration of genius.[27]

In the *Illustrated London News* it was remarked that 'His instrumentation is most elaborate, but his chromatic combinations become monotonous and heavy after a short time.'[28] Chorley indulged in more wholesale condemnation, observing:

the further we make acquaintance with his choral compositions, whether sacred or profane, the more thoroughly we are convinced that they are written on a mistaken system – or are mistakes because written *without* any system.[29]

But the criticisms in the *Morning Chronicle* were qualified by the statement: 'It is but an act of justice to record that our opinion appears to have been in a considerable minority, for nothing could exceed the enthusiasm of the audience.' Such enthusiasm was entirely in tune with the feelings of a writer in the *Morning Herald*, who was induced to exclaim:

We rejoice to find that Spohr is so honestly appreciated in this country, and that, in spite of the double allowance of Italian opera with which we are inundated, and the profusion of light unthinking tune which such flippant maestros as Verdi pour forth at the bidding of fashion, there is still a class of the community who can comprehend the infinity of his intellect, and are ready with the homage due to exalted and undying genius. In all branches of musical composition Spohr is equally great, and when the numerical abundance of his works is remembered . . . the wonder is that the conceptive faculty should have been so uniformly active, and that it should have originated so much to be admired and so little to be condemned.[30]

The association of Spohr with the highest ideals of art continued to be a powerful recommendation to those who deplored what they saw as the vitiation of public taste by the proliferation of unworthy music.

If, as seems likely, most of the critics had been motivated more by respect for the composer than by genuine enthusiasm for *The Fall of Babylon* on 9 July, they appreciated *The Last Judgement* on 23 July much more. However, the other two works performed with it – the 84th Psalm and *The Christian's Prayer* (the 1829 'Vater Unser') – according to the *Morning Chronicle* 'did not produce the slightest impression on the auditory'; but it went on to say that the oratorio '– Spohr's masterpiece in sacred writing – created a powerful sensation'.[31] The *Daily News* reported that 'Many of the movements were encored; and the illustrious composer, before leaving the orchestra, was loudly cheered for several minutes.'[32] There is little evidence in reviews to suggest that the sort of criticism which Chorley. and, to a lesser extent, Gruneisen had tended to level at *The Last Judgement*, along with the rest of Spohr's output, was accepted by the vast majority of critics and audience. The warm reception which the oratorio undeniably elicited provides clear evidence of a widespread rejection at this time of such remarks as had been made in *The Athenaeum* and the *Morning Chronicle* on the occasion of the oratorio's performance in November 1846.[33]

At the Beethoven Quartet Society the audience was of a very different kind from the huge audience which attended Exeter Hall, but it was no less favourable in its reactions to Spohr and his music. The *Illustrated London News* noted that 'The reception given to Spohr by his brother artists and the connoisseurs was most enthusiastic, Jenny Lind applauding most cordially.'[34] And *The Spectator* said of the same event that 'He received with his usual unaffected simplicity, but with evident pleasure, the homage which everybody strove to pay him.'[35] *The Atlas* too stressed Spohr's characteristic modesty, saying: 'To see a composer utterly absorbed in his art, and so little bent on making a market of his popularity that he hurries from the scene of his triumph before his audience have had time to thank him is edifying.'[36] This was undoubtedly a quality which aroused great admiration in the moral climate of the age.

Without hindsight it must have seemed to most of Spohr's contemporaries in 1847 that, in spite of some criticisms, Spohr's reputation was even more firmly established than it had been four years before. The verdict of the audience at Exeter Hall had been unequivocally given in his favour, while the respect, almost amounting to veneration, of his most distinguished colleagues could not be in doubt. There seemed every prospect that his works would continue to gain a wider circulation and that with the inevitable improvement of public taste which was seen as inseparable from the optimistic Victorian ideal of progress, more and more people would be brought to the level of Spohr's music. By those who held these views Spohr's work continued to be seen as a powerful weapon in their arsenal for use in the battle for the improvement of taste. In this vein *The Spectator* commented:

The present visit of this illustrious musician has been of great benefit to the progress of his art in England. He came to London on the invitation of the Sacred Harmonic Society, to superintend and direct their performance of two oratorios – *The Fall of Babylon*, and *The Last Judgement*. In doing this, he has enabled the Society to bring before the immense Metropolitan audiences who frequent the performances of Exeter Hall two of the greatest works in existence of the sacred musical drama . . . The enthusiastic reception of both these oratorios, and the demonstrations of personal admiration and respect for the author which accompanied the reception of his works, gave satisfactory proof of the growing taste and judgement of the great body of the London public. This taste and judgement will be still further increased by a more intimate knowledge of these as well as the other great compositions of Spohr, and of his younger brother Mendelssohn.[37]

His moral eminence was summed up in *The Atlas* with this statement:

Never was position more fairly and honourably won than that of Spohr, nor elevation possessed freer from detraction and amidst such an acclamation of good will. He is 'the last of the Romans'; following in the train of Beethoven, Cherubini, and Weber.[38]

All in all, therefore, this visit must have seemed not only a crowning triumph for a venerable composer, but also a new point of departure in the spread of his popularity; that this was largely an illusion would become clear only in the context of the next forty years.

XVI

Revolution: hope and disillusionment
1847–1852

When Spohr had arrived in England in July 1847 the Philharmonic season
was already over, but he was approached during his visit with the proposition to compose a new symphony for them for the following season. He
probably began to sketch his Eighth Symphony in G major op. 137 in London, but the bulk of the work was completed after his return to Kassel. On 9
September Spohr wrote to Hauptmann informing him that it was finished,
though the orchestration occupied him into October. In this work, Spohr
returned to the standard four-movement form (with slow introduction to the
first movement) without programmatic implications. There is an expansiveness about many of the themes in this symphony typical of Spohr's late style,
which seems often to have an affinity with Brahms. The principal theme of
the first Allegro is a characteristic G major theme (ex. 185) (cf. the first move-

Ex. 185

ment of op. 82 no. 2). The movement as a whole has a warm and unhurried quality, largely avoiding the nervous intricacy which disfigures some of Spohr's works. A nice tonal nuance is the recapitulation of the second subject initially in B flat; and a passage of harmonics accompanied by clarinets, bassoons and horns in the coda is an attractive touch (ex. 186). The Poco

Ex. 186

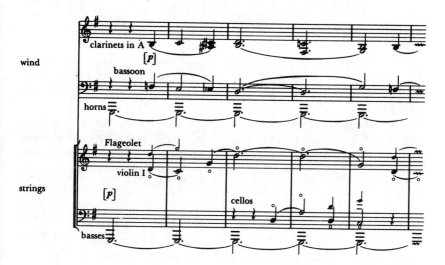

adagio is a deeply expressive movement whose opening theme seems an anticipation of Tchaikovsky (ex. 187). Later in this richly scored movement, trombones are extensively used in highly chromatic passages. The Scherzo is a lively movement in G minor 2/4, and the Trio introduces an agile solo violin part. The Scherzo is not recapitulated normally, for as he had done elsewhere (op. 123 for instance) Spohr combines the material of Scherzo and Trio, and the solo violin continues to play a prominent role. A 6/8 Finale concludes the symphony in high spirits. The scoring is finely judged as

Ex. 187

usual, and there is an air of playful lightness about the movement, as, for instance, in the second subject (ex. 188). The development, like that of the Finales of the Third and Fifth Symphonies, is dominated by a fugato.

Ex. 188

The new symphony received its first performance in one of the Kassel winter concerts on 22 December 1847, where it seems to have been appreciated but without rousing particular enthusiasm; a critic in the *AMZ* thought it not equal to his Second, Third or Fourth Symphonies. In London, where it received its official première at the Philharmonic Society on 1 May, it had a mixed reception. The *Morning Chronicle* wrote a laudatory article which began:

Now that Mendelssohn is dead, Spohr holds the position of the first composer of the day, without a possible rival. No master has done more to advance the art in the highest department of composition than he, and as he has excelled and produced masterpieces in every style, his genius may be pronounced universal, and a place be assigned to him by the side of Bach, Handel, Haydn, Mozart, Beethoven, and the lamented musician just mentioned, who may appropriately be called the kings of art.[1]

At the opposite end of the spectrum was Chorley in *The Athenaeum*, who concluded a very unfavourable account of the symphony with the observation that it was

a production which, did artists possess self-knowledge, Dr Spohr would not have sent to England; since there could be small doubt with anyone hearing it that it will be seldom, if ever, repeated. The ideas are old, and their treatment is precisely what everyone knew beforehand, who knows the master's tendency to incessant modulation – the cloying fullness of his score and the deficiency of that episodical matter which the Mozarts and Beethovens, even when their first thoughts have been ever so noble, loved to introduce in their composition.[2]

Other critics were somewhere between these extremes, the predominant opinion being that it was a masterly work but rather too predictably

'Spohrish'. According to *The Times*, 'The audience entered into the merits of the work with great warmth, and from the zealous reception it encountered, it may be safely registered as a future favourite with subscribers.'[3] In fact they were never to get the chance of a second hearing, for Chorley's prediction that it would not be repeated was vindicated by events. In Germany, too, it failed to gain any widespread popularity, despite an appreciative reception at its first performance in Leipzig on 14 December 1848. The *AMZ* critic echoed his London colleagues when he remarked that there were no new features to be found in the work but that it had a freshness about it despite its clinging to Spohr's accustomed manner.[4] Hans von Bülow expressed a similar opinion in a letter to Raff after hearing this performance, saying that it contained 'some beautiful parts, if not anything new'.[5] Von Bülow's feeling that this symphony was a clear example of Spohr's tendency to self-repetition is emphasised by an entry in a humorous 'Prophetic Musical Calendar' for 1859, where he wrote: 'Spohr composes his Eighth Symphony yet again without realising it.'[6]

During the latter part of 1847 and the first few months of 1848 Spohr was again active in composition, producing a number of songs and another important chamber composition. Of the songs, the most interesting is 'An Sie am Klavier', a poem by Braun von Braunsthal set as a 'Sonatine für Pianoforte mit Gesang' (op. 138). The poem of six stanzas is treated as a complete sonata movement with a Larghetto introduction (B flat minor, 3/4) and an Allegro (B flat major, 3/2) which is treated tonally and thematically in sonata form. The piano part is elaborate and effective, and the voice combines with it sometimes in quasi-recitative (in the Larghetto) and sometimes as an additional melodic part.

The chamber work which he composed between March and April 1848 was his String Sextet in C (op. 140) for two violins, two violas, and two cellos; it is significant both for the circumstances of its composition and for its intrinsic worth. He began work on it shortly after the outbreak of the revolution in France had sparked off unrest in his own land, and with lively hopes for a political regeneration of Germany. To the entry of the work in his catalogue he appended the comment 'written at the time of the glorious folk revolution for the reawakening of Germany's freedom, unity and greatness'. It would be fanciful, however, to see any direct link between the music and the events by which Spohr was inspired, except in its optimistic freshness and exuberance. In few others of Spohr's late works are these qualities so prominently displayed. This was noted in the *Musical World*, when it was first performed in England during Spohr's 1853 visit, where the reviewer described it as 'a work which, while showing all the experience of age, displays in an astonishing degree that freshness and spontaneity which are supposed only to belong to youth. One of the last chamber compositions of Dr. Spohr, this *sestet* is equally one of the finest and most captivating of them all.'[7]

Even Chorley's carping was silenced by it, for he remarked: 'the motivi . . . of the first allegro and of the scherzo have an eloquence, vigour and freshness rare in the late works of Spohr, and the writing throughout is in his freest and least mechanical style'.[8]

The sextet is certainly one of the finest of Spohr's late works, and is in every respect worthy to be classed among his best works of any period. It seems as if the composer had unexpectedly tapped a rich new vein of inspiration. This is partly to be accounted for, perhaps, by the optimistic frame of mind generated by the reforms of 1848, but also by the stimulation of tackling a new medium, which in the past had usually stirred him to produce fresh ideas. In his later chamber works Spohr had increasingly moved away from the hegemony of the first violin and towards a more genuine chamber-music idiom, with a fairer distribution of interest among all the members of the ensemble; in the Sextet it is only in the Finale that the first violin is allowed the customary cadential passagework, and its effectiveness there is increased by the restraint of the earlier movements. The first movement again shows the thematic expansiveness typical of Spohr's late works, which is close in spirit to Brahms, whose own decision to compose sextets was almost certainly a product of his admiration for Spohr's pioneering effort in the genre (ex. 189). An entirely Spohrish feature is the delicate filigree work, including extensive use of a trill figure, which runs through the first movement. The development makes a much greater impact than is usual with Spohr, partly because of the introduction of new material; and the coda, in which the trill figures are again prominent, brings the movement to a charming conclusion (ex. 190). The Larghetto is beautifully paced, beginning with a hymn-like theme to which the more energetic second subject provides an effective foil. The Scherzo has a poised and graceful character (ex. 191) and is highly original in form; there are no repeats; it begins with a

Ex. 189

(Ex. 189 cont.)

Ex. 190

311

Ex. 191

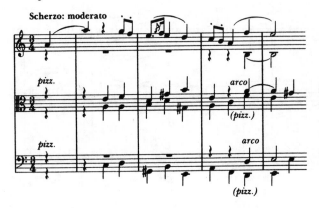

twenty-seven-bar section in A minor which gives way to a new waltz-like section in A major, marked 'con grazia'; the first theme reasserts itself followed by the beginning of the second, but this is dissolved after a few bars by the rising octave figure which had begun the movement. This figure then proves itself to be also the beginning of the Presto Finale (ex. 192), and continues to play a prominent part. At the point where a development section is expected, the Scherzo returns instead in a shortened version; the Presto is then recapitulated in the normal way, and a greatly curtailed version of the Scherzo usurps the place of a coda, only to be swept away by a short final Prestissimo which brings the work to an exhilarating conclusion.

On the completion of the sextet, Spohr found himself unable to concentrate on any further creative work for the time being on account, as he informed Hauptmann, of 'the excitement of politics and the constant reading of the newspapers'.[9] His attitude to events was neatly summed up in a letter of 3 April 1838 to Edward Taylor:

Germany's fate will soon be decided in Frankfurt! We have already been reassured over the apprehension that the republican party would get the upper hand. Only in South Germany do they support it; in North Germany they everywhere want a constitutional monarch, but with guaranteed free institutions such as we have now acquired. Here in Hesse we have already had a constitution since 1830 which leaves little to be desired, but because of the lack of press freedom the government was increasingly able to crush our freedom. Through bribery and influence over the elections the Diet became ever more servile and at last a tool of the government in destroying all constitutional freedom. The few liberal-minded men who dared to stand up to the despotism of the government became involved in lawsuits and were persecuted in every way. And these men now form our government! From this you can see what a reversal of affairs has taken place here! And yet all this has happened without any bloodshed thanks to the cowardice which overcomes such despots in the moment of peril! But we must be vigilant, for the German princes have only been forced to yield and would dearly like to take everything back at the first opportunity. But we know them now and will not let ourselves be duped again.[10]

Ex. 192

On 10 April the sixty-four-year-old composer was (according to his pupil Alexander Malibran) to be found manning the barricades with the Kassel citizens' militia. As soon as the theatre vacation began he travelled to Frankfurt, where he attended the lengthy debates of the German National Assembly, which had been convened on 18 May, with a perseverance that astonished even his friends; and in private circles he discussed politics with such men as the poet Ernst Moritz Arndt and the President of the Assembly, Heinrich von Gagern. Throughout the year his optimism for the future continued to increase, and after the popular celebrations in Kassel at which the Elector mingled with the citizens with the black, red and gold cockade of the 'new Germany' in his hat, Spohr wrote to Adolf Hesse:

It astonishes me that you will not believe in the favourable consequences of the revolution, for I am perfectly happy with the gains that have so far been made. Though the unity of Germany is not yet secured, freedom at any rate is quite certain and I am full of joy to have lived through such a time. Here in Hesse a wholly new spirit has awakened and we are as far in advance of the other German states as we earlier lagged behind them, despite our good constitution. Here the freedoms we have gained are already confirmed by legislation, and a new liberal administration has now been introduced in the country which will make all police interference impossible. In a few weeks we will also see the assembly of public proceedings and assizes, and everywhere the door is being shut on the former arbitrary rule.[11]

Spohr's only composition during the nine months after he had written the sextet had been a short *Rondoletto* op. 149 for piano, written at the request of Charlotte Moscheles for a proposed album of pieces that was never published; but in February 1849 he once again completed a more substantial work, his String Quartet no. 32 in C major op. 141. It is a far more successful quartet than its immediate predecessor, op. 132: the distribution of interest among the instruments is more satisfactory; the majority of the themes, if not so fresh as in the Sextet, are attractive; and the work as a whole, which is constructed with Spohr's usual skill, contains many highly effective ideas. The opening theme of the first movement provides a good example of Spohr's tendency towards more extended melodic writing with greater rhythmic flexibility which, combined with the rich harmonic accompaniment, gives these late works a warm and expansive quality (ex. 193). In the Finale some charming *pianissimo* passages lasting for almost thirty bars at a

Ex. 193

314

time introduce an element of light wit. The quartet's appearance, however, called forth a review from the *NZfM* which seems to encapsulate the growing feeling among many musicians that Spohr had essentially written himself out and was no longer capable of producing anything of note. The critic began: 'Spohr's 31st Quartet, 141st opus! This really says all that is necessary for our review. Whoever has become acquainted with the 141st opus of this composer has got what he expected!'[12]

A sojourn in Leipzig on his way to Karlsbad in May 1849 gave Spohr the opportunity to perform his new quartet and his Fourth Double Quartet there for the first time, and they roused such enthusiasm that he was persuaded to perform them a second time at the Conservatory. After he had enjoyed a reunion with Moscheles, Hauptmann and other friends and had been the recipient of the customary honours, he continued his journey to Karlsbad, where he stayed for several weeks discussing politics and enjoying the relaxing surroundings. During his stay, there occurred an incident that illustrates the enormous impact his music was capable of making on contemporaries, and provides a necessary counterpoise to the less enthusiastic criticisms that often appeared in the press. A young man also staying in Karlsbad who wished to meet the composer and express his admiration was so overcome with emotion on first seeing Spohr that he burst into tears, and only after some minutes was he able to tell him how deep and powerful an impression his music had made upon him.[13]

Spohr derived so much benefit from his holiday that his recurrent liver complaint was permanently cured and he returned to Kassel with renewed mental and physical vigour; his desire to engage in composition again was irresistible. In October, he wrote his Fifth Piano Trio, op. 142 in G minor, which, along with the Fourth Double Quartet and the Sextet, is among the best of the late chamber works; like them it is imbued with vigour and imagination, each of its four movements being on an equally high plane. The first movement has an abundant flow of ideas, but at the same time displays Spohr's liking for the unifying motif, the opening theme also providing an important element of the second subject (ex. 194), though the two themes are totally different in character. The development has a notable coherence, achieved largely by the continuous semiquavers in the right hand of the piano part, which bind together the thematic allusions in the string parts. The Adagio is one of those movements which confirmed Spohr's reputation for high artistic seriousness; it is in an exalted tone throughout, single-mindedly sustaining its initial mood. The Scherzo is whimsical, the ideas constantly changing their emphasis. In the Trio all ambiguity is set aside and Spohr is unashamedly skittish, contrasting helter-skelter triplets with staccato quavers (ex. 195). Earnest impetuosity and exuberance are the keynotes of the Finale. The first subject begins with a bold call to attention and continues with a figure which is clearly related to the first movement (ex.

Ex. 194

196). The second subject is in complete antithesis to the first, having a feeling of surging enthusiasm. These two moods jostle for supremacy during the course of the movement, the more sombre G minor mood finally gaining the upper hand in the coda where, after a number of explosive outbursts, the trio ends on a note of suppressed agitation.

In view of the reaction which had already set in against the revolutionary

Ex. 195

movements of 1848, it is surprising that Spohr should have remained even
guardedly optimistic in the autumn of 1849. As in 1831 he could not accept
that the cherished vision was proving to be a chimera. He wrote to Adolf
Hesse on 19 November: 'As far as the unity of Germany is concerned things
are now going so badly that one would certainly rather not speak about it.
Happily things are better with respect to freedom! At least here in Hesse we
have gained so much that our only worry will be to keep it!'[14] He was soon
forced to accept that the vast majority of these gains could not be preserved.
Fortunately he was able to immerse himself in artistic activities; a letter written to Speyer on 29 November 1849 gives a neat picture of his involvement in
and enjoyment of musical activities. He wrote:

The older I become the more I am overloaded with work. The sending of compositions which I must give an opinion on, of enquiries which I must answer, is certainly endless, so that I can only occasionally get on with work of my own. I have only, therefore, been able to carry on my biography up to the Italian journey, and since our return from Karlsbad have not written anything new except a piano trio (the fifth) and three duets for sopranos. – Our music parties have also begun again, and I chiefly play my latest compositions of the last years which you probably do not know yet. These are two quartets, a sextet for two violins, two violas and two cellos, and a double quartet (the fourth). – Our quartet music goes very well, and there can hardly be a better one in Germany. Besides the quartet parties there are now also several cir-

Ex. 196

(a) Finale

(Ex. 196 cont.)

(b) 1st movement

cles for piano music with accompaniment here in which I cannot refuse to participate. As a violinist, therefore, I have almost never been so much in practice as at
present although I gave up playing in public a year ago [this was in protest at the
political situation]. That I can, in these private circles, still compete so vigorously
with my pupils without any noticeable decrease of technical skill makes me very
happy and cheers my life, which now as before is wholly dedicated to art.[15]

The end of 1849 and the beginning of 1850 were clouded by domestic
problems. First, Marianne was dangerously ill for three weeks in December
and January, and then on 22 January Spohr had a fall on the ice resulting in
severe concussion from which he did not fully recover for several weeks.
During his convalescence, however, he planned another major composition,
his Ninth Symphony. Once again seeking inspiration in a programmatic
idea, he chose the title *Die Jahreszeiten* (The Seasons). The symphony is in two
parts, the first illustrating Winter – transition to Spring – Spring, and the
second, Summer – introduction to Autumn – Autumn. In reality the usual
four-movement form of the symphony is only thinly disguised. Winter is the
normal sonata-form first movement, Spring a scherzo, Summer a slow
movement, and Autumn a rondo finale. Winter (in B minor) is the weakest
movement, containing nothing which is graphically descriptive or even
evocative of that season; nor, taken without reference to its programmatic
intention, does it contain anything much to recommend it, for Spohr clings
pertinaciously to his stock melodic, rhythmic and harmonic formulae.
Spring has more life in it, and the Trio section in 2/4 is suggestive of a lively
country dance. Summer, using muted strings – divisi some of the time in
nine parts – effectively conjures up a picture of sultry heat and murmuring
insects, while Autumn, with its hunting calls and its quotation of a *Rhein-*

weinlied (from J. A. Schultz's *Lieder im Volkston*), has spirit, though it is perhaps too long drawn out.

Reviews of *Die Jahreszeiten* reiterated, with varying shades of emphasis, the usual opinions which Spohr's late works elicited. The *NZfM* observed: 'With all its harmonic and instrumental excellences, *Die Jahreszeiten* is a work showing the weakness of age, in the known Spohrish style and manner, full of reminiscences from the master's earlier period and provided with even more tone-painting than *Die Weihe der Töne*.'[16] In England, where it was conducted by Balfe at the Grand National Concerts on 25 November 1850, it was received unenthusiastically but on the whole respectfully. The *Morning Post* observed that

The Symphony is thoroughly Spohrish in character. It may be taken as a fair sample of the celebrated master's general style for it affords numerous examples of his peculiar beauties and defects. We remark in it the same luscious chromatic harmonies repeated to satiety, the same elaboration of details, the exquisite instrumentation and provoking monotonous phraseology which distinguish most of his works.[17]

On the other hand some critics, while frankly confessing the weaknesses of the symphony, took the opportunity to point out once again Spohr's preeminence in the musical world. *The Spectator* remarked: 'Spohr is truly "ultimus Romanorum" – the last of the great symphonists, the last successor of Bach and Handel in the oratorio, and the last dramatic writer of the pure German school of Gluck and Mozart. When he dies, these high walks of his art will be vacant, for no one seems coming forward to follow in his footsteps.'[18] In a similar vein the *Musical World* concluded its review: 'Spohr has taught us, by previous essays, to expect so much, that the announcement of a new symphony from his pen is almost tantamount to the promise of a new *chef d'oeuvre* for the art. That we have been disappointed on the present occasion cannot be denied; but if "Homer nods" at intervals, why not Dr Spohr?'[19]

The summer vacation of 1850 was devoted to a long-promised visit to Breslau, where Adolf Hesse was organist. On the way he stopped in Leipzig to attend rehearsals of Schumann's opera *Genoveva*, which left him with a higher opinion of Schumann's abilities than he had formerly held. This was due partly, no doubt, to the similarity of aims and methods which he detected between this opera and his own *Die Kreuzfahrer*. After hearing a performance of his Ninth Symphony at the Gewandhaus, Spohr and his companions travelled on to Breslau, where for two weeks he was regaled with a series of concerts, serenades, banquets and tributes of every kind. In a chamber concert he himself led his Sextet and Third Double Quartet, and a report in the *Breslauer Zeitung* testifies to his continuing command of the violin, noting that 'the master plays with the fire and energy of a young man, and throws off the greatest difficulties with a power and boldness that are astonishing'.[20] The climax of the visit was a production of *Zemire und Azor*, of which Spohr conducted the second performance. On the return journey to Kassel he visited Berlin and was entertained in the Conservatory by a performance of parts of *Des Heilands letzte Stunden* and his three Psalms op. 85.

As a distraction from the worsening political situation – his letters at this time contain no more optimistic prognostications – he threw himself once again into composition. In September he wrote a set of three songs to poems from Friedrich Bodenstedt's *Tausend und ein Tag im Orient*, and in October and November a seventh string quintet in G minor, op. 144. The songs are charming, but the quintet is disappointing, falling well below the level of the immediately preceding chamber works. Perhaps its lacklustre quality is partly to be accounted for by Spohr's growing concern about the political state of Germany at that time. He was profoundly disillusioned by the dismissal of liberal ministers by the Elector and the reappointment of the reactionary Hassenpflug to head the government. His view of the latter and of the Elector was unequivocal; he wrote: 'the whole country has been brought to an unparalleled state of confusion by this debased, infamous falsifier Hassenpflug, and one has not yet the least hope that he will give way . . . People abroad can hardly have any notion of how greatly the Elector and his clique are hated.'[21] On 8 December he informed Hauptmann of the worsening state of affairs:

Our situation is now truly desperate! In a few days the Elector will return together with Hassenpflug and his minions. Since they now have the upper hand they will not be content to rest until the constitution has been entirely destroyed and the most shameless arbitrariness put in its place. Should the Estates be called they will be dissolved again the moment they try to arraign the minister. The cowardice of the Prussian ministry has deprived us, along with the rest of Germany, of the freedom we had acquired, and unfortunately there is no prospect that the present generation will see a second, and one hopes more successful, resurgence of the German nation. If I were not too old I would emigrate to free America.[22]

The Silver Wedding of Spohr's daughter Ida, for which he wrote the only composition of these months – a *Festgesang* for alto solo, chorus and piano duet – was celebrated on 25 December amid the gathering gloom of this unsettled period, and a few days later Spohr wrote to his old friend Johann Friedrich Schwenke in Hamburg: 'During my whole life I have not spent such a sad New Year. After the splendid progress which the German nation made in the year '48, this trampling down of all laws and rights which has been experienced here in Hesse is absolutely intolerable.'[23] Worse was yet to come, however, and when he wrote to Hauptmann again on 9 January Spohr told a mournful tale of the quartering of troops and widespread intimidation of inhabitants who were known to have liberal sympathies. Among those who had soldiers forcibly quartered on them was Spohr's father-in-law, Wilhelm Pfeiffer; that Spohr himself was spared this indignity occasioned him some surprise, since, as he told Hauptmann, 'I know what the Elector thinks of me.'[24] As a householder, though, he was responsible for the billeting of a certain number of troops, and paying for them to be put up at an inn cost him a considerable sum of money. But the thing that troubled him most was the loss of the liberties gained in March 1848; he described the closure of all societies, (fearing that the St Cecilia Society might also be banned), the seizure of all newspapers except what he called 'Obermüller's shameful rag' (the state-controlled *Casseler Zeitung*), and the spying on those who expressed their opinions freely, in order to bring them before military courts. The extent of Spohr's disgust is neatly expressed in a letter of 10 March to Edward Taylor, where he exclaimed:

What do you think of our German condition, and particularly the Hessian? Is it not full of desperation? If I were not too old I would get out this instant with my family; but sadly I must stay and put up with things. But I still hope to live to see the German people once again throw off their chains and chase their demoralised princes out of the country.[25]

There can be little doubt that Spohr's international celebrity was to thank for preserving him from the same sorts of malicious persecution that the Elector vented on other state servants with dissident ideas. (It is noteworthy that he was serenaded on his birthday by the Prussian troops who had been sent to prop up the Elector's unstable regime.) The universal outcry that such measures would have provoked was a sufficient deterrent, but there were many small ways in which Friedrich Wilhelm could make his displeasure felt. Thus when Spohr put in the usual request for formal permission to take his summer vacation in 1851, it was refused without explanation, despite the fact that his original terms of contract stipulated his right to it. Spohr was not prepared to accept such treatment, however, and set off for his planned holiday in Switzerland and Italy without his *Urlaub*; then after returning to Kassel before the theatre vacation was over, he made a further journey to visit friends in Göttingen, where at a dinner in his honour 'Spohr's bold stroke' was boisterously toasted. As a consequence of his action, though, he found himself ordered to pay a fine of 550 thalers (more than a quarter of his annual salary); but when this sum was stopped out of his salary at the beginning of 1852, he took the Elector to court in a case which dragged on for three years. Judgement was eventually given against Spohr on the grounds that though he was entitled to the leave of absence he could not take it without permission! The whole incident can have done nothing to lessen his disgust with the arbitrary government of Hesse. The court of appeal did, however, state that from the very first day of his appointment Spohr had carried out the duties of his office loyally, punctually and conscientiously, and after that the Elector did not again refuse his leave of absence. But it was not the last time Spohr's plans were to be thwarted by electoral interference.

It is hardly surprising that these troubled times should not have been particularly conducive to creative work. Nevertheless, between February and August 1851 he completed another set of six *Salonstücke* op. 145, a duet for sopranos with piano, 'Wenn sich zwei Herzen finden', and in October and November a string quartet in G major, op. 146. The quartet is uneven in quality; its first movement shows the usual attention to detail, but the material has little intrinsic interest, and the customary abrupt modulations often sound forced. The Scherzo and Finale, without being outstanding, are more satisfactory. The finest portion of the work, though, is the Adagio second movement, which can stand comparison with the best of its kind among Spohr's output. Its principal theme establishes a mood of serene beauty that invests the whole movement (ex. 197).

Ex. 197

1852 was a much less productive year, seeing only the composition of recitatives to his thirty-nine-year-old opera *Faust* between January and March. The skill with which they are written, however, and the significant transformation of the opera which results make them highly interesting. The occasion for this major revision of *Faust* was the desire of Queen Victoria and Prince Albert to see it at the Royal Italian Opera, Covent Garden. This necessitated its being changed from its original form as a *Singspiel* to grand opera. The request for the alterations was conveyed to Spohr by the director of the Royal Italian Opera, Frederick Gye, during a visit to Kassel early in 1852. At first Spohr refused, feeling that the changes could not satisfactorily be made in many of the scenes, but having received several further pressing letters from London he agreed to undertake the task. Once he had begun to work on it he became completely absorbed, finding it a refuge from present realities. As he wrote to Hauptmann after finishing the recitatives,

This work has given me great pleasure and agreeably occupied me for a period of three months, during which I have been, as it were, completely transported back to the happy days of my youth in Vienna. At first with the assistance of my wife I had to alter the dialogue scenes in such a manner as to fit them for composition. In doing this I have tried to give them more interest than they previously possessed and to shorten those things which from the start had displeased me at many performances I had seen of this opera. I think and hope that I have succeeded in both. I then had to restore myself, as it were, to the same mood and style in which I wrote *Faust*, and I hope that I have succeeded in this too and that no one will observe a difference of style between the old and the new.[26]

In addition to modifying the dialogue and setting it to music – mostly in arioso style, or recitative accompagnato – Spohr recast the opera into three acts, ending the second act with the wedding feast and the death of Hugo and beginning the third act with a newly composed introduction, whose opening recalls the introductory Sinfonia to Part II of *Die letzten Dinge* (perhaps a subconscious association with the idea of impending judgement). He also sanctioned the inclusion of the aria 'Ich bin allein' from *Der Zweikampf mit der Geliebten* as a second aria for Kunegunde.

In this new form *Faust* was sent to London, where news of its impending performance under the composer's baton gave rise to a considerable degree of anticipation among English musicians.

XVII

'The Altmeister of the departing epoch'
1852–1859

With the advent of his summer vacation, Spohr travelled to England, and *Faust*, in its new form, was performed at the Royal Italian Opera under his baton on 15 July 1852. Anticipation was at a high level in advance of the first night, for as the *Morning Herald* observed there were 'few operas the component parts of which are in such general vogue'.[1] The *Musical World* also noted that many of the individual numbers were 'as familiar to the musical world, and to amateurs in general, as anything from *Der Freischütz*'.[2] The possibility of seeing it staged under its composer's direction, therefore, roused widespread interest. According to *Cocks's Musical Miscellany*, 'The "event" of the month has been the arrival of Louis Spohr in this country to conduct his own celebrated opera of *Faust*. The first performance took place . . . with a degree of perfection almost unprecedented in the annals of the Opera. To obtain that perfection, there were four full band rehearsals, under Spohr's own direction.'[3] And the *Musical World* reported of the performance: 'The house was crowded to suffocation. The event was a musical event in the strongest signification of the term, and almost all the musicians and amateurs of distinction, foreign and native, now in the metropolis, were present on the occasion. Dr. Spohr himself, the greatest conductor on the continent, presided in the orchestra.'[4] Despite numerous press reports of the opera's being, as the *Morning Post* put it, 'triumphantly successful',[5] and the *Musical World*'s confident assertion that '*Faust* is already ranked among the "classics" of the art, and is likely to survive so long as music continues to be cultivated', there were hints that the triumph might be more superficial than it seemed. The old comments about the non-popular character of Spohr's music were revived in some quarters and, notwithstanding the opera's continued success with the public during the remainder of the season, no English theatrical management seems to have been confident enough to produce the work subsequently. In Germany it enjoyed greater success, being produced by Liszt at Weimar and at many of the major German opera houses over the next decades, but it had fallen from the German repertoire too by the end of the century.

Spohr returned to Germany in the best of spirits after a stay of almost a month in London, during which he had also heard a fine performance of

Calvary (*Des Heilands letzte Stunden*) at Exeter Hall under Costa and spent many pleasant hours with his English friends. But his homecoming was marred by the serious illness and death of his old friend and father-in-law Wilhelm Pfeiffer; it was perhaps because of this that Spohr did not compose anything during that autumn, as he usually did after returning from his summer vacation. The pressure of his other duties was certainly not the cause of his artistic infertility, for at this time a second Kapellmeister, one of his favourite pupils, Jean Bott, was appointed to lighten the duties of his office. Spohr retained the direction of German operas while Bott took over the conducting of the lighter French and Italian works and undertook to lead the orchestra when Spohr conducted. Spohr was surprised at the arrangement, but perfectly content with it, and as he wrote to Hauptmann after seeing Shakespeare's *Midsummer Night's Dream* early in 1853 with Mendelssohn's incidental music, 'Bott rehearsed the music with great care, and it was a great pleasure for me to be able for once to attend a performance of good music without first having taken a multitude of rehearsals of it.'[6] He also informed Hauptmann that he had begun rehearsals of Wagner's *Tannhäuser*, which the Elector, having refused permission for its performance in 1846, had now permitted. Friedrich Wilhelm seems, however, to have regretted his decision, for in the middle of rehearsals he took steps to prevent any more of Wagner's operas being performed in Kassel, by sending an order to the theatre stating: 'Our general board of management of the Hoftheater must not buy any compositions in future from the composer Richard Wagner, formerly Kapellmeister and barricade fighter in Dresden.'[7]

Spohr's attitude towards Wagner's opera reveals much about his musical personality. During the rehearsal period he confessed: 'There is much that is new and beautiful in the opera, but much that is most distressing to the ear.' After the third performance he wrote again to Hauptmann setting out his thoughts about the opera in greater detail:

The opera has gained many admirers through its seriousness and its subject matter, and when I compare it with other things produced in recent years, I am in agreement with them. Much that at first was very disagreeable to me I have become accustomed to with frequent hearings; only the lack of rhythm and the frequent absence of rounded periods is still very objectionable to me. The performance here is truly a very outstanding one, and few will be heard in Germany which are so precise. In the enormously difficult ensembles for the singers in the second act not a note was left out last night. But for all that, there are several places where they make a truly horrifying music, particularly shortly before the place where Elisabeth throws herself on the singers who rush upon Tannhäuser. – What faces would Haydn and Mozart make if they had to listen to such a hellish noise which is now given to us for music! The pilgrims' chorus . . . was so perfectly in tune last night that for the first time I was able to reconcile myself to its unnatural modulations. It is remarkable what the human ear can become accustomed to by degrees.[8]

Reports of Spohr's reaction reached Wagner's ears, and in *Mein Leben* he remarked that he had heard that 'my *Tannhäuser*, when it was performed at Kassel, had caused him so much pain and confusion that he declared he could no longer follow me, and feared that I must be on the wrong road'.[9] These reports were not entirely accurate, for Spohr was still anxious to produce *Lohengrin* and made strenuous efforts both to perform parts of it in the winter concerts and to persuade the Elector to allow it to be produced in the Hoftheater. He also attempted unsuccessfully to hear it elsewhere, and as late as 1858, the year before his death, he wrote on 23 August to his former pupil Hubert Ries in Hamburg that he hoped to get to see a production of a new Wagner opera which he believed was to be given there in the spring.[10] Spohr's views on recent trends in music are further illustrated by his reaction to Berlioz's *Benvenuto Cellini*, which he heard in London in July 1853, and to an opera by Jean Bott, *Der Unbekannte*, which was produced in Kassel in August 1854. From London he wrote to Lueder:

It is with Berlioz as with all the other protagonists of the music of the future: they do not abandon themselves to their natural feelings in their work, but speculate on that which has not yet been. That is the reason why these musicians seldom write anything that is enjoyable particularly for people who grew up in the previous century with the music of Haydn, Mozart and Beethoven.[11]

Of *Der Unbekannte* he wrote to Hauptmann:

Bott's opera has indeed won a public here, and I am now anxious to see whether this will be the case abroad where people have no personal interest in him. It is certain that his opera, as a first attempt in the genre, deserves great attention. There are several good numbers, well-arranged form and rhythmic skill in it, as in Wagner's operas, and yet in the style one hears wholly the so-called music of the future! There is no reminiscence of Mozart, Beethoven or Cherubini; only Wagner, Meyerbeer and perhaps Marschner seem to have influenced him. In view of Bott's talent this is a riddle to me, for he has had the opportunity since earliest youth to acquaint himself with the masterpieces of the three first-mentioned composers; how is it now that he is not as inspired by them as we and all the artists of our period? Contemporary taste must be like the cholera; whoever is susceptible to it does not escape the infection.[12]

(It is interesting to note that in 1843 the *AMZ* had likened Bott's compositional style to Spohr's.[13])

Spohr's own artistic creed is clearly apparent in these comments: his fidelity to ideals of pure beauty based upon his early reverence for the music of his immediate predecessors; his almost obsessive aversion to anything which smacked of sensationalism, nevertheless counterbalanced by an intense interest in the experimental; a lively curiosity in current developments and a willingness to procure a hearing even for those things with which he could not wholly sympathise, so long as he believed the intention behind them to be sincere.

In the summer of 1853 Spohr made his last visit to England. The success of *Faust* in 1852 had encouraged the management of the Royal Italian Opera to

L'ANALYSE.

Souvenir of the Musical Union (Ninth Season), from a Lithograph.

Bazzini. H. Blagrove. Goffrié. J. Blumenthal. Vieuxtemps. Lazarus. S. Pratten. Jarrett. F. Hiller, Barret. Baumann.
Lindpaintner. Dr. Spohr. Molique. H. Berlioz. Ella.

Lithograph of musicians, including Spohr, who took part in the concerts of John Ella's Musical Union during the 1853 season

328

ask him to direct *Jessonda* during the next season, and in addition he had received an invitation to conduct the concerts of the New Philharmonic Society in Exeter Hall. It was the latter in particular that decided him to undertake the visit, for he welcomed the opportunity of ensuring a good performance of some of his larger orchestral works in front of a public which he believed was very well disposed to appreciate them. From press reports it seems clear that, at least in the case of his Seventh Symphony which he conducted on 8 July, he succeeded in kindling a notable degree of enthusiasm. *Cocks's Musical Miscellany* remarked:

> Dr Spohr's very remarkable symphony for two orchestras was excellently performed, and listened to with enthusiasm . . . the bands were placed in different situations to aid the effect, and the result was such as to exhibit this work as one of the greatest and noblest of Spohr's inspirations. Dr Spohr was greeted by the large assembly with a homage as sincere as it was unbounded. [14]

Only a few contrary opinions were expressed about the symphony or about the Quartet Concerto, which was performed at the same concert. George Hogarth, for example, who disliked programme music in general, described the symphony in the *Daily News* as 'the very coldest and driest of all his works', [15] and the *Morning Chronicle* was distinctly unmoved, though it was admitted that 'The audience applauded vehemently, and were evidently well pleased.'[16] Among the work's staunchest admirers was the *Musical World*, which observed: 'The conception of the whole symphony is in the highest degree poetical, and its general development worthy of Dr Spohr, among whose greatest and most lasting works it will undoubtedly rank.'[17] The *Morning Herald* commented that the treatment of the theme is 'richly varied, and the effect musically considered, is exquisite'. [18] But the *Morning Post* was perhaps the work's most eloquent partizan; its critic commenced with a long eulogy on the composer:

> were sufficient time and space allowed us, we know of no more profitable use to which it might be dedicated than that of duly celebrating the vast merits of one of the greatest of that noble line of classic composers which commenced with Haydn. Louis Spohr, like his renowned predecessors has excelled in every branch of musical art . . . It will be enough to state that his music is the best of the day, and that he is a complete master of orchestral resources, to prove his general superiority over all his contemporaries. [19]

In the event Spohr was not able to conduct the first performance of *Jessonda*. Its production was delayed because of the need to rehearse other operas to replace projected performances of Berlioz's *Benvenuto Cellini* which, having been roundly hissed, had to be withdrawn after only one performance, and Spohr had to return to Kassel before it could be brought out. When it was finally produced on 6 August it enjoyed considerably more success than Berlioz's opera, though it certainly did not create a furore of enthusiasm. A split in attitudes of different sections of the audience was noted by the *Musical World*:

Jessonda – like Faust, last season – obtained a *succès d'estime*. Liked and applauded by the connoisseurs and the general audience, it was patiently endured by the habitués of the stalls and grand tier boxes. Nevertheless, to the credit of all, it must be said, that even those who failed to understand and appreciate the music, listened to it with attention, and that no marks of impatience interfered with the execution and enjoyment of a work which has been acknowledged a *chef d'oeuvre* for upwards of 30 years, and belongs to the classics of the art.[20]

There is plenty of evidence that during these years taste was being very hotly debated along similar lines both in Germany and England. Those who admired and strongly supported Spohr were broadly in favour of the classical German school of which they saw him as the ultimate heir. They saw themselves as defenders of absolute canons of beauty in art against, on the one hand, the operas of the Italians and French schools which dominated the stage and, on the other, the propagandists of the 'music of the future'. Davison and a critic of the *Morning Post* are good examples of this attitude. The *Morning Post* critic launched an attack against those whom he saw as less responsible colleagues after the production of *Jessonda* (which he described as 'infinitely superior to the operas of Meyerbeer, Bellini, Donizetti or Verdi'):

The nonsense which is daily written about music is incredible . . . Everything that is good in musical art is rapidly passing away – vulgar meaningless tunes, uproar, and clap-trap, have taken the place of the pure beauties of the great masters, and are accepted by the general public as evidence of genius. Had our public critics been always competent, and done their duty efficiently, this state of things would have been crushed in the bud, and the popular taste directed to higher objects. We should never have seen the corrupt though occasionally clever music of Meyerbeer extolled to the skies, or the abominations of the modern Italian school spoken of as works of genius.[21]

The other group were belaboured in his review of *Irdisches und Göttliches im Menschenleben*, where he commented that Spohr had achieved far more than his 'present German contemporaries of the "aesthetical" school with all their hazy theories about poetical "inspiration", "Objective music" and contempt for technical rules and established models, have yet done or are at all likely to do. With those gentlemen the subject is everything, the execution nothing.'[22] The similarity of Davison's attitude is indicated by an article he wrote the following year, where he observed:

Within the last fortnight two of the symphonies of Dr. Spohr – the *Weihe der Töne* and the D minor (No. 2), – have been exposed to flippant animadversions, from those, on one side, who are nothing better than blind and bigoted past-worshippers, and on the other, from a very different class of critic, whose *beau idéal* is concentrated in a certain modern school of composition which might be properly styled the Music-run-mad School.[23]

In England the defenders of classical principles were to remain more influential and vocal than the protagonists of the new music for some time. In Germany there was already in the 1850s a strong and articulate sector in the musical press who were committed to the new aesthetic outlook; Hauptmann complained of them in a letter to Spohr in 1853: 'We want no *Neue Zeitung* [sic] to tell us that form is not the one thing needful for art, but it seems to ignore the fact that spirit alone will not do either.'[24]

Returning to Kassel in August 1853, Spohr set to work on a composition in which he once again affirmed his own undeviating fidelity to the ideals of classical perfection. While in London he had conceived the idea for a septet for piano, violin, cello, flute, clarinet, horn and bassoon. It was to be his first major composition (excepting the *Faust* recitatives) for almost two years, and into it he poured all his pent-up energy and imagination. It is one of that small group of late works which, while making no significant stylistic advance, achieve genuine vitality through the combination of vigour, charm and exquisite technical skill. As in so many other cases the challenge of an unfamiliar medium seems to have given a strong stimulus to his creativity. The first movement contains delicious passages of dialogue between the instruments which are rendered all the more piquant by offbeat accents (ex. 198) and provide a perfect foil to the sombre tone of the principal theme. Similarly sensitive scoring enlivens the Pastorale (Larghetto) second movement and saves the somewhat undistinguished material of the principal

Ex. 198

(Ex. 198 cont.)

theme from banality; the middle section and coda have a genuinely Romantic colouring. The Scherzo, hesitant and decisive by turns, has two Trios, the first with a prominent clarinet solo. A Finale of considerable power brings the septet to a worthy conclusion.

A contemporary review in the *NZfM* of the first Leipzig performance aptly summed up the qualities of the Septet when it observed:

As with all the master's works, one already recognises his individuality in the first bars, and this septet is suffused with that tender melancholy which manifests itself in all the productions of Spohr's pen. If, also, with respect to the content, there is little if anything new, and though indeed numerous reminiscences from the composer's earlier works are apparent, nevertheless the septet is very appealing and found a brilliant reception.[25]

His next compositions too were directly inspired by the visit to England, for during it he had heard and been greatly impressed by the brothers Alfred and Henry Holmes' performance of some of his violin duets. He thus determined to write some new ones and dedicate them to the two English violinists. The three duets opp. 148, 150 and 153 were composed in March

1854, December 1854, and autumn 1855. They are planned on a grand scale, each having four movements, and they once more affirm Spohr's unrivalled mastery of the medium, though it cannot be said that they have the drive and fire of his earlier duets.

The other substantial compositions of 1855 were a set of six songs for four-part mixed choir and his last published chamber work, the String Quartet in E flat op. 152. The quartet is interesting for it indicates that he was not closed to new ideas – that perhaps even at this late stage he was attempting to break away from the predictable paths which he had followed in recent years. The motive with which the slow introduction to the first movement opens reappears a few bars later over a pedal, where Spohr treats it in a quite uncharacteristic way, leaving the dissonance unresolved (ex. 199). As a whole, though,

Ex. 199

the quartet is not a successful work, for elsewhere the usual clichés are far too obtrusive.

Spohr's last significant published work was a set of six songs for baritone, violin and piano op. 154, which he wrote at the request of Prince Paul Friedrich Emil Leopold of Lippe. They too contain nothing unexpected, but are written with Spohr's usual care and attention to detail, and possess a beguiling charm. A curiosity is Spohr's setting of Goethe's 'Der Erlkönig', which has none of the anguished drive of Schubert's version. The sedate pace of the opening seems an almost unaccountable miscalculation, though the treatment of the Erlkönig's words, accompanied by delicate *pianissimo* violin figurations, is effective. The other songs of the set are much more convincing: 'Der Spielmann und seine Geige' is particularly attractive, with its appropriately virtuoso violin part (ex. 200). The final song of the set, a sim-

Ex. 200

ple and peaceful setting of Koch's 'Abendstille', though not in fact the last music which he wrote, could fittingly be taken as Spohr's swansong. The *Neue Berliner Musikzeitung* wrote an appreciative and fair review of the songs when they appeared in print in 1858, commenting:

It is from the intellectual mastery rather than the accumulation of new material that one recognises the master. And such a master, who does not merely experiment, but straightways rushes upon his true goal with a complete command of an admittedly somewhat individual technique. – Such a master is Spohr, one of the few who still live among us. The six songs in question, though they show no new side of Spohr's talents, have given us great joy.[26]

There had been a sharp decline in the quality of Spohr's output after 1850. One obvious reason for this was his preoccupation with and disillusionment over the failure of the 1848 revolution to achieve the freedoms which he believed in; it is true that from the autumn of 1853 he was more productive than during the previous eighteen months, but even then he was not composing with the fluency of earlier years. Perhaps this would have been surprising in a seventy-year-old composer, though there is plenty of evidence that his physical and mental powers were remarkably unimpaired. On the eve of his departure from England in 1853 Davison had written: 'His activity is remarkable, and his vigour and artistic enthusiasm are as extraordinary as though 40 instead of 70 had numbered the winters of his life.'[27] In 1854 he spent the summer vacation in a strenuous holiday in Switzerland and south Germany; the following spring he travelled to Hanover to direct his Seventh Symphony by royal command and during the visit was involved in constant activity, writing to Hauptmann that after a dinner lasting five hours 'I played two of my quartets, and as on the previous evening did not get to bed until two o'clock.'[28] After he had visited Hauptmann in 1856, during a summer in which he made excursions to Dresden, Switzerland, Prague and the Harz mountains, Hauptmann wrote to Hauser: 'Where is such another? I know of none. There are plenty of people who have grown old; he is the only one that is always young.'[29] And in September 1858, just over a year before his death, when he visited Speyer in Frankfurt for the last time, Speyer's son Edward recalled that 'At meal times . . . Spohr did not swallow while drinking but poured the contents of a wineglass into his wide-open mouth and straight down his throat,' and he described how after dinner, when the whole company took part in choral music with piano, Spohr 'sat right next to the pianist, conducted, with his glance directed to the score, in as energetic a manner as if he had a whole orchestra in front of him and sang valiantly with nothing less than astonishing fire and ardour in the chorus'.[30] That Spohr himself had begun to feel his age by this time, however, is evident from a letter which he wrote to his former pupil August Pott in March 1857, where he remarked that it was no pleasure to become old 'since it is a very sad thing to see one's mental and physical strength fade. And as an artist I particularly regret having to experience the present period when our excellent art is so perceptibly in decline.'[31]

In the years 1856 to 1858 he made several further attempts to compose substantial works, none of which satisfied him sufficiently to be considered wor-

thy of publication. The first of these was a string quartet in G minor, probably written during the autumn of 1856. After playing it through at his winter
quartet soirées he extensively remodelled it, changing the outer movements
to E flat major. Even in the new form, however, he was not satisfied, and
despite giving it the opus number 155 he laid it aside. The Tenth Symphony
in E Flat op. 156, composed in the spring of 1857, met a similar fate, for after
trying it out with his orchestra Spohr reluctantly decided that it was not
worthy to rank with his published symphonies and suppressed it. He came to
the same conclusion about a final string quartet in G minor, op. 157 – which
was his last substantial work to be completed – and withheld it too from
publication.

Spohr's increasing inability during the 1850s to compose anything which
satisfied him seems to have been more closely bound up with a crisis of
confidence than with the failure of his mental powers. His wife reported in
the *Autobiography* that musical ideas no longer flowed with the fluent unself-
consciousness of earlier days and that he himself expressed doubts as to
whether his later works would take equal rank with the earlier ones.[32] The
constant reference by critics to his mannerism and self-repetition could not
have failed to make an impression, as is evidenced by his attempts to open up
new paths in the String Quartet op. 152. Even the frequent letters of appreciation which he continued to receive, and the genuinely enthusiastic recep-
tions that were given to him whenever he travelled outside Kassel, could not
blind him to the fact that he was an artist who had outlived his time and now
found himself in an uncongenial environment which he no longer possessed
the power to influence.

The appointment of Bott as second Kapellmeister in 1852 had appreciably
lightened Spohr's duties; he was not happy, therefore, when in 1856, after a
disagreement with the Theatre management, Bott resigned. By September,
however, a successor was found in Carl Riess, Kapellmeister in Mainz.
Spohr was well satisfied with his new assistant, and wrote to Lueder praising
Riess' artistic qualities, telling him that he had 'even been relieved of several
more insipid and tedious operas' than when Bott had been there.[33]

In the summer of 1857 he made a journey to Holland on which he was
fêted everywhere in the customary manner; and returning through Cologne
he visited Ferdinand Hiller, at whose house he met the young Max Bruch, to
whom, after hearing extracts from his comic opera *Scherz, List und Rache*, he
gave friendly encouragement. On his return to Kassel after this invigorating
holiday, his spirits were dampened somewhat when he was apprised of a
rumour that the Elector intended to pension him off. Several friends advised
him to forestall such a move by resigning, but Spohr, confident of his ability
to carry out his duties, refused to contemplate that course of action. Even
though he had been forewarned, Spohr was hurt and angry when on 12

November 1857 he received a curt official notice informing him that he was to be 'permitted to retire' on account of his advanced age, with a pension of 1500 thalers per annum (three-quarters of his full salary). The original terms of his appointment had stipulated that it was for life, and Spohr briefly considered bringing a lawsuit against the Elector. He wrote to Bott shortly afterwards:

At first it gave me great pain, for I still felt perfectly competent to conduct the few operas which latterly fell to my share. But I soon learned to estimate my present freedom at its real value, and now feel very glad that whenever I choose I can get away by rail wheresoever my fancy takes me! I have also accepted the deduction from my salary, having been informed that I should not be able to secure the payment of the whole salary without a new lawsuit, and because it was repugnant to my feelings to take the whole amount without performing any service for it, since I can live very well with three-quarters of it by means of my savings![34]

On 22 November, after more than thirty-five years, Spohr took leave of the Kassel public with a festive performance of *Jessonda*.

At first he enjoyed his new-found freedom, continuing to take a lively interest in the Kassel opera and subscription concerts, and he embarked upon his usual winter quartet parties with enthusiasm; as he informed Lueder, 'I am happy to say that I am still all right at the violin, though I must always prepare myself a few days in advance, which was not necessary in earlier years.'[35] The impulse to compose was still strong, too, in spite of his misgivings as to whether he could now produce anything of value, and in December 1857 he began a Requiem which he intended as an appropriate termination to his *oeuvre*. His work on this was interrupted, however, by an accident which was to prove a serious setback to his hopes of a few happy years of retirement, for on the evening of 27 December, while on his usual visit to the reading room of the museum, he tripped over the stone steps at the entrance and broke his left arm. The fracture healed with surprising rapidity for a man of his age, but when able to take up the violin again he discovered after a few days assiduous practice that he could no longer play to his own satisfaction and reluctantly laid it aside for ever. During his convalescence he had continued to work for a while on the Requiem, writing optimistically to Speyer on 18 February 1858 that he was still composing fluently, but shortly afterwards he found himself unable to make further progress and gave it up at the beginning of the Lacrymosa. In a letter to Hauptmann on 6 April he mentioned plans for projected journeys later in the year, saying:

Whether all these journeys will be undertaken is not yet decided, but for the rest of my life my artistic enjoyments are confined to them, for I have now come to the conclusion that I cannot bring any more major works to fruition. I regret to say that my last attempt of the kind failed, and my Requiem remains a fragment.[36]

The termination of the Requiem at the Lacrymosa – the exact point at which

Mozart had broken off his setting – is appropriately symbolic of Spohr's lifelong allegiance to the ideals of pure beauty which Mozart's music embodied for him, and his reluctance, indeed refusal, to go beyond the bounds of what he understood as Mozart's aesthetic.

With the loss of almost all the activities which had been so important to him throughout his life, Spohr became increasingly subject to despondency. Neither the triumphant performance of *Jessonda* which he conducted in July 1858 in Prague – the city where his music had enjoyed such consistent popularity over many decades – nor the many other honours and compliments which were showered on him could compensate for the awareness of his artistic impotence and the realisation that nothing but increasing debility and death lay ahead of him. On his return to Kassel after his summer journeys of 1858 he sank into a protracted state of depression foreign to his normally resilient nature. Marianne recorded that whenever she attempted to cheer him

he would reply after a long and earnest silence that he was weary of life since he was no longer able to do anything positive; that he had enjoyed to exhaustion all that mortal life could offer, and had lived to see a more widespread recognition and love for his music than he could ever have hoped for; and now he ardently wished for death before the infirmities of old age entirely overcame him.[37]

Early in September 1858 he made one final attempt to compose. In response to a request for a contribution to Schad's *Musenalmanach* (for which he had written a setting of Walther von der Vogelwiede's 'Die verschwiegene Nachtigall' the previous year), he made a setting of Goethe's 'Neue Liebe, neues Leben'. At first he was pleased with his effort, but on looking at the manuscript again a short time later remarked sadly that it was worthless and regretted having sent it to the publisher.

Further excursions such as his visit to Speyer later in September temporarily lifted him out of his prevailing melancholy, but with the onset of winter his depression deepened. Physically, though, he was still active. In the spring of 1859 he travelled to Meiningen, where Bott was now Kapellmeister, and made his final appearance on the conductor's rostrum. The *Niederrheinische Musik-Zeitung* noted that 'the great master Spohr directed the whole of the first part of the concert throughout with a vigour and liveliness which considering his great age are frankly amazing'.[38]

The strain was considerable, however, and from this time on he showed more marked signs of physical debility. A few short excursions by rail were undertaken during the summer, but though he constantly yearned to continue travelling and kept his interest in music to the last, nothing could for long check his growing weariness of life. Each leave-taking of old friends and pupils and each performance of his own music provoked a painful nostalgia taking its toll in sleeplessness and nervous excitement. Finally on 16 October he took to his bed, refusing either to get up or to eat, and after a gradual decline lasting six days he died peacefully on 22 October 1859.

The funeral took place on 25 October with appropriate magnificence; the coffin was decorated with wreaths of palm and laurel sent by the Queen of Hanover, and the cortege, which was more than half an hour in length, included the members of the Hofkapelle and the opera as well as many of Spohr's former pupils who had come from all over Germany to accompany their master to his final resting place. With the eyes of the world upon him the Elector had committed the arrangements for the funeral to his Court Marshal, paying publicly, but with doubtful sincerity, a respect which he had seldom shown during Spohr's lifetime. He perpetrated one final act of spite, however, for two years later (probably after being acquainted with the liberal sentiments which were contained in the second volume of the *Selbstbiographie*) he forbade the musicians of his Hofkapelle to commemorate the anniversary of Spohr's death at the graveside.

XVIII

Reaction and neglect

The announcement of Spohr's death in October 1859 was not an occasion for searching assessments of his achievements and status; criticism was naturally muted by respectful appreciation. Nevertheless, a degree of ambivalence is apparent in reactions to the news. On the one hand, in German and English obituaries, Spohr's link with the great Classical tradition is almost universally stressed, the permanence of his achievement asserted and his position in the succession of great composers insisted upon; on the other, there are hints of uncertainty about his standing – a feeling that though he cannot be classed anywhere but in the first rank of great composers, he is not quite the equal of the greatest members of the pantheon. The *Casseler Zeitung* might be suspected of partiality in stating: 'Louis Spohr's creations are a legacy bequeathed to thousands, to be handed down by them to their posterity. His melodies still resound, and his name stands like a Memnonian pillar erected in the history of music', and claiming that the 'nobility' of his music 'has been surpassed by no German composer and indeed by no composer in the world';[1] but similar sentiments were widely echoed. In the *Musical World* J. W. Davison was even more emphatic in his assertion of the immortality of Spohr's music, confidently placing him among the very greatest creative minds of history:

What is especially worthy of notice in comparing the relative merits of the great masters is that they resemble each other in nothing except their common adherence to those irrefragable principles without which not only the musical art but all art must perish . . . They wrote after fixed principles, and as musicians of the present and future must of necessity write, if they would emulate, equal, or surpass them . . . Homer, Dante, Shakespeare, and Molière, Raphael, Buonarotti, and Turner, owed their supremacy not more to their transcendent genius than to their instinctive veneration for rules not less immutable than irrefutable. Spohr – like his illustrious predecessors, Handel, Bach, Beethoven, and Mendelssohn – was of these; and as one of their great fraternity was able to produce works that are immortal.[2]

From this passage it is plain why Davison and many others of a like persuasion should have valued Spohr so highly. The imagined threat to sanity in art posed by the 'aesthetic school' and the 'music of the future' can be seen to be underlying his sentiments. While he lived, Spohr had been the last embodiment of the Classical tradition, representing the supremacy of order and balance in musical composition; his death made these qualities all the more precious to those for whom the current trends in German music seemed like a wholesale rejection of all that was most important in their musical heritage, and appeared to border on artistic insanity. Davison had begun his obituary portentously with the assertion 'Spohr has died, full of years, crowned with glory, bending under the weight of laurels. The last of the Teutonic family of musical giants, . . . this remarkable man excelled in every branch of composition' – clearly revealing his opinion that music had entered upon a period in which no one was coming forward to equal the achievements of the great Classical masters.

This feeling is also expressed in a letter which Brahms wrote to Bertha Porubszky in October 1859, where he exclaimed, 'Spohr is dead! He was probably the last of those who still belonged to an artistic period more satisfying than the one through which we now suffer. In those days one might well have looked about eagerly after each fair to see what new and beautiful things had arrived from one composer or another. Now things are different'.[3] The *Neue Berliner Musikzeitung*, too, began its obituary with the observation that he was 'the last representative of that noble line . . . which had its roots fixed in Classical ground';[4] and despite some reservations about his mannerism, which all but Spohr's most fanatical worshippers admitted, this writer also took the view that he must be accounted 'one of the greatest tone-poets of all time'. But though more conservative musicians in the 1850s and 1860s valued Spohr as a bastion of tradition, they recognised that his claims to greatness were founded as much on his role as an innovator. His key position in the development of the techniques of Romantic expression were constantly commented upon; as Sir George Macfarren observed some years after Spohr's death, 'Few if any composers have exercised such influence on their contemporaries as Spohr did, and many living writers may be counted among his imitators.' He went on to say, however, that 'He is excluded from a place among the greatest masters by the fact of his constant employment of the same resources – his constant reproduction of the same forms and the same expression.'[5] It was this latter feature that was being mentioned with increasing frequency, and in an unfair overreaction the good began to be neglected along with the indifferent.

In the decade after Spohr's death, the chorus of denigration from those who considered his music outdated and irrelevant to modern developments grew more vocal. The criticism that had been stifled in deference to the venerable composer during his lifetime was not restrained by respect for his memory. Hauptmann remarked sadly after a performance of the Double Quartet op. 65 at the Gewandhaus in 1864 that he had heard 'a pack of unfledged critics . . . concluding that all such music is out of date' and added: 'If only we could give them an idea, how far above their criticism a work of art like this really is.'[6] The tide of opinion continued to flow strongly against

341

Spohr despite the efforts of historians like Schlüter, who regretted in his *History of Music* (1865) that he was being undervalued. He confessed that 'Spohr's later works, especially his operas and quartets, are mere repetitions of his earlier ones; and that which formerly made him appear original degenerated into mannerism and affectation'; but he went on to say:

These faults are only too evident . . . and have so warped the judgement of musicians on the subject of Spohr's music that not only have vigour and distinctness of expression been denied him, but also depth, imagination, and sentiment . . . Nevertheless, though even the most favourable opinion may find much that is onesided or deficient in Spohr's compositions, he is greatly to be respected as a sterling German musician – one who made no attempts to appear that which he was not; but, so far as he went, was genuine and entire.[7]

Eduard Hanslick made a similar point the following year when he observed, in a review of a concert at which Spohr's overture *Der Berggeist* had been performed,

The total disappearance of Spohr's music from the concert hall should certainly be lamented as a loss and an injustice. For our part, at least, we confess that with the increasing rarity of performances of Spohr's music we are agreeably affected whenever the estrangement from it is broken from time to time by a performance of a composition from his better period (before 1846). Spohr is not only an excellent master, but a truly appealing and characteristic individual; admittedly a onesided one who happily repeats himself, wherefore he who would enjoy him most must enjoy him moderately. It is hardly two decades since one had to warn against an all too zealous Spohr cult, and now already there needs to be a united effort to rescue the works of the master from the fate of total oblivion.[8]

The situation in the 1870s was paradoxical; for while Spohr was still conventionally included in a list of the ten greatest composers in history (see for instance F. Crowest's *The Great Tone Poets* (1874)), the criticisms that were levelled at his music were generally far more comprehensive than would have been aimed at that of any of the other composers on the list, and performances of his works were far fewer than of theirs. Nevertheless, there were still many whose admiration was considerable. T. D. Eaton observed in his *Musical Criticism and Biography* (1872):

We have always considered Spohr the finest and most original writer that has appeared since Beethoven. Less wild and eccentric than Weber, more solid and inventive than Mendelssohn, he is great in all styles of music. Yet it is much to be doubted whether he will ever become popular in this country owing to his inveterate predilection for artificial harmony. His melodies are often intensely sweet, as well as clear and simple, taken by themselves; but the harmony gives them a different character. Where the musician is delighted with an artful beauty, the common hearer is disappointed with an effect he can neither feel nor understand. The new relationships that are constantly starting up are too subtle and refined for him to trace.[9]

There is a great deal of truth in Eaton's judgement. Spohr's music had undoubtedly roused the enthusiasm of musicians and connoisseurs, but failed to win the wholehearted allegiance of the general public. And the continuing currency of this attitude is demonstrated by Philipp Spitta's assertion in 1904 that 'the present age is little suited to appreciate at his true worth a musician like Spohr.'[10] Reactions to Spohr's music continued to be equivocal during the 1880s, as many musical histories of the period indicate. F. L. Ritter in his *History of Music* (1880), for instance, observed that 'he created much that is fine and that may be counted among the best efforts of his time', but went on to qualify his judgement by pointing out the 'lack of energy and spontaneity' which cause his music to become 'monotonous and somewhat wearisome in effect'.[11] A similar balance of opinion was shown in numerous writings from this period. But whatever criticisms may have been registered, few writers seriously envisaged that within little more than a decade Spohr's works would have fallen into the almost total oblivion feared by Hanslick.

Indeed there are suggestions in many of these assessments that the neglect his music had suffered during the previous twenty years was a temporary aberration which was then showing signs of being righted. Emil Naumann in his comprehensive and popular *Illustrierte Musikgeschichte* (1880–5) remarked towards the end of a thorough and judicious consideration of Spohr's qualities and of his position in the development of Romanticism, 'Spohr's noble sentimentality and warmth of expression excited during his lifetime all the youth of Germany into an unusual enthusiasm. The composer's influence is now somewhat less than it was, and indeed latterly his productions have been underrated, but as all that is genuine resists momentary bias, Spohr's works are once more coming to the fore.'[12]

The resurgence of interest in Spohr at this time, prompted no doubt by the centenary of his birth in 1884, proved to be very short-lived. By the 1890s the convention of including Spohr in a list of the great composers had been almost entirely discontinued. The author of an article entitled 'Portrait Sketches from the Life' in the *Monthly Musical Record* in 1891 said of Spohr:

His position as a composer generally is not so easily determined; to relegate him to the second rank is repellant to one's feelings of veneration for him, and yet we cannot place him by the side of Bach, Handel, Haydn, Mozart and Beethoven. Not that his aims were less elevated or his workmanship less perfect, but because his emotional range was more limited.[13]

A similar point of view was expressed by J. W. Henderson in *Famous Composers and their Works* (1895), where Spohr nevertheless merited an eleven-page article with illustrations. He wrote:

'It is difficult for us at this day to fairly estimate the importance of Spohr as a figure in musical history . . . But though we with over half a century's perspective find the masterworks of Weber and Mendelssohn still in the foreground, while Spohr recedes into the middle distance, the contemporaries of these composers saw them standing apparently shoulder to shoulder at the front of the picture. Spohr's influence upon those who lived when he did was very considerable, and, more than that, there are certain features of his style which, it cannot be doubted, presented themselves as attractive models to his followers along the path of musical progress.[14]

A number of factors in addition to Spohr's often-cited mannerism contributed to the decline of his reputation. As has already been suggested, many of those who most strongly advocated his music during the latter part of his lifetime and in the period immediately following his death did so because he seemed the last representative of a school that had no worthy successor; however, the gradual acceptance of and growing enthusiasm for the music of Wagner, Schumann, Brahms, Verdi, Gounod, Dvořák, Tchaikovsky and others, and the rediscovery of the music of such major composers as Bach and Schubert, destroyed that position. Francesco Berger argued that the introduction of Russian music in particular had played an important part in displacing Spohr's music from the repertoire, suggesting that in England at any rate it had been eclipsed 'when the tide of Russian influence began to inundate this country, submerging much that was good and some that was better than what it brought us'.[15] To those who admired these more exotic blooms, Spohr's Classicism was a reproach rather than a recommendation. The originality of style which had cast a lifelong spell over many of Spohr's younger contemporaries during the 1820s and 1830s had long ago lost the appeal of novelty and made little impression on the generation of musicians who were coming to maturity after 1850.

Because Spohr had been the object of such extravagant adulation in his lifetime the reaction was all the more extreme when it came, and by the beginning of the twentieth century even the extent of Spohr's impact on his own epoch was being forgotten or misunderstood. In many of the histories of music written since the Great War he has scarcely been mentioned, and it is clear that where an examination of his importance has been attempted, judgements have usually been arrived at without an adequate knowledge either of his music or of contemporary attitudes towards him. There have been notable exceptions, such as Ernst Bücken and a number of other German scholars, but they are few and far between and their conclusions have been largely ignored; it was even possible, incredibly, for Eric Werner in *Mendelssohn: A New Image of the Composer and his Age* (1963) to write a chapter entitled 'The musical axes of Europe' without once mentioning Spohr, and he is not by any means alone in his myopia. But Spohr was central to the musical life of Germany and England during a period of more than forty years, and a clear picture of his output and his relationship to other musicians of the period is essential to any balanced view of musical developments at that time. As P. H. Lang observed in 1953 when reviewing a recording of the Nonet op. 31 (which he recognised as a 'near masterpiece'), 'If we persist in consigning the dim figures behind Beethoven to complete oblivion we shall never understand why Brahms developed as he did, while Berlioz, Chopin and Liszt went their own way.'[16] Spohr is undoubtedly one of the most significant of those dim figures. The evidence for his historical importance is unequivocal; it may well be argued that the judgement of posterity on his artistic achievement has been too severe. The best of his works are fine music which does not deserve the neglect it has suffered.

Abbreviations

A	*The Atlas* (London)
AMZ	*Allgemeine Musikalische Zeitung* (Leipzig)
An	*The Analyst* (London)
Ath	*The Athenaeum* (London)
BMZ	*Berlinische Musikalische Zeitung* (Berlin)
CMM	*Cocks's Musical Miscellany* (London)
DN	*The Daily News* (London)
Goethe–Zelter	*Briefwechsel zwischen Goethe und Zelter* (Berlin 1833–4)
H	*The Harmonicon* (London)
ILN	*The Illustrated London News* (London)
JD	*Journal des Débats* (Paris)
LLC	Hauptmann, M. *The Letters of a Leipzig Cantor* (London 1892)
LM	*The London Magazine* (London)
LSL	Göthel, F., ed. *Louis Spohr: Lebenserinnerungen* (Tutzing 1968)
MC	*The Morning Chronicle* (London)
ME	*The Musical Examiner* (London)
MH	*The Morning Herald* (London)
MMR	*The Monthly Musical Record* (London)
MP	*The Morning Post* (London)
MT	*The Musical Times* (London)
MW	*The Musical World* (London)
NBMZ	*Neue Berliner Musikzeitung* (Berlin)
NZfM	*Neue Zeitschrift für Musik* (Leipzig)
QMM	*The Quarterly Musical Magazine and Review* (London)
RGM	*Revue et Gazette Musicale* (Paris)
RM	*Revue Musicale* (Paris)
S	*The Spectator* (London)
Sb	*Louis Spohr's Selbstbiographie* (Kassel and Göttingen 1860–1)
SIMG	*Sammelbände der Internationalen Musik-Gesellschaft*
Spohr–Dorette	Göthel, F., ed. *Louis Spohr: Briefwechsel mit seiner Frau Dorette* (Kassel 1957)
St	*The Standard* (London)
T	*The Times* (London)
WS	Speyer, E. *Wilhelm Speyer der Liederkomponist* (Munich 1925)
ZVHG	*Zeitschrift des Vereins für Hessische Geschichte und Landeskunde*

Notes

I. Early life - 1784-1803

1. *Musical Truths*, pp.6-7
2. See Brown, *The Popularity and Influence of Spohr in England*, ch.IX
3. *MW*, xxix (1854), 252
4. *LSL*, i,2
5. *LLC*, ii,31
6. *LSL*, i,3
7. *LSL*, i,4
8. Müller, *Briefe*, p.15
9. Fitzmaurice, *Charles William Ferdinand, Duke of Brunswick*, p.18
10. *Ibid.*, p.19
11. *LSL*, i,8
12. *LSL*, i,9
13. *LLC*, ii,126 & 138
14. *LSL*, i,9-10
15. *LSL*, i,10
16. *LSL*, i,12-13
17. *LSL*, i,16
18. *LSL*, i,40
19. *LSL*, i,28
20. *LSL*, i,24
21. *AMZ*, v (1802/3), 667-9
22. *LSL*, i,52-3
23. *LSL*, i,59
24. *LSL*, i,321
25. *LSL*, i,14
26. *LSL*, i,14
27. *LSL*, i,15
28. *LSL*, i,15
29. *LSL*, i,321
30. *LSL*, i,31
31. *LSL*, i,59

II. First concert tours - 1803-1805

1. *LSL*, i,63
2. *LSL*, i,66
3. Spohr, *Violin School*, p.184
4. *Ibid*, p.196
5. Müller, *Briefe*, letter of 16 December 1804

6. *AMZ*, vii (1804/5), 201ff
7. *Ibid.*
8. *Ibid.*
9. *Ibid.*
10. *LSL*, i,85
11. *LSL*, i,82
12. *BMZ*, i (1805), 95
13. *LSL*, i,83
14. *LSL*, i,91

III. Konzertmeister in Gotha: marriage - 1805-1808

1. *LSL*, i,93
2. Weber, *Writings on Music*, pp.119-20
3. *LSL*, i,94
4. *AMZ*, xi (1808/9), 185
5. *LLC*, i,13
6. *AMZ*, x (1807/8), 90
7. *AMZ*, x (1807/8), 313-14
8. *LSL*, i,109
9. *AMZ*, xxv (1823), 458ff
10. *LSL*, i,112
11. *LSL*, i,114-15
12. Homburg, *Spohr: Bilder und Dokumente*, p.19
13. *LSL*, i,126
14. *AMZ*, xi (1808/9), 174-5
15. Reichardt, *Vertraute Briefe*, i,22
16. *LSL*, i,123
17. *LSL*, i,126-7
18. *AMZ* new series, ii (1867), 315

IV. Virtuoso and composer: spreading reputation - 1808-1813

1. *LSL*, i,119
2. *AMZ*, viii (1805/6), 230
3. *LSL*, i,132
4. *AMZ*, xii (1809/10), 745ff
5. *AMZ* new series, ii, (1867), 299
6. *AMZ*, xiii (1811), 379
7. *AMZ*, xiii (1811), 797ff

8. *LSL*, i,147–8
9. *LSL*, i,155–6
10. *AMZ*, xiv (1812), 722
11. *AMZ*, xiv (1812), 818
12. *AMZ*, xii (1809/10), 745ff
13. *AMZ*, xiv (1812), 601
14. *AMZ*, xv (1813), 53
15. *AMZ*, xv (1813), 115
16. *LSL*, i,161
17. *LSL*, l,168

V. Vienna – 1813–1816

1. *LSL*, i,170–1
2. Weber, *Writings on Music*, p.193
3. Goethe–Zelter, v,322
4. Weber, *Writings on Music*, p.193
5. *AMZ*, xvii (1815), 46
6. *AMZ*, xxii (1820), 239
7. *AMZ*, xix (1817), 153
8. *LSL*, i,180
9. Thayer, *Life of Beethoven*, iii,203
10. *LSL*, i,199
11. *AMZ*, xix (1817), 725ff
12. *AMZ*, xvii (1815), 218
13. *AMZ*, xvii (1815), 767
14. *AMZ*, xix (1817), 725
15. *AMZ*, xvii (1815), 218
16. *LSL*, i,197
17. *LSL*, i,227
18. *LSL*, i,228

VI. Italy – 1816–1817

1. *LSL*, i,296
2. *LSL*, i,288
3. *LSL*, i,267
4. *LSL*, i,266
5. *AMZ*, xviii (1816), 747
6. *AMZ*, xviii (1816), 883
7. *LSL*, i,274
8. *LSL*, i,280
9. *LSL*, i,305
10. *LSL*, i,305
11. In *AMZ*, xix (1817), 327
12. *AMZ*, xx (1818), 33

VII. Kapellmeister in Frankfurt – 1817–1820

1. *AMZ*, xx (1818), 335–40
2. Goethe–Zelter, v,319
3. *AMZ*, xxxi (1829), 829
4. *LSL*, ii,57
5. *AMZ* new series, ii (1867), 363
6. *AMZ* new series, ii (1867), 379
7. *AMZ*, xxi (1819), 27

8. *AMZ*, xxi (1819), 349
9. *LSL*, ii,58
10. *Die Wage*, vi (1819), 286
11. *WS*, p.116
12. *WS*, p.37
13. *AMZ*, xxi (1819), 874

VIII. London, Paris and Dresden – 1820–1822

1. *QMM*, i (1819), 400
2. *QMM*, i (1819), 400
3. *QMM*, ii (1820), 383
4. *LM*, iii (1821), 448
5. *LM*, i (1820), 89
6. *QMM*, i (1819), 406
7. *QMM*, iv (1822), 252
8. *QMM*, ii (1820), 376
9. *LM*, i (1820), 444
10. *QMM*, ii (1820), 384
11. *MC*, 13 March 1820
12. *T*, 22 April 1820
13. *QMM*, ii (1820), 384
14. *QMM*, iii (1821), 385
15. Cox, *Musical Recollections*, i,111
16. *WS*, p.55
17. *QMM*, ii (1820), 385
18. *MW*, xxxv (1860), 250
19. 'Spohr and the Baton', *Music and Letters*, xxxi (1950), 307ff
20. *WS*, pp.51–2
21. *MC*, 4 May 1820
22. *AMZ*, xxii (1820), 744
23. *H*, xi (1833), 96
24. *WS*, p.115
25. *WS*, p.49
26. *WS*, p.52
27. *LSL*, ii,75–6
28. *QMM*, ii (1820), 383
29. *MC*, 4 May 1820
30. *MC*, 12 June 1820
31. *QMM*, ii (1820), 385
32. *WS*, p.57
33. Chopin, *Selected Correspondence* (trans. Headley), p.55
34. *AMZ*, xxiii (1821), 650
35. *AMZ*, xxvi (1824), 29
36. *AMZ*, xxii (1820), 859
37. *AMZ*, xxiii (1821), 157–8
38. *LSL*, ii,118
39. *WS*, p.61
40. *LSL*, ii,109
41. *AMZ*, xxiii (1821), 181
42. *RM*, i (1827), 356
43. *RM*, i (1827), 351
44. *LSL*, ii,134
45. *WS*, p.62

46. *LSL*, ii,123
47. Gál, *The Musician's World*, p.23
48. *WS*, p.63
49. Spohr-Dorette, p.23

IX. Hofkapellmeister in Kassel: operatic triumph - 1822-1825

1. Holmes, *A Ramble among the Musicians of Germany*, p.276
2. Faulkner, *Visit to Germany*, pp.60 & 67
3. Spohr-Dorette, p.29
4. *Ibid.*, p.36
5. *Ibid.*, p.30
6. Malibran, *Louis Spohr*, p.156
7. Spohr-Dorette, p.30
8. *Ibid.*, p.43
9. Smart Papers, iv,102ff
10. Faulkner, *op. cit.*, pp.68-70
11. *WS*, p.65
12. Spohr-Dorette, p.29
13. *Ibid.*, pp.42-3
14. *Ibid.*, pp.40-1
15. *LSL*, ii,131-2
16. *AMZ*, xxv (1823), 458ff
17. *H*, ii (1824), 16
18. *AMZ*, xxvii (1825), 814
19. *MT*, xxv (1884), 445
20. Speyer, *My Life and Friends*, pp.102-3
21. *WS*, p.67
22. *AMZ*, xxvii (1825), 147
23. *AMZ*, xxx (1828), 746
24. *Allgemeiner Musikalischer Anzeiger*, i (1829), 41
25. *WS*, p.70
26. *WS*, p.78
27. *WS*, pp.78-9
28. *AMZ*, xxvii (1825), 235ff
29. *WS*, p.92
30. *AMZ*, xxvii (1825), 854
31. Smart Papers, iv,102ff
32. Goethe-Zelter, iv,119
33. *WS*, p.93
34. Holmes, *op. cit.*, p.277

X. Oratorio and opera: success and failure - 1825-1830

1. *WS*, p.91
2. *LLC*, ii,3
3. *WS*, p.94
4. *WS*, p.95
5. *SIMG*, v (1904), 253ff
6. *WS*, p.96
7. *WS*, p.98
8. *NZfM*, c (1904), 199
9. *Sb*, ii,176

10. *LLC*, i,14
11. *LLC*, i,24
12. *AMZ*, xxx (1828), 872
13. *ZVHG*, lxxv/lxxvi (1964-5), 553
14. *Berliner Allgemeine Musikalische Zeitung*, 17 March 1830
15. *AMZ*, xxxii (1830), 593
16. Letter from Döring to Spohr, 26 December 1826 (in the Murhardsche Bibliothek und Landesbibliothek der Stadt Kassel)
17. Homburg, *Spohr: Bilder und Dokumente;* Greiner, *Louis Spohrs Beiträge*
18. *NZfM*, c (1904), 199
19. *WS*, p.106
20. *RM*, i (1827), 356
21. *AMZ*, xl (1838), 882
22. *AMZ*, xxxiv (1832), 689ff
23. *LLC*, i,25

XI. Revolution and bereavement - 1830-1836

1. *WS*, p.106
2. *LLC*, i,63
3. *LLC*, i,68-9
4. *WS*, p.107
5. *WS*, p.107
6. *ZVHG*, lxxv/lxxvi (1964-5), 556
7. *Ibid.*
8. *LLC*, i,62
9. *WS*, p.105
10. Spohr, *Violin School*, p.96
11. *Ibid.*, p.121
12. Moser, *Joseph Joachim*, p.46
13. Joachim-Moser, *Violinschule*, iii,230
14. *Sb*, ii,190
15. Joachim-Moser, iii,196-7
16. *Erinnerung*, p.68
17. *WS*, p.121
18. *WS*, p.124
19. Schumann, *Music and Musicians*, p.312
20. *LLC*, i,81
21. *ZVHG*, lxxv/lxxvi (1964-5), 557
22. *LLC*, i,88
23. *AMZ*, xxxvii (1835), 495
24. Warrack, *Carl Maria von Weber*, p.204
25. *WS*, pp.143-4
26. *AMZ*, xl (1838), 163
27. *AMZ*, xl (1838), 611
28. *AMZ*, xxxv (1833), 497
29. *MW*, xiv (1840), 355
30. *WS*, p.141
31. *WS*, p.146
32. *WS*, p.145
33. *WS*, p.146
34. *SIMG*, v (1904), 253

35. *AMZ*, xxxvii (1835), 343
36. *LLC*, i,121 & 126
37. *LLC*, i,125
38. *SIMG*, v (1904), 294
39. *LLC*, ii,226
40. *Sb*, ii,203

XII. Remarriage and returning stability – 1836–1839

1. *WS*, pp.156-7
2. *WS*, p.159
3. *WS*, p.175
4. *LLC*, ii,185
5. *Sb*, ii,225
6. *Iris im Gebiete der Tonkunst*, xxi (1841), 47
7. *MW*, vii (1837), 250
8. *An*, viii (1837), 318
9. *NZfM*, viii (1838), 181
10. *Sb*, ii,215
11. *NZfM*, vi (1837), 145
12. Göthel, *Verzeichnis*, p.175
13. *Sb*, ii,216
14. *Ath*, xviii (1845), 637
15. *MW*, xiii (1840), 225
16. *A*, xv (1840), 236
17. *NZfM*, xiv (1841), 53
18. *MW*, ix (1838), 191

XIII. Renewed ties with England – 1839–1842

1. *H*, i (1823), 86
2. *Repository of Arts*, vii (1826), 353
3. *H*, ii (1824), 100
4. *H*, vi (1828), 166
5. *H*, iv (1826), 167
6. *Ath*, iii (1830), 252
7. *A*, v (1830), 524-5
8. *A*, vi (1831), 765
9. *A*, vi (1831), 140
10. *H*, ix (1831), 1
11. *A*, iv (1829), 749
12. *S*, xvi (1843), 636
13. *H*, viii (1830), 466
14. Naumann, *History*, ii,989
15. *MC*, 6 March 1831
16. *T*, 6 March 1831
17. *A*, vi (1831), 296
18. *MC*, 6 March 1831
19. *A*, vi (1831), 296
20. *An*, x (1840), 483
21. *MW*, vii (1837), 164
22. *Ath*, viii (1835), 171
23. *S*, viii (1835), 208
24. *MC*, 28 March 1837
25. *T*, 28 March 1837

26. *MC*, 16 September 1836
27. *Ath*, xiii (1840), 421
28. *MW*, xii (1839), 88
29. *T*, 23 September 1839
30. *MC*, 23 September 1839
31. *MC*, 23 September 1839
32. *T*, 21 September 1839
33. *MC*, 19 September 1839
34. *MW*, xii (1839), 338
35. *MC*, 20 September 1839
36. *MH*, 17 September 1842
37. *MC*, 17 September 1842
38. *T*, 17 September 1842
39. *AMZ*, xlvi (1844), 513
40. *Ath*, xv (1842), 893
41. *Sb*, ii,254
42. *MW*, xiii (1840), 332
43. *S*, xiii (1840), 590
44. *MC*, 22 June 1840
45. *Britannia*, ii (1840), 590
46. *T*, 19 June 1840
47. *RM*, vii (1830), 367
48. *JD*, 23 April 1830
49. *RGM*, ix (1842), 189
50. *Le Ménestrel*, 1 May 1842
51. *JD*, 30 April 1842

XIV. 'The great Spohr – the immortal while yet living' – 1841–1843

1. In *ME*, i (1842), 43
2. *Ibid.*, 83
3. *AMZ*, xlv (1843), 585
4. *AMZ*, xlvi (1844), 150
5. *ME*, i (1842), 83
6. *Op. cit.*, ii,29ff
7. *Sb*, ii,258
8. *NZfM*, xvi (1842), 36
9. *Foreign and Colonial Quarterly Review*, ii (1843), 14
10. *MW*, xvii (1842), 204
11. Bennett, *Life of William Sterndale Bennett*, pp.116ff
12. *WS*, p.257
13. *Sb*, ii,269
14. *LLC*, i,45
15. *LLC*, i,196
16. *Ath*, xv (1842), 774
17. *Punch*, iii (1842), 158
18. *WS*, p.258
19. *Sb*, ii,271
20. *Sb*, ii,271
21. *Sb*, ii,271-2
22. *Sb*, ii,272
23. *ME*, ii (1843), 253
24. *MW*, xviii (1843), 259
25. *Sb*, ii,277

26. *Sb*, ii,279
27. *MC*, 4 July 1843
28. *MC*, 4 July 1843
29. *S*, lxvi (1843), 636
30. *Examiner*, ii (1843), 264
31. *Ath*, xvi (1843), 637
32. *MC*, 22 June 1843
33. Smart Papers, vi,16
34. In *MW*, xviii (1843), 246
35. In *MW*, xviii (1843), 235
36. *Ibid.*
37. *Ibid.*
38. *MC*, 22 July 1843
39. *MW*, xviii (1843), 253
40. *Sb*, ii,281
41. *ME*, ii (1843), 288
42. *T*, 22 July 1843
43. *ILN*, iii (1843), 45
44. In *MW*, xviii (1843), 228
45. In *MW*, xviii (1843), 231
46. *MW*, xix (1844), 158
47. *The Maestro*, i (1844), 71
48. *The Maestro*, i (1844), 83
49. *MW*, xviii (1843), 373ff
50. *ME*, ii (1843), 342
51. *St*, 4 July 1843
52. In *MW*, xviii (1843), 228
53. *MW*, xx (1845), 422
54. *MW*, xx (1845), 171
55. *Ath*, xx (1847), 802
56. *S*, xix (1846), 187
57. Mendelssohn, *Letters, trans. Moscheles*, pp.220-1
58. *ME*, ii (1843), 253
59. In *ME*, iii (1844), 32
60. Anon., *Music*, London 1852 (essays reprinted from the *Quarterly Review*)
61. *Ath*, xvi (1843), 220
62. *Ath*, xxix (1856), 594
63. Von Bülow, *Briefe*, vi,90
64. *NZfM*, xvii (1842), 123

XV. An operatic finale - 1843-1847

1. *Sb*, ii, 289-90
2. *AMZ*, xlvii (1845), 558
3. *Sb*, ii,294-5
4. *AMZ*, xlvii (1845), 625
5. *RGM*, xi (1844), 250
6. *Sb*, ii,289
7. *Sb*, ii,298
8. *AMZ*, xlvii (1845), 742
9. Smart Papers, vi,16
10. *Ibid.*, vi,39
11. *Ibid.* vi,28
12. *Ibid.* vi,16-17
13. *WS*, p.299

14. *Sb*, ii,306
15. Wagner, *Mein Leben*, pp.348-9
16. *Sb*, ii,306; *LLC*, i,130
17. *Sb*, ii,321
18. *Sb*, ii,309
19. *MW*, xxiii (1848), 168
20. *S*, xxiii (1850), 132
21. *AMZ*, xlvii (1846), 123
22. *WS*, p.298
23. *MW*, xx (1845), 446
24. *MW*, xxii (1847), 471
25. *DN*, 10 July 1847
26. *MP*, 10 July 1847
27. *MC*, 10 July 1847
28. *ILN*, xi (1847), 42
29. *Ath*, xx (1847), 42
30. *MH*, 10 July 1847
31. *MC*, 24 July 1847
32. *DN*, 24 July 1847
33. *Ath*, xix (1846), 1147; *MC*, 5 November 1846
34. *ILN*, xi (1847), 59
35. *S*, xx (1847), 709
36. *A*, xxii (1847), 493
37. *S*, xx (1847), 709
38. *A*, xxii (1847), 492

XVI. Revolution: hope and disillusionment - 1847-1852

1. *MC*, 2 May 1848
2. *Ath*, xxi (1848), 467
3. *T*, 2 May 1848
4. *AMZ*, l (1848), 827
5. Von Bülow, *Briefe*, i,146
6. *Ibid.*, iii,245
7. *MW*, xxviii (1853). 443
8. *Ath*, xxvi (1853), 865
9. *Sb*, ii,325
10. *ZVHG*, lxxv/lxxvi (1964-5), 560
11. *Ibid.*, p.361
12. *NZfM*, xxxii (1850), 209
13. *Sb*, ii,331
14. *ZVHG*, lxxv/lxxvi (1964-5), 562
15. *WS*, p.342
16. *NZfM*, xl (1854), 162
17. *MP*, 26 November 1856
18. *S*, xxiii (1850), 1137
19. *MW*, xxv (1850), 766
20. *Sb*, ii,336
21. *ZVHG*, lxxv/lxxvi (1964-5), 563
22. *Ibid.*, p.564
23. *Ibid.*, p.564
24. *Ibid.*, p.564
25. *Ibid.*, p.545
26. *Sb*, ii,351

XVII. 'The Altmeister of the departing epoch' - 1852-1859

1. *MH*, 16 July 1852
2. *MW*, xxvii (1852), 458
3. *CMM*, i (1852), 68
4. *MW*, xxvii (1852), 458
5. *MP*, 16 July 1852
6. *Sb*, ii,356
7. *Reskript* of 28 April 1853, cited in *ZVHG* lxxv/lxxvi (1964-5), 565
8. *Sb*, ii,356-7
9. Wagner, *Mein Leben*, pp.348-9
10. In Sotheby's catalogue for sale of 14-16 April 1982, p.34
11. *Sb*, ii,360
12. *Sb*, ii,366-7
13. *AMZ*, xlv (1843), 884
14. *CMM*, ii (1853), 70
15. *DN*, 9 July 1853
16. *MC*, 9 July 1853
17. *MW*, xxviii (1853), 446
18. *MH*, 9 July 1853
19. *MP*, 9 July 1853
20. *MW*, xxviii (1853), 511-12
21. *MP*, 8 August 1853
22. *MP*, 9 August 1853
23. *MW*, xxix (1854), 252
24. *LLC*, ii,208
25. *NZfM*, xl (1854), 162
26. *NBMZ*, xiii (1859), 73
27. *MW*, xxviii (1853), 443
28. *Sb*, ii,369
29. *LLC*, ii,98
30. *WS*, p.403
31. *LSL*, ii,208
32. *Sb*, ii,378
33. *Sb*, ii,377
34. *Sb*, ii,384
35. *Sb*, ii,336
36. *Sb*, ii,388
37. *Sb*, ii,392
38. *Niederrheinische Musik-Zeitung*, vii (1859), 149

XVIII. Reaction and neglect

1. In *MW*, xxxiv (1859), 734
2. *MW*, xxxiv (1859), 713-14
3. Gál, *Johannes Brahms*, p.37
4. *NBMZ*, xiii (1859), 345
5. *The Imperial Dictionary of Universal Biography*, xiii, 104
6. *LLC*, ii,166
7. Schlüter, *History of Music*, pp.310-11
8. Hanslick, *Geschichte des Concertwesens in Wien*, ii,377
9. Eaton, *Musical Criticism and Biography*, pp.113-14
10. In Joachim-Moser, *Violinschule*, iii,196
11. Ritter, *History of Music*, p.428
12. Naumann, *History of Music*, ii,992
13. *MMR*, xxi (1891), 4
14. Henderson, *Famous Composers*, ii,382
15. 'Beethoven, Spohr and Hummel', *MMR*, li 248
16. *Musical Quarterly*, xxxix (1953), 234

Bibliography

A. Autobiographical writings

Spohr's memoirs (*Lebenserinnerungen*), which he began in 1847, at the request of Dr Friedrich Oetker, and continued intermittently until shortly before his death, are an invaluable source of information for details of his life and for his views on contemporary music and musicians. He completed them up to 1838, though the later part is less detailed than the earlier, which incorporates substantial extracts from his own diaries. After Spohr's death, his memoirs were edited, amplified to cover the years 1838 to 1859, and published by his family under the title *Louis Spohr's Selbstbiographie* (2 vols., Kassel and Göttingen 1860-1). An abridged version of this is available in a somewhat inaccurate English translation (London 1865, reprinted 1969; 2nd edn 1878); the earlier part of the *Selbstbiographie* is better translated in Henry Pleasants' *The Musical Journeys of Louis Spohr* (Univ. of Oklahoma Press 1961). A new edition of the *Selbstbiographie* edited by E. Schmitz was published in 1954-5. Spohr's *Lebenserinnerungen* (Tutzing 1968), edited by F. Göthel from Spohr's autograph, provides an authoritative text copiously and informatively annotated.

B. Correspondence and miscellaneous writings

Unfortunately no substantial collection of Spohr's letters has been made and published. A selection is to be found in the following sources:

Altmann, W. 'Spohrs Beziehungen zur Generalintendanz der königlichen Schauspiele zu Berlin', *NZfM*, c (1904), 199

Göthel, F., ed. *Louis Spohr: Briefwechsel mit seiner Frau Dorette* (Kassel 1957)

Homburg, H. 'Politische Äusserungen Louis Spohrs', *ZVHG*, lxxv/lxxvi (1964-5), 545

Istel, E. 'Fünf Briefe Spohrs an Marschner', *Festschrift Rochus Freiherrn von Liliencron* (Leipzig 1910), p. 110

La Mara [M. Lipsius]. *Musikerbriefe aus fünf Jahrhunderten* (Leipzig 1886)

—— 'Aus Spohrs Leben', *Klassisches und Romantisches aus der Tonkunst* (Leipzig 1892)

Rychnowsky, E. 'Louis Spohr und Friedrich Rochlitz', *SIMG*, v (1903-4), 253

Silhan, A. 'Louis Spohr a Jaho Styky s Prahou' (Louis Spohr and his contacts with Prague), *Hudebni revue*, ii (1909), 453

Speyer, E. *Wilhelm Speyer der Liederkomponist* (Munich 1925)

—— 'Briefe L. Spohr's an das Haus Peters in Leipzig', *AMZ* new series, ii (1867), 290

—— 'Letters of Spohr', *MW*, xxxviii (1860), 249

Most of Spohr's correspondence remains in manuscript. Many letters are scattered in libraries and private collections, but a substantial number are in the Louis-Spohr-Gedenk- und Forschungsstätte in Kassel. These include his correspondence with Edward Taylor and Adolf Hesse as well as many others. Also in this archive is a wealth of other manuscript and printed material, including the diaries of Spohr's second wife, Marianne.

Bibliography

Spohr contributed occasionally to music journals. His most important articles, published in the *AMZ*, are his report on the state of music in St Petersburg (*AMZ*, v (1802/3), 667-9), his open letters from Paris in 1821 (included in the *Selbstbiographie*), and his 'Aufruf an deutsche Componisten' (*AMZ*, xxv (1823), 458).

A selection of Spohr's works in ten volumes, including the complete Lieder, and selected symphonies, operas, oratorios and chamber music, is in the press (Garland Press, New York), edited by Clive Brown.

C. Secondary sources

Extensive bibliographies are to be found in *Die Musik in Geschichte und Gegenwart* and *The New Grove's Dictionary of Music and Musicians* (articles 'Spohr'); the following is a list of books and articles referred to in this book, together with a number of titles not to be found in the abovementioned bibliographies.

Altmann, W. (see section B)

Bennett, J. R. S. *The Life of William Sterndale Bennett* (Cambridge 1907)

Berger, F. 'Beethoven, Spohr and Hummel', *MMR*, li (1921), 248

Berlioz, H. *The Memoirs of Hector Berlioz*, trans. D. Cairns (London 1969)

Brown, J. C. A. *The Popularity and Influence of Spohr in England* (diss. University of Oxford 1980)

Bülow, H. von. *Briefe und Schriften*, ed. M. von Bülow (Leipzig 1895-1908)

Buckley, O. D. *Musical Truths* (London 1843)

Chopin, F. F. *Selected Correspondence of Fryderyk Chopin*, trans. & ed. A. Headley (London 1962)

Chorley, H. F. *Modern German Music; Recollections and Criticisms* (London 1854)

—— *Thirty Years' Musical Recollections* (London 1862)

[Cox, J. B.] *Musical Recollections of the Last Half Century* (London 1872)

Davison, H. *Music during the Victorian Era. From Mendelssohn to Wagner* (London 1912)

Eaton, T. D. *Musical Criticism and Biography* (London 1872)

Faulkner, Sir A. B. *Visit to Germany and the Low Countries in 1829, 30 and 31* (London 1833)

Fitzmaurice, Lord E. *Charles William Ferdinand, Duke of Brunswick. An Historical Study, 1735-1806* (London 1901)

Gál, H. *The Musician's World: Great Composers in their Letters* (London 1965)

—— *Johannes Brahms* (London 1975)

Giehne, H. *Zur Erinnerung an Louis Spohr* (Karlsruhe 1860)

Glover, W. *The Memoirs of a Cambridge Chorister* (London 1885)

—— *Reminiscences of Half a Century* London 1889

Goethe, J. W. von. *Briefwechsel zwischen Goethe und Zelter in den Jahren 1796 bis 1832*, ed. Dr F. W. Riemer (Berlin 1833-4)

Göthel, F., ed. *Louis Spohr: Briefwechsel mit seiner Frau Dorette* (Kassel 1957)

—— ed. *Louis Spohr: Lebenserinnerungen* (Tutzing 1968)

—— *Thematisch-bibliographisches Verzeichnis der Werke von Louis Spohr* (Tutzing 1981)

Greiner, D. *Louis Spohrs Beiträge zur deutschen romantischen Oper* (diss. University of Kiel 1960)

Hanslick, E. *Geschichte des Concertwesens in Wien* (Vienna 1870)

Hauptmann, M. *Briefe von Moritz Hauptmann an Franz Hauser*, ed. A. Schöne (Leipzig 1871)

—— *Briefe von Moritz Hauptmann an Louis Spohr und andere* (Leipzig 1876)

—— *The Letters of a Leipzig Cantor*, trans. & arranged [from the two preceding] by A. D. Coleridge (London 1892)

Hogarth, G. *The Philharmonic Society of London* (London 1862)

—— *Musical History Biography and Criticism* (London 1835)

[Holmes, E.] *A Ramble among the Musicians of Germany* (London 1828)

Homburg, H. (see section B)

—— *Louis Spohr: Bilder und Dokumente seiner Zeit* (Kassel 1968)

Jacobs, A. 'Spohr and the Baton', *Music and Letters*, xxxi (1950), 307

Joachim, J., and Moser, A. *Violinschule* (Berlin 1902-5)

Lang, P.H. 'Editorial', *The Musical Quarterly*, xxxix (1953), 232-9

Macfarren, Sir G. A. article 'Spohr' in *The Imperial Dictionary of Universal Biography* (London n.d.)

Malibran, A. *Louis Spohr* (Frankfurt am Main 1860)

Mendelssohn, F. *Letters of Felix Mendelssohn to Ignaz and Charlotte Moscheles*, trans. F. Moscheles (London 1889)

Moscheles, I. *Aus Moscheles Leben: nach Briefen und Tagebüchern*, ed. C. Moscheles (Leipzig 1872-3)

Moser, A. *Joseph Joachim*, trans. L. Durham (London 1900)

Müller, A. *Briefe von der Universität in die Heimat* (Leipzig 1874)

Naumann, E. *History of Music*, trans. F. Praeger, ed. F. A. G. Ouseley (London 1882-6)

Neumann, W. *Louis Spohr* (Kassel 1854)

Phillips, H. *Musical and Personal Recollections* (London 1864)

Prout, E. 'Spohr's *Jessonda*', *MMR*, xxxiv (1904), 121

Reichardt, J. F. *Vertraute Briefe geschrieben auf einer Reise nach Wien und den österreichischen Staaten zu Ende des Jahres 1808 und zu Anfang 1809* (Munich 1915)

Ritter, F. L. *The History of Music*

Rychnowsky, E. (see section B)

Schletterer, H. M. *Ludwig Spohr. Ein Vortrag* (Sammlung musikalischer Vorträge, 29), ed. P. Graf Waldersee (Leipzig 1881)

Schlüter, J. *History of Music*, trans. R. Tubbs (London 1865)

Schumann, R. *Gesammelte Schriften über Musik und Musiker* (Leipzig 1854)

—— *Music and Musicians; Essays and Criticisms*, trans F. R. Ritter (London 1877)

—— *Erinnerung an Felix Mendelssohn Bartholdy*, ed. G. Eismann (Zwickau 1947)

Smart, Sir G. Papers in the British Library Department of Manuscripts

Speyer, E. (see section B)

—— *My Life and Friends* (London 1937)

Spohr, L. *Violinschule* (Vienna 1832)

—— *Spohr's Violin School*, trans. J. Bishop (Royal College Edition, London n.d.)

Taylor, P. M. *A Memoir of the Taylor Family of Norwich* (privately printed 1886)

Thayer, A. W. *The Life of Ludwig van Beethoven*, rev. H. E. Krehbiel (London 1960)

Wagner, R. *Mein Leben*, ed. M. Gregor-Dellin (2nd edn, Munich 1976)

—— *My Life*, trans. A. Gray, ed. M. Whittall (Cambridge 1983)

Warrack, J. *Carl Maria von Weber* (2nd edn, Cambridge 1976)

Weber, C. M. von. *Writings on Music*, selected & ed. J. Warrack (Cambridge 1981)

Zelter, C. F. *see* Goethe

Index of names and subjects

355

Index of Spohr's works

INSTRUMENTAL MUSIC

(1) FOR ORCHESTRA

(A) SYMPHONIES

(B) OVERTURES

(C) OTHER ORCHESTRAL WORKS

(D) WORKS FOR SOLO INSTRUMENT(S) AND ORCHESTRA

(i) Violin concertos

(ii) Clarinet concertos